An Arch

The Hardy Boys Casefiles™

Books in The Hardy Boys™ Casefiles Series

Too Many Traitors
The Number File
The Borderline Case

Franklin W. Dixon

AN ARCHWAY PAPERBACK
Published by SIMON & SCHUSTER

New York   London   Toronto   Sydney   Tokyo   Singapore

An Archway paperback
first published in Great Britain
by Simon & Schuster Ltd in 1993
A Paramount Communications Company

Simon & Schuster Ltd
West Garden Place
Kendal Street
London W2 2AQ

Simon & Schuster of Australia Pty Ltd
Sydney

A CIP catalogue record for this book is
available from the British Library

ISBN 0-671-85220-5

Printed and bound in Great Britain by
HarperCollins Manufacturing, Glasgow

Too Many Traitors

Chapter

1

"COME ON, FRANK, show a little life," Joe Hardy said. "We're landing soon."

He glanced out the plane window, his blue eyes eager for a glimpse of the Spanish coastline. Joe loved the rush of takeoffs and landings. And, as he stretched, he was glad that the long flight from New York was almost over.

"Hey, *Frank!*" Joe repeated. A year older than Joe, Frank Hardy bore little resemblance to his brother: Frank was slim and an inch taller than Joe. Frank's hair was brown, Joe's was blond.

Finally Joe shook Frank's arm, and Frank opened his eyes. He'd been listening to music on his new Walkman. Now he slipped the headphones off his ears and let them dangle around his neck. "Take it easy, Joe," he said. "That's

1

what we're on vacation for, remember? To relax.''

"You're right," Joe admitted. He was tense because he was expecting trouble. Lately trouble had been coming to them out of seemingly innocent situations. A visit to the mall had thrown Frank and him into an assassination plot. A plane ride had become a hijacking. Even a simple party had turned into a bizarre murder attempt in their last case, *The Borgia Dagger*.

Even though they were only seventeen and eighteen Joe and Frank Hardy had fought more crime than most big-city policemen. They just seemed to fall into it—either in their hometown of Bayport or anywhere that they traveled.

"I'd have more fun if you'd talk to me, Frank. You've barely said two words since you won that Walkman. All the way across the Atlantic, you've just sat there, plugged into—"

"I like listening to music." Frank held an earphone to one ear so he could listen to Joe with the other. "Besides, this is a prize—just like this trip. And I intend to enjoy *all* my winnings."

Joe slouched in his seat and looked over at his brother and smiled about Frank's recent good fortune. Frank had entered a contest while he was ordering some computer supplies by mail. Several weeks later he learned he was the winner of an all-expense-paid trip for two to the sunny Spanish paradise called the Costa del Sol.

The first prize included the trip, complete with guided tour. But among the other goodies were the Walkman and a supply of tapes to play in it.

Joe spoke again. "I think you brought me along only because Callie wasn't free."

"Come on, you know that's not true," Frank said, shrugging off Joe's teasing. He knew Joe finally had a grudging respect for his girlfriend, Callie Shaw. Because even Joe had to admit that it was Callie who'd saved them all during the Borgia Dagger case.

Frank teased his brother back. "I'd have offered the trip to Mom and Dad if they hadn't gone to Chicago. Lucky for you they took Aunt Gertrude with them."

"She doesn't like the beach. All that sand is bad for her shoes." He grinned. "Boy, I hope the Spanish beaches live up to their reputation." He closed his eyes and imagined the girls.

The wheels touched down on the tarmac of the airport runway. Within minutes the plane had taxied to the gate. Soon Frank and Joe were heading down the aisle toward the door.

"So long, Joe," said a smiling red-haired flight attendant as they stepped through the exit. "Hope I see you on the flight home."

"Me, too, Cindy," Joe replied. Waving at her, he followed his brother along the exit ramp.

"When did you two get so friendly?" asked Frank in surprise.

Joe tugged lightly on the headphones dangling around Frank's neck. "There's a lot you miss when you have these things plastered to your ears." He winked at his brother and set off for the customs line.

After clearing customs, they walked into the terminal.

Joe glanced around. "I thought somebody was supposed to meet us."

Frank grabbed Joe's arm and pointed. "There's our man."

Ahead of them stood a sandy-haired man of about thirty, his arms and face well tanned. The man wore black slacks and a red- and white-striped shirt, and he held a handwritten sign. The scrawled letters read "Hardy."

"Here we are," Frank called. The man spotted him and lowered his sign as the brothers approached. "I'm Frank Hardy," Frank said. "This is my brother, Joe."

"Welcome to Spain," the man said, smiling. "I'm Martin Chase—call me Martin. I'm your guide. For a minute there I wasn't sure I'd find you."

"But I thought this kind of thing was everyday stuff for you guys," Frank said.

Martin shrugged, embarrassed. "Not for me. I'm a writer, and Málaga is a nice place to write. I guide English-speaking tourists to keep the roof over my head and feed myself."

4

"What do you write?" Joe asked.

"Journalistic stuff," Martin said. "Which reminds me—you are Fenton Hardy's sons, aren't you?"

"How'd you know that?" Frank eyed him.

Martin smiled sheepishly. "You'll have to forgive me. I do a lot of crime writing, and I'm something of an armchair detective. Your father is one of my heroes, a really exceptional investigator. I've read about all of his cases." Martin studied their faces. "You know, you both look a little like him."

"Well, what do you know?" Frank said. "Dad's reputation grows all the time."

Martin nodded. "Is that all your luggage?"

"This is it." Joe picked up one of their two overnight bags. "We like traveling light."

"Let's go, then," Martin said. He led the way through a crowd of perplexed tourists, blasé world travelers, and relaxed residents. Outside, Martin stopped beside a long black limousine.

The driver hopped out to open the back door. He wore a dark suit and chauffeur's cap. A thick black beard masked his face, and sunglasses hid his eyes. While the Hardys got into the backseat and Martin climbed in front, the chauffeur loaded the bags into the trunk. Then he climbed behind the wheel again. All this he did without uttering a word.

"To the hotel," Martin ordered. Soon the big

car was weaving through the fast-moving traffic, heading toward downtown Málaga.

The city amazed Frank. He had expected the old stone buildings, but the park-lined boulevards and the plazas with outdoor cafés and fountains were a surprise to him. It wasn't the quaint little village he had expected, but a beautiful city that mixed the Old World with the new.

The local bullring, the impressive Plaza de Toros, came into view. Then it gave way to baroque-style churches whose ornate towers gleamed hot white in the bright sun.

"Know much about Málaga?" Martin asked, turning in his seat to look at the Hardys.

"Just what we read in the brochure," Frank began.

"This place is an old port founded by the Phoenicians some three thousand years ago," their guide said. "There's a lot of history in this old town."

Joe said, "I was hoping they'd have discos here too."

Martin laughed. "Don't worry," he assured him. "I suggest you work off your jet lag with a good night's sleep. Then tomorrow we'll start on the *real* tour—including a couple of the better discos."

The big black car rolled to a quiet stop in front of an impressive old stone building with a red-tiled roof. They slid out of the car and Martin escorted them into the large, cool lobby of their hotel. They passed sturdy wood and leather chairs, tall urns filled with bright flowering plants, and huge oil paintings of Spanish nobles of centuries past. At the oak front desk, the hotel clerk welcomed the Hardys and handed them registration forms.

Frank set his tape player on the counter. Before he started filling out the form, he noticed Martin admiring it. "Want to try it?" Frank asked. "I won it as part of the contest. It's the latest model."

Nodding, Martin slipped on the earphones and switched on the machine. "Thanks." He grinned as the music began to play, and as Frank and Joe registered, Martin paced the lobby, listening.

"This is great," Martin said as the Hardys approached him moments later, room keys in hand. He started to hand the player back, then pulled it away just before Frank could touch it. "I don't suppose you'd part with it?"

"Not a chance," Frank said. He put out his hand and Martin reluctantly handed it back. Frank clipped it to his belt.

"Our rooms are on the third floor," Joe said.

"So is mine," their guide replied. "This way." He led them to an elevator and pressed the button next to the wrought-iron gates. "Your tour will work like this—tomorrow we'll check out the city of Málaga itself."

He nodded excitedly. "You've got to visit the cathedral, Gibralfaro Castle, Picasso's birthplace, the Fine Arts Museum, and, of course, a bullfight and a flamenco club. And, you can't miss eating paella at Pedro's."

"That sounds like a week's tour, Martin," said Joe.

"There'll be days to take it easy," Martin assured him. "There's the beach, and some little towns—Torremolinos, Fuengirola, and Marbella—and a stop for fish at La Carihuela, an old fishing village that—"

The elevator arrived and Martin paused, tugged the door open, and held it as the Hardys carried their luggage in.

As the door slid shut, Joe heard footsteps running for the door. Without thinking, he pushed it back open.

Two pretty blond girls got in and smiled at Joe. Then they started whispering together, sneaking peeks at him. Joe couldn't make out what they were saying, except for an odd word here or there. German? Swiss? Swedish? He couldn't decide.

He smiled back at the girls, about to say something to them, but then Martin started in again.

"For the rest of the week," the guide said, "there'll be day trips to Granada, Seville, and Ronda, and you don't want to miss the hydrofoil over to Tangier. Then there's—"

"Hey, I thought this trip was for relaxing," Frank said, smiling. "You're going to run us ragged."

"Only one way out of this," Joe joked. "Martin, we're going to have to kill you."

The elevator opened on the third floor, and Martin and the Hardys stepped out. "I'm right over here," Martin said, moving to the room opposite the elevator.

Joe turned back for a final glimpse of the blond girls. They giggled and waved as the door slid shut. "Nice town," Joe told Martin. "I'm definitely going to like it here."

"Wait till you get to know it," Martin said. "Tomorrow we'll meet at eight o'clock in the lobby. We'll have breakfast and then we'll begin the tour. I'll leave you on your own about noon. The car and driver are yours to use for the next couple of days. Go anywhere you want."

"Great," Frank said, glancing at his key. "Which way's three-thirteen?"

Martin pointed to the left. The Hardys headed for a bend in the hallway. "Remember, eight sharp," he called after them. Then thcy were gone.

Martin closed his door and crossed the room to a large window, opening it wide. He stood for a moment, inhaling the sea air. Then he moved back to a small desk. On top of it were a handful of pens and a ream of writing paper in a large wooden box. Martin pulled the paper from the box and set it to one side.

Hidden in the bottom of the box was a compact shortwave radio. Martin put on the earphone and picked up a small mike. He touched a switch on its side and raised it to his lips.

''The couriers are now in place,'' he said into the microphone. ''Tomorrow's rendezvous will go as planned.''

''Plans change,'' said an unfamiliar, accented voice behind him.

Startled, Martin turned and stared for a second at his attacker. Something hard cracked against his temple. The mike slipped from his fingers. And then he slowly toppled to the floor.

Chapter

2

FRANK HARDY LOOKED at his watch and frowned. It was seven past eight the next morning, and he was eager to begin the tour of the city. Instead, he was sitting on a couch in the hotel lobby, rhythmically tapping his fingers on the arm as he watched the stairs, waiting for Martin to appear. Joe sat across the lobby, watching the elevator. But there was no sign of their guide.

The minutes ticked by. By a quarter past eight Joe walked over to Frank and said, "He's not coming."

"Why?" Frank asked. "Do you think he missed his wake-up call?"

"He sure missed mine," said Joe. "I rang his room five minutes ago. No answer. Maybe he went out last night to check some of those discos he talked about. I bet he's dead to the world."

Frank heard his brother's stomach growl, and the sound made him smile. "Just a minute," he said, and walked over to the hotel desk. After a few words with the man behind the desk, he returned to Joe.

"What was that all about?" Joe asked.

"Breakfast," Frank replied. "The desk clerk says there's a little café around the corner. I left word for Martin to meet us there."

"Think he'll mind if we start without him?"

Frank glanced again at the empty stairs and then at his watch. Eight twenty-five. "He knows where to find us—and I feel like having more than a hotel breakfast."

"Great," Joe said. "Let's go."

They stepped outside and walked down the narrow street to the corner. On the other side of the street was their limousine, the driver leaning against it with a newspaper in his hands. Dark glasses still hid his eyes. And from the angle he held the paper, Frank wasn't sure if he was reading or watching the street. Either way, he never moved.

The Hardys went into the café, and soon a waiter brought a tray of sausages, toast, and oranges and set it in front of them.

"Let's hit the beach this afternoon," Joe said after finishing an orange.

"Mmmm?" Frank said, his mouth full of toast.

"When the tour's over. We've got the afternoon free, remember?" Joe held up a hand and studied his skin. "I've got to work on my tan."

"And the girls," Frank said.

"And the girls," Joe admitted, laughing as he called the waiter over. He got the bill, dug a handful of Spanish pesetas from his pocket, and dropped them on the table.

The sun had already made the city hot. It was cooled only by an occasional ocean breeze. The street was busy, clogged with cars in the road and pedestrians on the sidewalk. Despite the antiquity of many of the buildings, Málaga was as modern as any city.

Which is what Martin would tell us, Frank thought. If he were here.

As they passed their car, the driver waved at them and then crossed the street. He drew a long white envelope from his pocket and handed it to Frank without a word.

"It's from Martin," Frank said after tearing the envelope open. He had several sheets of paper with typing on them. The top sheet read:

Dear Frank and Joe,
  Sorry I can't be with you this morning. Continue without me. The driver knows where to take you. Good luck.
                                    Martin

Under the first sheet were more papers, detailing the tour and the special features and history of the places they were scheduled to see. "Does this mean we can go straight to the beach?" Joe asked.

"We've got the car for only a couple of days," Frank said, slipping the notes into his shirt pocket. "Plenty of time for the beach later. Let's go see the town while we can."

"Can we get a new driver?" Joe whispered as they crossed the street. "This one's not my choice for tour guide of the year. He looks like his face will fall off if he smiles."

"I know what you mean," Frank whispered. The driver opened the back door for them. Frank and Joe slid in. "He doesn't smile, he doesn't talk, and I still haven't gotten a good look at his face," he said so only Joe could hear. The door slammed behind him. "But think of it this way: Who looks a gift horse in the mouth?"

The driver got in and turned on the ignition. The limousine roared to life, then pulled into the traffic. In seconds the Hardys found themselves swept along through the streets of Málaga.

As they neared the city's waterfront, traffic thinned out, and the car cruised the Paseo del Parque beside the harbor. "Look," Joe said, pointing at the palm-shaded walkways that lined the marina. "It looks like California."

"But there's something you won't see in California," said Frank, reading the tour notes. He pointed to an ancient limestone church crowned by two towers. "That cathedral dates back to the sixteenth century."

To Frank's surprise, the limousine drove right past the cathedral and turned a corner, heading back to the center of town. "Hey!" shouted Frank. "We were supposed to stop there!"

"No time," said the driver, his voice a harsh whisper.

"What do you know?" Joe said. "He talks."

"Great." Frank gave the driver a sour look, then studied the notes again as the car traveled the Málaga streets. "Can you see where we are now?"

Joe craned his neck. "The Plaza de la Merced. Any idea what that is?"

The limousine screeched to a halt at the curb. "Thirty minutes," the driver muttered.

"This isn't exactly the tour I had in mind," Joe said as they climbed out of the car.

Frank pocketed the notes. "According to Martin, the birthplace of Pablo Picasso is right near here. Let's go find it."

Joe shrugged, and together they crossed to the far side of the plaza. After a short walk they found a small building. Like many other buildings they had seen, this one had old wooden shutters on its windows and small balconies on every floor. A small sign was tacked up next to the door, and among the Spanish words was the name Pablo Picasso.

"This must be it," Frank said. "You'd think it would be a lot less ordinary looking, wouldn't you?" He squinted at the notice. "I wonder what this says."

Joe gently nudged his brother aside. "Let an expert translate. I've been waiting to try my high school Spanish."

"A memorial is to be erected here to commemorate the birth of the great artist Pablo Picasso," said a soft voice behind them. "This will become an official historical site."

The Hardys turned. And Joe smiled. A pretty young Spanish woman, dressed in a print blouse and denim skirt, was standing and staring at them with large brown eyes.

"Thank you," Frank said. He held out his hand. "I'm Frank Hardy, and this is my brother, Joe. We're Americans."

The woman's eyes narrowed, and she made no move to shake Frank's hand. "The sky is bluer in Barcelona," she said.

"That's very interesting," Frank replied.

"The sky is bluer in Barcelona," she repeated, tension sounding in her voice.

The smile faded from Joe's lips, and he looked bewildered. "Want to get something to drink, Frank?"

"Sounds like a good idea," Frank answered.

To the girl he said, "Thanks again for your help." Before she could react, the Hardys moved away from her.

"The sky is bluer in Barcelona!" she shouted desperately, but they were already halfway across the plaza. Curious stares from passersby silenced her.

"What was that about?" Frank wondered aloud. "It almost sounded like some sort of code."

"Beats me," Joe said. "Nice looking, but—" He shook his head and sighed. "Why do I always run into crazy ones?" Wistfully, he glanced over his shoulder for a last look at her.

At first he thought she was waving. Then he realized she was pointing. That's when he saw a man, dressed in a dark suit and sunglasses, step from a doorway.

As he looked around, he saw three similar men moving into position all around the Plaza de la Merced. They were all closing in on the Hardys.

"We've got trouble," Joe yelled. "Head for the limo. Quick!"

Frank nodded and broke into a sprint. In seconds they had reached their car and scrambled into the back seat. The four men were only yards away. "Windows up," Frank ordered. He pressed the button on the window control, but nothing moved. "Driver!" he called. "Get us out of—"

He stopped. Their driver wasn't in the car.

"Are the keys in the ignition?" Frank asked Joe. He glanced out the window. The four men were closing in.

"Nope," Joe replied, leaning over the front seat. His hand scooped down and came back up with a false beard and latex nose in it. "But I found *part* of our driver."

"A disguise?" Frank's bewilderment changed to anger. "We've been set up!"

A hand thrust through the open car window. In it was a small-caliber pistol. Frank looked up to see a man in sunglasses grinning unpleasantly at him. The man's three companions stood around the car, each guarding one door. Another limousine, with a diplomatic license plate, appeared from around the corner.

In a thick Russian accent the gunman said, "You are to be coming with us. Now."

"Any idea of what's going on?" Joe asked Frank as the men outside began to pull open the doors.

"I'm not sure," Frank said, "but I have this weird notion we're being kidnapped by the KGB!"

Chapter

3

"THE KGB?" SAID Joe. "Well, I hope they get a real kick out of *this*." He slammed his heel into the unlocked car door, smashing it open. It struck the man outside, knocking him backward into the gunman behind him.

Joe barreled out of the car.

The man standing outside Frank's door raised his gun. Instantly, Frank drove his fist through the open window and into the man's stomach. Caught off guard, the Russian doubled over.

The fourth man swung his pistol toward Frank, but it was too late. Frank caught his wrist and hauled up. The man flew into the car, banging his head against the roof. As he fell away, Frank swung his door open, leaping out of the car.

"This way!" Joe shouted, and Frank followed

him toward the corner of the block. Already, the Russians were recovering, and Frank knew they'd be after them in seconds.

"I think we can lose them," Frank told his brother as they ran down a narrow street. Just ahead was a busy intersection. The traffic made it almost impossible to cross. "If we can just get to the other side—"

He scanned the intersection for a break in the traffic, but there was none. The rapid footsteps behind them raced closer, and Frank could hear words muttered in Russian. There was no time to wait, he knew. They had to make their move now.

He hurled himself into traffic. Tires screeched and horns blared as drivers slammed on their brakes. *"Turistas locos!"* someone yelled, and others joined in. Frank ignored them, focusing on nothing but the other side of the street. Out of the corner of his eye he could see Joe keeping pace with him.

At last they jumped over the far curb. "Made it," Frank said breathlessly.

"Keep running," he told Joe, and both broke into a sprint again. Their gamble hadn't worked too well for them. Traffic had now ground to a stop, and the Russians were crossing the street with ease.

The Hardys reached an alley. Ducking into it, they slowed down. The alley was damp and littered with piles of garbage, and the buildings it ran between were close enough together to shade it from the sun. "Shhh," Frank said. "I'm pretty sure they didn't see us come in. If we're quiet, they might pass by."

As Frank spoke, the Russians appeared at the end of the alley. Frank and Joe crouched against a wall, dropping out of sight behind a garbage pile. Cautiously, they peered over the top of the garbage. They hadn't been spotted.

The four Russians were standing on the street, arguing. One pointed into the alley and another pointed down the street. Finally, two of them went down the street.

The other two drew their guns and stepped warily into the alley, slowly moving toward the Hardys. One of the Russians kicked at a garbage pile, scattering it everywhere. He shook his head at his partner, and they cautiously moved closer.

"They must think we're hiding in the garbage," Frank whispered to Joe. "They underestimated us at the car, but I doubt that's going to happen again."

"Let's make it happen," Joe whispered back. As the shadow of a gun fell over his face, he dug into the garbage and flung it into the air. Instinctively, the Russians spun and took aim at the flying rubbish.

Joe rushed between them, catching each of them around the waist with an arm and forcing them back against a wall. Before they could react, Joe threw a punch at the Russian to his left. The man toppled to the ground.

As he whirled to deal with the other one, Joe felt the sharp smack of metal against his temple, and he staggered back, pain exploding behind his eyes. Through the haze he could see the Russian's gun. It was what had hit his head, he knew, and now it was aimed at his chest.

"Hiii-ya!" Frank shouted, and his foot lashed out, kicking the gun from the startled Russian's hand. The heel of Frank's hand smashed into the Russian's jaw, and the man dropped.

Joe rubbed his head, clearing his vision. "Two down, two to go," he said. They ran for the far end of the alley.

"I'd rather we didn't meet the other two again at all," Frank replied. "Let's try to get back to the hotel."

"Do you hear something?" Joe asked.

Frank listened. Circus music, but distorted, he thought. Tinny, like guitar music. He didn't know what it could be.

The alley opened into the back of a churchyard. "Through here. It'll be quicker," Joe said, and they entered the church. Its high, domed ceiling was painted with angels. Set into the walls were wooden statues of saints.

Frank pulled open the front door of the church, and he and Joe froze.

In the street in front of the church was a parade. The sidewalks were lined with spectators. *"Buenos días,"* said a voice behind them.

They turned. A priest stood in the aisle, dressed in a traditional black cassock. He smiled at them and said, "Every year we have a street festival at this time. Come! You are welcome to join us."

With a slight bow he closed the doors of the church and led them down the steps to the street. Halfway down, Joe nudged Frank in the ribs.

"Look," Joe said, nodding toward the street.

Frank peered through the crowd, and his heart sank. Across the street, on the other side of the parade, were the other two Russians. They were watching them.

"Keep going," Frank told Joe. "They won't try anything with this many people around, and it'll be easy to lose them in the crowd."

They left the priest and started walking beside the parade. Frank could see the Russians on the other side keeping pace with them. But the brightly dressed marchers and rows of carts pulled by oxen and decorated with streamers and flowers kept the Russians from crossing the street.

"That keeps them in *their* place," Joe said, laughing. "They'll never get to us."

"We have to go to them sooner or later. Our

hotel is in that direction. We'll have to cross over.''

A squad of musicians, mostly drummers, followed the lines of carts. Frank stared down the length of the marchers until he saw the end of the street. "It looks like the parade's coming to another plaza. Maybe we can get across there.''

On the other side of the street, the Russians shadowed them step for step.

At the plaza, people in traditional Spanish costumes danced on the pavement. Women in long, full dresses, flowers in their hair, twirled arm in arm with men in short vests, white shirts, and tight black slacks.

As the Hardys were passing them, the dancers went into the crowd and pulled spectators into the dance with them.

"This way," Frank told Joe. "I have an idea.''

The Hardys skirted the circle of dancers, watching the Russians move around on the other side.

"Now," Frank said, and he stuck out a hand. A woman caught it and tugged him into the circle. Almost before he knew what was happening, Frank was passed from woman to woman. Dizzy from the spinning, he kept his eye on the Russians as he drew nearer and nearer to them with each step. Behind him, Joe was also dancing, waiting for Frank's next move.

As he passed the first Russian, Frank grabbed

the man's wrist and pulled him into the dance, handing him to the next woman in the circle. The woman laughed and pulled the Russian along, and Frank stepped out of the dance and into the crowd.

The last man turned to reach for Frank, but Joe caught the man's arm and repeated his brother's trick.

"Run," Frank said, pushing through the crowd. Joe followed, laughing as he thought of the Russians caught among the dancers.

They reached the open street and ran. When they had run several blocks, cutting from street to street, they stopped to catch their breath. No one was following them. "We finally lost them," Frank said. "I figured they'd want to keep a low profile and not cause a scene around the locals. That gave us the edge we needed."

"We'd better not run into those guys again," Joe replied. "I think we're all out of edges. I can't wait to get my hands on Martin and find out what this is all about."

"You think he had something to do with it?"

"He vanishes, our chauffeur does a disappearing act, and suddenly there are goons crawling all over us," Joe said. "Hey, he was supposed to be with us today. Maybe they weren't after us— maybe they were looking for Martin."

"There's only one way to find out." Frank

glanced around one last time but saw no sign of the Russians. "Let's get back to the hotel."

They entered the hotel through the back door and climbed the back stairs to the third floor. The walk back had been long and difficult.

"If you want to go to our room, I'll bring Martin around," Joe suggested. "We'll meet you there."

"Fine," Frank said. "He's got a lot of explaining to do." He left Joe and turned the corner, walking down the corridor to their room.

Frank stopped, ducking into a doorway. A policeman was standing in front of their doors. Frank slipped along the corridor, heading back to the stairs.

Joe was waiting, a look of dread on his face. "Frank," he said, "there's a cop in front of Martin's door, and a sign on it saying only police are allowed to enter. What's going on?"

"I don't know," Frank replied. "But we're in the thick of it. The cops are watching our room too." He started down the stairs. "Maybe we can find something out from the front desk."

"Looks like rush hour, doesn't it?" Joe said as they reached the main floor. Dozens of people, guests at the hotel, milled around the lobby. Scattered among them were policemen handing out photographs. Near the front desk were two pretty blondes. "Those are the girls who were on the elevator last night. Maybe they've heard something. Let's go ask—" He started moving toward them.

Frank pulled him back, around a pillar. "Let's not," Frank said. "Look who they're talking to."

Joe peered around the pillar. The young women were speaking to a tall, burly man with dark hair. He wore a dark tailored suit and tie. He nodded, recording the girls' words in a small notebook.

"Cop?" Joe asked Frank.

"Plainclothes," Frank answered. "He's probably the one running the show here."

"Let's go talk to him, then," Joe said, and started around the pillar. The man with the notebook had closed it and turned to the desk clerk.

The man spoke to the clerk in a deep voice that cut through the din. *"Hermanos."* Joe heard the Spanish word for "brothers." He strained to catch more, and was lucky. The policeman spoke clearly and slowly. He was easy to understand. "They were seen with the man just before the time of death, and were heard making threats against him."

The anxious clerk spoke quickly, but Joe caught something about murder being bad for the hotel.

"It will be over soon," the dark-haired policeman said, "when I arrest Frank and Joseph Hardy for the murder of Martin Chase."

27

Chapter

4

JOE DUCKED BACK behind the pillar. "Big trouble, Frank," he said. "We've got to get out of here."

Frank glanced over his shoulder at the back door, but it was no longer unguarded. A policeman stood there, checking the tourists who came in. "If we go, we go out the front," Frank muttered. He scanned the lobby. The other guests were chatting with one another, acting as if a party were going on. On the wall to the Hardys' left was a small newsstand. "Follow me," Frank said. "If we act naturally and don't attract any attention, we should be able to pull this off."

Casually, he strolled over to the kiosk, picked out a paper, and handed some coins to the vendor. Frank opened the paper, folding back a page and holding it up so that it blocked the lower half of his face. He turned to face the room.

No one noticed him. The policeman in the dark suit was speaking to the young blond women again. And next to them a uniformed policeman worked on a sketch. He's drawing us from their descriptions, Frank thought. The police will have pictures of us in no time.

Behind the cover of the paper Frank jerked his head to one side, signaling Joe to make his move. Then Frank began to walk, apparently aimlessly, toward the front door, flipping through his newspaper like a tourist looking for somewhere to go.

Frank walked through the front door and onto the street and breathed a sigh of relief. He tossed the newspaper into a trash basket. Where was Joe? he wondered. Had they finished the sketch and recognized him before he could escape?

No, there was Joe, coming out the door.

"Now what?" Joe asked, joining him in front of the hotel. "All our stuff is in our room, and we can't get to it. What are we going to do?"

Before Frank could answer, a cry of *"Alto!"* sounded behind them. They turned to see a uniformed policeman with a paper in hand. He spoke to them rapidly in Spanish.

He's got us, Frank thought. That must be our picture in his hand. As if hearing Frank's thoughts, the policeman thrust the paper into their faces and started asking more questions in Spanish.

The picture he held was a photograph of Martin.

"He wants to know if we know the man in the picture," Joe said, and then, to the policeman, *"No. Dispenseme. No comprendo."*

The policeman nodded, shrugged his shoulders, then went back toward the hotel.

"Come on," Frank said. "Let's hit that café where we had breakfast. We can rest and sort things out there."

The Hardys entered the café and sat at a back table that was partially hidden by lush green plants. Seconds later a waiter appeared with menus. It was the same waiter who had served them at breakfast, and his lean face brightened when he recognized them.

"You are back," he said slowly in English. "I am Francisco. What may I bring you, my friends?"

"Dos Coca-Colas, por favor," Joe answered.

The waiter spun around and vanished into the kitchen.

"He sure is friendly," Joe said, grinning. "I must have tipped him better than I thought."

"Great." Frank rubbed his eyes tiredly. "Someone else who can recognize us." He looked around the room. Besides the door they had come in through, there was a door to the kitchen. Good, we can reach that easily if we have to, Frank thought. "Why are the cops looking for us anyway?"

Joe stared at his brother. "I thought you heard. They think we killed Martin."

"What?" Frank looked angry. "Where did they get *that* idea?"

"How should I know?" Joe said. "Maybe we should turn ourselves in. After all, we *are* innocent."

"I don't think so," Frank responded. "This whole thing is starting to smell like a setup. If someone fingered us for Martin's murder, who knows what evidence they've manufactured? We're not in America, Joe. I have a feeling we'd better be able to *prove* our innocence before we start talking to any police."

Francisco reappeared with the drinks. "Mind if we sit here a bit?" Frank asked. "We'll order some food in a little while."

"Sí!" the waiter said, flashing his smile at them. "Stay as long as you like. Eat! Eat!" He wandered toward the front of the restaurant.

Sure that they were alone again, Joe sipped his drink and said, "You've got a point. We're probably better off on the streets." He chuckled. "Besides, we don't want to make it too easy for the Russians to find us, do we? You don't suppose *they* set us up?"

Frank shook his head. "There wasn't time.

31

You know who I bet could give us a few answers? Our chauffeur. He's the one who gave us Martin's note. And he led us to the Russians. Maybe he's working for them—at least, his disappearance was awfully well-timed."

"You're right," Joe agreed. "But we don't even know what he looks like. I never got a good look at his face, and his face wasn't his real face anyway. He could be anyone."

"We can't even be sure he's a he," Frank said. "It could possibly have been a woman."

Joe's eyes widened. "You don't suppose that Spanish girl at the plaza . . ."

"I doubt it," Frank said with a shrug. "Too slight. The chauffeur's height and build would be hard to fake. No, I'd guess he was a man. I wish he'd had a scar, some peculiar mannerism, *something* we could identify him with."

"We're not finding him unless he wants to be found," Joe said. "And we can't walk up to the Russians and ask them what's going on. I don't see any way we can help ourselves until we get a handle on the situation."

Suddenly Frank snapped his fingers and said excitedly, "There's *one* person who might be able to clue us in!"

"Who?" Joe asked. "The girl?"

A broad grin spread across Frank's face. "Martin."

"Martin? But he's—"

Frank waved a finger, cutting off his brother's thought. "Right. But the police have sealed off his room, so odds are everything he had is still in there."

"Of course!" Joe said. "If he left any information in his room—but how do we get in?"

"That's what we've got to figure out," Frank replied. "One thing's for sure. We'll have to wait until dark. Till then, we might as well eat." He picked up the menu and studied it, then raised his hand to flag the waiter to the table.

Despite the bright spotlights that lit up the front of the hotel at night, the rear of the place was dark, except for the parking-lot lights and ground lamps that marked the edges of walkways.

Frank and Joe slipped around to the back of the hotel, staying in the shadows. There were no signs of police in the parking lot, and guests were coming and going now as they pleased.

"I don't know if we should have spent so much time in that café," Joe whispered. "All that food is starting to weigh me down." A car sped by them, catching them in its headlights, and the boys turned their heads to hide their faces.

"We can make up for it by eating light for the rest of the trip," Frank answered. "Besides, if this doesn't work, we may not get another chance to eat at all. Did you leave a big tip?"

"Sure. Never know when we'll have to hide out there for a few hours again."

Following his brother, Joe crouched down and darted across the parking lot until he reached the safety of the darkness on the other side. Now they were at the bushes just in back of their hotel, and he looked up to the third floor, counting silently to himself. "There's our room," he said, pointing to a window on the third floor. "Four rooms in from the end."

Frank nodded. "That's good to know for when we have to get in there."

Joe walked to the corner of the building and turned up the side, counting carefully. Finally he stopped under two balconies, one above the other, and looked up. The top balcony was dark, and he could see no shadows on the shades drawn inside the room there. "Martin's."

Frank cupped his hands together and held them down at his knees, palms up. "Ready?" he asked Joe.

"Ready," Joe said. He broke into a sprint, heading straight for Frank. His last step landed in Frank's cupped hands, and Frank jerked upward, hurling Joe into the air. Joe stretched out his arms, and his fingers locked onto the balcony above him. Straining, he pulled himself up and over the railing and rolled with a thud onto the balcony.

Joe flattened himself on the balcony floor and

reached down through the railing until Frank gripped his hand. "Hold on," Joe said. Slowly, he lifted his brother up. Finally, Frank grabbed the bottom of a rail and dragged himself onto the balcony.

"One down," Frank said breathlessly. "Care to try for another?"

"Why not?" Joe said, gathering his strength. Frank cupped his hands together again, and in seconds Joe had disappeared over the railing of the top balcony.

For a long minute Frank watched in vain for some sign of him. But there wasn't even a sound.

"Joe!" he whispered. "Are you all right?"

As if in answer, an arm extended down from the top balcony. Frank grabbed it and hung on as he was lifted.

"You know, you could have answered me," Frank complained as he came over the railing. "I thought something had hap—"

That's when he realized Joe wasn't alone. Two policemen were holding his arms. Standing in front of Frank was the man who had been interviewing the blond girls that afternoon.

"You are Frank Hardy?" the man asked in accented English. "I've been waiting to meet you. I am Police Inspector Melendez.

"You and your brother are under arrest."

Chapter
5

"YOU CAN'T ARREST US," Joe said. "We haven't done anything."

Police Inspector Melendez clutched Frank's arm and shoved him inside the room beside Joe. "Sit down," he said. The Hardys sat on the bed. "Men who haven't done anything don't come creeping into dead men's rooms through the balcony in the middle of the night. Perhaps in America murder is considered nothing—"

"That's not what I meant," Joe interrupted.

"But in Spain we take it very seriously," Inspector Melendez continued as if Joe had said nothing. "What was your relationship with the dead man?"

"You mean Martin?" Frank said. "We met him only once, yesterday. He was supposed to be our guide around Málaga. I'd won this contest—"

Inspector Melendez cut him off. "Then what was your motive for killing him?"

"You're crazy if you think we did it," Joe said.

Inspector Melendez scowled. "I would be crazy to think you did not. You were the last persons to be seen with him before his death and the only persons ever seen with him in this hotel."

"What about the chauffeur?" Frank asked.

"Chauffeur?" Inspector Melendez repeated. He pulled out his notebook and leafed through it. "No one else has mentioned a chauffeur. Please describe him."

Frank swallowed hard. "We can't. He had disguised his face."

"I see." With a sigh of exasperation Inspector Melendez flipped the notebook closed and returned it to his pocket. "You were overheard to threaten Martin Chase in the elevator."

"That was a joke," Joe said. "A figure of speech."

"And we have this," Inspector Melendez replied. With a tweezers he held up a piece of writing paper. On it were bloodstains and three handwritten words: "Frank and Joe." "The dead man's handwriting. The paper is covered with his fingerprints. The pen that wrote those words was in his hand when he was found."

"None of that proves anything," Frank said.

"Perhaps," Inspector Melendez replied. "I think he was trying to name his killers but never got the chance to finish. Have you another explanation?"

Joe started to stand, but a policeman put a hand on his shoulder, forcing him to sit. "He could have been leaving us a note."

"With his dying breath?" Inspector Melendez said. "I find that unlikely."

"All right. A warning then."

The inspector dropped his cigarette to the floor, ground it out with his heel, and looked at Joe with new interest. "Oh? Of what would he need to warn you?"

He'll never believe us, Frank thought. Everything we say just makes us better suspects. "We were chased by Russians this morning and spent all day trying to stay out of their way," he said in a weary voice. "He might have been trying to tell us about them."

With a burst of laughter Inspector Melendez asked, "Russians? You are spies, then?"

"No, but—" Frank began.

"Then what," the inspector continued, "would Russians want with you?"

The Hardys looked at each other. Their last card was played, and it was useless. They were beaten.

"We don't know," Joe said.

Inspector Melendez snapped his fingers, and

the two policemen stood up straight. One grasped Joe's shoulder and the other took hold of Frank. "One last thing," Inspector Melendez asked. "What did you expect to find here?"

Joe shook his head. "Something to prove our innocence, I guess."

"Take them to headquarters," Melendez ordered. "We will get some *real* answers from them there." The policemen shoved Frank and Joe to the door of the room.

The whole situation was hopeless. No one would believe their story—unless *they* did something to prove it. Frank glanced at the door, and Joe nodded. As they were going through the door, Frank said, "Now!"

Together they spun, and each shoved one of the policemen back into the room. "Run," Frank shouted, and together they headed for the front stairs.

Next to the stairs the elevator had stopped and was letting people out. Behind them Frank could hear Inspector Melendez and the policemen coming out of Martin's room. Inspector Melendez yelled in Spanish, and Joe could hear a pistol cock.

"The elevator!" Joe said. "They won't shoot while there are other people around." He pushed through the crowd coming off the elevator and grabbed the door, holding it open. A second later Frank jumped into the car, and Joe let the door slip closed. As the elevator sank in its shaft, Joe could see Inspector Melendez furiously ordering his man down the stairs.

On the main floor the elevator door slid open. The Hardys raced across the lobby with Inspector Melendez and his men only a few yards behind them. "Outside!" Frank said. "We'll lose them in the dark."

But as they stepped through the door, they were greeted by the glare of the lights that lit the front of the building. "We're better targets out here than in there," Joe said reasonably. Three steps at a time, they sped down the front steps to the relative darkness of the street.

They were halfway across the street when a dark van screeched to a halt between them and the police. Before Joe or Frank could react, the side door of the van was slid open and strong arms gripped them, dragging them inside. A damp cloth pressed against Joe's face, and the stench of chloroform burned into his nose and mouth, filling his lungs. The last things he saw before plunging into unconsciousness were his now sleeping brother and the face of the girl who had spoken to them at Picasso's birthplace.

A coarse cloth patted Joe's cheek, and he tried to open his eyes. "Frank?" he called out. "Are you there?"

"Your brother is here," said a rough, cold

voice, and Joe's eyes snapped open. Sunlight glared into them, and he raised a hand to shield his face. There were bars on the windows of the room. He rolled his head to see Frank seated on a chair a few feet away. Another chair stood in front of him. Except for a small table with a lamp on it, the rest of the room was bare.

Morning, he realized. He remembered the police and the van and the sting of chloroform fumes. Captured, he thought. But who?

The girl from the plaza knelt beside him, a cloth in her hands. "Are you all right?" she asked, with genuine concern in her voice.

"Silence, Elena! Move away from the boy," ordered the cold voice. The girl backed off. Joe stared up at a bald man with a heavyset build. Standing behind him, one on either side of the door, were two of the Russians who had chased them across Málaga the day before. The bald man scowled at Joe impatiently. "Tell me the name."

Joe looked at Frank. "KGB?"

Frank nodded. "His name's Vladimir. The boss, I guess. He keeps asking about some name."

The man called Vladimir gave them a frosty smile. "The Network should not employ babbling children."

Joe stiffened. He and Frank had worked with the supersecret government agency called the Network in the past. But there had been no contact between them for several months. Now, it seemed, the Network was back to haunt them.

"What network are you talking about? NBC?" Frank said. "And who are you calling children?"

"Do not play the fool." Vladimir's voice was cold and flat, but his eyes glittered with menace. "You will not get your agent back until we have received the name. We had an agreement, your masters and mine."

"I'm starting to get it," Frank said to Joe. "The *Network* set us up. I gather Martin was working for them—"

"Of course he was," Vladimir told them impatiently. "Just as you are. He reported he had passed the name to you. And now I want it."

"The Network pulled a fast one on you, pal," Joe said. "We've got nothing to do with them."

"Ah." Vladimir shrugged and turned away. Then he pivoted, throwing his weight into a slap aimed at Joe's face. But it never connected. Instinctively, Joe reached up and blocked the blow. Then he clenched his fist and drew back his arm. At the door safeties clicked off two pistols.

"No!" shouted Elena. She flung herself between Vladimir and Joe, pushing them apart. To Vladimir she said, "You promised it would not be like this." Then to Joe she whispered, "Strike him and they will shoot you."

Vladimir shoved her away. "They will cooperate—or suffer." He pushed Joe off his chair. "I would think carefully," Vladimir said as he grasped Joe's arm and tossed him back in the chair. "Your only hope of leaving this consulate alive is to give me answers."

Joe shook his head and said nothing.

Vladimir shrugged. "Perhaps they don't believe me." He went to the gunmen by the door and took one of their pistols. "We do not need both of them. If this one will not cooperate, perhaps his death will convince the other one." He sighted along the barrel, aiming at Joe's head.

"Don't move now." Smiling at his little joke, he slowly squeezed the trigger.

A black-gloved hand reached in the door and seized Vladimir's wrist, jerking his hand back and up. The bald man whirled around, furious, then he jerked back in surprise. "Konstantin!"

Whoever this Konstantin might be, it was obvious that Vladimir wasn't expecting him and wasn't happy to see him. The tall blond stranger, on the other hand, was calm and completely at ease. His piercing blue eyes twinkled over his confident smile.

"Vladimir, Vladimir," Konstantin said as he took the gun away. "Exile to this lonely country has not changed your ways?"

Vladimir rubbed his bruised wrist, still glaring. "What brings you to Spain, comrade?" he asked. "Have you come to invite me back to Department V?"

"Department V?" Frank whispered to Joe. "That's the KGB's assassination bureau!"

"No, Vladimir." Konstantin put a restraining hand on the big man's shoulder as he studied the Hardys. "The department is no secret—not among *professionals*." He emphasized the word as Vladimir's eyes narrowed angrily. "However, we prefer stealth and skill, not the brute force you demonstrate here."

Furious, Vladimir shrugged off Konstantin's hand and headed for the door. "Very well, I leave them in *your* hands. We shall see whose methods are most effective." He turned on his heel and stormed off, slamming the door behind him.

Sighing with relief, Elena picked herself up off the floor and approached Konstantin. "Thank goodness you arrived when you did, comrade. He was about to torture them, I'm sure."

Konstantin shook his head. "How terrible. Brutality solves nothing. There are more appropriate techniques." Casually, he walked to the table, picked up the lamp, and ripped the wire from its base. The lamp cord, still plugged into the wall, sprayed a shower of sparks as the exposed wires met.

With the look of a scientist who has performed the same experiment many times, he moved the sparking wires toward Joe's face. "Now," he said, "we shall get our answers."

Chapter
6

"Don't!" Elena screamed. "How can you think of such a thing? Who *are* you?"

Konstantin blinked at Elena as if noticing her for the first time. To one of the gunmen he said, "One of ours?" The gunman shook his head, and Konstantin faced Elena again. "Ah! One of Vladimir's local puppets. This is beyond you, girl."

"You can't—" she began, but Konstantin cut her off.

"I *can*. I am Vladimir's superior. While he may permit you to question his decisions, I will not. Perhaps your loyalty to the Party is insincere—"

"I am loyal," Elena insisted. "But torture—"

"This is incentive," he said, tapping the live wires together, creating a fat spark.

45

"You don't need that wire," Frank told him. "We've been telling the truth."

Nodding, Konstantin rested the cord on the table so that the ends dangled off without touching. "But one must make certain, no? Let us put together a picture of events.

"One: My government graciously accepted a proposal from your agency to exchange a captured agent for a piece of information of extreme interest to us. Your agent had been caught in the midst of treacherous action against the Soviet Union."

"Agency?" Joe asked. "You're talking about the Network?"

"Two: You were chosen as couriers to deliver this information to us. Your own contact radioed that you had received it. Yet, when *our* go-between"—he waved a thumb at Elena—"contacted you, you refused to speak with her or turn over the information. I wish to know why."

"We still don't know what you're talking about." Frank sighed.

Konstantin shrugged and lifted the cord from the table. "So you say."

"Perhaps," Elena said uncertainly, "they *are* telling the truth."

"And perhaps *you* betrayed us. You could have ruined the exchange." Konstantin turned toward Elena, the sparking wires in his hand now pointing at her.

Elena backed away in horror, fiercely shaking her head.

Konstantin turned away from her, disgusted. "Get the fool out of here." One of the guards stepped forward and grasped Elena's shoulder. He shoved her toward the door.

"Leave her alone!" Joe shouted. Without thinking, he leapt from his chair, fists clenched. The gunman released Elena, and he and his partner spun, their pistols out and aimed at Joe.

With a shriek Elena threw herself against the gunman next to her, knocking him off balance. As he stumbled, her hand snaked out, and before Konstantin or the other guard could move, the pistol was in her hands.

"Now let them go!" she ordered.

Konstantin set the cord down again. "You are free to leave," he told Frank and Joe.

The second gunman lunged for Elena, but she pivoted and aimed at him. He stood flat-footed and scowled. "Your gun," Elena said to the man. "Give it to him." She pointed to Joe.

Konstantin sat casually on the edge of the table and joined his hands behind his head.

"Let's go," Frank said.

Konstantin smiled and shook his head. "You may leave this room, but you will not escape the consulate."

"We'll see," Frank said as Joe and Elena slipped from the room. He joined them in the hallway a second later, then slipped the outside bolt on the door, locking Konstantin and the gunmen in the room.

The long hallway was lined with doors, and they were at the end of it. At the other end was a stairway. "Any other way out?" Joe asked Elena.

She shook her head sadly. "No. There are three floors below us. I am sorry. This is all my fault."

"We'll discuss that later," Frank said, taking the gun from Elena and pocketing it. "We've got to get out of here before they sound the alarm." They ran for the stairs. "How many people does Vladimir have in here?"

"I don't know," Elena said. "A dozen, two dozen perhaps. It is the Soviet consulate. I'm sorry."

"Oh, great," Frank said.

A Russian voice shouted from the stairs they were running toward. A guard stood staring at them. He pulled back the bolt on his AK47 assault rifle.

A stream of bullets from that, the Hardys knew, would cut them in half before they could even reach the Russian—and the guard looked only too eager to shoot.

Joe shrugged, took the pistol he carried by its barrel, and started to raise his hands.

The Russian grinned—then stared in confusion

as Joe's hand kept going up, hurling the pistol at the guard's head.

"Down!" Joe warned, falling to the floor as Frank tackled Elena.

The hurtling pistol caught the Russian in the head. He tumbled forward, riddling the ceiling with bullets before he collapsed.

"Joe," Elena cried. Her eyes brightened as he got to his feet. "I thought you were—"

"I'm okay," Joe answered, flashing her a smile. He picked up the AK47.

They heard heavy boots pounding up the stairs toward them. "This way!" Elena said. She flung open one of the many heavy oak doors. They dashed inside and she slammed it behind them, slipping the locks into place.

"Where are we?" Frank asked. The room was paneled in dark wood. One wall was lined with bookshelves while the opposite wall was lined with file cabinets.

"Vladimir's private office," Elena said as someone began pounding on the other side of the door. "He is very concerned with security. The door will hold."

"It's only a matter of time before someone shows up with the key."

"There is only one duplicate," Elena said.

Joe looked over the room, stopping at a glass door set in the wall. Behind the door was a fire extinguisher, hose, and ax. "Get a load of this."

Frank pulled open a file drawer and started rifling the files. "Let's see what he keeps in this. Any way out of here, Joe?"

"Maybe." Joe drew aside the thick curtains covering the windows and rapped on the glass with his knuckles. "Bulletproof. A cautious guy, this Vladimir." Joe looked out the window and smiled. Outside was the fire escape he had hoped to find.

"Bingo!" he said. "Our ticket out of here." Joe slid the window open and looked down. Far below, men were scrambling over the lawn. "Maybe not. They're already waiting for us down there."

Frank grabbed a handful of files as the pounding on the door grew louder. He walked to the window and looked up. The fire escape continued up and curved onto the roof. Keys were now jingling outside the door.

"We've got no choice," Frank said. "We go up." They climbed onto the fire escape, which wobbled under their weight. But it seemed as if no one below saw them as they scaled the ladder to the roof. The roof was flat, with several pipes sticking out of it, and a large shedlike structure in one corner. In the structure was a door.

Stairs from inside, Frank realized. So they'll be coming at us from two directions. If only we could wreck the fire escape, he thought. But that would take tools they didn't have.

"Bad move, brother." Joe stood at the far edge of the roof, looking down and holding the AK47. "It's too long a drop to the ground—" He stared glumly at the nearest building, twenty feet away. "And the next roof's too far to jump to."

Anxiously, Frank turned in a circle, studying the roof. There had to be some way to escape, he insisted to himself, but he knew he was wrong.

His shoulders slumped. "I hate to say it," he said finally. "But unless we grow wings in the next few seconds, we're trapped."

Chapter
7

JOE PEERED OVER at the roof next door, so near and yet so far. "Look at those pipes," he said. "If only we had a rope or cable, we could lasso a pipe on the roof next door and run a line across to it."

"We can!" Frank cried, excited. He dropped the files to the roof. "I need the rifle."

Puzzled, Joe threw the AK47 to his brother. Frank snatched it in midair as he ran to the fire escape. "What are you doing?" Joe asked.

"No time to explain," Frank answered. He pointed at the door to the stairs. "Whatever you do, keep that door closed!" Then Frank was gone, climbing down the fire escape as it bounced beneath his feet.

He slipped back into Vladimir's office. Out-

52

side, keys clanged as the doorknob rattled. They're trying to find the right key, Frank realized. Vladimir must not be in the building any longer. Frank opened the fire closet in Vladimir's wall and pulled out the fire hose.

He turned the metal ring attaching the hose to the wall until the hose came free. The tough canvas hose would make as good a line as any.

As Frank gathered up the hose, he heard a key finally turning in the lock. He had to keep the guards from coming through the door.

His glance fell on the heavy bookcases with their thick books stacked around the doorway. With a grin he pulled the trigger on the AK47, spraying the top shelves. The books absorbed the bullets.

But the guards outside didn't know that. Frank could hear frantic commands as the men threw themselves to the floor.

Frank snatched the ax, and with a swift flick of his wrist he spun the wheel in the fire closet. A jet of water rushed from the wall where the hose had been and sprayed across the office. That ought to slow them down, he thought as he dashed to the window.

He was wrong. Like trained combat troops, the Russians rolled into the room and took positions on the floor. As Frank stepped onto the fire escape, they locked their sights on him and fired.

Vladimir's window fell into place behind Frank, and the shots bounced harmlessly off the bulletproof glass. Seconds later Frank climbed onto the roof.

"Great!" said Joe when he saw the fire hose. Frank handed him the ax instead.

"They're right behind me," Frank said. "But that fire escape's about to go. I don't think anyone's checked it in years. Try to pry it loose from the building with the ax."

"I do not understand," Elena said as Joe worked at the bolts holding the fire escape to the building. "How do we escape?"

"We're going to go hand over hand across this hose to the next building," replied Joe.

"I can't do it, my arms are too weak," Elena said.

"You'll hang onto me, and I'll take us both across. But right now I need some help. . . ."

Frank knotted one end of the hose around a pipe and tested it. The hose held. He tied the other end of the hose in a slipknot.

Joe groaned. "It's too late." The first Russian was slipping out of the window onto the fire escape. He grinned viciously up at Joe. The Russian's foot slammed down on the first rung of the ladder.

Under his weight the fire escape gave way. Flailing amid the falling metal, the Russian grabbed the window ledge and stopped his fall, but the fire escape crashed down to the ground.

"False alarm," Joe said. "How's it going on your end, Frank?"

"I think I've got the range," Frank said. He swung the looped end of the hose over his head like a lariat, then let go and flung it across to the other roof.

It bounced off a pipe, slipped off the building, and fell.

"Here," said Joe, taking the hose from Frank. "Let me show you how it's done."

"Hurry!" Elena screamed. Footsteps were pounding up the inside stairs.

We only need another minute, thought Frank. He studied the door to the stairwell. It had no lock. Metal braces stuck out of either side of the doorframe, but they were useless without a bar to hold the door closed.

A bar! he realized. He snatched up the ax and ran to the door. "Get back!" he ordered Elena, and she moved to the side. The door swung open, and Frank kicked out, driving a man back into the stairwell. Elena threw her weight into the door and slammed it shut, and Frank rammed the ax handle into place across the two braces.

"That won't hold them long," he told Joe. "Any luck?"

Joe focused on a curved pipe on the far roof.

He threw the hose across the alley. It caught the pipe. He pulled it taut.

"Let's go," he said. Frank scooped up the files as Elena rushed to Joe's side.

"Grab onto me," Joe said to Elena. "And hold tight." He lowered himself and Elena onto the hose and started to inch across the rope.

After only a foot of very slow going they heard the sound of wood splintering. The ax handle was breaking.

"You'll never make it all the way across," Frank whispered. "You'll get gunned down."

"We have to try," said Joe.

"Maybe not," Frank answered. And he signaled them to hurry back.

As Joe worked his way back the short distance, Frank said, "Here's my plan. . . ."

With a crack the ax handle split and shattered, the door swung open, and Russians swarmed onto the rooftop. They stopped, staring at one another in confusion.

Aside from the Russians, the rooftop was deserted.

Konstantin strolled onto the roof, and the Russians snapped to attention. He walked to the hose, still stretched to the far building, and looked over the edge of the roof. On the ground, halfway across the alley, were files and the AK47. On the far roof were more scattered files.

"How could you let them escape?" roared an angry voice behind him. Konstantin turned to see Vladimir standing in the doorway.

He waved Vladimir to the roof's edge. "They have reached the next house. Your men should search the streets. On foot they cannot get far." Almost as an afterthought he added, "They seem to have some of your files."

"What are you waiting for?" Vladimir told his men. "Bring them back."

The Russians raced down the stairs. Vladimir followed them slowly. On the roof Konstantin gazed at the nearby houses in the peaceful Spanish morning. Below, a wave of Russians broke through the streets. "Clever boys," Konstantin said, chuckling, then abruptly turned and went downstairs.

"All gone," Frank said. He rolled off the top of the structure that housed the stairwell, landed on the roof, and stretched his legs.

"I was so afraid," Elena said as Joe helped her down. "Lying so still, trying not to make a sound—"

Joe dropped to the roof. "You did fine. That was a good idea, Frank, throwing the files and rifle off the roof to make them think we'd made it to the other side."

"There was almost nothing in the files we could use," Frank said. "And the rifle wouldn't have done us much good against all those men. We didn't have anything to lose. This place should have cleared out by now. How can we get away from here?"

"I have a car parked just a block away," Elena said.

"Sounds like our best shot," Frank agreed. Going downstairs, they moved cautiously through the almost deserted consulate.

Elena turned onto a narrow dirt road. A short distance farther she pulled the Audi to a stop. "Well, where do we go?" she asked.

"Let's get out of the car for a minute and then discuss it," Joe answered her.

"We have to find the Network—if we can," Frank said. "They're at the bottom of this whole mess."

"You're right," said a deep voice. "But the Network found you instead." Both Frank and Joe recognized the man who appeared just behind them. Usually he wore a gray suit and a rumpled trench coat. That day he was in short sleeves, with a camera around his neck—a typical tourist. His specialty was appearing completely unremarkable, just one more face in the crowd. But he really was a dangerous agent.

"The Gray Man!" Joe said. Whenever they dealt with the Network, they had always worked through him. "Are we glad to see you! You've got to help us clear our names."

"I can't, Joe." He drew his hand from his slightly baggy pants. He held a small pistol. "I have my orders," the Gray Man said. "You're coming with me."

Chapter

8

"YOU'RE KIDDING!" JOE said. But the Gray Man's expression told him it was no joke. "Take us in for what?"

"Washington thinks you killed our agent here," the Gray Man explained. He waved the gun to signal them to raise their hands. "I'm to bring you in before the Spanish grab you. We don't want this to become more of an incident than it already is."

Frank slowly edged left. "Do you think we did it?"

The Gray Man shrugged. "What I think doesn't matter. To the Network you're outsiders. And that makes you suspect. The theory is you got greedy, stole the data Martin gave you, and decided to go into business for yourself. He tried to stop you and you killed him.''

"Business?" Frank said. As the Gray Man's eyes followed Frank, Joe eased to the right. "Like *selling* the data? We don't even know what it is. How are we supposed to sell it?''

"You're not stupid, Frank, so don't play dumb with me,'' the Gray Man said. "In his last message, Martin said he passed the data on to you. If he said he did, he did.''

Frank pondered the Gray Man's words. Had Martin passed the information to them without their knowing it? Was it in something he said? Or something he gave them? He reached for his pocket, and the Gray Man took aim at him.

"Slowly,'' the Gray Man said. "Two fingers.''

Frank nodded, and dug into his back pocket with his thumb and index finger. Their itinerary was still there. He pulled it out. "This is the only thing Martin gave us,'' he said. "If this isn't it, I don't know what it is.''

"Give it to the girl,'' the Gray Man ordered. Frank handed the paper to Elena. "Bring it here.'' She walked to the Gray Man, who took the paper in his free hand. As Elena returned to Frank, the Gray Man shook the paper open and studied it.

"This was printed from a computer,'' the Gray Man said. He crumpled the paper and threw it to the ground. "That wasn't Martin's style. To keep

61

up his cover as a writer, he used a battered old manual typewriter. The *E* and the *J* were crooked. He didn't write this. Stop playing games."

"The chauffeur said Martin gave it to him to give to us," Joe insisted, taking another step to the right.

"Chauffeur? The Network didn't arrange for a chauffeur."

Frank's jaw dropped. "Arrange? It was part of the contest I won."

"You won because you were the only entry," said the Gray Man. "It wasn't my idea. The Network needed a go-between for this exchange, someone who wasn't publicly connected to us.

"One of our people suggested you. When I told them you wouldn't go along with it, they created the phony contest. Once you were in Málaga, Martin would handle you."

He sighed. "I objected to the plan, but I was outvoted."

"Because your agent *had* to be rescued," Frank said. "I can understand that, but the Network still had no right to involve us."

"Who told you about our agent?" The Gray Man asked, suspicion creeping into his voice. "I thought you didn't talk to Martin about it."

"As a matter of fact, it was a guy named Konstantin," Frank said, inching left.

It was the Gray Man's turn to be surprised, and

for a moment it showed on his face. "Konstantin's here?" he said.

Joe nodded. "Do us a favor," he said. *"Talk* to us. Pretend for a minute that we walked into the middle of this, and tell us what's going on. Maybe if we know what this information is, we can tell you where to find it."

"I owe you that much," the Gray Man replied. "Martin had discovered the name of a mole—a double agent—inside the KGB. He was working for the Chinese too. That's why they were willing to let our man go.

"Stop it," he said suddenly.

Joe and Frank froze. They were standing directly opposite each other, with the Gray Man in the middle. The Gray Man knew that they had been trying to outflank him all along. "We're not going back with you," Joe said. "The only way to take us is to shoot us."

The Gray Man shook his head. "Don't be stupid."

"We've been set up," Joe said. "And our only hope is to prove that."

"I want to believe you. But I've already spent too much time talking about this." His face hardened. "Now, take out your pistol and throw it down the hill, Frank. Yes, I can see you've got one."

With two fingers Frank pulled the pistol from

his pants pocket and cast it away. "We don't want to hurt you," he said.

"That's nice," the Gray Man said. "I'd hate shooting you too."

Joe took a deep breath and charged. Maybe the Gray Man's reluctance would slow down his trigger finger. . . . He leapt in, feinting with his left. As the Gray Man slapped Joe's left arm aside, Joe drove a powerhouse right at the Gray Man's stomach.

But before the punch could land, the Gray Man swerved. His elbow hooked down around Joe's wrist, and the Gray Man's hand wrapped around Joe's shoulder. He spun on his heel and jerked forward. With a loud slap Joe slammed facedown into the dirt. The Gray Man had decked him without even using his gun.

Elena screamed and scampered off.

Frank circled slowly around the Gray Man. Their eyes locked and focused. He's going to beat me, Frank thought as he stared at the look of confidence on the man's face. No, he told himself. He's psyching me out. I'm going to win. I *have* to win. With a sharp cry Frank hurled himself forward, kicking out at the Gray Man's gun hand.

Once again the Gray Man didn't use his gun. His free hand shot out and cracked into Frank's chest, knocking him backward. Frank landed on his back with a thud.

"Finished?" the Gray Man asked. Angrily, Frank and Joe got to their feet. "Let me put it another way. You *are* finished." The gun was pointing dead at them. "Prove your innocence when you get home."

"No!" Elena shouted. She stood a few feet away. In her hand was the gun Frank had thrown away. "Get your hands up," she told the Gray Man. "Now!"

The Gray Man dropped his gun and cupped his hands together in back of his head. Joe scooped up the gun, and Frank yanked the camera from around the Gray Man's neck. With Elena keeping the gun aimed, the Hardys led the agent to a tree.

"Sorry we have to do this," Frank said. He pulled the Gray Man's arms back around the tree and tied them with the camera strap.

"We'll have a chance to talk again," the Gray Man called after them as they ran back to their car. "Real soon."

Moments later the car screeched back onto the main road, passing a gray sedan parked at the junction. "The Gray Man's," Frank said. "He's a very slick tail. I was looking, and never knew we were being followed."

"Think he'll be all right up there?" Joe asked. "Maybe we shouldn't have left him tied up."

"Him? He's probably free already," Frank said, rolling his window down. "You know, we're running out of time. We really have to figure this thing out."

"I've been thinking about this mole in the KGB," Joe said, glancing out at the rocky hillside as they rushed past. "Suppose he found out about the exchange? If I were in that guy's shoes, I'd want to stop it."

Taking one hand off the steering wheel, Frank snapped his fingers. "Sure, that makes sense. He could learn a lot by putting himself close to Martin—maybe in disguise."

"Exactly, he could disguise himself as a chauffeur," Joe said. "Yeah, why else would that chauffeur pass a note to us and claim it was from Martin—for that matter, what other reason would he have for going around wearing a false beard and nose? He killed Martin, and *he* probably got the information everybody seems to think we got."

"Maybe not," Frank said. "This guy didn't take off. He hung around after Martin was dead. Remember the next day? Why would he do that if he had the data? I'm betting our mole doesn't have it yet."

Joe thought about it. "So we can still catch him."

"Right." To Elena in the back seat Frank said, "We're going to head back to our hotel. We'd better split up at that point. You're in this thing too deep as it is."

"Too deep to leave," Elena told him. "The Russians think I betrayed them. If they find me now, they'll—" She shuddered. "No, I'm safer staying with you two."

"We won't let anything happen to you." Joe glanced in the rearview mirror. A small red car was speeding along on the empty stretch of road behind them. "Frank? I think we might have company," he warned.

After looking in the mirror, Frank frowned. "Yeah, I noticed that car before, right after we left the Soviet consulate. Could be nothing, but then again—"

The red car sped up, zipping suddenly to the left to pass them. Frank glanced at it suspiciously, reaching for one of the pistols.

But a woman he'd never seen before was driving the red compact. Her eyes were hidden by sunglasses, and long dark hair swirled over her face and fell to meet a high collar that covered her neck.

She smiled warmly at Frank, and she raised a cigarette holder with a long cigarette in it to her lips.

Frank relaxed. "Nothing to worry about," he decided.

A thick swirl of smoke spat from the tip of the cigarette and shot across the space between the two cars. The smoke hit Frank in the face.

He coughed, suddenly let go of the wheel, and clutched at his throat with both hands.

The red car was already past them, speeding away.

For an instant Joe stared at his choking brother. "Frank, what's wrong?"

Frank tried to catch his breath but couldn't. "Smoke," he gasped. "Poison—" He fell against the steering wheel of the speeding car. "Woman—KGB—poisoned me—"

From the backseat Elena pointed and screamed.

Joe glanced up through the front windshield and grabbed for the steering wheel.

The road ahead took a sharp curve around a cliff. Far below the road was a stretch of bright blue sea. If Joe didn't get control, they'd be off the road and in the air.

Desperately, Joe tried to steer the careening Audi.

The car swerved wildly across the road. Its motion threw the unconscious Frank against his brother.

Joe lost his grip on the wheel.

Right in front of them now was a low wooden rail. The car was rushing straight at it.

The rail was all that stood between them and the long drop to the rocky beach.

Chapter
9

JOE SHOVED AGAINST his brother's unconscious body and got one hand on the steering wheel.

He gave it a sharp twist and with his other hand yanked at the emergency brake.

The Audi rattled, shuddered, and scraped against the wooden railing. Then it groaned and jerked to a stop, just inches from the edge.

Joe jumped out and glanced down the road as he hurried around the front of the car. "There's a truck blocking the road down there—holding up that red car. We can still catch her."

He ran to the driver's side, opened the door, and tugged Frank out from behind the wheel.

"I'm going to put him in the back, Elena. You drive," he told her.

A moment later they were off.

The road ahead was clear again, and the red car was growing ever smaller in the distance.

Elena slammed the gas pedal to the floor. "We should take him to the hospital," she suggested. "He may be dying."

"I'm sure he is," Joe said in a low voice. "But if he was right about that woman being a KGB assassin, a hospital won't help him. By the time they find what poisoned him, he'll be dead. No, our only hope is to catch up to the assassin."

They were reaching more heavily traveled roads now. The red car moved slower, but even so, the distance between it and the Audi kept growing.

"She is losing us," Elena cried. "How can she help your brother?"

"When KGB assassins use poison, they always carry an antidote, in case they should accidentally poison themselves," Joe replied grimly. "She's got it, and it's the only thing that will save Frank."

The street widened into a boulevard, with a grassy strip between the two sides of the road. The red car was still in view, far ahead. "You *are* a spy!" Elena said to Joe. "How else could you know so much about the KGB?"

Joe chuckled in spite of himself. "We're not spies, Elena, just ordinary Americans. There are plenty of books published about the KGB and how they operate. I've read one or two of them."

His smile faded as the red car vanished from sight, and he looked at his brother.

Frank was still breathing, but in a shallow, uneven way. His skin was tinged with blue. "He's suffocating." Joe's fists clenched as he looked for the red car. But it was gone. "We've failed."

"Not yet!" Elena said, determined. She spun the steering wheel left and hit the gas again. The Audi bounced on the low curb and sped onto the boulevard's center strip. The Hardy's car skidded wildly on the grass, its tail swaying back and forth, but Elena gripped the wheel and kept control.

They sped along the center strip, passing the traffic clogging the road, tearing through shrubs and flower beds. The red car came back into view—still far ahead. Joe bent forward in his seat. "Go," he urged Elena, and she sped even faster. Frank's life was in Elena's hands.

"Look out!" Joe shouted suddenly. Elena took her eyes off the red car and saw a clump of trees dead ahead, covering the width of the center strip. There was no way through it, and no time to stop. Elena slammed her foot on the brake and froze. Barely slowing, the car hurtled on toward the trees.

Joe reached over, spinning the steering wheel. The car swerved left, ran off the median, and sped headlong into the oncoming traffic. Cars ran off the road to avoid the Audi, and horns blared as it zipped past them. Elena stared straight ahead, her hands still gripping the wheel.

"Snap out of it!" Joe barked. "Frank needs you." At the sound of his voice Elena shook as if waking from a dream. With a gasp she slammed the brake and turned the wheel, and, tires screaming, the Audi pulled back onto the median, on the other side of the trees.

"The red car," she said, pointing to a compact on the right side of the median. Joe saw the dark-haired woman in it and smiled without humor.

"She's slowed down," he said. "She must think she lost us. Is she in for a surprise!"

The Audi jumped off the median and swung into traffic, sideswiping the red car. The woman looked up, startled, her face still obscured by sunglasses and wisps of black hair. But her lips tightened in anger as she saw Joe's face, and she aimed the cigarette holder toward him.

"Hit her again," Joe ordered, and Elena rammed the Audi into the red car a second time. The cigarette holder tumbled from the woman's fingers in the impact. It hung in midair for a second as she desperately grabbed for it. She missed. The holder fell out the car window and shattered on the ground, spewing glass pellets which broke and gave off wisps of poisoned smoke. In trying to catch the holder, the woman let go of her steering wheel.

The little red car screamed across the lanes and

smashed into a storefront, scattering fruit and vegetables all over the street. As the Audi pulled to a stop behind it, Joe looked at Elena admiringly. "Where'd you learn to drive like that?" he asked.

"American television," she replied. Then her eyes widened as the woman scrambled from the red car. "She's getting away!" Elena shouted.

"Not if I can help it," Joe replied. "Stay here with Frank." He leapt from the Audi and ran after the woman, who sprinted down the line of stores.

Joe closed in. The woman turned into the nearest alley and vanished from sight for a moment, but Joe wasn't worried. He knew she couldn't outrun him. He rounded the corner—and stopped.

The woman was gone.

It's not possible, he thought. The alley ended at a brick wall, and there was no way over it. Cautiously, Joe tried the doors on the alley. None opened. The woman couldn't have escaped.

Finally, he tried a pair of old wooden doors set into the ground. They swung up to reveal wooden steps and a dark basement below. He listened. From deep in the darkness came a muffled panting.

The woman was there.

He slowly moved down into the pitch-black of

the basement. There was no sound now. Two steps, and no sign of the woman. Three steps.

Strong hands grabbed his ankle, tugged, and Joe pitched down the last stairs. He rolled, landing faceup, and in the dim light he caught the faint gleam of a small revolver aimed at him.

"You will not live to blackmail me," came a gritted whisper from the dark. "You, your brother, Martin—you should never have played games with me." A finger tightened on the trigger.

Joe kicked fiercely and knocked the gun into the air as the shot rang out. He did a backward flip and landed on his feet as the woman started up the steps. Without thinking, Joe lunged at her, grabbing at her purse and her hair. Both tore loose in his grip, and he fell back down the stairs, landing on the basement floor with a thud. The woman vanished into the alley.

Seconds later Joe emerged into the light. He started back to the Audi.

"Quick," Elena said as she saw him. She held Frank, whose breathing had all but stopped. "You got the antidote from the woman?"

Joe opened the purse, rifled through it, and brought out a small clear bottle with Russian lettering on it. "This had better be it," he said, and handed it to Elena, who opened it and forced the contents through Frank's lips.

Frank sputtered and convulsed as the liquid

74

flowed into his mouth. With a great spasm he went limp in Elena's arms.

"He's not breathing," Elena said, terrified. "I think he's dead!"

"Am—not," Frank mumbled, and opened his eyes. "What happened?"

"Oh, nothing," Joe said, relieved. "You just got poisoned by a KGB agent."

"Joe caught her," Elena said excitedly.

Joe flushed and shook his head. "No, I didn't," he admitted. "And it wasn't a her."

"What?" Frank and Elena said at the same time.

Joe held up the wig. "A disguise. When she spoke, she had a man's voice—also disguised— and she wore men's shoes. I got a pretty good look at them. It was a man disguised as a woman."

"The chauffeur was a disguise too," Frank said. He sat up weakly in the car. "Probably the same person. And that assassination attempt means he's probably a member of Department V."

"Or was," Joe said. "It could have been Vladimir."

"We must go somewhere so you can rest," Elena told Frank. "Your hotel?"

Frank shook his head weakly. "The police might be waiting for us there. Any way we can get out of town without running into cops?"

"Certainly," Elena said. "We can follow the dirt roads along the hills and go south along the Costa del Sol. There is a resort village called Marbella not too far away."

"Anywhere we won't get chased or shot at is okay with me," Joe replied. Elena started the car, and they wound through the foothills of the Sierra Nevada Mountains. They could see the highway that hugged the coastline but were far removed from it. The hillsides were dotted with small pastel-colored houses.

"I cannot believe Vladimir is an assassin," Elena said after some time.

"So why'd you save us from him at the consulate?" Joe asked.

"It was that man, Konstantin," Elena said. "Electricity." She swallowed in disgust. "He would have killed you."

"I don't think so," Frank replied. He thumbed through the one file he had taken from Vladimir's office. "Konstantin just wanted to scare us."

"That doesn't make him a nice guy though," Joe said.

Frank pulled a map of the Spanish coast out of the file. On it, the town of Torremolinos was circled in red. He held up the map so Elena could see it. "Does this mean anything?"

"Vladimir's villa is there," Elena replied, glancing at the map. "I went there once."

"Hmmm," Frank said, setting down the map

and picking up another piece of paper. "Here's a memo from some KGB agent accusing Vladimir of anti-Soviet activities. He probably intercepted before it got to his superiors."

"Maybe they did get the message. That could be why he's stuck in Spain," Joe said, chuckling.

Then he stopped laughing, his eyes opening wide. Joe looked at Frank. He had the same expression on his face.

"Vladimir's the mole!" they said at the same time.

Frank settled back in his seat. "That would explain why the KGB sent Konstantin in to look after things. They suspect Vladimir." He made a fist and chewed on his knuckle as he thought. "Elena, who brought you in to contact us?"

"Vladimir," Elena said.

"And who were you supposed to give the information to?"

"Vladimir," Elena replied.

"Where was he the morning of the contact?" Frank continued.

"I don't know," she said uncertainly.

"Yeah, he could have been the chauffeur," Joe said. "What's that noise?"

Frank heard it too, a soft whirring growing louder each second. He stared out the window at the sky.

"Helicopter!" Frank shouted over the noise. "No markings. It's not the police."

Something flashed from the side of the helicopter and screamed toward them.

The ground erupted in smoke and thunder, throwing Frank out the window as the car swayed on two wheels. It crashed back to the ground as the helicopter fired another missile.

An explosion in front of the Audi brought it to a halt and spattered it with dirt. The car half vanished in the gathering smoke.

As Frank watched helplessly from the roadside, a third missile screamed down. Shock waves hurled him back as the car went up in a ball of fire.

"Joe!" Frank called as he picked himself up off the ground. "Joe!"

No sound came from the Audi except a steady crackling, and no movement but the dancing of the flames.

Chapter

10

"Joe!" Frank cried out again. He tried to reach the burning car, but the heat and smoke forced him back.

I've got to keep yelling so Joe and Elena can find their way out of the flames, Frank told himself. Joe has survived worse than this. I can't give up. I can't. But even as he shouted, Frank wondered how long he could keep convincing himself.

The beating of the rotors drowned out his voice as the helicopter landed on the road a few yards from the wreck. The pilot got out, holding a rifle. Out from the other side stepped an agent Frank recognized. The agent flashed Frank an unpleasant smile, and Frank could feel his grief burn away into anger.

"Your foolishness cost your brother his life,"

the pilot said. "Do not resist, or the same will happen to you." He cradled the rifle in the crook of his arm, leveling it at Frank.

Frank clenched his fists. Just stay cool, he told himself. They had killed Joe, and they had to pay for it. Hot anger wasn't going to help him. He had to cool down. He had to stay alive and make them pay.

The Russians walked toward him, and Frank backed away from them. "Stop," ordered the pilot, his finger pulling back on the trigger.

"Go ahead," Frank said, surprised by the coldness in his own voice. "Shoot. You'd like that. Vladimir would like that. Then he'd never get the information he wants, would he? It'd be out there, waiting for someone else to find it. I can just imagine what he'd do to the men who kept him from getting it."

The smile faded from the agent's lips. He shot a worried glance at the pilot, who seemed unconcerned. Frank turned away from them and began walking, but as he took his fifth step, the pilot fired. The shot sprayed up a jet of dirt just inches in front of Frank's feet. He stopped.

"But Konstantin will not mind," the pilot said, laughing. "Hands up, please." Frank raised his hands. "Come here."

Frank marched toward them. His bluff had failed, he realized, and if he tried to run from the rifle, it would cut him down. He stared bitterly at the burning car as he headed back.

All of a sudden Frank stopped, startled. "Come," the pilot repeated, and Frank began walking again, his face toward the ground to keep them from realizing what he had seen.

In the smoke something had moved, then vanished behind the helicopter.

With the rifle the pilot nudged Frank toward the helicopter. He circled in front of Frank to lead the way, backing up to keep Frank covered. The silent agent followed on Frank's heels, ready to block any escape attempt. At last the pilot backed through the helicopter door, signaling Frank to follow.

But something moved behind the pilot, inside the helicopter. Joe! His face was streaked with smoke, and he looked grim as he slammed into the pilot's back, knocking him out of the helicopter. Frank grabbed the rifle with both hands, rolled into a backward somersault, and, kicking upward, threw the surprised pilot over his head and into the silent agent.

They tumbled to the ground, and then Frank and Joe were on them. When Frank and Joe stood, the pilot and the agent were unconscious.

"Am I glad to see you!" Frank said, giving his brother a hug. "How?"

"Luck, mostly," Joe replied. "When you got knocked out of the car, I guessed what was coming next, so I grabbed Elena and pulled her out the other side." He whistled. From behind a bush Elena appeared. "I'm not sure what happened next. An explosion, I guess, and when I woke up, I saw those jerks hauling you off. So I snuck around to the other side of the chopper and got in to surprise them."

"You saved my life," Elena said.

"No problem," Joe said, a bit embarrassed. He looked at the remains of the Audi. The fire was almost out, leaving a blackened husk. "It's a cinch we're not going anywhere in that. Maybe we ought to turn back."

"No," Elena said. "Marbella is only five kilometers more. Perhaps less."

"About three miles, then," Frank said. "We'd better get walking." Joe and Elena stared at him. "It's safer and less conspicuous than hitchhiking," he explained. "And none of us knows how to fly a chopper, right?"

"When you're right, you're right." Joe picked up the rifle in both hands, twirled it over his head, and let it go. It disappeared into a tree. "No sense leaving it for the Russians. Should we tie them up with their belts?"

Frank nodded.

As soon as they were finished, they began the long hike to Marbella.

* * *

82

"I hope this works," Joe said the next day. He was basking in the morning sun, refreshed after a good night's sleep in a soft bed. It now seemed like the day before had never happened. But he did remember everything. They had reached Marbella, checked into a hotel, and made plans over dinner.

"I don't see why it won't," Frank answered. They stood on a crest overlooking the harbor of Marbella, which was filled with yachts. "Elena kept up her end. A family's willing to take us back to Málaga on their private boat, so that'll get us past all the roadblocks."

"Think the desk clerk bought our stories?" Joe asked.

"After I asked him all those questions about how to get from Algeciras to Morocco?" Frank said. "Sure. He'll be able to identify us to the police all right."

"But will they buy it?" Joe wondered out loud.

"After we phone in a tip to Inspector Melendez, they ought to. While they're trying to keep us from getting to Africa, we can search our hotel room and Martin's in Málaga."

They walked past a row of boutiques and restaurants. Stopping in front of a swimwear shop, Joe studied the window. "You know," he said, "the boat ride to Málaga will last awhile. If I bought a suit, I could work on my tan on the way. And I did come to Spain to work on my tan."

"Dream on, brother," Frank said. He glanced at his watch. "Elena said we have to be on that yacht at nine A.M. sharp, or we'll get left behind." He stiffened. "Joe, look straight ahead, and whatever you do, don't turn around."

Puzzled, Joe stared in the window and gasped. On the other side of the street, reflected in the shop window, was a policeman. "He couldn't be looking for us, could he?" he whispered to Frank.

"I don't know," Frank whispered back. "Start walking. Slowly."

They sauntered down the street, leaving the policeman behind. As they turned a corner, they saw another policeman ahead of them, and, a block farther along, another.

The Hardys ducked into a doorway and waited for a third to pass.

"The harbor's crawling with cops," Joe realized when the policeman had walked by. "They *must* be after us."

"It's not possible," Frank said as they returned to the street. He looked at his watch again. It read 8:55. "Not unless— What if Elena sold us out?"

"Couldn't be," Joe replied. "Not after all we've been through together. More likely the hotel clerk got itchy and called the cops."

"We'll find out when we reach the harbor," Frank decided. "Or sooner." Another policeman walked straight toward them. There was no time to duck out of sight, and turning around would attract his attention. They would have to brazen it out.

He looked them up and down as they passed, but did nothing. Joe breathed easier. It had been simple, almost too simple, and he looked over his shoulder to get another look at the policeman's reaction.

He saw the policeman raise a whistle to his lips.

"Run," Joe yelled as a shrill whistle pierced the air. The Hardys sprinted off with the policeman close behind. Ahead lay the harbor, and the Hardys could see swarms of boats, all shapes and sizes, as they neared. But there was no sign of Elena.

Other policemen joined in the chase. "We're in luck," Frank said as he ran. "If you can call this luck. I don't think they've sealed off the harbor yet. That means all the cops are behind us."

They reached the harbor and dashed from pier to pier, looking for the boat. Where's Elena, Joe wondered. Maybe she did set us up.

No, he thought, and put the idea out of his mind. But they couldn't find Elena or the boat. More whistles sounded from all directions. The police were closing in.

"Look!" Frank shouted. "There she is!"

Elena stood in the stern of a large boat with

sails of aqua and gold. She was staring sadly at them.

Between them and the boat were fifty feet of water.

Trapped at the end of a pier, the Hardys watched the sailboat drift away, moving out to sea.

Chapter

11

THE HARDYS SLOWLY turned around. A semicircle of policemen had formed at the other end of the pier. They linked hands, barring any path of escape, and walked slowly toward the Hardys.

"Great," Joe said. "What do we do now?"

"The way I see it," Frank replied, "we fight or we surrender."

"What's the worst that could happen if we surrender?" Joe asked, though the grim humor in his voice told Frank he wasn't really serious. "We get thrown in a Spanish jail for what? Twenty, thirty years? Life maybe?" He clenched his fists and stood shoulder to shoulder with his brother, ready to do battle with the cordon of policemen.

Frank studied the crowd that was gathering to

watch on the dock. "If we fight, we could probably break through. But the police might start shooting. Someone could get hurt."

"Us, more than likely," Joe growled. The policemen were ten feet away, and closing in. "I guess there's only one thing to do."

Frank nodded. "One—two—three . . ."

At the count of three the Hardys took two steps back and dropped from the pier into the ocean. The policemen broke ranks and dashed to the end of the pier. There was no sign of the Hardys, only ripples on the water. Two policemen dived into the water, stayed under for a few seconds, then bobbed to the surface, shaking their heads. Others ran back down the pier and scattered the length of the harbor, their eyes on the water. They, too, had nothing to report. The Hardys were gone.

Air trapped in his puffing cheeks, Joe swam underwater, moving steadily away from the land. The water above him looked golden with the morning sun shining on it, but below was darkness. His lungs burned, and he desperately needed to breathe.

He clamped his lips, holding the air in as he passed under something long and dark. The hull of a boat, he realized. Ahead he saw a soft glow, and he knew that there, on the other side of the boat, he could surface and breathe again, hidden from the harbor.

Joe reached up, clawing toward the light. His chest ached. How long had he been under, he wondered, and he knew it was too long. His mouth burst open with a rush of air, and saltwater came flooding in. It stung his lips and tongue, and pushed down his throat, choking him. His water-logged clothes were dragging him down, but he kicked desperately, forcing himself up toward the light.

Sputtering and coughing, Joe broke through the surface of the sea, arching his back so that his face remained above water. As he floated and gulped the warm Mediterranean air, the sea churned in a bubbly froth, and a small wave splashed over him. From the middle of the wave burst Frank, gasping for life. Joe grabbed his brother's arm and held him up until Frank caught his breath too.

"Any sign of the cops?" Frank asked, still choking on the sea. They bobbed in the shadow of a moored yacht, hidden from the shore by it. Joe peered around the yacht's bow and studied the harbor.

"No," he said. "But it won't be long before they send boats out to look for us." Joe turned toward the open sea and saw the sailboat they should have been on drifting away from them, its gold- and aqua-striped sail waving at them like a flag. "Think we can catch it?"

Frank dabbed a finger on his tongue and stuck

the finger in the air. "Not much wind," he replied. "What choice do we have?"

Kicking off from the side of the yacht, they propelled themselves toward the drifting sailboat. With powerful strokes the Hardys cut through the warm blue water, moving farther and farther out to sea.

"Think there're any sharks or octopuses out here, Frank?"

"Let's hope we won't find out," Frank said, his eyes on the sailboat. It was closer now, carelessly washing eastward on gentle winds and currents. He could see Elena on the stern, still staring back at the harbor. "Only a few more yards."

"Hey!" Joe yelled as loud as he could, and Elena stiffened and looked around. Again he yelled, "Over here!" He treaded water and waved frantically. Elena shielded her eyes from the sun with her hand and gazed out over the water. A second later she stepped out of sight.

"Did she see us?" Frank asked. But before Joe could answer, he answered himself. "I wonder. I'm not sure we can trust her, Joe."

"We can trust her," Joe said. "Look at how she's helped us so far." But doubt was creeping into his voice. The sails on the boat had shifted, and the boat picked up speed, cruising away from them. Had she seen them, he wondered. Had she told the captain to leave them adrift there? It was the only explanation he could think of.

"Look!" Frank said excitedly. "It's turning." The wind had caught the sails and was moving the sailboat rapidly back toward them. "I take it all back," he told Joe. "Elena's great."

Ropes were tossed down as the sailboat cruised past them, and the Hardys grabbed the ropes and tied them around their waists. One by one they were pulled onto the deck, and Joe smiled at Elena as he rose.

"You were lucky the little lady saw you, boys," said one of the men who had brought them aboard. He was tall and red-faced, and his voice had a familiar twang. "And here we thought she was fooling us when she said some fellow Americans needed a ride. You oughtn't to have been late though. Made her look like a liar."

"Sorry about that. We ran into a little trouble. You're Texan?" Joe asked, unable to believe his ears. "I'm Joe, and this is my brother, Frank."

Frank nodded and peeled off his wet shirt.

"Sam," the Texan replied. He pointed to a rugged-looking man at the wheel. "That's Jimmy Luke. You boys easterners, hey? Well, I guess not everyone can be born lucky. You better get out of those wet clothes. The sun'll dry them out by the time we hit Málaga, and there are some swim trunks in the hold you can wear in the meantime."

"Thanks," Frank said. "When do you expect we'll reach Málaga?" He and Joe walked toward the hold.

"A couple hours at the rate we're going," Sam replied. "You all just relax and enjoy yourselves, y'hear?"

"Thanks again," Joe said. "We really appreciate this."

Sam winked. "Think nothing of it. What are countrymen for, right?" As the boat straightened out its course, he called after the Hardys, "But the next time you go swimming, you ought to dress for it."

"Is there something wrong?" Elena asked Frank as they climbed onto the pier at Málaga. Frank had been frowning.

"I'd still like to know how the cops knew to expect us at the harbor," he said. "You never explained that."

"I *cannot* explain," Elena said desperately. "I had nothing to do with it. You must believe me."

"We do," Joe said, stepping between her and his brother. "Inspector Melendez probably notified every cop on the Costa del Sol to be on the lookout for us. All it would have taken was for one to spot us. For all we know, they think we're in Algeciras by now, just as we planned."

"Look, I'm sorry," Frank said to Elena. "But

this is a life-or-death situation. We can't afford to ignore all the possibilities.''

"I forgive you." But Elena's voice trembled as she spoke. She pressed close to Joe, and he put a comforting arm around her. "I only wanted to help."

"You have," Joe said, and he glowered at Frank. "A lot. If that's settled, we'd better figure out where we go from here."

"The bus," Frank said, and both Joe and Elena stared at him in surprise. "We're running out of money," he explained, "so we'd better get to the hotel and try to get our travelers' checks. It'll be risky, but if the police are convinced we're on our way to Africa, security might be lax."

"Plus," Joe said, "if Martin really gave us something, it's got to be in our stuff. I think the only way we're going to crack this thing open is to find the information. So where do we catch a bus?"

"Right this way," Elena said.

After a slow, crowded ride back into central Málaga, they arrived in front of their hotel.

"It's quiet," Joe said as he stepped off the bus. "Too quiet. It might be a trap."

"No," said Elena. "Siesta time. It's customary during lunch for the stores to close up. Everyone goes home to eat and sleep. The hotel should be just as quiet."

They reached the front door and Frank looked

in. In the lobby three people sat in armchairs, reading papers. Only one man stood behind the main desk. "We've got to get in without being seen," he said. Then, to Elena he said, "Can you distract them?"

"Yes," Elena said. She left them and walked around the hotel until they could see her framed in the rear exit. "Help!" she screamed. "*Socorro!* Help!"

The desk clerk ran to the hall, and Elena disappeared from the back door as he rounded the corner and moved toward the exit. The guests in the lobby turned their heads toward the screaming.

In a flash Joe dashed through the lobby and slipped behind the front desk, grabbing the key to their room. He joined Frank at the stairwell, and together they sprinted up to the third floor. No one else was in the hallway.

Carefully, they leaned around the corner and looked down the hall. "They've taken the guard off the door," Frank said. "Let's go." They slipped silently to their room. Joe put the key into the lock, quickly turned it, and swung open the door. They darted in, shutting the door behind them.

Frank let out a sigh as he opened the closet door. Then he froze.

None of their luggage was there.

He frantically went over the room, then turned

to his brother. "The police took everything," Frank said, dismayed. "We've hit a dead end."

"That's a good way of putting it," said a voice behind them. As the Hardys turned, the door slammed shut.

"Now," the Gray Man continued as he stood in the narrow entrance hall. "Where were we?"

Chapter

12

JOE HURLED HIMSELF at the Gray Man. In the cramped area Joe hoped the Network agent wouldn't have space to maneuver.

The Gray Man ducked under Joe's swing, stood up, and drove his arm against Joe's back. Joe slammed into the wall and bounced off. The Gray Man caught him behind the knees, and then Joe was flying across the room. He sprawled on his bed as the Gray Man, hands in his pockets, sat in a chair near the door.

The government man sighed. "Frank, sit on your brother while we have a little chat."

Frank leaned on a wall and put his hands in his own pockets, keeping his eyes on the Gray Man. "What's there to talk about? You've got to take us in, right?"

"Maybe," the Gray Man replied. "Maybe not."

"Does this mean you believe we didn't kill Martin?" Frank asked.

"I wrote up your profiles for the Network, remember? Cold-blooded murder's just not in your makeup. Even if you had a motive, which you don't."

"Yeah," Joe said, sitting up on the bed. "But you said your boss wouldn't be satisfied."

"I've been thinking about that," the Gray Man said. "I had a lot of time to think yesterday. You might remember. Someone left me tied up to a tree."

"Sorry about that," Frank said. "We had to. You understand."

The Gray Man shrugged. "I would have done the same. But let me explain something to you. It doesn't matter if you're innocent or not. A deal with the Russians got messed up. The Network won't take the rap for that; it would look bad for our side. If they can lay the blame on the go-betweens, well, it's what happens sometimes when you use freelancers."

"That's not fair," Joe protested. "We didn't ask to get in the middle."

"Welcome to the spy business," the Gray Man answered. "Face it. You're what we in the business call 'out in the cold,' unless you can pull a rabbit out of your hat."

"Or a killer and a name," Frank said. "We sort of figured that out already. Why are you telling us all this?"

"I feel responsible for you," the Gray Man admitted. "I got you involved with the Network in the first place. So I'm going to help."

"Won't that upset your people?" Joe asked.

"We won't tell them," the Gray Man said. "They won't suspect anything for another twenty-four hours. That's our time limit. What have you got so far?"

"A theory," Frank replied. "Our most likely suspect for the murder is the KGB mole."

"Who is—?"

Frank shook his head. "That's the problem. We can't know for sure until we get our hands on Martin's information. Do you have any idea what it looked like?"

"None," the Gray Man said. "No one in Washington does either. That was Martin's department. He was a strange guy, a real loner." He rubbed his chin, thinking. "What's your girlfriend's role in this anyway? Ever consider that she might be your suspect?"

"We considered it," Frank began.

"No, we didn't," Joe interrupted angrily.

"No offense, Joe," the Gray Man said, "but I'll take Frank's word over yours in this case. You're a sucker for a pretty face." Joe reddened with embarrassment. "Frank, go on."

"We dismissed it," Frank said. "She's as innocent as we are. We think it's Vladimir, the KGB agent. And we think Martin did slip us the information to prove it—without telling us. But the cops got all our stuff, so how are we going to find it?"

"That is a problem," the Gray Man agreed. "Unless you knew that it was probably in the local police storage warehouse and that the warehouse is half a mile from the harbor."

"How did you know that?" Joe asked.

"It's my business, remember?" the Gray Man said. "If I showed you where it was, you think you could sneak in and get your things?"

"You make it sound so easy," Joe said.

"You'll find a way," the Network agent replied. "You have to. The mole's probably as eager to get his hands on the information as you are. You'd better get to it first."

"You're right. Let's go," Frank said. "It's still siesta for a couple of hours. We may as well hit the place now. They won't be expecting it, and it makes more sense than waiting around here to be caught."

"Elena goes with us," Joe insisted. "I'm not abandoning her. Not while the Russians are after her too."

The Gray Man stood and chuckled. "See what I mean. A pretty face." He opened the door and peeked into the empty hall, then waved the Hardys toward him. "Sure, bring her. The more the merrier."

The police storage warehouse was a long windowless hut made of steel. It had a curved roof and was surrounded by a chain-link fence. "Electrified?" asked Frank as he studied the building from across the street. The Gray Man nodded and put a finger to his lips, signaling Frank to keep silent. In front of the gate to the warehouse an armed policeman stood, waiting at the checkpoint, and just inside the gate were parked a dozen empty police cars.

"How do we know how many cops are in there?" Joe whispered.

"We don't," the Gray Man whispered back, pointing his finger at the gate. "That's the only way in. And out."

"How are we supposed to get by *him?*" Frank asked, nodding toward the sentry.

"I'll handle that," the Gray Man said. He took Elena by the arm. "You just get ready to make your move."

The Hardys watched Elena and the Gray Man vanish down the street. For long minutes they waited.

A shrill squeal pierced the air, then turned into a growing mechanical rumble.

"What's that?" Joe asked, and then he saw it. The Gray Man's car was racing down the street, swerving wildly. The guard looked up, shocked, and unbuttoned his holster. Before the Hardys' eyes, the car skidded off the pavement and rammed to a stop against a telephone pole.

The car burst into flames, and from the fire came a pleading female voice, pitifully calling, *"Socorro! Socorro!"*

"Elena!" Joe gasped, and started out from his hiding place. This was a special nightmare for him. He'd lost one girlfriend in a burning car. But Frank grabbed his arm and held him back. "She's in trouble, Frank. If you don't let go, I'll—"

"No," Frank said. "Look." The guard ran to the burning car, and from the hut came two other policemen. They, too, went to the car, but all three were forced back by the flames. "I don't know how they're doing it, but it's just her voice. It's our diversion."

Joe's face brightened. "Come on," he said. While the policemen's backs were turned, the Hardys sneaked across the street and through the gate. They ran into the building, slamming the door behind them. Two offices were on either side of the doorway. From there the hut opened into a giant warehouse filled with file cabinets and rows of steel shelves.

"No time to figure out the filing system," Frank said. "Look for our suitcases. They can't store too much luggage in here."

"You think so, do you?" Joe asked as he

moved down one of the aisles. He stared at a rack filled with baggage. Then he smiled.

On the top shelf was his carry-on bag, and Frank's sat a shelf down. "Over here," he called.

Quickly they dragged the bags down and opened them. "It's all here," Frank said as he rifled through his things. "Nothing's been taken out, but nothing's been added to mine either. What about yours?"

"Nothing," Joe muttered. "I was so sure this would be it. We'd better get this stuff back in place so the cops won't suspect we've been here."

"Let's make a couple of changes," said Frank. He peeled back the upper lining of his suitcase and pulled a stack of traveler's checks from behind it. Then he picked up his tape player, strapped it to his belt, and stuffed a couple of tapes into his pockets. "If I'm going to be on the run, I'm going to enjoy myself," he explained.

A nearby voice shouted in Spanish. Frank and Joe looked up the barrel of a gun.

"What's he saying?" Frank asked as he stood and raised his hands.

"A rough translation?" Joe replied, his hands also in the air. "We're going to a jail for a long, long time."

Chapter

13

"DON'T SHOOT," FRANK told the policeman. His hands outstretched, he took a step toward the cop. Puzzled, the policeman fixed his aim on Frank and barked out an order. But Frank slowly moved closer.

"He wants you to stop, Frank," Joe said. "He doesn't understand English."

Frank jerked to a halt and raised his hands again, staring wide-eyed at the policeman. He looked innocent, but his words weren't. "That's all I need to know. When I tell you to, hit the floor. Fast."

"Don't make a move. He'll shoot." Joe translated the cop's words, his eyes on the gun aimed at his brother's chest. Without thinking, he moved toward Frank. Startled, the policeman pivoted, pointing the gun at Joe.

"Now!" Frank shouted. He clutched the shelf to his right and pulled. The shelf toppled over, burying the policeman in a flood of boxes and stolen merchandise. The loot literally swept the cop off his feet, the gun flying from his hand and sliding under another set of shelves without going off.

"That was lucky. One shot and this place would have been crawling with cops," Frank said, digging the policeman out from under the boxes. He checked the cop's pulse and held a finger beneath his nose to test his breathing. Both were strong and steady. "He'll be all right, except for this forced siesta."

"Great," Joe said. "Let's get out while we have the chance."

Cautiously, they crept toward the door. Frank opened the door a crack and looked out toward the checkpoint and the street. Though a thin trail of dark smoke still rose into the air, the fire in the car was out.

The two policemen who had rushed out to help were coming back in.

Frank and Joe looked at each other. They were trapped. Three cops blocked the only way out of the warehouse. And behind them was another guard, who sooner or later was going to wake up and start hollering.

"Things can't get worse," Joe whispered.

He was wrong.

"More trouble," Frank said, still looking outside. "Take a peek at who just showed up."

Joe glanced out. Then he closed the door. "Vladimir and Konstantin. What bad timing!"

"And it doesn't take a genius to guess what they want," Frank said. "The same thing we wanted—Martin's information. They must've come to the same conclusion we did."

"But we were wrong," Joe said. "It wasn't in our stuff."

"But they don't know that." Frank opened the door a sliver and looked out again. The guards were arguing with the Russians, barring the entrance while Vladimir kept pointing at some sort of document and thrusting it into their faces.

"Another chance to put your Spanish to the test, Joe. Can you make this out?"

Joe put his ear to the door and listened. "As near as I can make out, Vladimir has an order from Inspector Melendez giving them access to our stuff. The head guard wants them to wait until Melendez verifies the order."

The talking outside slowly turned to shouting. "Sounds like Vladimir doesn't care for that idea."

"His authorization order is probably a forgery." Frank grinned. "I bet Vladimir's getting pretty nervous by now. Until he gets and destroys

105

the information, his freedom's hanging by a thread.'' Outside, the voices rose.

"Konstantin seems to be taking the whole thing in stride.'' Joe peeked out. "This argument may be our best chance to get out of here—if we make our move quick.''

"If we can de-electrify the fence, we can climb over it. They don't even have to see us," Frank said. He gazed around for a switch but saw nothing. "The control must be outside, at the guard post. That lets that out. We'd never get to it without being spotted.''

"Something's happening," said Joe. At the checkpoint one guard was picking up a phone and reaching for his revolver.

Shaking his head, Konstantin held out his attaché case. It flipped open, and a cloud of gas burst out to envelop the three guards. They staggered back, then fell to the ground. Vladimir and Konstantin were both holding pads over their noses and mouths.

"Konstantin," came a voice outside the gate. The single word was punctuated by the telltale click of a bullet being jacked into the chamber of an automatic. Vladimir and Konstantin stiffened. They turned slowly.

The Gray Man stood there with an automatic trained on them.

"This is very foolish, my friend," Konstantin

scolded. "After we worked so well together in Paris."

"True, we'll always have Paris," the Gray Man replied. "But don't think we're friends. We're business associates, and we have problems to work out like civilized men."

Vladimir angrily pointed at the Gray Man. "You had your chance to save your agent," he said. "You will not see him again."

"Take it easy," the Gray Man said. "We can still work things out to everyone's satisfaction. Let's not abandon the swap over a silly misunderstanding."

"Misunderstanding?" Vladimir repeated coldly. "I for one do not—"

Konstantin raised a hand to silence him.

"Always you are the soul of logic, and I agree completely," Konstantin told the Gray Man. "We must, however, have some sign of your good intentions. A hostage, perhaps."

"I see three at your feet," the Gray Man said.

"We need someone more *personally* involved," Konstantin replied without blinking. "One of the young men. Where are they?"

"Right here," Frank said, throwing open the door behind the two Russians. "No hostages."

Vladimir whipped around at the sound of Frank's voice. When he saw the Hardys, his lips formed a hard line. But other than that he showed only icy calm. "These two young fools have stolen the name. Turn them over to us."

"Not true," the Gray Man said. "They've told me they didn't steal it, and I believe them. Someone else killed Martin. Your mole."

"Lies. A Network smear tactic," Vladimir said flatly. "You can prove nothing."

"I think we can, right now," the Gray Man replied, and to the Hardys he said, "Over here." They moved in a wide arc around the Russians. To Vladimir the Gray Man said, "I think we can. Tell us what you found in your luggage, Frank."

"Whatever Martin had, it wasn't there," Frank mumbled.

Vladimir's voice cut like a knife. "Even now they lie. We must not let them leave."

"Silence!" Konstantin barked. "Anyone can see these are honorable men." He smiled at Frank, saying, "I bow to your honesty," and he made a deep, comic bow, his head going almost all the way to his knees.

"Frank!" the Gray Man warned. "Look out!"

It was too late. From the bow Konstantin swept up one guard's revolver, and as his hands touched the ground, he balanced on them and swung his body around, catching his ankles in Frank's and knocking Frank off his feet.

They rose a second later. But now Konstantin stood behind Frank. His right arm wrapped tightly around Frank's neck, the other hand held the revolver.

"Ah. Now I have my hostage," Konstantin told the Gray Man.

Frank grabbed the arm across his throat and chinned himself on it, bringing his heels up against Konstantin's shins as hard as he could. The tall Russian howled and loosened his grip. Frank dropped to the ground, and he and Joe sprinted across the street.

"Stop!" Vladimir warned. He tore the revolver from Konstantin's grip and fired it recklessly.

"Get out of here!" the Gray Man ordered. He pushed Elena at Joe and fired back at Vladimir. "I'll handle this."

"We can't leave you," Frank said.

"I'll find you again, don't worry," the Gray Man answered. "If we take off together, they'll catch us in no time. If I hold them off, they'll lose your trail. Go." He stepped behind a tree and fired another shot around it.

"He is right," Elena said, and she tugged on their arms, pulling them away. Reluctantly, they left the Gray Man behind.

Siesta had ended, and crowds of people were back on the streets. "I wish we hadn't had to leave the Gray Man," Frank said.

"Say, how'd he pull off that car-crash stunt

anyway? I was afraid you were in the car," Joe said.

"A receiver," Elena admitted. "Part of the surveillance equipment he carries with him. I spoke into the microphone. He jammed the steering wheel of the car so it would move in a straight line when it rolled."

"Let's swap stories later," Frank said. "We're sitting ducks out here on the street. But where can we go?"

"I have friends," Elena said wearily. "I did not want to involve them, but now . . ." She sighed. "It is too far to walk." She went to the curb and stuck her thumb out.

"Hitchhiking's dangerous," Joe said. Elena ignored him. Three cars cruised by her, but the fourth came to a stop. She ran to it and scrambled into the front seat. The back door swung open, and Joe began to climb in. He stopped as he saw Elena trembling in front.

"Get in," Konstantin said, seated behind the steering wheel, a triumphant smile on his lips.

Chapter

14

KONSTANTIN STEPPED OUT of the car and spoke over the hood. "I do not have a gun," he said. "Please step into the automobile. You will not be harmed."

"What do you think?" Joe asked Frank. Frank shrugged and stared suspiciously at Konstantin.

"You may leave at any time," Konstantin continued. "It is important that we talk. Alone, far from Vladimir and his agents. Your lives may depend upon it."

"Come over here," Frank ordered. Konstantin walked around to the curbside. "Hands on the side of the car. Spread your feet wide apart."

As Konstantin stood in that position, Joe frisked him. "He's clean," Joe said. "No gun, just as he said."

"All right. Get in back." Frank motioned at the back door. "Elena will drive. Joe, you get in the front seat."

"Agreed," Konstantin said as he slid to the far side of the car. Frank got in after him.

The car pulled into traffic.

"Okay," Frank said. "Talk. What do you want?"

"To work with you," Konstantin answered. "To help you, so that you may help me."

The Hardys exchanged surprised glances. "Why would we want to help you?" Joe asked.

"To catch the killer of Martin Chase. Let me come to the point. You and I, we are on the same side, though you do not know it. I am a special operative, dealing with special problems."

His voice deepened. "Problems such as Vladimir."

"What's that to us?" Frank said.

"We have had our eye on Vladimir for some time," Konstantin continued. "Some months ago our agent in London disappeared after suggesting an investigation of Vladimir. His official report never arrived. That made us suspicious."

"I found the report," Frank said. "It was in Vladimir's files. Your agent recommended that Vladimir be recalled."

"You have this file?" Konstantin asked anxiously.

Frank shook his head. "Up in smoke in a bombed car. Go on."

"When Vladimir informed us that an exchange was about to take place, it was decided that I should come here. I arrived during your interrogation and took steps to take over. On determining that you were telling the truth—"

"I don't quite remember it happening that way," Joe said. "Seems to me you were about to fry me."

"He wasn't, Joe," Frank said. "He spoke to the gunmen in English so that we'd understand what he was saying. And he dawdled with the interrogation until we decided to make a break for it. He *wanted* us to escape."

Joe stared. "He *what?*"

Konstantin gazed at Frank with new respect. "Why should I wish that?"

"You want me to guess? I'd say you figured we had the incentive to find the information everyone was looking for, and you wanted us to lead you to it. Am I close?"

"It seems I am a better judge of character than I suspected," Konstantin said, laughing. "Vladimir sees you only as enemies or victims. He failed to see that you have the makings of a fine agent."

"Thanks," Frank said. "Now let's cut to the chase. You still haven't convinced us that we should work with you."

"Ah." Konstantin scratched his head. "I see.

113

Would it surprise you to know that I already know who the mole is? That I know it is Vladimir.''

"Yeah," Joe said. "We figured that out a long time ago. But convince us to work with you."

"Vladimir is desperate to save himself. That is why he was willing to confront the police."

"I thought that was a little dumb back there at the warehouse. But you seemed as involved as he was," Frank said.

"An act," Konstantin assured them. "If I did not act, he would have grown suspicious. Your escape from me was most convincing. But do you think a trained KGB agent would use such an elementary ploy?"

"Sure," said Frank moodily. He could still feel the grip on his throat, and he hoped the Russian's shins still smarted as well. "I like to think so."

"You would be wrong," Konstantin answered. "Vladimir will not stop until he is safe from you. I think you will also not stop until you find Chase's information, and when you do, I want it. I promise your names will be cleared, and I will prove Vladimir disguised himself as your chauffeur to assassinate Chase and watch you."

"And you get to put Vladimir out of commission," Frank said. "If we agree to work with you, you'll keep the KGB off our backs?"

"Agreed." Konstantin pulled a business card from his pocket. "You can contact me day or night at this number. Have we a deal?"

"We'll let you know," Frank said. "Elena, pull over." The car stopped at a curb and the four of them got out. "You keep up your end as a gesture of good faith, and we'll be in touch."

As he opened the driver's door, Konstantin asked, "Can I trust you?"

"You're such a student of human nature," Frank answered. "You tell me."

Konstantin smiled slowly and shook his head. "You Americans." He climbed into the driver's seat, then leaned over to the passenger's window. "One warning. Do not remain on the streets. The Spanish police are not interested in our deals."

The car pulled away. For long seconds they watched until it disappeared in traffic.

"He's got a point," Joe admitted. "We'd better not hang around where we can be spotted." To Elena he said, "Does the offer to stay with your friends still hold?"

"Of course," Elena said, fear in her voice. "But you said you cannot find the information. How can you make a deal?"

"Konstantin doesn't need to know that," Frank said.

He turned to Joe and Elena. "It's time we changed tactics. If we can't use Martin's information to prove our innocence, we'll use Martin's killer."

"Now that we're pretty sure who he is," Joe said. He stepped into the street to flag down a cab. "I can't wait to see the look on Vladimir's face."

"Neither can I, brother," Frank replied. "I can't wait to see the look on a lot of faces."

The taxi drove down a tree-shaded street, heading toward the house of Elena's friends.

They all sat in the backseat, Elena wedged between the Hardys. Joe stared out the window at the setting sun. Frank, his Walkman over his ears, listened with his eyes closed.

"How can he enjoy himself at a time like this?" Elena asked Joe.

"Music relaxes Frank," Joe explained with a grin. "It helps him think sometimes, and we have to think up a trap for Vladimir in a hurry. We've been lucky so far, but that can't last forever." He turned to look into Elena's eyes. "You've really been a lot of help to us."

She lowered her eyes. "I—they said no one would be hurt. When they tried to hurt you, I had to . . ." Giving in to exhaustion, Elena dropped her head on Joe's shoulder and began to cry. "How could I have trusted them?"

"Because you thought they believed in what you believe in," Joe said softly, putting a comforting arm around her.

The cab pulled up in front of a small house which sat on top of a hill. A long flight of stone steps led up to the house.

Joe let Elena out. "I'll get the fare," he said as she ran up the stairs. Joe reached back into the car and shook Frank. "Come on. We're here."

Frank opened his eyes and took off the headphones as Joe dug into his pocket for money.

Elena rang the doorbell. "Rafael," she called through the door. "It's me. Elena."

The door swung open, and Elena gasped.

"Stand still," said Inspector Melendez, who was standing inside the house. "Did you think the police were unaware of your activities? We have long kept track of your friends." He stepped back into the shadows and stared down at the Hardys. "Signal them to come up. Do not alarm them."

Slowly, forcing a smile, Elena turned. From the street Joe waved, and she waved back.

"Do nothing foolish," Inspector Melendez whispered. "Or you will be jailed in their place."

The inspector's words stinging her ears, Elena continued waving as Frank and Joe started up the stairs.

Chapter

15

ELENA TOOK A deep breath and lowered her hand.

"What are you doing?" Inspector Melendez whispered angrily.

"I will not betray my friends," she said. She cupped her hands around her mouth and shouted down the stairs, "Run! The police are here! Run!" Furious, Inspector Melendez clapped his hand on her shoulder and pulled her into the house.

"Arrest them!" he called out the door. At his command half a dozen policemen leapt from their hiding places among the trees and bushes along the stone steps.

"Melendez," Frank muttered. He glanced at

the cab rolling down the street. It hadn't yet reached the corner. "Let's get out of here."

On the steps Joe hesitated. "Elena—" he began. He could see Inspector Melendez holding her in the doorway as she struggled to break free, but the policemen barred Joe's path.

Frank tugged him back to the sidewalk. "They're cops," Frank said. "Good guys. She'll be all right with them. Come on." The police barreled down at the Hardys.

Joe took a last look at Elena. "We'll be back," he yelled. Then he spun and ran after Frank down the street.

"Taxi!" Frank shouted as he ran. "Wait!"

The taxi came to a stop, then began to back up. Frank and Joe ran to it, opened the doors, and jumped in. *"Vamos! Pronto!"*

Frank flung a fifty-dollar traveler's check on the front seat. "Tell him it's all his if he puts lots of distance between us and Melendez. Hurry."

The cab driver looked at them over his shoulder. His eyes widened as he saw the policemen bearing down on his cab; he slammed his foot down on the gas pedal. With a screech the cab roared away, leaving the policemen coughing and covering their eyes in the cloud of dust kicked up by the tires.

"We've lost them," Frank said, looking out the back window. "They must've parked their cars far away so we wouldn't know they were at the house. By the time they get to them, we'll be long gone."

"*Dónde?*" the driver asked in Spanish as he handed the traveler's check back to Frank. Frank began to sign it.

"Don't worry about the money yet," Joe told his brother. "He wants to know where we're going. I'd like to know that myself."

"Just tell him to drive around for a while." Gloomily, Joe relayed the message. "As long as the cops didn't get the license number, we're as safe here as anywhere. What's eating you?"

"I wish we didn't have to leave Elena like that," Joe replied. "She shouldn't have been caught."

"I'm sure Melendez will let her go once we prove we're innocent," Frank said. "If there's no crime, there're no grounds for holding her."

"That's kind of optimistic, isn't it?" said Joe. "Frank, we've never been in as bad a spot as this. Even if we live there's no way we can stay out of jail. We've run out all our leads."

"We can't give up," Frank said. "I know we're overlooking something. Let me think." He put on his headphones and slipped a Rolling Stones cassette into his tape player.

"Listening to music isn't going to help," Joe continued, although he knew Frank could barely hear him. "What are we overlooking? We can't go searching all over anyway. Every cop in Málaga is after us, and probably every Russian in the south of Spain—except Konstantin. And him I wouldn't trust any farther than I could throw him.''

Frank leaned his head back and closed his eyes, the steady throb of rock music beating in his head. The cab cruised aimlessly, heading west out of the city.

"And don't forget we've probably gotten the Gray Man in trouble, and the Network wants to hang us out to dry,'' Joe said as Frank hummed softly. "We're stuck in a foreign country with no way out. I don't see how we're going to walk away from this one.''

Frank began to laugh.

"I don't see that there's anything to laugh about,'' Joe said.

Frank pulled off the headphones and grinned at his brother. "I do. I just figured out where the information is.''

"What? Where? Let's go get it.''

"That's the best part,'' Frank said. "There's no need to.'' He glanced out the window as they passed a road sign. "What did that say? Torre-molinos?''

Joe nodded. "Four miles away, yeah. Are you going to tell me, or what?''

"Trust me,'' Frank replied. "Torremolinos is where Vladimir's house is. Tell the driver to head there.''

121

His smile got grimmer. "We're going mole hunting."

Like the rest of the towns on the Costa del Sol, Torremolinos was a resort town. Though far smaller than Málaga, the town had many discos that glittered under the Mediterranean night sky.

By late evening the Hardys stood in front of the Tortuga Club. Built of stone and stucco, water stains smeared its outer walls, and Joe wrinkled his nose in disgust.

"The cab driver told us this was the worst disco in the town," he said. "Why did you insist that he bring us here?"

"We don't want a place with a lot of people," Frank explained. He pulled open the door and they went in. "But they'd better have a phone in here."

"Over there," Joe said, pointing to a dark alcove off the door. He stopped. No music was playing. Only a waitress and a disc jockey were in the whole place.

"Want to tell me what's going on?" Joe asked.

"Take a table," Frank said, and Joe sat at a table just to the left of the door. Frank took out Konstantin's card. "I've got to make a couple of calls," he said, walking to the phone.

Several minutes passed as Frank made call after call, and Joe watched curiously. A couple entered, ordered drinks, finished them, and left.

The waitress hovered around Joe, waiting for an order, but Joe smiled uncertainly until she went away. At long last Frank returned.

"What was all that about?" Joe asked. "Who were you calling?"

"I started with Konstantin," Frank began.

"Konstantin?" Joe stared at his brother. "Are you out of your mind? We should be trying to get in touch with the Gray Man."

"We don't know how," Frank reminded him. "With his connections, I'm sure he'll arrive about the time Melendez and Vladimir get here."

"I think maybe I'm missing something," Joe said. "You'd better explain."

"I called both Melendez and Vladimir and told them we'd be here at midnight to turn over the information that will clear us," Frank said, looking at his watch. It read 10:25. "I told Vladimir to come alone. Melendez is bringing Elena."

"Great!" Joe said, his eyes brightening. Then a look of doubt swept over his face. "So they all come here at once. How will that help us?"

"Konstantin's coming right over. He's going to bait the trap for us." Frank eyed the disc jockey. "We should get some music going. You think the deejay takes requests?" He got up and walked to the far end of the floor just as Konstantin stormed in.

There was a flush of excitement on Konstantin's face, but when he saw Joe, he calmed down and walked over to his table.

"You have good news?" he asked.

"Your guess is as good as mine," Joe replied. He waved a thumb at Frank, who was deep in conversation with the disc jockey. "Ask him."

As the sound of the Rolling Stones filled the room, Frank came back and sat down. "We found what Martin left us," he said.

"We did?" said Joe.

From his pocket Frank dug two Rolling Stones cassette cases. He slid them across the table to Konstantin. "Identical in every way. Except I had one copy when I left New York and two after Martin used my tape player." He opened one of the cases. It was empty. He put it into his pocket. "The deejay's playing my tape. The other tape has Martin's info. I didn't know it until I took the tapes from the police warehouse."

Konstantin slowly tapped his forehead, thinking, then dropped a finger on top of the remaining case. "Ingenious. You have listened to the tape?"

Frank shook his head. "I thought I'd leave that to you."

"Good." With a flick of his wrist Konstantin flung the case open. The cassette inside crashed to the floor. Before Joe or Frank could react, he stamped it with his heel, tearing tape and sending bits of plastic flying in all directions.

"Much better. So much off my mind," the Russian said.

Joe stared from Konstantin to the wrecked cassette on the floor, his eyes growing wide with sudden realization. "It was you," he said slowly. "Vladimir isn't the mole! It was you all along."

Chapter

16

JOE LUNGED ACROSS the table, grabbing at Konstantin. The Russian's laughter faded, and from under the table came the telltale click of a revolver hammer being cocked. Joe froze, his fingers inches from Konstantin. And trembling with frustration, he let his hands fall back to the table.

"Sit down," Konstantin said. Joe sat. A dozen men and women came in together, smiling and laughing, and walked past the table to the dance floor. "Do not move. Do not attempt to speak to anyone," the Russian warned.

"What are you going to do with us?" Joe asked.

"We'll disappear," Frank said. "Just like our

chauffeur disappeared. You'd know more about that than we would, right, Konstantin?''

Konstantin gave him a cold stare.

"Funny how you knew about him," Frank continued. "We told the Gray Man about our chauffeur, and we told the Spanish police. But we never told Vladimir. And we never told you. There's only one way you could know."

"You're right," said Joe, studying Konstantin as if seeing him for the first time. "Dark wig, fake mustache, sunglasses. *Konstantin* was our chauffeur!"

"Shut up," Konstantin said.

"What are you going to do? Kill us here?" Frank asked as another group entered. "You'll have a lot of witnesses. It won't do much good to save yourself from the KGB only to have the Spanish police throw you in jail for the rest of your life. Seems to me we have a stalemate."

A man from one of the groups stepped to the bar and ordered a drink. Like his friends, he was dressed in tight black slacks and a bright silky shirt. But his hair had gone prematurely gray.

As he picked up his drink, he turned slightly and raised it to Frank and Joe, catching their eyes. Before Konstantin noticed, he turned back to the bar.

It was the Gray Man.

"No stalemate," Konstantin replied. "I would prefer not to cause trouble here. But should it be necessary, I can be out of the country within the hour. Please do not force my hand."

"It won't work," Joe said. "Frank called Melendez and Vladimir, and they'll be here any minute. You don't have time to do anything to us. You barely have time to get away."

Konstantin cocked an eyebrow. "You arranged for both to arrive at the same time?"

"That's right," Frank said confidently.

"Did you not think I would have Vladimir's phone monitored?" Konstantin said, looking at his watch. "You told Vladimir you would meet him at midnight. It is now ten to eleven. No, they will not arrive in time to save you."

His revolver glinted for an instant in the light from the revolving mirrored ball. He deftly transferred the gun to his jacket pocket, keeping his finger on the trigger. "Up," he said. "Time to go."

Frank looked over his shoulder at the door. "And if we don't?" he asked calmly. The outline of the gun appeared in Konstantin's pocket.

"Then you die now," Konstantin replied.

Joe sprang from his seat, his hands gripping the edge of the table, and as he stood, he began to tip the table into Konstantin. It didn't budge. He looked down to see Konstantin's foot pressed down on one of the table's feet, keeping it from moving.

"I am ready for any trick," Konstantin said.

He motioned again for Frank to rise, but Frank stayed in his chair.

"I should probably tell you the Gray Man is standing to your right," Frank said.

"A desperate lie," Konstantin said, his eyes fixed on Frank. "Get up."

"You found me out," Frank answered, pretending to be exasperated. "I lied about the Gray Man. I lie about everything. I even lied about not listening to the tape."

Konstantin looked puzzled. "You knew? Then why—"

The Gray Man started to rush Konstantin, but before he could reach him, the Russian spun, pulling his gun from his pocket. He aimed it at the form running toward him.

Joe slapped out, driving Konstantin's hand down, and with a crack a bullet smacked into the disco floor. The Gray Man slammed against Konstantin, knocking him off his feet and throwing him back against the wall.

At the sound of the gunshot, the music stopped. The couples on the dance floor stared at the three men grappling at the table. Then slowly their attention was directed toward the door.

Vladimir and eight Russians rushed in, guns drawn. When he saw Konstantin fighting with the Gray Man, Vladimir snarled rapid orders to his agents. They moved toward the table.

Frank stood.

All at once a voice came over the loudspeakers. "A top agent for the KGB has actually been a mole working for the Chinese for the last eight years," Martin's voice said. "His name is Konstantin. He was recruited while still in training by Wong Wah Lum, head of China's Third Directorate. Konstantin has since—"

Joe, Vladimir, the Gray Man, Konstantin, and the Russian agents stopped and listened as the voice droned on, outlining Konstantin's acts of treason against the Soviet Union.

Then the voice broke off, replaced by the sound of Konstantin speaking to someone in Chinese and a Chinese voice answering him. By the look on their faces, Frank knew both the Gray Man and Vladimir had recognized the voice of the man called Wong Wah Lum.

Konstantin looked icily at Frank. "You—all the time you—" Fiercely, he kicked aside the wrecked cassette on the floor. "You gave me the wrong tape."

Frank nodded. "Yeah, I sort of lied about that too."

Vladimir pointed to Konstantin. "Take him." He looked over at Frank, Joe, and the Gray Man. "Them too."

"Halt!" came a commanding voice from the doorway. It was Inspector Melendez accompanied by a small army of policemen. He held out his badge for everyone to see. "You are all under arrest."

"Policía!" someone on the dance floor cried out, and in panic the dancers rushed for the door, scattering the policemen. Vladimir clapped his hands, and his agents spread out across the bar. Policemen raced in to grab them.

"I can clear everything up," the Gray Man called to Inspector Melendez. But as he turned his head, Konstantin decked him. The Russian moved for the door. Vladimir flung himself into Konstantin, grabbing the tall Russian around the waist. And Konstantin rammed his fists against Vladimir's back.

In the midst of all this, Inspector Melendez spied the Hardys. "You have made a good run of it, but you are finally caught." He reached for them, but Joe overturned the table, hurling it into the police officer's path.

"That's the guy you want, Inspector," Frank said, pointing at Konstantin. *"He* killed Martin. We have to go."

Vladimir and Konstantin came stumbling by like a pair of clumsy dancers doing a waltz. Frank leaned forward, pushing them both toward Inspector Melendez. Then he grabbed a chair and threw it through a window. Before the inspector could push through to them, Frank and Joe had climbed through the broken window and landed on the street outside.

"What are we running for?" Joe asked. "They've got Konstantin. It's all over."

"Not quite," Frank said. He looked down the street, empty when they entered the disco but now lined with police cars and autos with diplomatic plates. A policeman stood vigilantly outside one of the police cars. Inside, in the back seat, sat Elena. Frank tossed Joe a ring of keys.

"What are these?" Joe asked, amazed.

"Vladimir's keys. I took them from him when he passed by," Frank said. "Get Elena and Vladimir's car. I'll distract the cop."

Joe crept along the line of cars, staying out of the policeman's sight. From the disco the sounds of fighting continued. The noise caught the policeman's attention, and nervously he drummed his fingers on the squad car's dashboard.

From his hiding place down the street, Frank called to the policeman. The policeman looked around but saw nothing. Frank called again, louder. The policeman got out of the car.

Joe popped his head in the window on the opposite side of the car, startling Elena. He put a finger to his lips, warning her to be silent. Frank called again, and Joe opened the car door with a soft click. Elena slid over and crept from the car. Signing for her to crouch, Joe led her away. They ducked out of sight behind a limousine as the policeman returned to his car.

"Which car is Vladimir's?" Joe whispered. A

shrill police whistle pierced the air. Elena pointed out a BMW on the other side of the street, and they all ran to it. In seconds Joe unlocked the doors and they slid in, Elena taking the wheel. She put a key in the ignition and turned it.

The ignition wouldn't budge.

She tried another key, frantically watching in the mirror as the policeman began a car-by-car search for her. "It will not work," she said, trying another and another. Finally, she tossed the ring in Joe's lap, reached under the dashboard, and brought out two wires. She touched them together. The car started.

"Where'd you learn to do that?" Joe asked, as the car pulled onto the street. Ahead, Frank stood in the road, waving at them.

"American television," she replied. The policeman spotted the car and began to run beside it, grabbing at the handles.

"If we stop, he'll catch us," Joe said. They raced toward Frank. Joe reached over the back seat, unlatched the back door, and flung it open. "You'll have to jump for it," he yelled at Frank through his open window.

As the car passed, Frank leapt, snatching at the doorframe. His heels scraped the pavement as he was dragged along, and, straining, he drew his knees up to his chest, lifting his feet off the ground. Twisting, he swung into the back seat of the BMW and slammed the door behind him.

"Glad you could make it," Joe quipped. "Mind telling me *now* what's going on?"

"In a minute, Joe," Frank said. "Elena, you mentioned Vladimir had a house in Torremolinos. Know where it is?"

"Yes," Elena said.

"Great. Take us there," he replied. "Sorry I couldn't let you in on my plan, Joe. I wanted you to react the way you did in front of Konstantin."

"Let me guess," Joe said. "When you realized what the tape was, you gave it to the disc jockey with instructions to play it over the loudspeakers when you gave the signal."

"Right," Frank said. "He had his own Stones album to play, so it seemed like I gave him the real Stones tape. When I stood up, Martin's tape went on. All I had to do was stall until Vladimir and Melendez got there."

"Good thing they were early."

Frank grinned. "No, they were right when I expected them. If you were trying to catch someone, and they said they'd meet you in a certain place at a certain time, wouldn't you try to get there first? I figured if I told them midnight, they'd be there by eleven."

"I still don't understand what we're doing," Joe said. "Everyone heard the tape. They know Konstantin's the mole, and when it all gets put together, Melendez will let us off the murder charge. So why did we need Elena, and why did we take Vladimir's car?''

"Because it's not over," Frank answered. "The Network played us for fools. Wouldn't you like to pay them back?"

Joe smacked a fist into his other hand. "I sure would."

"This business started because the Network was trying to trade for one of their agents. Now that the tape's public knowledge, it's useless as trade. But Vladimir still has the Network's agent."

"I get it," Joe said. "Vladimir would have him stashed somewhere near, but not in the consulate. So the likeliest place would be—"

"His house," Elena interrupted. They neared a two-story house with curved red tiles on the roof. Around the house was a gate, and as the car approached, a man stepped out of the gate and shut it behind him. He held out his palm, signaling the car to stop.

"Right," Frank said. "We needed Elena to show us where the house was, and Vladimir's car to get us through the front gate. Stay cool."

The car rolled to a stop, and the man, carrying a machine gun, walked up to Elena's window. "Vladimir told us to wait inside," Elena said, bluffing.

The man studied them for several moments,

then said something in Russian, his finger nervously tightening on the trigger.

"What does he say?" Elena asked, puzzled.

"He's on to us," Frank began. "Hit it—"

His words were cut off as a hail of bullets ripped into the car.

Chapter

17

THE BULLETS DENTED metal and smacked against glass, but they all bounced off.

"Vladimir must have bulletproofed his car too!" Frank said. "Quick! Roll up your window!" he ordered Elena.

But she sat, trembling, as if she'd never heard Frank speak. The man outside started turning his gun on the open spot. Joe reached over Elena, slapping the window control. The bulletproof glass rose swiftly.

"Hold on," Joe cried. From the passenger seat he stepped hard on the gas pedal and grabbed the steering wheel. The BMW lurched forward, speeding toward the gate.

Frank flung his door open. It clipped the man outside as they passed, knocking him off his feet.

He didn't get up. The car crashed through the gate and careened toward the house.

"The brake," Frank shouted. "Hit the brake!"

"I can't," Joe said. "It's too far. Elena!"

All at once Elena snapped her head up. She's in shock, Joe realized. "Elena! Get with it! Hit the brake!" Gasping in surprise, she seized the wheel and slammed on the brake.

The BMW skidded sideways and smashed into a glass-enclosed porch. In a flurry of shattered glass and scattered furniture, it came to a stop.

"Everyone okay?" Frank asked.

"I am," Joe replied. Elena still held the steering wheel, staring straight ahead and shaking. "I think Elena's had better times, but she wasn't hurt." He patted her on the shoulder, and she turned fearful eyes toward him. "Stay here and calm down, Elena. Honk the horn if you see anyone coming."

"She'll be all right," Frank said as he and Joe got out of the car. "We all are, thanks to Vladimir's mania for security."

In the light by the gate Joe could see the armed man's chest rising and falling rhythmically. "He's okay too. Just knocked out."

"Good," Frank said. "Let's go. If there's anyone inside, they couldn't have missed all that noise." He darted into the house. It was simpler than Frank had expected. Just a porch, small dining room, tiled foyer, and sunken living room. There was a tiled stair leading to the second floor.

At the top of the stairs were two Russians. One was slender, but the other bulged with muscles and stood over six feet tall. At a command from the slender man, the big man started down the stairs.

"Trouble?" Joe asked as he caught up with Frank. He spied the giant lurching toward them. Trouble, he thought.

The slender man disappeared down the hall.

"There's no time to waste," Frank said. Together, the Hardys sprinted up the stairs, startling the huge Russian.

He grabbed for Frank, and Joe slammed into him, making him stagger back. Frank ducked under the giant's grasp, stepped past him on the stairs, and slammed his fists against the back of the Russian's knees. The big man's legs buckled, and he toppled.

His hand reached out and caught Joe's shirt-sleeve. Over and over they tumbled down the stairs, landing with a thud in the foyer. Frank looked at the twisted bodies below. Neither moved.

"Joe!" Frank called. He started back down the stairs. "Joe!"

Joe, dazed by the fall, lifted his head. "Don't worry about me. Go." He flashed his brother a pained grin, and Frank dashed to the upper landing to follow the slender man. Joe began to disentangle himself from the giant.

The giant lashed out, clamping his hand around Joe's throat. Joe clawed uselessly at the Russian's wrist, and as the Russian stood, he lifted Joe off his feet.

Joe let go of the giant's wrist and clapped his palms as hard as he could against the Russian's ears. The Russian dropped Joe to the floor and cupped his hands against his head. Joe scrambled to his feet.

But with a sweep of his hand the Russian knocked Joe back into the living room against the fireplace. The giant charged at him.

Joe bounded to his feet, backing away from the Russian's punches. "There's no need to fight," Joe said. "My brother has everything under control upstairs, so you've already lost. Let's just call it quits, okay?"

Smirking, the giant raised a meaty fist and swung down at Joe. Joe dived and tackled the Russian. With an astonished look the huge man fell forward and cracked his head into an armor breastplate hanging on the wall. He twirled twice, then crashed to the floor.

Relieved and exhausted, Joe slumped against a wall and wondered what had become of his brother.

* * *

Frank Hardy kicked open a door. It was one of four on the top floor, but behind it was neither the slender Russian nor the Network's agent. He unclenched his fists. The room was virtually a duplicate of Vladimir's office in the consulate, down to the file cabinets and the heavy oak desk. He checked the center door on the desk, and it slid open. He smiled. Inside were several small black books. Remember what you're here for, he told himself, though he suspected the room held a lot of information.

Almost absentmindedly, he pocketed the black books and left the room. Something moved at the opposite end of the hall, and he ducked back into the office. Frank did not understand the Russian words he heard, but the tone was clear. Hands raised, he stepped back into the hall.

At the far end stood the slender Russian, holding a pistol to the head of another man. The prisoner was slightly taller than the slender KGB agent, and his face was covered with an unruly thatch of beard. His hands were tied behind his back, and strips of surgical tape covered his eyes and mouth. Judging from the paleness of the man's skin, Frank guessed he'd been kept out of the sun a long time.

"The Network's man, I presume?" Frank said. In answer, the Russian aimed his gun at Frank's chest, and his finger tightened on the trigger.

Suddenly the Network agent's head lashed

back, and his skull conked the Russian's jaw. Frank sprang down the hall. The prisoner stepped aside, and Frank spun, kicking out with his foot. The slender Russian collapsed.

"You're the American agent?" Frank asked as he helped the second man to his feet. He ripped the tape from the man's face. "What's your name?"

The man nodded. "My code name's Donner. It's about time the Network sent someone for me." His eyes slit with suspicion. "You should know that. Aren't you from the Network?"

"Yes and no," Frank replied. He unknotted the cords binding Donner's wrists, and Donner rubbed the circulation back into his hands. "It's a long story. We'll fill you in on the way out."

Donner limped slightly as they headed downstairs, and Frank offered him an arm. At the foot of the stairs they found Joe, patiently waiting.

"What took you so long?" Joe said.

"That's just what *he* said," Frank replied, waving a thumb at Donner. "Everyone's a wise guy."

"Who are you?" Donner asked as they cut through the dining room.

"I'm Joe Hardy, and this is my brother, Frank," Joe said. They moved across the ruined patio, heading for the wrecked BMW.

"I've heard of you," Donner said. "The Gray Man's protégés. You're supposed to be untrustworthy."

"If you don't trust us, you can always stay here," Frank suggested, but Donner winced and shook his head. Elena came out of the car as they approached. "Let's get to safety before anyone else shows up."

They ran to the gate. The man they had left there still lay on the ground, unconscious. They passed through the gate and onto the darkened street.

"We did it," Joe said. "We showed the Network how it's done."

"Wait!" Donner shouted, but it was too late. The night exploded in light, blinding them, and as Frank's eyes refocused, he saw they were caught in a semicircle of car headlights. There was nowhere for them to go but back. A bald man stepped from one of the cars.

"Very good," Vladimir said with cold pleasure. "Now I have you all."

Chapter

18

"YOU ARE MY prisoners," Vladimir declared, a satisfied smile on his face.

"What do you need us for?" Joe asked. He stepped between Donner and Vladimir. "You've got the name you wanted; we've got the Network's man. That was the deal."

"Silence," Vladimir said. "The exchange never took place. I am not bound by that bargain." He snapped his fingers, and two Russians shoved Konstantin into the semicircle of light. The blond man curled his lip in rage, but Vladimir laughed.

"You have given me much more than a name," Vladimir continued, staring Joe in the eye. "For the capture of this one"—like a circus barker, he swept his arm extravagantly, motioning at Konstantin—"I will become a hero of the state, with pay to match." His eyes flashed with anger. "But you annoy me, young man. You disrupt my plans, destroy my car, invade my house. You are too dangerous, you and your brother. I must be rid of you."

Vladimir pointed at Donner and Elena. "Take them." Two Russians stepped into the circle of light and grabbed them, forcing them to Konstantin's side. "They have further uses." He grinned at the Hardys. "But *these* two—"

"I'm surprised you managed to get out of the disco in one piece," Frank said. "You must be better than I thought to get away from Melendez."

"Yes." Vladimir glared at him icily. "Escape was a simple matter." He patted his coat pocket. "And I now have the tape. I have Konstantin. I have all I need.

"I do not need *you*." Two Russians appeared on either side of Vladimir. "Take them somewhere and dispose of them."

Two shots rang out, and the headlights of the car Vladimir stood next to spat glass and went dark. Desperate to stay out of the line of fire, Vladimir threw himself to the ground.

"No one goes anywhere," the Gray Man said from the darkness. His voice seemed to come from all directions at once. Frank and Joe could see no sign of him. "Didn't you think I'd follow you, Vlad? Let Donner, the Hardys, and the girl go."

"You are forgetting," Vladimir said. "My men have the Hardys in their sights. Show yourself or they will kill the boys."

"I have *you* in my sights," the still-invisible Gray Man said. "This is a Sterling assault rifle. I could put three bullets in you before you finish telling your men to shoot them. Is that the way you want to play it?"

Vladimir licked his lips thoughtfully. He waved his men back. "And if I give you these four," he called to the Gray Man, "I keep Konstantin?"

"Sounds fair."

"Wait!" Konstantin suddenly called out. He shook himself free of his captors. "Gray Man! I wish to defect!"

Vladimir sputtered, unable to find words to voice his anger. From the darkness the Gray Man said, "You killed Martin, right?"

"Of course," Konstantin casually admitted. "You would have done the same in my place. I wish to defect."

"You make a big mistake, Konstantin. You and I aren't alike at all," the Gray Man retorted. "I don't like moles, and I don't like killers. If I had my way, I'd send you back to your KGB masters and let them deal with you." There was a long pause. "But you can tell us a lot about both Chinese and Russian espionage, and I can't overlook that. All right, I'll help you defect, but you try anything and you'll be sorry."

"No!" Vladimir shouted, and he lunged forward, grabbing Frank. "Konstantin stays here! If I were to lose him, I would suffer in his place." A spring-operated knife popped out of his sleeve and into his hand. He pressed it against Frank's throat as they backed toward the wall. "Shoot now if you choose, Gray Man. You will hit your friend, not me. And my men will gun down your other friends. Give up."

"Seems to me like you have a stalemate," Frank said, feeling the cool sharp touch of steel on his throat. He reached into his pocket and came out with a small black book. "Maybe this can break it."

Vladimir stared, then inhaled sharply as he recognized what Frank held. "My bankbooks." Enraged, he prodded Frank under the chin with the point of the knife. "Where did you get this?"

"Same place as all the others," Frank replied. "There were a lot of them, and they all seemed to refer to bank accounts. Lots of bank accounts. Skimming funds from the KGB, Vladimir?"

Vladimir said nothing.

"Yeah, that's what I thought," Frank said. "That's why the KGB's London man reported you, isn't it? Your own private retirement fund, at KGB expense."

Vladimir's arm fell away from Frank.

147

"Let us go, and I'll tell you where the other bankbooks are."

The knife slid from Vladimir's fingers and clattered on the ground. "Let them go," Vladimir ordered wearily. He was a beaten man, Frank knew. "Let them all go."

"Uh-oh," Joe said. "Frank, I think you overplayed our hand." Beyond the semicircle of light the other Russian agents moved forward. Two roughly shoved Elena and Donner at Vladimir and the Hardys, and a second later Konstantin joined them.

"You are traitors," a Russian outside the circle said to Konstantin and Vladimir as the others took aim. To everyone in the light he said, "You are all enemies of the state. Ready—aim—"

An arc of light ripped through the night, exposing and blinding the Gray Man and the Russians. "This is the police," came a deep Spanish-accented voice over a bullhorn. "Drop your weapons and put your hands up."

Two Russians spun and trained their weapons on the voice. Two shots exploded from the night, and the Russians jerked back, flopping to the ground. When the other Russians and the Gray Man had let their guns fall, a tall, burly man with dark hair walked into the light.

"Inspector Melendez," Joe cried. "I never thought I'd say this, but am I glad to see *you*."

"You are all," the inspector replied, "under arrest."

Frank left the ticket counter and pushed his way through the airport crowds. Ahead, Joe chatted with the Gray Man, and as he caught his brother's attention, Frank waved the tickets at him. As Frank reached them, the Gray Man was saying, "It's all cleared up. Good thing Melendez was already listening when Konstantin admitted to killing Martin. That made it much easier to get you off the hook."

"I thought you had it planned like that," Joe said.

"Don't I wish! Sometimes you just get lucky."

"Yeah, it's about time," Joe answered. "You just make sure the Network knows we beat them at their own game. They couldn't shake Donner free and we *did*. Let them think about that the next time they want to take us for a ride."

"I don't think that'll happen again," the Gray Man said. "Donner told me to say goodbye, by the way. He's got his hands full right now."

"Is he taking care of Konstantin's defection?" Frank asked.

"No," the Gray Man replied. "Konstantin's staying here to stand trial for Martin's murder. That was part of our deal with Melendez. No, the person defecting is Vladimir."

"What?" said both Hardys in unison.

The Gray Man chuckled. "He feels he'd be safer in the decadent West, especially with his bank balance." He spotted two familiar figures entering the airport. "Company coming."

"Elena!" Joe shouted as she ran to him. Behind her Inspector Melendez walked at a steady pace.

Frank cocked his head at Joe and Elena. "Let's let them say goodbye to each other." He picked up the suitcases and, sandwiched between the two men, started for the departure gate.

"I'm surprised you came by to see us off," Frank told Inspector Melendez.

"I wished to be certain you were truly leaving," Inspector Melendez answered, a trace of a smile on his lips. "If you should ever choose to return to Spain—"

"Yes?"

"Do me a favor. Go to Italy," the inspector concluded. "Goodbye, Frank Hardy. Say goodbye to your brother for me." Frank and Inspector Melendez shook hands, and without another word Inspector Melendez turned and left.

Joe ran up as the line of passengers began filtering onto the plane. After a quick round of farewells with the Gray Man, they joined the line and headed up the ramp to the plane. Within minutes they were seated.

Frank took his Walkman from his suitcase and put it on as the plane taxied out to the runway.

"Sorry the vacation got cut short," he said apologetically to Joe.

"It's okay," Joe replied. "We met girls, we went swimming, we went boating, we saw a lot of scenery and sights. I've had enough vacationing for a lifetime."

Frank smiled and slipped on his headphones. Joe put his head back and closed his eyes. As the plane left the ground, Joe dreamed of Bayport and its quaint, quiet streets. He was looking forward to going home, he realized.

He would finally get to relax!

The Number File

Chapter

1

"JUST ONE SHOT LEFT," Joe Hardy muttered. "I'd better make it count." His blue eyes narrowed in concentration as he sighted along the barrel of his gun. He squeezed the trigger, then his hand whitened on the gun stock. Joe knew he'd missed.

"You're through!" Laughter came from behind Joe, and he turned. His brother, Frank, stood there, grinning in triumph, his teeth bright against his tanned face. "That was your last clay pigeon—I win!"

Frank patted Joe's blond hair, which the early-morning sea breeze had tangled into curls. "Nice aim, Joe," he teased.

Joe shrugged. "My aim was better yesterday—when I shot Kruger."

1

"There's a big difference between shooting a camera and shooting a gun," Frank answered.

Joe silently agreed and cracked open his shotgun to eject the spent shell. The Hardys had recently found themselves on both sides of guns—being fired at and firing when desperate.

Joe was remembering their last case, *Line of Fire*. They'd both been targets, trying to keep a sharpshooting friend from becoming a murderer.

"Well, this case is a lot easier than that last one," Frank said. "Just observe, take pictures, and enjoy the sun."

Frank and Joe were on the island of Bermuda, in a small town called Somerset Village. They were doing a surveillance job for their famous detective father, Fenton Hardy. For the past few days they'd been staying with an ex-colleague of their dad's, Alfred Montague, and his daughter, Alicia.

Montague, as he preferred to be called, had been a detective with Scotland Yard, and had helped Fenton Hardy with several international cases. He was only too glad to give his friend's sons a base. And he'd been giving the boys some pointers on trap-shooting during their few free hours.

"Want to try another round?" Joe suggested.

Frank glanced at his watch. "We should be heading for Kruger's villa."

"Why? We haven't gotten anything yet," Joe said. "Nothing but a bunch of pictures of Kruger and his house and a tan. If our source was right, in just two days a batch of counterfeit credit cards is going to the U.S. from here. And we have nothing new to tell Dad."

Frank ran a hand through his brown hair. "So you think we'll accomplish more blasting clay pigeons?"

"Well, I'll feel better, beating you."

Frank drew himself up to his full six-one and grinned at his slightly shorter, slightly younger brother. Joe was seventeen. "You're on." Then he turned to wave to the trap house across the carefully tended lawn as Joe reloaded. Montague was inside, running the machinery that would catapult the clay pigeons into the air.

Joe stood seemingly at ease, the shotgun loose in his hands. Frank knew he was tenser than he looked. Joe loved action—and the past few days he'd seen little of it.

Loading his gun, Frank said, "Do you want to take every other shot?" Joe nodded as Frank continued, "At least the stakeout's easy. We sit on a rock under a cedar tree and take pictures of a house by the ocean—"

Joe yelled, "Pull!" The clay pigeon soared

into the sky. Joe's gun rose smoothly to his shoulder, barked, and the clay disk shattered into hundreds of pieces.

"Three shipments with fifteen thousand credit cards already left here," Frank mumbled to himself. "And we only find out about it by accident."

"What did you say?" Joe asked.

"I was just thinking about our source—that counterfeiter who got caught and talked."

"Yeah, if he hadn't supposedly been one of Kruger's couriers, we wouldn't know anything." He smiled, then yelled, "Pull!"

Caught off-guard, Frank jerked up his gun—and missed. He gave Joe a dirty look and added, "Supposedly?"

Joe shrugged. "Well, there's no proof, remember. They only found this guy with the cards made from stolen plates. He rolled over and named Kruger. But we don't have *proof* that Kruger's involved. I mean, who's going to believe that sleaze? Pull!"

Another clay pigeon soared. Joe blasted it and went right on talking. "All we know is that he said there was going to be another shipment on Friday."

"The whole racket better be stopped soon. Dad said they cost the real cardholders more than two million bucks so far," Frank added. "They're pretty smart—buying stuff with the

4

fake cards, and then selling it at half price. They only use the duplicates for a couple of days, so there's almost no chance of them being caught. We've got to stop it at this end— before the cards get to the U.S."

Joe yelled "Pull!" again, but this time Frank was ready and hit the clay pigeon.

"And that means checking Kruger out, even if there's no hard evidence against him. So it looks like we're stuck sitting outside his walls, taking pictures," Joe said.

"Speaking of pictures," Frank said, "is that Alicia coming out of the darkroom with the latest batch?"

Always willing to look at Montague's dark-haired daughter, Joe turned toward the sliding glass doors in the white bungalow behind them.

No one was there.

Frank took advantage of his distraction to yell, "Pull!"

Joe whipped around, but his shot missed. Now it was his turn to glare at his brother.

Frank smiled, saying, "Now we're even." He signaled Montague that they were through.

Montague walked toward them from the trap house, carrying a manila envelope. Tall and slender, he looked fifteen years younger than his almost-seventy years. The only sign of age was his soft voice which sounded worn down after years of relentless interrogations of British villains. "Alicia left these pictures for you before she went to town," he said, handing them to Joe. "I thought you'd like to see them before you go."

The shots were all too familiar to Joe—trees, the top of Kruger's fence, his villa with the beach below. "Low tide," he said, fishing one picture out. "High tide," he added in a sing-song. He fished out another. "And the big cheese himself." Joe held up a picture of Kruger. "This guy *looks* mean."

Joe's telephoto lens had caught Kruger's square face head-on. A pair of steel gray bushy eyebrows pushed their way up onto the man's forehead over a pair of calculating eyes. Kruger looked like a man who'd just been struck by a wonderfully sinister idea. He was smiling slightly, deep creases showing up in his leathery tanned face. Kruger wore a turtleneck with a sport jacket over it.

Montague grunted as he looked at the picture. "Hasn't changed much since he was captured back in forty-three. Still looks like a U-boat captain."

He slid out a photo from under the pile in Joe's hand. "I had Alicia make a copy of this from an old file." It was another picture of Kruger, showing a much younger man. His hair was dark instead of gray, and his face was lean. But his cold blue eyes looked just as evil.

"We'd just caught his sub sneaking into a quiet cove here in Bermuda," Montague explained. "I never knew what made him decide to settle here after the war."

"The climate's better than Hamburg's," Frank said.

"Maybe the *legal* climate," Montague said. "The local chaps say your man always made frequent trips to Miami and New York. I suspect Kruger's had his fingers in lots of pies."

"Better get moving," Joe said. "Who knows? Maybe we'll get lucky today."

Montague tossed them a set of car keys. "Take the old bus, but be careful—those Yank tourists are always driving on the wrong side of the road."

Laughing, the Hardys drove off, heading for Kruger's villa. The ride was beautiful along the North Shore Road to Kruger's place. After they passed the dirt road leading down to the house and the beach, they pulled the old red MG off the road into the cover of some trees. They yanked the convertible top up and locked it in place.

Hanging a pair of binoculars around his neck, Joe made his way up the rocky hill that overlooked the walled estate. "Guess I'll find my favorite rock," he said, feeling sorry for himself. He was already peering through his glasses when Frank joined him, carrying the camera with the 400mm lens.

They had a great view of the rambling, whitewashed building and the bay below them. There were no boats at the small dock, but a red-and-white buoy peacefully bobbed up and down about one hundred feet out in the calm blue-green water.

Joe was slowly scanning the house and paused at the bay window of Kruger's living room. He refocused the glasses. Then his shoulders stiffened.

"See something?" Frank asked.

"Yeah." Joe's voice was grim. "A guy— with binoculars looking at me." He turned to Frank. "We've had it for today, bro'. Should I wave bye-bye?"

"Let's just get out of here—fast!"

They tore down the rocky hill to the under-brush, where Montague's little "bus" was hidden. In minutes they were on their way back to Somerset Village.

"What do we do now?" Joe asked, rolling up his window. A stiff breeze had just come up. "If they're on to us—"

"There's nothing we can do," Frank finished for him. He pulled onto one of the many bridges that connected Bermuda's six islands. "It's so peaceful here," he said, looking at the water shimmering all around him. There were no guard rails to block his view.

Near the end of the bridge a powerful black BMW started to pass them on the right. Dark-tinted windows on the sleek performance car made it impossible to see if the driver was male or female—or if there were any passengers.

The BMW held its position, creeping toward the MG. "Why doesn't this idiot pass?" Joe grumbled.

"He's not passing!" Frank shouted suddenly. "He's trying to drive us off—"

Before Frank could hit the brakes, four thousand pounds of BMW slammed into the side of the little MG.

"Watch out!" Joe shouted.

Frank fought to stay on the bridge, but it was a lost battle. The little car spun out of control, jumping over the small curb. It rammed into the rocky slope on the left that the bridge had led up to.

The brothers were tossed forward as the car plummeted backward down the steep incline. Finally they splash-landed in thirty feet of water! As they drifted down into the crystal clear depths, Frank shook his head. Sunk, he thought. We're really and truly sunk.

Chapter

2

"I can't get the door open!" Joe rammed a forearm against the metal.

"Don't touch the door or windows!" Frank's voice was firm, but calm. Water was coming under the doors and floorboards.

Joe shook his head, groaning. "I think I must have bumped my head." He still looked a bit dazed as he took a deep breath, trying to relax himself. He hung on tightly as the little MG sank toward the soft ocean bottom and finally settled, in slow motion, onto the driver's side. Frank was moving quickly now, unbuckling both seat belts and checking out the position of the car.

"There's too much pressure from the water on your door," Frank said rapidly. "Breathe

10

deeply and stay cool. You have to open your window just a crack.''

It was hard for Joe to remain calm as he turned the car into a perfect watery grave. But he knew he had to do it. Because of the way the car had settled into the mud, Joe's window was facing toward the surface.

The water streamed in, and in less than a minute the two brothers were submerged up to their shoulders. They both pressed their faces into the narrowing air pocket above them.

"Okay," Frank said. "Take a deep breath— now open your door and then just swim toward the surface.''

"Can't," Joe said, leaning into the door. "The frame's bent.''

"Then open the window. Easy—don't panic. I'll be right behi—''

Frank's last words were drowned out by the water which had now filled the entire MG. Joe started cranking the handle. Slowly the window started to open more. One inch, two inches, three— His cranking came to a stop. The window was jammed!

Frank knew immediately that something had gone wrong. He leaned over his brother and began pushing down on the window. Joe continued to press against the handle. Finally the window gave way.

Joe squeezed through the tiny opening diagonally. Frank started to follow, hunching his shoulders as they scraped against the twisted frame. But a sharp piece of metal snagged a shoulder seam of his shirt. He was caught—his shoulders jammed against the two sides of the window and his arms pinned at his sides.

With his knees slightly bent, Frank planted his feet against the door on the other side of the car. Then he straightened his legs and inched his body forward. His shirt sleeve ripped as he continued forcing his way through the opening. He knew he could make it, but would he make it in time? He was almost out of oxygen.

Joe was already halfway to the surface, his head throbbing and his heart beating rapidly. He glanced behind him, expecting to see Frank swim up to him.

He instantly reversed direction when he did see Frank. Joe reached the MG in two seconds and forced his hands under Frank's arms. Then, bracing himself against the side of the car, he pushed off with his legs.

Frank was free! His face was a frightening deep red. As he kicked feebly, he prayed his natural buoyancy would carry him to the surface.

Joe pushed off against the car and made like a torpedo for the surface. He, too, was out of air.

"Uaahhhh!" The sound of the two brothers gasping for air seemed unnaturally loud after the deadly underwater silence. They bobbed up and down in the water as they gulped in great lungfuls of air.

They were only a short distance from the embankment and slowly dog-paddled to it. They pulled themselves up onto the rocky slope and collapsed onto their backs.

Their chests were still heaving when Joe spoke. "That was a close one." He coughed, then grinned. "Good thing that car didn't have electric windows!"

Frank finally smiled. "You're all right?"

"Yeah. You okay?"

"Uh-huh—but this was my favorite shirt." Frank looked at the shredded left sleeve, then grinned at Joe.

"Well, now it can be your favorite *short*-sleeved shirt," Joe offered, and the two brothers laughed.

"Whooaahh," Joe groaned as he tried to stand up, but only toppled back onto the rocks. "I guess I'm a little dizzy from punching the windshield of the car with my head. I wonder how many of my brilliant little gray cells died from the battering and the lack of oxygen?"

"I'd worry more about the damage your head did to the window," Frank said.

"My only worry right now is getting home

and getting dry.'' The bump on the head had done nothing to affect Joe's impatience.

''What's your hurry?'' Frank asked. ''It's a long climb up and then a long walk back to the village. I think we should just take it easy for a few minutes.''

Frank glanced up to the road to see if anyone was observing them. Joe lay back with his eyes closed, still taking long, deep breaths and occasionally rubbing the spot on his forehead, which was working its way into a lump. Frank broke the long silence.

''No one around. Nobody would have even known we went off the bridge.''

''Except whoever was in the BMW,'' Joe reminded him.

''Did you get a look at anyone?'' Frank asked.

''Couldn't see a thing through those windows, and he, she, or it was already alongside us by the time I looked. I don't even know if the car followed us from Kruger's. But somebody tried to kill us, and that means we *are* getting close to something.'' Joe frowned.

After the brothers had rested, they climbed up over the rocks to the road.

''We can either walk back to those stores we passed and phone Montague, or try to hitch,'' Frank said.

Joe stuck out his thumb and started walking

backward toward Somerset. "I don't think I want to tell Montague on the phone that the car he's loved since 1968 is thirty feet underwater."

"But I don't know who's going to pick us up looking like this," said Frank. "We look so disheveled."

" 'Disheveled'?" Joe repeated. "I think you were underwater too long—you sound like Aunt Gertrude!"

As Joe stretched out his thumb again, a pickup truck bounced by and came to a wobbly stop.

"Need a lift?" the long-faced, unshaven man behind the wheel shouted.

The brothers ran toward the truck and started to jump in the back.

"You can ride up front," the driver insisted. "A little water isn't going to hurt this baby. What happened to you guys?"

"You know how it goes," Joe answered, hoping his vague reply would do.

The lean man nodded his head and grinned. He dropped the brothers at the driveway that led up to Montague's villa.

As they were closing the door to the house, Montague called down from upstairs. "That you, boys?"

Joe cleared his throat, which suddenly had become dry. "Uh, yes, we're back."

"I didn't hear the car pull up. I'll be right down."

Frank and Joe looked at each other in awkward silence. They had no idea how to tell Montague what happened to his "bus." But their host made it easy for them—the moment he walked downstairs he knew something was wrong. He cut off Frank's explanation about the MG. "Never mind the car—are you boys okay?"

"We're fine," the boys assured him, relieved that Montague was more concerned about them than his car. They told him about the attempted killing.

"You'll have to report this to the Hamilton police," Montague told them. *"And* you'll need some way to get around. There are no rental cars on the island, but you can rent mopeds. There's a place in Hamilton. Let's see . . ." He looked at his watch. "Alicia said she'd be back at four—that'll give you time for a wash-up and rest.

"Alicia and I have a five o'clock engagement we can't break, but we can drop you at the ferry to Hamilton."

Later they heard a car pull into the driveway, and in a minute Montague's eighteen-year-old daughter burst in. Her sparkling dark brown eyes widened in concern as she listened to a

16

recap of the boys' story. It left her pale under her smooth tan. Her short black hair danced as she turned from Frank to Joe, her eyes drawn to the bump on Joe's head. "You're hurt!"

"Not enough to slow me down," Joe told her. "We'd better hurry, so we can make the bike rental place before closing."

The quiet of the ferry ride to Hamilton was shattered by the sound of the ferry crunching against the dock. After the brothers left the boat, they walked the three blocks to the moped rental place.

The bikes were all the same—squat-looking scooters with small, fat wheels—so the choice was easy. Frank handed the burly attendant his father's credit card, which had been given to him for emergencies.

"I'm sorry," the salesman said after making a phone call. "I cannot allow you to have the bikes. Your credit card is more than three thousand dollars over the limit, and I've been instructed to cut up your card."

"We haven't spent anywhere near that much!" Frank stared at the man.

"You can't destroy our card," Joe said, leaning into the counter as if he'd push his way right through it. "And you've got to give us those bikes."

"Sorry, chum," the attendant repeated in

his flawless British accent. "You must take it up with the credit card company."

"The card!" Joe demanded, his hand stretched out.

"Take it easy," Frank cautioned. "It's not his fault."

"Yeah, well it's not *our* fault, either, and why should—"

"Come on, Joe," Frank said, interrupting him and grabbing him by the arm. "We'll straighten this out later. It's getting late and we still have to see the police."

Frank and Joe walked through the narrow two-lane streets and watched as the shops were beginning to close. When they were two blocks from the station, they heard the sound of a car behind them picking up speed. A maroon sedan shot past them, then screeched to a halt, its red brake lights flashing on. Then, the two clear backup lights came on as the car roared back to them.

Two large, well-dressed men jumped out of the car and approached them. One of them, a tall black man wearing a conservative pin-striped suit, pulled back his coat to reveal a gun tucked into his belt. The other man, shorter, opened his dark blue suit and drew a small revolver from a shoulder holster.

"Just hold it right there," he said. "Don't do anything stupid."

The blue suit stood in front of the Hardys as the tall man with the hat walked behind them. Joe, standing in front of Frank, could hear the click-clack as the tall man snapped handcuffs on Frank's bare wrists. Two more clicks and Joe, too, was handcuffed. Finally the tall man spoke:

"You're under arrest for fraud, conspiracy to defraud, and credit card counterfeiting."

Chapter

3

"COUNTERFEITING! WHAT'RE YOU talking about?" Joe turned his head back and forth between the two men.

"Who are you?" Frank asked.

Blue suit holstered his gun with one hand as he reached into his back pocket with the other. "I'm Bill Baylis," he said as he produced identification. "And this is Walt Conway. I'm from the Interagency Banking Commission, and Detective Conway is with the Bermuda police, assigned to work with me."

"We happened to see you leaving Bernhard Kruger's," the man called Conway chimed in. "And we know about the faked credit card you just tried to use."

"There must be some mistake," Frank insisted.

"Where've we heard *that* one before?" countered Baylis. "Let's go to police headquarters. You can tell your story there."

"We were just on our way there," Joe admitted, realizing how phony it sounded.

"We're private investigators," Frank told them, "staying with Alfred Montague."

"Into the car." The tall man's tone made it clear he wasn't interested in any more conversation. He opened the back door and ushered them in.

Within minutes they were seated in the office of Chief Boulton. The blond police chief with his dark walrus mustache was bigger than Biff Hooper and very impressive in his immaculate, all-white uniform. He seemed out of place in an office where every flat surface was cluttered with papers, books, and boxes. He looked at the boys with cold blue eyes. "May I see some identification, please?"

"We do get one phone call, don't we?" Joe asked, half-joking.

"Of course," the chief responded. "Local or long distance?"

"Local. We're staying with Alfred Montague. He's a retired policeman—do you know him?" The chief nodded. "He'll vouch for us." Joe dialed Montague's number. After the seventh ring, he hung up, remembering Montague's five o'clock appointment.

Frank explained to the three men the purpose of their visit to Bermuda and why they had the Kruger villa under surveillance. He told them about Fenton Hardy's involvement in the case back in the U.S. and how ironic it was that they were now being held for a crime they were trying to stop.

"I know of your father," the chief said, lightening up a little. "Shall I ring him?"

The boys hated to use their dad to bail them out, but after exchanging a brief look, they nodded their agreement.

Chief Boulton called Fenton Hardy, spoke briefly with him, and turned the phone over to Frank. Frank filled his father in on everything that had happened so far. He learned that his father hadn't put more than two hundred dollars on the credit card that the merchant confiscated.

The chief got back on the phone. "Makes sense to me," he said after listening silently for a long time. "Fine, then. I'll call Chief Collig in Bayport. Then if everything checks out, I'll be happy to release your boys and give them all the help I can." After a quick goodbye, the chief hung up.

Frank asked why they had been arrested when they hadn't done anything but try to use a card over its limit. And Chief Boulton confessed that they thought Frank and Joe might be couriers for the counterfeit credit card gang because they had been seen leaving Kruger's earlier. And then, when they tried to use the overdrawn card, they had decided to bring the Hardys in with the hope of sweating information out of them about Kruger.

Before they were released, Frank and Joe officially reported the incident with the black BMW. Although they couldn't connect the attempt on their lives with their investigation of Kruger, there didn't seem to be any other explanation.

Chief Boulton gave Frank and Joe some additional information about the counterfeiting racket. The police thought that stolen blank cards were being shipped to Bermuda—possibly from Puerto Rico. They were "punched" in Bermuda and then sent to the U.S. for distribution. The police suspected Kruger, but they didn't have enough evidence to search the man's house.

"That's it," the chief said. "That's everything I have on Kruger. I can't get your credit card back, but if you're going to continue your investigation, I'll call the moped agency and arrange for you to rent two bikes. Meanwhile, your father said he would arrange to get you a different card."

"Thanks," the brothers replied.

"And if you're short of cash in the meantime, just let me know."

Frank and Joe smiled, pleased that the chief had turned out to be so good-natured.

"Now just fill out these accident report forms," the chief continued. "And list everything that was in the car when it sank."

"Oh no!" Joe blurted out. "I completely forgot about the stuff in the trunk." Joe's face fell as he realized out loud that both cameras were thirty feet underwater.

"And the binoculars," Frank added.

"You can rent scuba gear across the street," the chief suggested, "if you're in the mood for a do-it-yourself rescue. But I don't know how good the cameras will be after *that* dunking!"

"One of them was an underwater camera," Joe explained. "We used it when we went diving near Kruger's dock a couple days ago."

"I'll ring the scuba shop and make the arrangements."

It was almost six-thirty by the time Frank and Joe loaded rented scuba gear on the back of the mopeds to ride out to the MG. It was a pleasant ride. The summer light made the pastel ice-cream colors of the houses outside Hamilton shimmer. The temperature was still warm, even though an ocean breeze blew across the narrow highway.

"Here's the spot," shouted Frank, pointing down to where he knew the little car lay. Joe pulled up next to Frank, parking beside a pile of rocks.

"Do you want to set up on the flat rock down there?" Joe asked, extending his arm toward a flat rock below them.

"Looks good." Frank nodded.

In fifteen minutes the boys were ready. Joe had stuck a spare key to the trunk into a small pouch attached to his weight belt.

"The water's so still," Frank said.

"Yeah. It's hard to believe it almost buried us."

Frank and Joe slipped into the warm water and dived. It didn't take long to spot the MG, which had sunk another two feet into the soft sand. Joe motioned to Frank to check the inside of the car for the binoculars while he swam around to the trunk.

Frank was able to force the passenger door open very slowly, granting him easy access to the car's interior. He found the binoculars and was looking to see if anything else had been left inside when he heard a sharp bang against the metal frame of the car. He turned to see Joe waving his arm for Frank to come.

Joe's eyes were opened wide under the small

mask, and Frank knew instantly something was wrong. He swam to Joe at the rear of the MG.

The trunk lid was wide open and bent out of shape. Frank saw that the lid hadn't gotten twisted from the accident. Someone had forced it open. The two cameras were gone!

Joe could understand why they had been run off the road—if Kruger was behind it. But why would he order someone to dive thirty feet underwater to take two cameras from the submerged car? Was he afraid of what the film might show? But would the film even be all right after getting wet?

As Joe's mind was wandering, searching for answers, Frank was swimming around the MG, looking for clues. Trying to get his younger brother's attention, Frank clanged the base of his knife against Joe's tank, snapping him out of his daydream. Joe nodded after Frank made a swirling motion with his hand indicating they should scour the area.

The water was so clear that there was enough light to see even at thirty feet, although Frank was using a flashlight anyway.

They finished their underwater search, and Frank gave Joe a thumbs-up sign. It was time to surface. The two brothers swam toward the darkening sunlight above and climbed out near the rocks where they had left their gear.

"That was a waste of time," Joe said, pulling off his face mask.

Frank shook his head, disagreeing. "I don't think so. We learned that Kruger's really afraid that we might have something on him."

"That's what I figured. A picture of something," Joe said.

"Could be. Or maybe he just wanted our stuff to see if they could learn more about us. What else *was* in the trunk? Do you remember?" Frank asked.

"Let's see," Joe replied, closing his eyes and trying to visualize the trunk. "My bag, which had a change of clothes and our towels and swim trunks, and some shells—maybe . . ."

"What about that lifesaver we found on the beach near Kruger's villa?" Frank was talking about a ring-shaped life preserver that must have fallen from a boat and been washed ashore.

"That's right." Joe nodded, then stared at his brother. "But what would anyone want that for?"

"Nothing—unless it belonged to them in the first place!"

Frank and Joe gathered up their gear for the trek back up to the mopeds. They checked the ground carefully for any signs left by the underwater thieves during their approach or get-away.

"Someone might have walked over here, but that doesn't tell us anything," Joe mused, talking to himself.

"I don't see anything," Frank said.

When they reached the bikes, they checked for tire tracks or footprints—anything that might help them later in establishing the thieves' identity.

After Joe loaded his gear onto the moped, he scanned the surroundings. "They had to leave something behind," he said. "No one's that good."

"Looks like they were careful. Pros always are."

"But maybe not careful enough!" Joe had just noticed something glinting under a low bush.

Frank followed Joe's gaze about fifteen feet from where they had climbed down to the water. A small object was shining, reflecting the early-evening light. "I see it!"

"I hope it's not just a pack of cigarettes or something," Joe said as he jogged over to the bush. "Whoa—this just might be our first clue. Looks like a credit card!" Joe smiled.

"Well?" Frank said.

"Well," Joe mimicked, "it *is* a credit card, a Bank Eurocard." The sun was gleaming off the card's hologram. As Joe looked closer, his triumphant grin disappeared.

"Well?" Frank urged.

"It'll be very easy to track down the person who owns this," Joe continued. "According to the name on the card, it belongs to—Alfred Montague!"

Chapter

4

"MONTAGUE?" FRANK REPEATED, complete disbelief on his face.

"Alfred Montague. That's what it says. I can't believe he's involved in this."

Frank agreed. "Me, neither. There must be *some* explanation."

"If there isn't?"

"If there isn't"—Frank paused—"we might be staying in the home of someone who's trying to kill us!"

"What do we do? How do we find out?"

Frank thought for a second. "We'll ask him." He made it sound as if it would be the easiest thing in the world. But Frank knew the confrontation with Montague would be awkward—and possibly dangerous.

"Okay. But I'd feel a lot better if Alicia wasn't around when we meet with Montague." He looked at his watch. "Almost eight o'clock. They should be home by now. Why don't I give her a call—think of something to get her out of the house," Joe suggested.

Frank nodded and got on his moped to join his brother. After a few minutes of riding, Frank pointed out a pay phone next to a small roadside restaurant. Joe dropped two coins into the box, then slowly dialed. He was still trying to think of some reason to get Alicia away from the house.

"Hello? Alicia? . . . Hi . . ." Joe was thinking in double time. Maybe he could ask her to meet him somewhere, then he and Frank could go to the house when she left. But he rejected that idea because it would leave her stranded. "Do you, uh, feel like coming out to meet me?" he asked, still fumbling for words. ". . . Oh . . . Where? . . . Could you give that to me again? . . . Wait, let me write it down." Joe fished for a pencil and then jotted something down as Alicia talked. "Thanks," he concluded. "I—we'll see you soon."

Thoughtfully Joe replaced the phone on its hook and walked back to where Frank was waiting, straddling his moped.

"Could you get her out of the house?" Frank asked.

"She can't go anyplace because Montague had to borrow her car. But she did say she got a strange call about half an hour ago from some guy she didn't know. He said that Montague was supposed to be meeting with him, but he hadn't shown. And this guy"—he paused to check his notes—"Martin Powers, said the meeting was urgent. He left her his address."

"Well, where is he? Let's go check it out." Frank was ready to take off.

Joe checked his notes again. "Saint George's Harbor." He handed the note to Frank on which he had hastily scrawled "Martin Powers, #1 Blue Vista."

The two scooters lurched forward as Frank and Joe sped off toward St. George.

It was dark when the Hardys drove down into town. They parked their bikes and carried their scuba gear into a small café.

"Yes, I do know where that is," said the proprietor after looking at the address. "You can leave your gear in the back room and then I'll accompany you outside and set you in the right direction."

Joe and Frank found a clear corner for their stuff, then followed the proprietor outside.

"Just go through the square there," the man explained as he pointed, "and take a right out onto the quay. It should be one of the boats out on the left of the dock."

"Boats?" both brothers said simultaneously. Joe stared at the man. "You mean this address is a boat?"

"Definitely! *One Blue Vista* is the name of a boat. Happy sailing!"

Sailing wasn't what they were thinking of when Frank and Joe located the boat that had the name painted in bright blue letters across its stern. Martin Powers's boat took up an entire corner of the dock. "That's no sloop," Joe remarked. "That's a full-size yacht."

"I wonder where this Powers guy is. Doesn't look like anybody's on board." Frank's observation was pretty obvious—there wasn't a light on.

"You want to have a look?" Joe asked.

"It's trespassing," Frank reminded his younger brother.

"Yeah, but we're trying to find out what happened to Montague. Maybe he's on board—hurt or something. We should check it out."

Joe took out his small underwater flashlight. He was going on board, with or without Frank.

"Okay," Frank finally agreed. "But let's make it quick—someone may come soon, and there's no back door to *this* house." He followed Joe onto the deck of the large boat, walking silently in case someone really was on board. The sound of the water lapping against the side of the boat drowned out the creaking of the deck under the boys' weight.

"Here's the door that leads down to the cabins," Frank whispered.

Joe's flashlight lit up the small latch on the cabin-house door. Frank pulled on it, and the small door swung open.

"I'll go first," Joe said. Frank checked to make sure no one from shore could see what they were doing. The dock was empty. "Follow me," Joe said, forcing Frank's attention back.

The two brothers moved stealthily down the few steps into the small living compartment. "Watch yourself," said Frank from behind.

Just as Frank spoke Joe tripped over something, stumbling noisily forward. The flashlight flew from his hand, to make a hard landing against the wooden floor.

Frank winced as he heard the sound of breaking glass, followed by the lopping sound of the flashlight as it rolled across the floor. The light winked on and off with each turn of the flashlight. "You okay?"

Joe had landed on one knee, but recovered quickly. "Yeah. The lens on the flashlight broke, but the light still works." Joe reached down and picked it up, shaking it gently every time the small light flickered out.

"Are you clumsy, or what?" Frank asked his brother.

"I tripped over something," Joe said, annoyed.

Joe shone the light on the steps that had led down into the cabin. "But there's nothing on the stairs." Just then the light reflected off a thin wire that ran across the last step.

"Uh-oh," said Frank. "I don't think that's a regulation part of the boat."

Frank took the light from Joe and followed the wire with it. The dim glow barely illuminated the corner of the cabin, where the wire eventually led to a small box about fifteen inches square.

Frank's worst fears were realized. He now could hear the faint ticking of a clock. "Is that what I think it is?" Joe asked, knowing what Frank's answer would be.

"Yep. It's a bomb," Frank said, moving quickly to examine it more closely. "You triggered it when you tripped on that wire."

"Then why didn't it go off?" Joe asked.

Frank was shining the light on two wires that ran from the little box to a small digital clock set in its face. "It's a time delay." Frank stared at the changing numbers on the clock. "And we have less than six seconds! Hit the deck! It's going to blow!''

Joe dived into the darkness, overturning a small table, which he scrambled behind.

Frank had gingerly picked up the bomb when he shouted for Joe to take cover. He had had to drop the flashlight, and the room was now in total blackness. For only a fraction of a second Frank stood motionless. Then he noticed the light coming in from the outside through a small porthole. Four seconds left.

Praying that the porthole was open, Frank rushed toward it.

Two seconds.

"Here goes!" He pitched the small box toward the light. But just before the bomb reached the small, circular opening, Frank saw a reflection on the glass, and he knew the tiny porthole was closed!

One second later the room filled with a flash of hot, bright whiteness as the bomb exploded—inside the small cabin!

Chapter

5

THE ROAR OF the explosion was deafening. Within seconds an entire side of *One Blue Vista* was blown out and engulfed in flames.

"Frank! Frank!" Joe cried out, pulling himself free of debris.

There was no reply.

Joe tried to push down his thoughts of losing Frank. He had been protected, in the far corner behind the collapsed table. But Frank had been in the middle of the room, completely exposed.

Fire was spreading rapidly through the tiny cabin. Furniture, books, and papers had been thrown around the room by the force of the blast. Shattered glass covered the deck, and heavy black smoke fell from the ceiling. Joe saw their plastic flashlight melted into the floor.

Only a moment earlier Joe had been in desperate need of light. Now the glow from the flames was blinding.

"Frank! Where are you?" Joe knew his brother would answer if he could.

Then Joe saw him. Frank's legs were sticking out from under a door just a few feet away. Obviously he had tried to protect himself by crouching between the bulkhead and a closet door, which he'd pulled open just before the blast. The door must have been blown from its hinges, and now lay on top of Frank's lifeless body.

"I'll get you out!" Joe yelled as he moved on all fours through the rubble toward his brother. Frank continued to lie motionless. Smoke was beginning to fill the room from the ceiling down. Joe tore the door off his brother, then he grabbed Frank under his arms and crawled through the smoke, dragging him.

"We'll make it," he said, not even knowing if Frank was dead or alive. "Here we go." He stood up and threw Frank over his shoulder and charged up what remained of the steps.

Aware that when the fire reached the fuel tanks for the engines there would be another explosion, Joe darted to the guard rail. He shifted Frank so he lay across his shoulders, clambered over the rail, and plunged into the oily waters.

"Got to swim clear," he kept saying. Side-stroking with one arm around Frank's chest, Joe swam parallel to the main dock toward the next pier. Joe suddenly realized he was getting some help. Frank was moving his legs and kicking feebly! "That's it!" Joe cried, as they moved a little faster. "Swim, swim!"

The wailing of the fire engine and ambulance sirens cut through the crackle of the flames. Then all sound was drowned out by a tremendous roar. The fire had reached the boat's fuel tanks.

"Down!" Joe yelled, pulling his brother underwater with him. They felt the force of the new explosion ripple through the cushioning effect of the water, but they were safe. They had swum far enough away from the yacht.

When they came up for air, Joe checked Frank out to see how badly he was hurt. He could see numerous cuts and bruises on his brother's arms, but Frank's face was okay except for a large bump over his left eye. "Are you all right?"

Frank groaned. "What happened?"

"You were on an exploding boat," Joe reminded him.

"Ohhh," Frank groaned, stretching his arms and neck. "I forget, does that make us flotsam or jetsam?"

Joe smiled. "How do you feel?"

"Like a soccer ball—after a game. Are you okay?"

"I think so, but I've been too busy saving you to check!"

Exhausted, the brothers were slowly dog-paddling toward a pier when suddenly they were bathed in a circle of bright light. It was coming from a spotlight bobbing up and down in the water. It had to be a boat, the boys knew, even though they couldn't see a thing beyond the blinding glare. The source of the light reached them in a few seconds, and the two Hardys could hear excited voices over the roar of the boat's engines.

"Grab my hand!" a voice ordered as the boat pulled beside them. "Come on, son, I've got you," said one man as he grabbed Frank and pulled him up over the side of the boat. "You next, friend," another man said.

"Easy does it!" the first voice said. "You boys all right?" And before anybody could answer, he added, "Just lie there and take it easy."

Both Joe and Frank could tell from the crew's brisk, precise movements that they'd gone through this drill often. The uniforms on the crew members and the blinking blue and red light on the stern told the Hardys they were aboard a police boat. Joe spoke first. "So what happened after I took cover?"

"I tossed the bomb and then realized that the porthole was closed," said Frank. "The bomb must have exploded just before it hit the porthole—it blew the glass right out and then released its full force outside the boat."

"Yeah," Joe agreed, "that must be why the room wasn't trashed more than it was." He shook his head. "Good timing. A few seconds sooner and the bomb would have bounced off that glass right back at you. A few seconds later would have been *too* late."

"I took a dive for the corner just after I threw the bomb," Frank explained. "I didn't have time to get into the closet, but I was able to yank the door open. And then the lights went out."

The two had almost forgotten they were surrounded by a small group of police and Coast Guard. One of them leaned over to question the brothers. His eyes narrowed and he stared directly at Frank. "Now, why were you trying to plant a bomb on Martin Powers's boat?"

"Are you kidding?" Joe said, exasperated. "We were trying to get the bomb *off* the boat."

"How did you know there was a bomb *on* the boat?" the harbor policeman continued.

"I tripped over it," Joe confessed, before he realized how silly it sounded.

"Just what were you doing on the boat?"

But before Joe could answer, the police boat

had reached the pier and the two brothers were helped onto the dock, where a few curious onlookers had gathered. Six or seven people stood around immediately in front of them, one taking pictures. Someone shouted from the back of the small group, "Arrest these two! Arrest them! They blew up my partner's boat! They've killed him!"

"Oh, no," Frank said. "Here we go again." He could see the man's fist waving above the heads of the others.

"Arrest them," the stranger kept insisting.

"No need to worry, we've got them now, and we'll take care of them," one of the officers said as he handcuffed the two brothers.

"Hold it," Joe objected, turning his head away from the blinding flashes of the photographer's camera. "We didn't *do* anything." But no one listened.

Then the stranger, a squat man with bushy, steel-gray eyebrows, emerged from the back of the small crowd. "Lock them up!" he yelled, staring at the two of them as he moved closer.

Joe immediately recognized the well-dressed, gray-haired man from the photos he had been looking at earlier that same day. "Kruger!" he shouted.

The sinister-looking German curled the corner of his lip into an evil smile. "Yes, Kruger— Bernhard Kruger." He let out a short laugh, and then turned and walked toward the burning boat.

"*He's* the one that should be arrested!" Joe yelled, pointing into the crowd. But no one was listening as he and Frank were being towed toward the waiting police car. Joe was furious. "Wait a minute!" he objected, struggling to turn around. But as he looked back, he saw that Kruger had disappeared into the curious crowd.

Joe and Frank were quickly checked by one of the medics who had arrived and then were escorted into the waiting patrol car. As they were pulling away, they turned and could still see the glow from the fire. Fifteen minutes after their ordeal the two Hardys were sitting in the St. George police station, wrapped in blankets and drinking hot tea.

Joe and Frank sipped their tea and explained to the officers who they were, what they were doing on the boat, and what their connection was with Kruger.

Within a few minutes a heavyset, dark-skinned man with short, curly hair that looked as if it had been flecked with white entered the small interrogation room. "I'm Captain Hodges," he said to the Hardys. He listened to the boys' story from his chief officer, then immediately called Chief Boulton.

"George Hodges here," the brothers heard

him say. "Sorry to ring so late, but we had a little fire here on the docks. I have a couple of kids with me who claim to be friends of yours."

Joe put his face in his hands as he listened to Chief Hodges explain the situation to Chief Boulton in Hamilton. "Great!" he mumbled. "We managed to get arrested not once, but *twice* in less than a week."

"We haven't arrested you—yet," Captain Hodges said as he hung up the phone. This time he finished his comment with a broad smile. "You're just here for questioning. It *seems* your story checks out. Your identification looks legitimate. I suggest you lay these out overnight on some paper toweling," he said as he returned the Hardys' ID cards. "And I think once you fill out some papers and sign a statement, we can let you go."

"You mean we're being released?" Frank asked, still somewhat dazed.

"Yes," Hodges assured them. "But remember that even the famous Hardy brothers can be arrested for trespassing and illegal entry."

The brothers nodded, aware that he could have detained them if he wanted.

"Chief Boulton asked me to tell you to watch out for yourselves," Hodges said with a smile. Joe grinned and shifted in his seat.

"But," he said softly, his tone turning more

serious, "I also have some bad news. Walt Conway, a detective from our force, wasn't so lucky. He was shot this afternoon and is in critical condition."

"Shot?" both brothers chorused.

"He was ambushed a couple of hours ago as he was getting out of his car in front of his home."

"Did they catch the guy?" Joe asked.

"All we know is that there were probably two men. An eyewitness said the shooter's car pulled away at just about the same time the shot was fired, so we assume one person drove while another handled the gun." His chest heaved as he took a long breath. "The doctors removed one slug from him—a twenty-two."

Hodges paused a second to reflect on the outbreak of violence on his usually peaceful island. "These incidents are starting to get out of hand. And if they are all related as you say—" He paused again, shaking his head in frustration. "If only we could get something on this Kruger fellow."

It was almost midnight when the boys drove up to the Montague house on their mopeds. Alicia was up, waiting at the screen door. She was standing rigid, pale and distraught. "Are you all right? I heard what happened on the news. When I called the Saint George police, they said you had already left. I thought Dad might be with you. Was he in the explosion?"

"Whoa," Frank said, interrupting her. The boys were still standing outside. "Slow down. May we come in?"

Alicia didn't realize that she was blocking the doorway. "I'm sorry. Come in, sit down." Although normally in control, Alicia was terribly excited and tense now. "I'm so worried," she confessed. "Did you see Dad? He hasn't come home. And he was supposed to have been at that boat that blew up. I'm terrified something's happened to him!"

"We didn't see him. But I'm sure he's fine." Joe tried to sound very confident. "He wasn't on the boat—I'm positive." He was worried about Alicia's father, and almost forgot that Montague might have been the one who tried to have them killed!

"Let's change our clothes," Frank suggested, still damp from their evening plunge. "And then we'll go out and see if we can find him." But he knew that with nothing to go on, their search would probably be fruitless.

"Did you call the police?" Joe asked.

"I mentioned it when I spoke with the Saint George police, but they didn't know anything. And if the Hamilton police knew something happened to Dad, they'd call me." Alicia sounded much calmer now.

"Shh!" Joe said, interrupting her. "I heard a noise outside."

The three listened in silence.

"Sounds like we have visitors," Frank said. "Maybe our friend from the boat wants a second chance."

Joe reacted quickly. "I'll go out the back and circle around."

"Go upstairs," Frank whispered to Alicia.

"But what's going on?"

"I'll explain later." He moved quietly toward the front door.

Alicia backed up the stairs as Frank positioned himself behind the front door. He could hear someone approaching the house very slowly.

Joe peered out from around the side of the house. He moved forward silently and crouched behind a low bush on the side of the driveway as he watched someone crawl along toward the front door. The person, on all fours, was moving stealthily across the front lawn.

Joe stole out from behind the bush, then sneaked around behind the prowler and moved up on him without a sound. With the accuracy of a mountain cat, he lunged forward, knocking the man flat.

"Got you!"

Frank burst through the front door, ready to help.

But the man trapped under Joe wasn't putting up a fight at all. He just lay there, motionless. Joe had lifted himself off the limp body and was flipping the man onto his back as Alicia thrust her head out an upstairs window.

She screamed. Frank looked up at her silhouette in the window, then turned back to Joe when he heard his brother gasp. Joe's prisoner was Alfred Montague!

Chapter

6

"MONTAGUE! CAN YOU hear me?" Joe asked the semiconscious man.

Frank turned to see if Alicia was still at the upstairs window. But she was already at the front door, running toward them.

"Oh, no!" Alicia exclaimed as she saw the limp body of her father. "He's bleeding!"

Blood trickled down the side of Montague's face from a cut just above his left eye; his eye was swollen and turning black and blue. His chin was cut but had stopped bleeding. Montague's eyelids began to flutter open.

"He's coming to," Joe reported.

"Let's get him into the house." Frank took Montague by the legs while Joe carefully lifted the wounded man under the shoulders. Alicia wanted to help, so she ran ahead and propped open the front door, then cleared off the living-room sofa. "Put him right here."

They laid him down on the couch, propping his head up with one of the cushions. Alicia went to get some water and a washcloth. Besides the bruises on his face, he had a large lump on the back of his head, and a two-inch spot of his hair was matted down with dried blood.

Returning from the kitchen Alicia asked, "Is he all right?" There was a slight tremor in her voice.

"I don't think there are any broken bones," Joe announced, "and hopefully no internal injuries."

Montague lay still, moving only his eyes. Although fully conscious, he still looked dazed and bewildered. "What happened?"

"That's what we were going to ask you," said Frank. "Boy, that must have been some fight!"

"I don't remember any fight," Montague wheezed. "I just remember being hit on the head and then waking up on the front lawn with *everything* hurting. I don't know if someone was trying to kill me or not."

"I don't think so," Joe said. "If someone had been trying to kill you, you'd have more than a bump on the head. It looks to me as if someone wanted to teach you a lesson—"

"Or make you look bad," Frank added.

"Dad—"

"I'll be all right, honey. Now, don't you worry." Montague tried to calm Alicia. His words were clear, and they all knew he hadn't been badly hurt. He then turned his attention to Frank and Joe. "What happened to you fellows?"

"Never mind us, what happened to *you?*" It had been a trying day—an endless day—a day that was making even Frank impatient to find answers.

"I went out to try to help you fellows after I heard you were kidnapped."

"Heard what?" Frank and Joe said together.

"I received a phone call when we got home from our five o'clock appointment. The voice—some man's, I didn't recognize it—said the two of you had been kidnapped and that if I didn't believe him, he would send me Frank's ring—still attached to his finger. He told me to meet them at the Gibbs Hill Lighthouse, alone."

"Then?" Frank asked.

"Well, I don't remember exactly what he said, but I just assumed it would have taken more than one person to subdue both of you. Anyway, I drove out to the lighthouse without even telling Alicia, and as I was waiting, someone cracked me on the head. That's the last thing I remember until I woke up on the front lawn.''

Frank hesitated a minute, unsure whether Montague was a victim or a mastermind. He brought out the credit card Joe had found. Frank knew the card had been found *before* Montague's abduction, but he wanted to hear his host's reaction—or excuse. "Did you lose your Bank Eurocard?" he asked, trying not to make it sound like an accusation.

"Don't know," Montague replied. "Let me check my wallet." He reached beneath him as if he were going to pull his wallet from his back pocket, but his hand returned empty. "I seem to have lost my entire wallet," he said. "I could have lost it at any time today, because I don't know when I checked it last."

Joe's mouth tightened as he listened to Montague speak. Frank could see that Joe was having difficulty believing Montague, and although Frank really liked the man, he didn't know *what* to think.

"We'd better call the police," Joe said after Montague had finished his story.

"No," Montague said. "There's nothing they can do now. And I'm too tired to handle any questions right now anyway."

Frank and Joe tried to convince Montague

to call them, but their host insisted on leaving the police out of it. "I'm going to bed now," he announced, rising suddenly from the couch. He turned and walked toward the stairway.

Alicia jumped up and went over to her father, gently taking his arm above the elbow. "See you in the morning, boys," she said, helping her father up the stairs.

"What do you think?" Joe asked his brother.

"I don't know what to think," Frank admitted. "His bruises were real, that's for sure."

"*I* think it's time to check out this house. If Montague's involved in any of this, there might be a clue."

"Maybe you're right, but I've done enough for one day." Frank could no longer hide his weariness. "And what if we're wrong? I really don't feel comfortable going through his drawers and closets. We *are* his guests, you know."

"His guests *or* his victims," Joe quickly pointed out.

"Fine," Frank muttered as he headed upstairs to the guest room. "Let me know what you uncover—in the morning."

Joe decided he would work on his own. He tiptoed around the living room, opening drawers, searching behind curtains and under seat cushions, lifting lamps, and moving books, not knowing *what* he was looking for.

Then he went into the small study off the living room and opposite the kitchen. He crossed to an easy chair with a small end table next to it and pulled open the drawer in the table. His question was answered when he saw—on top of the pens—a small revolver.

Joe reached for the gun, not concerned with protecting fingerprints since it was undoubtedly Montague's gun and his prints would be on it. He lifted the gun to his nose. It's been fired recently, he thought. The .22 revolver still had two bullets left in it. Although he and Frank hadn't dodged any bullets yet, Joe remembered that Walt Conway had been shot that afternoon with a .22.

He brought the gun upstairs, excited to show his brother, but Frank was already fast asleep. No point waking him now, Joe decided. Can't do a ballistics check until tomorrow, anyway.

Joe took off his shoes and lay down on the bed next to Frank's, thinking about everything that had taken place since early morning. He held the gun, after making certain the safety was on, and turned it over again and again. He was thinking about Kruger, the black car, the boat—and Montague—and as he lay there trying to put some of the pieces of the puzzle together, he shut his eyes and fell fast asleep.

* * *

"Let's go!" Frank said, what seemed like only moments later to Joe.

He moaned. "I just fell aslee—" He stopped short when he saw it was light outside.

"Let's go," Frank repeated. "Nine o'clock! You want to slip on some pajamas so we can go into town?"

Joe didn't understand his brother's joke until he realized that he had fallen asleep with his clothes on. "I feel awful," he said.

"You look it. And since when have you taken to sleeping with a gun?"

"A gun? Why would I— Oh, *that* gun." Joe saw the revolver on the bed next to him and realized he must have fallen asleep with it. "I found it last night in the end table in the study. I know it's Montague's gun, and the interesting thing is, it's been fired recently. I thought we could take it down to the police lab today."

"Good. And then I think we should head back to Kruger's."

"After being spotted yesterday?"

"Maybe they won't expect us." Frank picked up a towel that had been tossed over the arm of an easy chair and threw it at Joe. "I called the police in Hamilton and Saint George just a minute ago. Divers went out early this morning to check out the MG, and experts sifted through the rubble of *One Blue Vista*. Nobody came up with anything. So, Kruger is still our best lead." He paused and put both hands on his hips. "Now, wouldn't you like to get ready for the day's detective work?" he asked, kidding his brother.

Joe hung the towel around his neck, smiled, and headed groggily into the bathroom. "Another day, another adventure," he mumbled.

It didn't take Joe long to get ready, and he soon joined his brother and Alicia in the kitchen for a light breakfast. Alicia agreed to let them use her car, since neither she nor her father had any plans for the day.

By nine-forty-five they were on their way. They went into Hamilton first and stopped off at the police station to drop off Montague's gun. Then they drove on to Kruger's.

They pulled off the road into a small clearing behind a clump of trees, about a hundred yards in front of the place where they had parked the day before. "Let's leave the car here," Frank suggested, "and walk the rest of the way. It should make it harder for them to spot us," he added. He stopped and pointed at a small boat he noticed heading into shore. The all-white boat looked about twenty-six feet long. Frank couldn't see any crew.

"It's aimed right for Kruger's dock," Joe said. He paused and stared at the boat and dock, a puzzled look on his face. "I took a picture of that dock the other day. Something's not right." He tried to remember how everything had looked the last time they were there. "Wait a minute! Do buoys move?"

"Sure. They bob up and down all the time."

"No, I mean from one spot to another," Joe explained.

"No," Frank said. "They're anchored down, so they can be used as markers."

"Or signals!" Joe felt a rush of excitement. "When I took a picture last time, that buoy was on the other side of the dock. I'm positive. It was closer to the shore and on the right side."

"We can be positive of another thing—that boat definitely is headed for the dock. Can you make out the name of it?" Frank asked. Joe shook his head.

As the boat drew nearer, Frank read the name on its bow out loud. *"Sea . . . Mist. Sea Mist."*

Joe noticed that Frank was no longer looking at the boat but was trying to remember something.

"That's it!" Frank exclaimed. *"Sea Mist* was the name on the life preserver we found on the beach—one of the things that was taken out of the trunk of the MG!"

Chapter

7

THE *SEA MIST,* a large, oceangoing pleasure craft, glided in toward shore, closer and closer to the dock used by Bernhard Kruger. Then, about a hundred yards from the dock, it stopped.

"Looks like they're anchoring out there," Frank observed. "The flag's from Panama, but then a lot of American boats and ships have Panamanian registry."

"I can see someone on deck," Joe interrupted, looking through a pair of binoculars. "He's lowering a dinghy." The purring sound of the engines had now stopped. High rolling waves came in as the winds started to pick up just then.

"There's another guy," Frank said. He took

the field glasses from Joe. "They're going over the side. It looks like they're going to come ashore in the dinghy." He scanned the rest of the yacht with the binoculars. "I don't see anybody else on board." Dark clouds began passing in front of the sun, casting shadows over the scene. Frank watched as the men climbed into the dinghy and began rowing ashore. The dinghy swayed and bounced in the surf.

"The wind's starting to kick up a bit," Joe observed. "If there's a storm brewing, it probably means that no one will be taking the boat out again for a while."

"You've got that look on your face," Frank said. "Don't tell me. I know exactly what you're thinking."

"Well, look at it this way," said Joe through a broad grin. "The odds against getting blown up on two boats in two days are pretty high."

"Here we go, breaking and entering again. Just don't tell Chief Hodges."

Frank focused on the two men as they reached the dock. But the passing shadows made it difficult to see their features clearly. Neither guy would stand out in a crowd of other men in their late thirties or early forties. One had a well-trimmed, curly black beard. The other sported a knitted watch cap perched on the back of his head. Frank watched them as they pulled the dinghy out of the water and tied it securely to the dock.

They were close enough for Joe to see them clearly without the binoculars. "I tell you what," he said, "you keep tabs on those two, and *I'll* sneak aboard the boat alone. That way at least one of us will be following orders."

Frank sighed in agreement. "But we'll meet back here in thirty minutes." He watched as the two men from the boat walked up the beach to Kruger's door. "I'll make a dash for the house. As soon as they're being let in, I'll go over the wall. Less chance of someone looking out the window right then."

"Okay . . . now!" Joe said, seeing the door open.

"Thirty minutes," Frank reminded his brother. Then he broke into a sprint.

Joe slipped into a pair of trunks and then swam out to the boat. The water was choppy, and Joe found it easier to swim underwater as much as possible; that way he avoided the crashing waves above him. Swimming came naturally to him, and in very little time he'd reached the *Sea Mist*. He swam around to the stern of the boat so he wouldn't be seen boarding her if anyone happened to be looking out of Kruger's villa. Straining upward, he was able to grab hold of a rail and hoist himself onto the deck. The wind had picked up now, and the water slapped against the sides of the ship in regular bursts.

Joe took a moment to get his sea legs, steadying himself against the rail as the boat bounced and tipped. Then he walked forward along the deck, into a passageway that ran down the middle of the boat. The second door on the right was marked *Captain*. He opened it and looked in.

The first thing he noticed was a table full of papers against the right-hand wall. He checked the rest of the room—a bunk on his right, a little sink on the left, metal lockers across from him. Then he went inside. Maps and charts for all the waters and islands from Puerto Rico to Bermuda were strewn on the tabletop. Pencil markings on the maps showed that somebody was more interested in staying within the cover of little islands than taking more direct open-water routes. He left the chart table and walked across the cabin to a small desk beside the captain's locker.

Joe sifted quickly through the haphazard piles on the captain's desktop. "Notes, papers, checkbook stubs, computer disks—" Then he looked in the drawers beneath. "And here we have"—he opened a medium-size file—"a stash of blank credit cards. Jackpot!"

He had just picked up one of the blank cards when he heard noises above him on deck. He froze for a second, listening intently as the sounds became distinct—footsteps! There was a crew member on board—probably left behind to look after the boat. Joe was annoyed at himself for taking it for granted that the boat was deserted. But he had *worse* problems.

The footsteps were coming right toward the captain's cabin! Joe grabbed the check stubs and one of the disks on the desk and crammed it into the waist of his trunks. Then he made a dash for the cabin door—just as it began to open.

Joe pressed himself against the bulkhead behind the door as a tall, muscular man stepped into the room. His hair was cropped close, and the back of his neck was all lines and wrinkles. Joe stiffened, but the man never noticed him, going straight for the desk. He leaned over, his back to Joe, and opened the bottom drawer.

The boat was still swaying from the turbulence, and the cabin door was swinging on its hinges. Joe knew that if the door slammed shut, or if the tall man turned around, he'd be a goner. His only chance was to slip out right then. He stepped around the door and soundlessly backed out the open doorway, his eyes fixed on the big man.

The burly guy closed the desk drawer and stood up. Now! Joe told himself, turning to bolt.

Then he froze, staring at a short, broad, powerfully built man who gave him a nasty stare back.

"Hey, Mickey! We've got company." The stocky man's voice was a growl as he shouted to his partner in the cabin. His dark blue turtleneck sweater made it difficult to tell whether or not the squat man really did have a neck. But he definitely had a four-inch black switchblade handle in his hand. At the touch of a button, the handle sprouted a four-inch silver blade.

If Joe hadn't stopped short of the gravelly-voiced thug, he might have bowled him over and had a chance of getting away. Now he was trapped between Mr. Big and Mr. Broad. Moving back into the cabin meant four walls and the guy called Mickey; moving forward meant the man with the knife, but beyond him was the ocean. Joe decided to take a chance on getting past that switchblade.

The armed man had a two-inch gash across his left cheek, which told Joe this was definitely not the thug's first knife fight. And even though Joe stared into the man's eyes, he could see the extended right hand moving back and forth in front of his body with the shiny knife.

Then the muscleman made his move, lunging forward, the length of his right arm extended by four inches of sharp metal. His move was quick, narrowly missing Joe. The blade actually sliced his shirt as he twisted aside. But Joe had more than evasion in mind. Now his adversary was off-balance, leaning forward on one foot with his right hand out, his fist clenched tightly around the knife.

With the back of his left hand, Joe swung at the raised arm of his assailant. Then Joe quickly turned his body so that his right shoulder pinned the man's arm against the bulkhead until he dropped the knife. Joe's back was to the squat guy, who had grabbed Joe around the neck. Joe drew his elbow back, hard, and hit his target—the man's stomach.

"What the—" Mickey exclaimed as he stepped out of the cabin. "Hang on, Croaker!"

"Great name." Joe grinned as he backed up and slammed Croaker into the bulkhead. He could hear the thud as Croaker's head made contact with the metal. Croaker finally let go of his stranglehold around Joe's neck.

Joe backpedaled as he watched the man called Mickey move toward him now.

Mickey didn't look much more attractive from the front than he had from behind. He looked as if he shaved his head rather than cut his hair. And his eyebrows, which were also short, met just above his long, crooked nose.

The big guy was undoubtedly strong but slow

on his feet. And the rolling motion of the boat didn't help him.

Croaker, who was on his knees, reached out and wrapped his arms around Joe's left leg as Joe turned to race away from Mickey. Joe tried to shake him off, but Croaker held fast. He kept Joe back just long enough for Mickey to reach them.

"Hey, tough guy," he heard Mickey say from behind. And then Joe felt a hard object slam into the back of his head. The world went red and hazy. Then a crashing blow connected a second time behind Joe's ear. He buckled, then sank into blackness.

A gallon of seawater thrown into his face brought Joe around.

"Are you awake now?" a raspy voice said. "Or would you like another drink?"

When Joe could focus, he saw Croaker standing above him with a bucket. Joe started to go for his rival, but couldn't move. His hands and feet were bound tightly. His body aches were capped by a throbbing pain in the back of his head. "Now what are you going to do?" he asked.

"I'm not sure," Croaker replied. "I wanted to cut you up for shark bait, but I'll let Mickey decide."

"Has he said anything?" the big man asked as he walked over.

"Nah, we were just talking about the fish."

"What were you looking for?" Mickey demanded, turning his attention to Joe.

"Nothing," Joe replied. "I thought this was someone else's boat."

Mickey kicked him in the side. "What were you looking for, I said?"

"Nothing—are you going to kick me again?"

"Forget him," Croaker growled. "Let's toss him."

Mickey persisted. "What were you looking for? Who are you working for?"

Joe knew that whether he talked or not, he wasn't going to get out of this one. "I told you," he said, "I got on your boat by mistake. I'm not looking for anything, and I don't work for anybody. I'm just a tourist."

"Aw, do what you want with him," Mickey told Croaker. "I've got stuff to take care of." He turned and walked away, leaving Joe in Croaker's hands.

"Well, well," the muscleman said, "I guess it's just you and me now." He flicked out his switchblade, pressing the blade under Joe's chin. "Nah, I don't want to dirty my good knife. I tell you what—you swam out here, right? I'll let you swim back."

He left for a minute and then came back with

a small anchor. "This ought to give you some exercise." He tied the anchor to Joe's waist. "You can do the *dog* paddle," he said, grinning. "But pretty soon you'll be a dead *duck*."

His laugh was more like a frog's croak as he picked up Joe and the fifty-pound anchor. With the strength of a champion weight lifter, he lifted Joe above his shoulders and tossed him into the ocean, like a fisherman throwing back an undersize fish.

Chapter

8

THE ANCHOR FASTENED around Joe's waist did its job perfectly. It sank rapidly to the twenty-five-foot ocean bottom, dragging Joe along like a fish on a line.

Every muscle ached as Joe tried to squirm free from the ropes that bound him. His head was throbbing. He tried to remain calm and conserve his oxygen. But his fear and his struggles caused his heart to race faster and faster, burning up precious oxygen.

He could feel the binding loosening around his legs, and he kept rubbing his feet together, trying to slip an ankle free. The wet rope stretched, and finally Joe did pull his legs loose. But his hands had been tied more firmly—they wouldn't budge. And no matter how hard he kicked his legs, it wasn't enough to overcome the weight attached to his waist. He was almost out of air.

Joe gritted his teeth, forcing his mouth shut so the water wouldn't rush in as he started to black out. Something rasped against his lips! A heavy stream of bubbles rose in front of his eyes. Someone was trying to force something into his mouth. It was Frank, trying to get him to take the regulator of his scuba tank. Joe opened his mouth and started breathing rapidly into the regulator, his teeth clamping down on the hard rubber mouthpiece. Frank stood by holding his breath, one hand on the regulator, the other on his brother's shoulder.

It seemed like an eternity before Joe pulled himself together enough to realize that he and his brother had to share the same regulator. He inhaled deeply, then motioned for Frank to take the mouthpiece back.

Frank took a deep breath, gave the regulator back to Joe, and then, using a knife he had tied to his weight belt, cut the ropes to the anchor. He and Joe started swimming slowly for the surface, sharing the oxygen supply on the way up. Frank cut the ropes that bound Joe's hands.

The Hardys surfaced. All around them the sky and water were black. The wind had blown in rain clouds and was tossing the waves violently against the boys. Joe threw his head back and sucked in the fresh air. A bullet whizzed past his ear.

"Down!" Frank said. The men on the boat must have seen the air bubbles from the scuba apparatus.

With only one tank between them, Joe's first impulse was to try to swim clear of the bullets. But he knew there was too great a chance of one of them being hit.

Like it or not, they had to return underwater to share the scuba mouthpiece. Although they were still close to the surface, the light made it difficult for the men on the boat to find their mark. The two brothers dived even deeper. A minute earlier the ocean depth meant danger— now it offered safety.

Even underwater the Hardys could hear the *zing* of bullets cutting through the waves, but they were far out of range. The storm was blowing in full fury now, and Frank and Joe knew their attackers would be unable to see them. They swam among the reefs, looking for a safe spot behind rocks where they could crawl back onto land.

After they pulled themselves up on the rocks they lay back for a moment, catching their breath. The waves were crashing against the rocks, covering them with spray and filling the air with a sound that was almost hypnotic.

Frank unhooked himself from his gear and said, "That was close. Do you need a minute more to rest?"

"No, I'm okay," Joe responded. He coughed a few times, then got to his feet. "We better split. They'll come for us and the rain's going to start any second."

As they climbed over the slippery rocks, Frank explained why he had swum out to the boat with the scuba gear. "I could hear the men talking inside the house. They said something about the guys still on the boat. I knew you'd be in trouble, and I thought the best place for me to be was underwater by the boat. I returned to the car, and then—" He stopped short as the clouds finally released their load. Fat, pelting drops drove holes into the water and beat a steady, heavy rhythm against the rocks.

Frank ran his arm across his eyes to clear the view. "Look!" he exclaimed. "Back on the boat."

Frank and Joe watched through a sheet of rain. Mickey and Croaker began unloading ordinary-looking, tarp-covered boxes from the boat into a second dinghy. "Rain or no rain," Joe remarked, "it looks like they're going to get that boat unloaded—pronto."

"They probably figure that we can lead the cops back to them."

"Right. And if they do go on board, they don't want to get caught with the goods, whatever they are."

"It's got to be blank credit cards!" Joe told Frank how he'd found a drawer full of the blanks in the captain's cabin.

"Well, there's nothing more we can do. Let's get out of the rain," Frank suggested.

Joe laughed. "Don't tell me you're afraid of getting wet!"

The brothers found themselves laughing heartily as they headed back to Alicia's car. Then Joe's laughter stopped suddenly. "Wait a minute!" he said. "If the goons on board guess we made it back to shore, they'll call the house to let them know. Then the guys inside will be waiting for us—at the car."

"Right," Frank agreed. "We'd better separate and circle around in case it's being guarded."

As they were moving silently through the few trees that separated the rocky shore from the roadway the rain let up to a steady shower. They both reached the car about the same time. Everything seemed to be normal. No one was around.

"Put the gear in the trunk," Frank said, "while I get the car started." He shook himself off, climbed in, and started up the engine. Then he looked in the rearview mirror. The trunk

was open, obliterating his view. He looked in
the sideview mirror—to find the image of a
familiar car. The BMW! Frank saw that the
black car was heading straight for them. But
Joe couldn't; his back was to the rapidly approaching car and the light rain was muffling
the sound. He was a perfect target.

Frank moved like lightning. He shoved open
the car door and stepped out, screaming, "Joe!
Behind you! The car!"

Now Joe heard the racing engine at his back,
and knew immediately what was happening.
He reached into the trunk and yanked out the
metal scuba tank; in one move he turned and
hurled the heavy tank at the windshield of the
black BMW.

The car was only ten feet away when the
heavy tank crashed into the large windshield,
creating a spider's web of cracks before breaking all the way through the glass. Joe was
poised to dive into the mud on the side of the
road, but his fast action and deadly aim had
worked. The BMW screeched to a halt. The
tank had landed in the lap of the driver. Joe
saw his arms folded in front of his face, the
knitted cap still perched on his head.

"Take off!" Joe shouted to his brother.

Frank knew what Joe had in mind. He
jumped back in the car, put it into gear, and
stepped on the gas. Just before the car sped

off, he felt Joe thumping into the trunk. It all happened so fast, and the little car squealed so noisily as it peeled out, that Frank didn't even know if they were being shot at or not.

He looked into the sideview mirror and saw one man scramble out of the passenger side of the BMW. He knew the pursuit was over—for now. He kept watching the mirror until the man, too small to identify, became a tiny speck. Once the coast was clear, Frank stopped to give Joe a chance to get out of the trunk. "Want to ride up front?" he asked.

Joe climbed out of the trunk, stretching his arms. "I was just starting to enjoy the view from the rear." He grinned.

"Did you learn anything else at Kruger's?" Joe asked as they drove back to Hamilton under the now clearing sky.

"When I got up to the side of the house, I stood under an open window. One of the guys from the yacht was called Gus, and the other Del—I think he was the one that you nailed with the scuba tank. Anyway, the first thing out of Gus's mouth was something about the other two guys on the boat. We didn't figure there was anybody else left. I didn't know what to do. I wanted to stay and listen to Kruger, but I was afraid that you were headed for trouble. So I sneaked back to the car, grabbed the gear, and headed out."

It was two-thirty when the Hardys got back to Hamilton. Joe suggested they stop at the police station to get the ballistics report on Alfred Montague's gun and to find out how Walt Conway was doing.

"Hello, Chief Boulton," the brothers said as they entered his office.

"Hi, boys." The chief looked the boys up and down, almost hesitant to ask about their damp attire. They had quickly pulled their jeans on over their wet trunks. "How's the crime-fighting business?"

Frank and Joe exchanged a look. Joe spoke first and then they both filled the chief in on the specifics of what they discovered at Kruger's house.

"How's Conway?" Frank asked.

"He's recovering quite well," the chief responded. "And I suppose you want to know about the report on the gun you brought in?"

Frank and Joe just nodded.

"Well, Montague's gun was *not* the gun used to shoot Conway—or anybody else that we know of, for that matter."

"That's a relief." Joe sighed.

"One curious thing, though," Chief Boulton added. "Joe's fingerprints were the *only* prints on that gun. Before he handled it, it had been wiped clean!" He pulled the gun out of his drawer and handed it back to Joe.

Joe screwed up his face, puzzled. "The gun had been fired, but why would someone wipe the prints off?"

The chief just shrugged.

Joe leaned against the wall, trying to figure it out. "Wait a minute! I completely forgot!"

"You mean you know why the gun was wiped clean?" Frank asked.

"No," he said as though he couldn't care less about it. "I forgot the stuff I took from the boat!" He pulled something from the waistband of his trunks that looked like a soggy piece of paper on a square plate and tossed it on the table, a wide grin on his face. "Check stubs and a disk, from the *Sea Mist*."

Chapter

9

FRANK AND JOE took the check stubs and computer disk with them, certain that some information could be retrieved. They wanted to check them over carefully when they got back to Montague's house and could use his computer.

There were things bothering them—little unresolved things—including why Montague's gun was wiped clean of fingerprints. Why had his credit card turned up on the cliff overlooking the wreck of the MG? And the larger questions, such as, what happened the evening Montague was supposedly kidnapped, and was he holding back anything? There were so many unanswered questions—and so little time left.

"We've spent the past two days getting

bruised and battered and out of breath." Joe sagged back in his seat as the brothers headed for home.

"But we're not even close to solving this case," Frank said. "And if we don't by tomorrow, we won't deserve a vacation."

Joe scowled. "All we have are names, some pictures, and a good idea who's behind the credit card scam and trying to kill us off."

"Maybe Montague can help," Frank suggested.

"Montague?"

Frank shrugged. "He's either for us or against us. If he's *for* us, then maybe we can get him to help in solving this thing. If he's *against* us, then it's time we confronted him and forced his hand."

"Okay, here's your chance." Joe cocked his head, indicating that they were back at Montague's house.

"I didn't realize we were home yet," Frank said, surprised.

"That worries me," Joe mused, "considering *you're* driving."

They parked Alicia's car and headed for the house.

"Oh," said Frank, remembering something. "We should get the stuff out of the trunk."

"The only thing in the trunk was *me;* the scuba gear's in the front seat of the BMW."

"But what about the second tank?"

"Oh. Guess you missed that. I threw it at the front tire of the BMW after I got in the trunk. There wasn't enough room in there for the two of us, and it looked like a good way to slow them down when they chased us."

"But they didn't chase us," Frank reminded his brother.

"Maybe the tank under the tire worked!" Joe said with a big grin on his face.

Montague and Alicia had come to the front door to greet them.

"Hello!" they both said.

The brothers said "Hi" as they walked up to the door. Then Joe added another "Hi!" and a broad smile as he looked at Alicia.

They were ushered into the living room, Montague and his daughter anxious to hear how the day had gone so far.

Joe started in without even waiting to sit down. He was uncomfortable pretending to be the friendly guest while he still had doubts about his host. "There are some things we have to talk about." He thought it sounded unusually cold and began to feel even more uncomfortable when he noticed Alicia staring at him, a look of worry on her face.

"Yes, I know," Montague said without hesitating. His manner was relaxed and friendly, and it helped ease the tension. "There's some-

thing I have to tell you boys first. Sit down."
He motioned for the brothers to have a seat on
the couch as he sat down on an easy chair
opposite them. Alicia grabbed a cushion from
the couch and sat on the floor.

Frank and Joe listened to what started like a
confession.

"I know more than you think about this
Kruger affair," Montague began. "And I'm
not exactly a retired copper."

Frank watched as Joe fidgeted in his seat.
Alicia looked up at the younger Hardy, but for
the first time since their arrival at the villa
almost a week earlier, Joe was unaware of her
presence.

"I wasn't able to say anything until now,"
Montague continued. "In fact, even Alicia
didn't know all the details until this morning."
He paused, looking from Frank to Joe. "I'm
only semiretired, and I'm not really a detective. I work for British Intelligence. And for
the last month, I've been on loan to your FBI."

Joe sat still, staring at Montague. Of all the
confessions he'd been preparing himself for,
this was the one he least expected. Frank
smiled broadly, with a look that showed he was
eager to hear more.

"You see," Montague resumed, "the FBI
knows of my work with British Intelligence,

and I'm the only agent who's an established local."

"And the government here? Do they know about you?" Frank asked.

Montague nodded. "They're aware—unofficially. The Bermuda police haven't made any progress on the activities of Kruger's group, especially since the consequences of his actions are felt primarily *outside* of Bermuda, particularly in your country. The credit card distribution scam is operating mostly in the United States. But the FBI is more interested in where the credit card blanks are stamped than they are with the distribution. If they close down the counterfeiting operation, then the distribution stops."

"Then you've been working on this case all along," Frank stated.

"Yes, but I wasn't allowed to tell Alicia or you until today. Even Alicia thought I could be involved with Kruger in some way!"

Frank turned to Alicia. "*You're* the one who wiped the fingerprints off your father's gun."

Alicia gave an embarrassed nod. "I was in such a state that I didn't know what to do. Dad was so suspicious, so secretive. When I heard that a Bermuda policeman had been shot, I really got nervous. I knew Dad kept a gun. It was always in the study and always spotlessly clean. When I saw it had been fired, I didn't know what to think."

"I had practiced with the gun on Tuesday," Montague interrupted. "Simple as that."

"So I wiped the prints off the gun." Alicia looked down, the beginnings of a blush rising to her cheeks. "It was a rather stupid thing to do."

Joe gave her a sheepish grin. He took the revolver out of his back pocket and placed it on the end table. "Welcome to the club," he said. "You weren't the only one who thought your father might be working with Kruger. Remember that credit card we found?"

"Only too well," Montague said. "I knew you boys had your suspicions then, especially when you never told me where you found the card."

"At the scene of the crime," Joe said and raised an eyebrow. Then he laughed at himself. "It was right where our car—uh, *your* car— was forced off the road."

"Ah." Montague nodded, thinking. "So, Kruger planned it so I was to be your primary suspect. You see, Kruger doesn't know I'm with British Intelligence, or that I'm involved with this case in any way. However, he knew about you and your investigation, and somehow you must have worried him. He decided to arrange an 'accident.' But you boys surprised him—you survived.

"So he had to try a bigger production—a bomb on board *One Blue Vista*. A murder, complete with someone to blame. Kruger expected you to be eliminated. And he thoughtfully supplied the police with a suspect." He tapped his finger lightly against his chest. "Me. I was the only choice since you boys had no connection with anyone else on the island, and since he made sure I had no alibi."

"Then the whole bit with Martin Powers was a setup, too," Joe suggested.

"Right. I was lured out of the house under the pretext that your lives were in danger."

"They were!" Joe interrupted.

"Yes, but the idea was to keep me out of sight during that time so I would have no alibi. Then you boys were led to believe that I was on Powers's boat. Kruger knew that once you got to the boat and found out that no one was on board, you wouldn't pass up the chance to search it. You were supposed to go out in a blaze of glory."

Alicia picked up a newspaper. "I guess you must have missed today's *Nassau Guardian*." She held up the front page. "You two really look cute!"

Joe grimaced and Frank laughed as the two of them looked at the photo of Joe on the front page. It showed the fire in the background, while up front was a furious, soggy, handcuffed Joe with his mouth wide open. "That must have been taken when I was yelling for the police to arrest Kruger instead of us," he said.

"Well, here's a picture of Powers being interviewed, safe and sound—and not dead, as Kruger said. And here we are, *still damp*," Frank said.

Joe stood up and reached into his pants pocket to pull out the wad of soggy paper and the computer disk. "I took this from the boat this morning," he said, directing himself to Montague.

"What is it?" Montague asked.

"A checkbook—I mean, the stubs that were attached to checks—and a computer disk."

"Now all we need is an underwater computer so we can read the disk." Frank grinned. "And the ink on the check stubs has all washed out."

"We won't be able to read the check stubs," Montague cut in, "but we may be able to retrieve some information from the disk. Why don't you boys go up and change, and Alicia and I'll work on it."

When Frank returned, he found Alicia and her father at work on a computer in the library. A bottle of cleaning material, some swabs, and a hair dryer sat on the desk, along with tweezers and a knife. Sunlight was dazzling the cozy room. All was quiet, except for the whining and clicking of the computer.

"We've cleaned and dried the disk," Alicia explained, "but a lot of the data has been lost."

Joe appeared and looked at the computer screen. "Looks like you're breaking a code."

"We're using a program that will fill in some of the missing information by running through plausible letter and word combinations," Montague explained. "There are still a lot of complete words or names missing, but at least we can make some sense of it."

He pointed to the top of the screen. "The disk is titled 'The Number File.' It contains hundreds of names, addresses—"

"And credit card numbers," Joe said, staring at the flickering columns. "Some of the entries even include a listing for 'mother's maiden name'!"

"They're all real people, and real card numbers," Frank explained. "That's one of the things that's making it so hard to crack this case—the crooks are using real credit card numbers—like a second card. None of the numbers are phony."

"But how do they get the numbers?" Joe wanted to know.

"I think it's possible for someone to tap into

a company's computer line and retrieve information without removing it from where it's stored," said Frank. "Something like going into an office and reading files without taking the files out of the office."

"It's a new kind of theft," added Montague. "They're stealing *information* rather than goods. It makes it a much harder crime to crack."

"I guess we should pass this information on to Boulton," Frank suggested.

"I'll take care of it," Montague said. He dialed the phone next to him. After a pause, "Hello, Chief Boulton, please. This is Alfred Mont—Hello—Hello!" He clicked the button up and down. "The line's gone dead."

"Could have been the storm." Alicia sounded as if she wanted that to be the reason.

"Sure." Joe quickly agreed to keep her from getting anxious. "Must have been the storm."

"I still think we should take a copy of this disk to Chief Boulton," Frank said. "Will you and Alicia be okay here alone?"

"Sure," Montague replied. "I've got the revolver, remember?" He slipped another disk into the computer and hit some keys. "Here's a copy. In the meantime I'll try to clean up some more information from the original."

"Since the rain has stopped," Joe said, "we

can take the mopeds. You two can have the car in case anything happens.

"Fine," Montague agreed.

They said their goodbyes, and once again the two brothers were on the road, headed for Hamilton.

Not five minutes from the Montagues' villa Frank saw the all-too-familiar black BMW in his rearview mirror. A piece of lightweight plastic had been secured over the hole in the windshield.

"Joe," he shouted over the roar of the two bikes, "we've got company!"

Joe looked over his shoulder. "I guess they cut the phone lines just to get us out of the house." He let out the throttle on his bike.

Frank couldn't hear his reply over the roar of the two bikes going full out. But at a top speed of fifty miles per hour, they were no match for the BMW. The boys were exposed and defenseless on their bikes.

The strip of road they were driving along was narrow, with no placc to turn off. They were riding single file now, Frank's bike faltering a little and lagging behind.

Frank looked over his shoulder and saw that the BMW had closed the distance between them to less than fifty feet. He leaned over the front of the bike to cut wind resistance and to make himself a smaller target for the bullets he expected would be flying at him.

He didn't expect what did happen. The car, going at least thirty miles an hour faster than the bike, rammed into the back of Frank's moped. The bike flipped. And suddenly Frank found himself spinning in midair, flying over the top of the speeding BMW.

Chapter
10

JOE CRINGED AS he heard the sickening crash of his brother's bike flipping over again and again until it bounced off the highway and stopped. He turned in time to see the black car come to a halt. He jammed on his brakes, leaned far to the right, and turned the bike 180 degrees. He twisted the throttle, downshifted, popped the clutch, and lurched forward in the direction of the crumpled bike.

Then he noticed his brother, who was lying motionless in a large bush by the side of the road about forty feet behind the BMW. Mickey and Croaker had gotten out of the car and were sauntering over to Frank's body.

"Hold it!" Joe yelled in rage as he sped toward them.

"I knew we wouldn't have to go after you!" Mickey shouted. "You'd come back for what's left of this guy." He lifted Frank behind the legs, and Croaker was ready to take his arms.

Joe drove right up to the two men, flying off his bike and landing on Mickey like a rodeo star in a bulldogging contest. His bike went sailing past them. It leaned over until it fell to the pavement, sending sparks everywhere and sliding off the side of the road. Mickey hit the ground hard. Joe lashed out with his fist and caught him with a blow to the jaw. Then he spun around as Croaker was about to grab him from behind. He threw a right into the short thug's midsection. His arm was back, ready to land a knockout blow when someone grabbed his arm.

"I got him, Del," his new attacker announced.

"Nice work, Gus." The two thugs had joined Mickey and Croaker. As Joe struggled to break the hold on his arm, he remembered those two names. Frank had said they were back at Kruger's. With a desperate yank, Joe pulled free—just in time for Del to put a chokehold on him.

"For old times," Gus said, lashing out and punching Joe in the stomach—knocking all the air and fight out of him.

"Lock him in the trunk before I kill him," Croaker ordered as he got up off the ground, his voice even gruffer than usual. "And hide the bikes." He pointed to a small clump of greenery near where Frank's bike had landed. "This time the Hardys are going to disappear without a trace!"

"What about this one?" Mickey asked, standing over Frank's body.

"Throw him in the back seat. He won't give you any trouble—he's dead!"

Joe tried to look over his shoulder at his brother as Mickey opened the trunk. Gus spun him around, and Joe twisted frantically, struggling to see.

"I've had enough of this," Croaker growled as he placed his hand against a nerve on Joe's neck. Joe collapsed, unconscious.

When Joe awoke, his stomach ached, and his shoulder felt as if it had been stepped on. His head was swimming. And he was rocking back and forth, back and forth. Then all at once he knew the rocking wasn't in his imagination. He was on a boat, thrown in the bilge. Looking at the emptiness of his surroundings, he thought about Frank then for the first time.

Before he could go over what had happened, or try to figure out what was about to happen, a door opened on the other side of the room. Joe recognized Mickey. "Enjoy your trip!"

The thug cackled as he shoved a body into the room with Joe.

"Frank!" Joe yelled. In spite of the fact that his older brother was bruised, bloodied, and dazed, he'd never looked more welcome to Joe. "I thought you were dead!"

"I know" were Frank's first words. "Mickey was gloating about the way Croaker announced I was dead. That was Croaker's idea of a joke. He knew I hadn't been killed, but he was trying to get to you."

"He's a real piece of work—" Joe swallowed the rest of his words. "But you're okay?"

"I'll live, maybe." Frank forced a grim smile. He said he was black and blue, and his body hurt all over. "They said they didn't want me to die before they had a chance to kill me properly." He looked at his brother. "*You* all right?"

"Yeah. I wasn't hurt or anything. I was just given a nice, long nap." He paused, running his teeth over his lower lip. "Well, what do we do now?"

"I don't know," Frank admitted. "I checked out this room thoroughly before they brought me topside for a few questions. Did you see what's in those boxes?"

"No." Joe shook his head, still a little groggy. "I just got here." He got up and walked over to one of the boxes his brother had pointed out. "Wha-do-ya-know!" he said as he pulled out a handful of bright new credit cards, all stamped with names and account numbers.

"And all the other boxes are filled with the same," Frank informed Joe, pointing out the other ten or so boxes that were scattered throughout the room. "There wasn't enough time to stamp the load of credit card blanks you found on the *Sea Mist* earlier. So this is probably the delivery we were supposed to get Dad the information about."

"Well, we're certainly right on top of things." Joe scratched the back of his neck. "If the *Sea Mist* did come from Puerto Rico, like it showed on the maps I saw, then the boat brings in a load of blanks from there, drops them at Kruger's, and then takes a load of stamped cards wherever we're going now."

"Yeah," Frank added. "Wherever."

"Any ideas?" Joe asked.

"Feels like we're on the open seas, and when I was topside I saw we were headed right into the setting sun, so we're either going due west or southwest."

"Are we on the *Sea Mist?*" Joe asked.

"Couldn't tell. The only close-up look I ever got of the *Sea Mist* was from underwater. I'd guess from the way she rides that she's about a sixty-four-footer."

"We must be headed to the U.S. mainland, though," Joe figured.

"Quite right, boys!" Mickey had opened the door just in time to catch Joe's remark. "But you won't see the mainland again. We have a scientific project in mind for you. You're going to get a firsthand look at how things—and people—disappear in the Bermuda Triangle!" Mickey let out a sinister laugh as he gave the brothers time to understand what he meant.

Joe hated Croaker, but he liked Mickey even less. He slowly started to move away from Frank. Maybe while Mickey's attention was centered on one of the brothers, the other could somehow overcome him.

A revolver appeared in Mickey's hand. "You keep moving like that," he said to Joe, "and you're never going to hear the end of my story."

Joe froze while Mickey continued. "You've caused us a lot of trouble. We even had to send a diver down to fetch your camera from that MG, in case you happened to get a picture of the boat. And we got a bonus—the life preserver! I didn't even know that was missing."

He grinned at them nastily. "Too bad you didn't hold on to it. You'd find it handy where you're going. Before we rendezvous tomorrow with some friends, we're dumping you overboard. This time we'll *know* there's no chance you'll show up again. And without any bodies, the police can't be sure of a crime." His laugh echoed off the bare walls. "And the final joke is that we'll buy a couple of thousand dollars' worth of merchandise in *your* names with *your* credit cards before anybody even knows you're missing!"

He looked crazed as he backed out of the room and stopped suddenly in the doorway. "I almost forgot. They say bad things happen in threes. Well, tomorrow by this time there'll be three of you sharing an ocean grave."

The sound of the slamming door echoed throughout the room until it was finally muted by the sound of rushing water outside the bulk-head. Joe and Frank looked at each other without speaking. There was one light in the dim room—a bare bulb hanging from the ceiling attached to a long cord plugged into the far wall. There wasn't much they could use to escape and overcome their captors.

Frank was the first to break the silence. "Who do you suppose the other person is?"

Joe's face was tight. "Think about it. Who else do we know who's working on this case? Montague!"

As if on cue, the door opened again, and someone was shoved into the room. "Company!" a voice yelled out. Frank and Joe watched as the person stumbled into the light.

"Alicia!" they shouted simultaneously. Joe rushed up to her and grabbed her by the shoulders. Her eyes were red, her face pale, but she didn't seem to be hurt. "Did they—"

"I'm fine," she interrupted. Her smile assured the brothers that she was okay.

"What happened? How did you get here?" Frank asked.

"After you left, I started wondering about the phone line. At first I thought maybe it had been cut to trap us in the house. *Then* I wondered if Kruger's plan was to get both of you *out* of the house.

"You couldn't go very fast on those bikes. I decided to follow you in the car in case you needed to get away quickly. Dad said he'd wait at home in case something happened and we missed one another.

"I practically rammed into that black BMW you had told me about, and then I saw your bikes. But I didn't see either of you. I tried to turn around, but before I could get out of there, the passenger door swung open, and this big guy turned off the ignition key and grabbed me.

"They forced me into their car and asked me a lot of questions. I didn't say anything, so then they took me with them. They questioned me topside, and when I wouldn't tell them anything again, they brought me down here."

"I'm glad to see you, but I'm unhappy that you're here," Joe burst out. "Does that make any sense?"

Alicia grinned. "I understand."

"They didn't try any rough stuff?" Frank asked in a soft, concerned voice.

"No—they didn't even search me." Alicia's grin grew wider as she reached behind her. "I've had this all along." She pulled something out from her baggy jeans.

"The revolver!" Joe stared in amazement.

"Dad said I should take it just in case."

"Fantastic! Let's invite Mickey back in here, threaten him with the gun, and then take over the ship," Joe said.

"Not so fast," Frank cautioned. "If Mickey forces us to use this gun, that would warn the others. Besides, remember what Mickey said about a rendezvous tomorrow. We need to find out where that meeting is."

"But they're going to dispose of us *before* then."

"Look. There's no way we can reach Florida by tomorrow, so the rendezvous must be at sea."

"We've got to figure out where the rendezvous is, and *then* find a way out of this mess.

It shouldn't be too difficult to pick the lock on this door—the only real problem is how to overcome the crew."

"Are there just the four of them?" Joe asked.

"I only saw two," Frank answered.

"There are three," Alicia confirmed. "The short, fat guy with the funny voice stayed behind."

"Croaker," Joe said. "Did you happen to notice the name of the boat?" he asked excitedly.

"The *Sea Mist*."

"Great. Then I know how to get to the wheelhouse and the captain's cabin."

"Good," Frank said, feeling more confident now. "Tonight the boat will probably be on automatic pilot, and we'll know the direction of the ship. Picture that as a straight line from Bermuda to someplace on the U.S. mainland—"

"But you said we won't reach the mainland," Joe interrupted.

"That's not the important thing," Frank said. "If one of us can get to the wheelhouse and reset the pilot—heading us off course—we'll be able to find the rendezvous point."

"How?" Joe wanted to know.

Frank drew a line in the dust on the floor with his finger. "Let's say this is the original route." He ran his finger partway along the same line, then turned off at an angle. "Here's where we turn the ship during the night." He extended the line.

"But tomorrow morning they'll discover they're miles off course," Joe said.

Alicia chimed in, understanding Frank's plan, "And they'll have to plot a new direction. And where that course crosses the original course is where the rendezvous is set."

As Alicia spoke, Frank drew a new line that intersected the first. "X marks the spot!"

"It's a big triangle," Joe said.

"That's why it's called the triangulation method. It's really nothing more than geometry."

"Once we know where the meeting place is," Frank added, "we can contact the authorities and head back to Bermuda. Got it?"

"Got it!"

The three were not interrupted again as they sat quietly and discussed their plans. No one had even brought them any food. It was after five when Frank said it was time to move. He picked the lock on the door in about fifteen minutes, using the wire from one of Alicia's barrettes. Joe crept out and found his way up to the wheelhouse. Everyone was asleep, and he wasn't seen. The wheelhouse was empty, and Joe had no trouble setting the automatic pilot for a different course. He then returned to their prison.

"Done," he said when he reentered the room.

"Any problems?" Frank asked.

"The only problem I had was coming back here without going after those hoods. It seems crazy not to take care of them now that we're free."

"We need to know that rendezvous point," Frank emphasized once again. "We're too tired to think clearly now anyway—let's get some sleep. Then we'll figure out a plan in the morning before anyone comes back."

There was nothing to do now *except* wait. The three captives flattened out some boxes to lie on. Joe took the revolver from Alicia and slipped it under one of the boxes. Then they all huddled together on their hard, makeshift bunks and went to sleep.

The sharp sound of a piercing alarm woke them a couple of hours later. "What's that?" Alicia asked, startled.

"The radar warning system," Frank informed them. "It probably means there's something in the boat's path. It's a warning to the captain to take the boat off automatic pilot and steer a new course.''

"Then they'll find out the automatic pilot has been tampered with.''

"Let's see—'' Frank looked at his watch. "It's almost seven A.M. We've gone far enough off course to calculate the rendezvous point once they set the new course.''

The alarm stopped, and the trio could feel the boat turn sharply to port. Then, without warning, the door to the room was unlocked and slammed into the bulkhead.

Mickey burst into the room, gun in hand. "So, somebody was playing captain in the middle of the night, huh? Did you really think that if you set a course for the Carolinas, the boat would reach land before we got up in the morning?''

Joe was searching for the gun he had taken from Alicia a few hours earlier, but it had slipped under one of the box flaps. He started to reach for it.

"You! Tough guy!'' Mickey said, looking at Joe. "Stand up!''

Joe got slowly to his feet as Gus and Del stalked in.

"Over against that wall. Gus, tie him up. Now you, handsome,'' he said, nodding at Frank. "Stand up, turn around, and put your hands behind your back. Del, take care of him.''

"I'll take care of him, all right.''

"Just tie him up—that's all.''

"Why don't we just toss them overboard right now?'' Gus asked.

"Because we want to wait for local radio contact with the other ship. What if the FBI found out our rendezvous point, and our boys aren't there but the Coast Guard is? We might need some bargaining power.''

Frank and Joe were securely tied with rope, then thrown down on the deck like sacks of potatoes. Then, after Gus and Del left, Mickey went over to Alicia, grabbed her by the arm, and pulled her toward the door.

"We'll take care of your girlfriend, lover boy. The next time you see her, you'll both be twelve thousand feet underwater!''

Chapter

11

"A FINE MESS your plan has gotten us into,"
Joe grumbled. "I should have nailed them all
last night when I had the chance."

"Stop griping and try to get out of your
ropes," Frank said, cutting him off. "We
haven't got much time."

"They tied me so tight I can't move anything
except my fingers."

"Good. Then get your fingers over here and
try to loosen *my* ropes."

Joe rolled across the room, mumbling. "Is—
won—irks—mooss."

"What?"

"I said, this only works in the movies."

"It'd better work now," Frank said. "Or
we'll never see another movie."

103

The two brothers rolled and kicked until they were lying back to back. Joe tried to slip his fingers into the knot that secured Frank's hands.

"It's no use," he said, his voice showing as much anger as frustration. "These guys are all seamen. That's a sailor's knot. I can't work it loose."

"Wait a minute," Frank said. "I think Del's the pilot, and Mickey's a sailor, but I don't know about Gus. He's the one who tied you. Let's see if I can loosen *your* knot."

Frank maneuvered until his fingers could grasp the main knot that bound Joe's hands. "It's just a lot of loops, I think. If I pull on it near the end, I think I can open one loop at a time." Frank struggled to undo Joe's bonds bit by bit.

"There," he exclaimed, his fingers raw, "that should do it. Open your fist and slip your right hand up."

Joe turned and twisted, and the ropes burned into his wrist. "Got it!" he whispered triumphantly as his hand came free. Thirty seconds later he was standing, a coil of rope on the deck beside his feet.

He leaned over and untied the sailor's knots that held Joe. "Even with two hands this knot is hard to undo," he remarked. "There! Now to find the gun."

Joe searched for the gun under the broken boxes while Frank shook himself loose from his ropes.

"It's not here!" Joe shoved the credit card boxes across the deck.

"It's got to be," Frank insisted as he joined in the search. "Where was it?"

"Right here under a box, next to Alicia and me."

"Alicia!" Frank figured that must be the answer. "When Mickey ordered you to stand up, Alicia was still sitting. She probably took the gun."

"Great. Now who's going to rescue who?" Joe muttered. "We've got to get out of here. I hope Alicia doesn't try anything foolish."

"Maybe she can get the drop on them."

"And maybe not." Joe's voice was grim.

Frank hurried over to the door and tried the handle. "It's open!" He peered out, then stuck his head back in and closed the door. "There's no place to hide between here and the upper deck. If we get spotted, we're done for. Unless we get a gun."

Joe shook his head. "I'm sure they're not going to send Alicia down here with hers! They didn't bring us anything to eat yesterday, so I doubt they'll come this morning—except to dispose of us."

"Then we have to *coax* someone down

here," Frank suggested. "If we make a commotion—"

"And then one of us hides behind the door and bops them when they come in? I don't think so. That's a good way to get shot. No one's going to open that door more than an inch until they see us still tied up on the other side of the room."

"I have an idea," Frank said. "Help me get that light bulb down." Frank clasped his hands together to give him a foot up. Joe unhooked a spool of wire that was hung over a nail in one of the beams.

"What are you going to do with a light bulb?" Joe asked.

"Not the bulb—the wire. The cord is long enough to stretch from the wall outlet to the door. If we remove the wires from the socket and attach them to the inside metal doorknob and plug it in, anyone touching the outside knob will get a shock."

"But it won't be enough to knock anyone out," Joe pointed out.

"The ship is two-twenty volts, and that should stun him long enough for us to make a move. We just have to hope that only one guy comes down."

Joe was still not convinced. "And what'll we use to cut the wires?"

"I still have my watch. I can smash the

crystal, and use the broken glass." Frank un-buckled his watch strap and rammed the watch face against the deck until the glass cover cracked. He picked up a large piece and held it.

"Sounds good—except for one thing: once we start working on this, we'll have no light. It'll be pitch-black in here."

"Can't have things too easy," Frank said. "Now get your bearings—remember where everything is. Ready?" He pulled the plug, and the room was plunged into darkness.

A half hour later, at eight-thirty A.M., the men could hear a faint banging sound coming from the hold.

"Gus, check our guests," Del ordered. "If they've gotten loose, knock them out! I've had enough of those two."

"All right." Gus walked below to the room that held the two captives. He pulled his gun and started to turn the doorknob.

"Now!" Joe whispered.

Frank was ready. He pushed the wire into the socket, and the Hardys heard a muffled shriek followed by the sound of Gus hitting the deck.

Gus had been prepared for what the brothers might have tried after he got into the room, but he never expected anything before he even got the door open. Joe sprang into action, jerking the cord free, swinging open the door, and throwing a fist into Gus's jaw almost in one move. The shot to the mouth kept the muscle-bound thug from shouting out.

Frank was in the doorway now, and with one karate chop to the back of Gus's neck, Gus slumped to the floor.

"We've got to work fast, before they decide he's been gone too long," Frank advised. He dragged the body into the darkened room while Joe picked up some of the rope that had been used to tie them. He fashioned a gag out of part of Gus's shirt, and in no time the thug was bound so securely it would take machetes to cut him free. "Now, *those* are sailor's knots!" Frank said to the still-unconscious Gus.

Joe picked up Gus's gun from the passage-way. "Let's do it," he said to Frank.

The two brothers sneaked along the passage-way and up the stairs onto the main deck. They tiptoed past the captain's cabin, checking to see if it was occupied.

"They're probably all in the pilothouse," Frank whispered.

"There's only two of them and two of us now," Joe reminded his brother.

"But we have to be careful Alicia doesn't get caught in the middle," Frank said cautiously. Joe nodded in quick agreement.

The two brothers made their way to the wheelhouse without being seen. Del and Mickey sat in the middle of the room, laughing and joking. Alicia was on a stool directly inside the open doorway.

Frank and Joe rushed the wheelhouse, Joe's gun drawn. As soon as Del saw them coming, he spun the wheel and the boat turned sharply, throwing Joe slightly off balance. This gave Mickey just enough time to draw his gun. He pointed it straight at Alicia.

"One more step and she's dead!" he said, grinning sadistically.

Mickey was watching Frank—not Alicia—and she used this time to drop down behind her stool. The few seconds it took for him to look her way and get her in his sights again was all the time Frank needed.

He kicked out sharply, his entire body horizontal to the deck. His body had become one long weapon. His foot landed against Mickey's gun hand with such force that the gun flew into one of the wheelhouse windows, cracking it in two. Mickey reeled backward, tripping over the stool. He crashed against the deck, his head hitting the hard wood floor.

In the meantime Del lashed out at Joe, who was momentarily distracted checking out Alicia. The pilot grabbed Joe's gun hand, and the two wrestled. Joe was as strong as his opponent, but Del was at home on the rocking boat, and that was all the advantage he needed. He jerked back on Joe's hand, sending Joe down. The gun went flying out the door and splashed overboard.

Mickey's gun had landed behind Del, and Frank had to get by him to retrieve it—he lurched forward. But with Joe down, Del had the seconds he needed to pull his own gun from inside his jacket.

Before Frank could reach him, Del had drawn a bead on Frank.

"Say goodbye!" Del cackled as he wrapped his finger tightly around the trigger.

Joe watched in horror as the would-be killer took deadly aim at Frank.

"Nooooo!" he yelled. But his cry was drowned out by the roar of an exploding bullet.

Chapter

12

THE GUN FLEW out of Del's hand. He grabbed his hand in pain as Joe and Frank looked at Alicia, still crouched behind the stool, with the revolver grasped firmly in her hand.

"Where did you learn to shoot like that?" Joe asked, flabbergasted.

"You don't think you and Frank were my dad's *only* students, do you?" she asked, keeping a watchful eye on both Del and Mickey. "I've won the Bermuda women's trap-shooting championship two years in a row."

"That was as close as I ever want to come—" Frank's face was just beginning to get its color back. "I owe you, Alicia."

"Me, too," Joe chimed in.

"Don't mention it," she said to Frank,

slightly embarrassed. Then she grinned at Joe and said, "But from *you*—I might collect."

Frank picked up Mickey's gun, while Joe managed to shut off the engines. After Joe revived Mickey and bandaged Del's hand, he escorted the two downstairs and tied them up and laid them to rest beside their colleague.

"I'm sorry it's dark down here." Joe grinned at them. "But there's a cord, a socket, and a bulb around someplace." He locked the door with the key he had taken from Mickey, and they all went topside again.

Frank stretched his arms and took a deep breath. "It's good to be free and out in the fresh air."

"Yeah. And there's only one thing on my mind right now," he said as he looked at Alicia with a glint in his eyes.

"What's that?" she inquired.

"Food!" We haven't eaten since breakfast yesterday!"

"That's right. It's ten-thirty already. Why don't you two see if you can scrounge up some breakfast while I figure out how to get us home," Frank said.

"I'll take care of it," Alicia offered. "I've been on deck all morning while you two were penned up below." She smiled, then turned and went looking for the galley.

"I've figured out the rendezvous point,"

Frank said, once he had Joe's attention. "See this point, where our present course intersects the course we were on yesterday?" He pointed to a spot on one of the charts he found in the wheel house. "It's about four miles off the coast of Florida, somewhere up by Jacksonville."

Joe studied the map. "Kruger probably uses a local fishing boat or something to pick up the cards at sea. That way there's no chance for customs officials to find anything on a boat coming in directly from Bermuda."

"The data is probably sent to Bermuda directly on disk," Frank continued. "The Number File that was on the disk you found had only American spelling. I noticed that eye color was spelled c-o-l-o-r and not c-o-l-o-u-r, so the disk was probably made up in the states."

He stopped to gather his thoughts. "The credit cards must either be manufactured in Puerto Rico or stashed there after they're stolen. Then they're taken by boat to Bermuda. The disks are small enough to be sent by mail without arousing suspicion, but the credit-card blanks need to be hand-delivered. Otherwise, it would be too easy to trace where the packages come from or where they're going."

Joe nodded. "Then the operation in Bermuda only stamps the cards."

"And they put on the holograms."

"Then the *Sea Mist* takes the finished cards to another boat, which sails into U.S. territorial waters."

"Right." Frank agreed. "After that, the cards are distributed through a network of operatives." He shook his head. "There're so many links in this chain that it's no wonder the police can't get enough evidence to stop the scam."

Frank and Joe sat silently for a moment. They were pleased that they had finally figured out Kruger's operation and captured three of his henchmen. But they also knew their job was not done—they still had no hard evidence against Kruger.

Frank turned the boat around to head back to Bermuda. He radioed the Coast Guard and explained how he'd calculated the rendezvous point with the other ship. The Coast Guard said they'd meet the other ship and notify the Bermuda police that the brothers and Alicia were safe and were returning with three of Kruger's band.

With the current against them, the journey back was nearly three hours longer than the trip out. They took turns sleeping and keeping watch, so by the time they arrived back in Bermuda at six A.M. on Saturday, they all were relaxed and well rested. They were met in Hamilton by Chief Boulton.

"Nice work, boys," Boulton said. "When I got the call from the Coast Guard, I did some checking on the names you gave them. Since this Gus fellow has his official residence listed as Kruger's villa, we now have sufficient cause to examine those premises. I woke the judge and just got a warrant a few minutes ago."

"Can Joe and I come?" Frank asked.

"Certainly. Although you'll have to stay back. And we'll have to keep your weapons." The chief turned to Alicia, whom he had known for a long time. "I'll keep the gun as well, if you don't mind, Alicia. I'll return it to your dad when I see him."

"Where *is* he?" she asked, glancing around. She had expected he'd be there to greet them.

"I don't know," the chief replied. "We tried to call yesterday, but the line was dead. We sent a squad car out, but there was no sign of him. The officers left a note for him saying that you were all right and that he should contact me. But I haven't heard from him." Chief Boulton couldn't hide his concern.

"Then let me go with you to Kruger's," Alicia pleaded. She knew if her father had disappeared, Kruger was behind it. Chief Boulton gave his okay.

A procession of four cars and two motorcycles left for the Kruger estate. The Hardys and Alicia rode with the chief, but nobody said much. They were all thinking about Montague.

When they reached the villa, the officers surrounded the house while Frank, Joe, and Alicia waited in the car. Chief Boulton banged on the front door of the villa. When no one answered, he ordered his men to break down the door.

Chief Boulton and one officer carefully entered the villa as Joe, Frank, and Alicia watched from the car. Then the chief came outside again and waved for the three to join him. They ran quickly to the front door.

"The place is empty," the chief informed them. "And it doesn't look like its occupants are planning to return."

They entered the living room. Against the front wall stood a fireplace that looked as though it had never been used. There was furniture throughout the house and pictures were still hanging on the walls, yet the house seemed deserted. The closets were empty, desk drawers and file cabinets had been cleaned out.

By now Chief Boulton had ordered his men to search the house thoroughly. "We might as well head back," he said, purposely avoiding Alicia.

Suddenly one of the officers called from the kitchen. "Chief! Chief! Come quick!"

The four of them ran into the kitchen. They looked around to see what the officer had discovered, but nothing looked out of the ordinary. The policeman, a thin man not much older than the Hardys, stood in the middle of the room. Before the chief could ask, the officer said, "Listen. Listen carefully." They stood silently in the middle of the kitchen listening. Not a sound.

"Wait," the officer whispered, seeing that the chief was about to speak. The group stood motionless, and finally the silence was broken.

Thump—thump—thump! The sound was below them. It stopped, then started up again.

"It's almost directly below us," Joe said, dropping to his knees. He popped up, looking around the room. "Here, help me move the refrigerator," he said to Frank.

They slid the refrigerator out from its place against the wall and surveyed the area where it had been. All they found was a bare wall and floor. The knocking had stopped.

"There's a room under here," Joe insisted. "And there must be a way down." He walked over to the stove. "Come on, help me move this."

"A stove has all sorts of connections in the back," Chief Boulton said.

Joe hopped onto the countertop next to the stove, then peered behind it. "Not this one," he said. He turned on one of the gas knobs for a burner, but nothing happened. "This one's not connected to anything!"

The chief and his officer pulled out the stove, which revealed a trap door.

"This is it," said Joe, reaching for the handle.

"Just a minute," the officer said. "There's someone down there." He pulled his revolver and slowly opened the trap door, then he leaned over and peered down a short staircase leading into a shallow basement. "There's a light on," he whispered.

Chief Boulton stepped over to the opening. "All right, whoever's down there, come out quietly, there's no escape."

But instead of a voice, the response was the knocking again. "It's coming from under the stairway," the officer announced. He stole down the stairs cautiously, and then looked beneath them. "Chief! There's a man tied up down here!"

The group thundered downstairs until they reached the bound and gagged body. Alfred Montague was on his back against the wall and apparently had been banging his heels against the stairway.

"Dad!" Alicia cried out as soon as she recognized him. She pushed past the men and pulled the gag from her father's mouth.

"Alicia!" he exclaimed. "I thought Kruger had you!"

She summed up their adventure in less than four sentences, anxious to hear her father's story. "What happened to you? Are you all right?"

"Yes, I'm fine. A little stiff, and pretty hungry." As Montague spoke, the young officer cut off the ropes that bound him.

"Kruger became suspicious of me, especially after he found out you two were using my place as your base." He glanced at Frank and Joe. "After his men picked up you boys and Alicia, he paid me a visit to find out how much I knew—saying he would trade information for Alicia's life. He went through all my files and found papers linking me with British Intelligence. Then he really started questioning me. He knew we were closing in on him, but he wasn't sure just how close we were. But he realized it was time for him to clear out."

"Then what happened?" Joc asked, hardly giving Montague time for a breath.

The intelligence man walked around the small hidden basement, shaking his legs and stretching out his arms as he continued his story. "Kruger's men had all gone, though some fellow named Croaker came back later.

Anyway, Kruger and I were alone. I think he was used to having his men do all the dirty work, so he wasn't about to do away with me himself. And he didn't like the idea of killing a government man, even though it was probably he who ordered the hit on Conway. Besides, Kruger had nothing to gain by killing me—*he* knew that everything *I* knew was already on file with headquarters.''

Montague was still pacing, rubbing the back of his neck and shoulders, his eyes fixed on the gray concrete floor. "He wasn't going to kill me, but he couldn't just leave me free. He had to keep me out of the way for a while. So he brought me to the villa here, tied me up, and stuck me down here in the basement. He figured I'd be found eventually, but not until he was long gone.'' He looked up at Alicia, then at Frank and Joe, and smiled proudly. "He never thought you'd turn the tables on the boat.''

Joe grinned back. Then, anxious to learn more, he asked, "Did Kruger take all his equipment with him?''

"Ah, you haven't really *seen* this place yet.'' He led the group to a door opposite the stairs, then reached in the room and switched on a light before ushering the group in.

"Wow!'' Joe blurted out. "Just look at this setup!'' The room was filled with printing presses, stamping machines, sorting devices, computers, file cabinets, and loads of tools. "This is an entire credit-card factory!"

"And yet it took only two or three people to run the operation," Montague said. "Kruger, and his partner, Powers, handled the computer while a couple of goons operated the machinery."

"That would be Croaker and Gus," Joe offered. "They probably worked the machines and took some of the boat trips. Then he had two more delivery men, Del and Mickey, operating the boat. Them plus the U.S.–based crew." Joe was making a mental count as he spoke.

"Oh, I almost forgot," the chief broke in. "The U.S. Coast Guard picked up four men in a boat off Jacksonville. The FBI was afraid they wouldn't have any evidence against the men since you boys foiled the drop, but then they found three hundred thousand dollars in cash on board. Most of the bills were marked and came from a deal that went down between an undercover agent and two crooks involved in the distribution of the phony cards.

"The undercover man had bought some of the cards. The FBI decided not to arrest the crooks—there was a better chance of being led to the kingpin if they paid them off in marked bills and waited to see where the money showed up."

"That means we have seven of the gang members so far," Frank calculated out loud.

"No, eight. We picked Powers up earlier today, and we're holding him," Boulton said.

"But what about Croaker and Kruger?" Frank asked.

"Goodness!" Montague exclaimed. "What time is it? And what day?"

"Saturday, exactly seven-fifty-two."

"A.M. or P.M.?"

"A.M."

Montague seemed agitated. He spoke rapidly. "How long did it take you to get here from the harbor?"

"About twenty minutes. Why?"

"Kruger told me he was going to take the *Bermuda Star* to New York. That's his main U.S. distribution point. Even if I was found before the ship left, Kruger knew I wouldn't say anything as long as his men had Alicia."

"When did the boat leave?" Chief Boulton asked.

"It hasn't yet," Montague said, rushing his words. "Kruger said the *Bermuda Star* leaves at eight o'clock this morning, in eight minutes."

Chapter

13

"CAN WE MAKE the ship on time?" Joe asked, concerned that they might lose their last chance to pick up Kruger.

"Not even if we raced the whole way," the chief said.

"Well, what about calling and holding the ship until we arrive?"

"No, the *Bermuda Star* always leaves on time. If anything out of the ordinary happens, it's likely to spook Kruger. If he panics and goes into hiding, it'll take that much longer to fish him out."

"Besides," Montague added, "it'll be better if we let Kruger think he's getting away. We know he's the top man in this credit card ring, and he'll be met by the head of the U.S. operation when the ship arrives in New York. We'd like to get our hands on the New York chieftain, too. Even with Kruger behind bars, the New York head could probably keep the distribution operation going for another six months."

"Even though we found all the machinery and know how the whole operation works?" Alicia asked.

"The machinery is replaceable," Chief Boulton said. "And the organization still has a large stockpile of illegal cards that haven't been used. The key is to arrest the leaders—none of the other gang members will be able to carry on the operation without them."

"What if we just let Kruger leave and then notify the FBI to catch him when he arrives in New York?" Alicia asked.

"No, that's too risky," Montague said. "You can be sure that anyone in the business of counterfeiting credit cards will have a forged passport as well. With a disguise and a name change, Kruger could walk right through customs.

"I think it's important for someone to take the cruise with Kruger. We can't take a chance on losing him." Montague shook his head.

"I have no jurisdiction outside of Bermuda," Chief Boulton reminded them. "That leaves it up to you lot."

"I can go," Montague suggested, and nodded at Frank and Joe. "And so could the boys."

"And Alicia," Joe insisted. "We wouldn't be here now if it weren't for her."

Montague was concerned about letting his daughter accompany them on what could be a dangerous voyage. But finally he relented.

"We're losing precious time," Frank broke in. "How can we get on that boat?"

"I just thought of something," Chief Boulton broke in. "If we start right now, we can get to Hamilton before the pilot boat leaves. That's the boat that brings the pilot back to port once he has navigated the *Bermuda Star* into open waters. We can call ahead and arrange for you to get aboard. When the pilot transfers back onto the pilot boat—you can get on the *Star*."

"Sounds good." Montague nodded. "Now, what can we do about your appearances?" He looked at each of the three teens. At first Joe and Frank thought he was talking about some sort of disguise. But Alicia realized that her dad was referring to the clothes the three of them had had on for the past couple of days.

"I'll have one of the officers at the station pick up some supplies for you," Chief Boulton offered. "There are some shops right near the station. He'll meet us at the pilot boat."

"He'll need to hurry," Frank reminded him.

"And so will we!" Joe nodded at Frank, then turned and threw a quick wink at Alicia.

The group ran to the car. They raced back to town, sirens blasting, led by a motorcycle escort.

They arrived just in time to catch the pilot boat. The *Bermuda Star* was already in open water; the pilot was waiting to be picked up.

"I was just about to leave without you," the pilot boat captain said. He was an elderly man with a heavy gray beard and a heavier British accent. "But the officer here kept delaying me, insisting you wouldn't be but another minute." He was referring to one of Chief Boulton's men who stood next to the captain on the dock.

"I hope these things fit," the uniformed man said to Montague and the three youths. "I picked up a variety of loose-fitting clothes and some toilet articles. Anything else you need you should be able to buy on the boat." He handed them three large plastic bags. "I hope you'll find the things satisfactory, miss," he said to Alicia.

The figure of the policeman on the dock became smaller and smaller as the pilot boat bumped across the choppy waves of the harbor. They reached the *Bermuda Star* nearly two miles from port. The pilot climbed down before the four new passengers went up the ladder. The transfer was a bit difficult because of the wind that had come up forecasting a new storm. The three youths and Montague were happy to finally be on board. They were ready for a luxury cruise to New York.

"I'm glad there were a couple of cabins empty," Alicia said. "I'd hate to spend another night in the hold."

"And they're connecting cabins, too!" Joe had a twinkle in his eye as he looked at Alicia, then turned bright red as he remembered that Montague was there, watching and listening to it all.

"Let's get settled in our connecting cabins," Montague suggested with a grin. "We can change and freshen up."

"Then we'll have to go over the passenger list and see if we can spot Kruger."

"Remember, though," Frank cautioned, "we can't let Kruger spot us. He thinks we're dead, and if he knows we're on to him, he'll give us—and the police—the slip."

The four were led to their cabins on C-deck by a proper and polite purser who had been instructed to cooperate with them. Only the purser, the captain, the ship's doctor, and the ship's radio operator had any knowledge of the group's mission. The purser produced a map of the ship, announced he would be at their service should they require assistance, and returned to his office.

The two connecting cabins were near the end of a narrow corridor, slightly aft of the middle of the ship. Montague and Alicia took C-111, and the Hardys took C-112, which was closest to the door leading to the deck.

"I hate to stay cooped up," Joe said, complaining almost instantly. "Oh. We forgot to ask the purser for the passenger list."

"And—since there's no telephone service— *one* of us has to go to the purser's office to get the list," Frank said. "I wonder who should go?" he asked innocently. "Well, I guess it might as well be you, Joe, right?" he said, laughing. "Think you can make it there and back without wandering off in search of adventure?"

Joe opened the cabin door and checked the corridor before leaving the room. He hurried along the passageway, then proceeded cautiously toward the front of the ship and up to B-deck.

"There was no Kruger on the passenger manifest," the purser said. "So I have compiled a list. These are the men traveling without families who fit the description given us by the Hamilton police. There are eight names and room numbers."

"Thanks very much."

"One of the men—this one here," the purser said, pointing to a name on the list, "is in the dining room right now having breakfast; I saw him sit down a couple of minutes ago."

"Weisberg," Joe muttered, reading the name on the list. "I guess he's as good to start with as anyone. Can you point him out to me?"

Joe and the purser slowly made their way to the dining room. The boat was rolling more than usual—a storm was definitely going to kick up. "There," the purser said, nodding with his head. "The man eating alone."

Joe could see a partial profile of the diner's face. He had a full head of dark hair, glasses, and the beginnings of a beard. Joe remembered Kruger as clean-shaven and with gray hair and no glasses. This man didn't look like Kruger. But there was something familiar about him. Joe kept watching. Then the man turned to order something from the waitress, and Joe got a good look at his full face.

Bingo! It *is* Kruger! The eyes. Those were the same eyes, and they gave him away. "Yeah, that's him, all right! There's no way to disguise those eyes."

There was no doubt in Joe's mind that the man he was looking at was Kruger masquerading under the name of Weisberg. For the first time, it seemed, something was going right.

The first person on the list of possible Krugers was the head man himself.

"That's great," Joe said when they were back in the purser's office. "Thanks very much. If anything happens, we're in cabin C-one-twelve."

"Yes, I know," the purser said. "I have the passenger list, remember?" He paused long enough for a quick smile. "And the other gentleman, Mr. Weisberg, is in cabin B-thirteen on the deck above you—this deck—and farther forward."

Joe started back for his cabin. Kruger just sat down to eat, he thought to himself. So there's no way I could run into him if I went past his cabin. I'll just take the long way back to my cabin, get some fresh air.

He pushed hard against the door and went out on the deck. The wind was blowing hard, and the voyage was very rocky now. The passengers had already gone inside, and Joe found himself quite alone. He held on to the railing that ran along the side of B-deck beneath the lifeboats. He pulled himself forward and decided to go back in. There was a door. He staggered toward it and yanked on the handle. A burly man flew out and rammed right into him.

"Sorry," the man grumbled in a gravelly voice. He was stocky and muscular, dressed in a blue turtleneck. He looked up, then froze, glaring up into Joe's astonished face.

Joe had been so busy concentrating on Kruger that he had forgotten about Kruger's murderous henchman—Croaker!

Chapter

14

THE TWO OF THEM just stood there. Croaker thought Joe was dead—thrown overboard on the *Sea Mist*. And Joe had forgotten about Croaker. Now the two were face-to-face.

Croaker was stunned—unsure what move to make on a ship that offered no escape. He blocked the doorway with his stocky frame, preventing Joe from entering the passageway.

Joe stood fast. He controlled his first impulse to slug the crook. For all Joe knew, Croaker could be carrying a gun. And although the deck was empty for the moment, a passenger or ship's officer could walk by at any time.

"There's no way out of this one, Croaker," Joe told the thug. "No place to go." He paused, his tone and his stare unwavering. "Give yourself up."

Croaker's eyes never left Joe's. Without changing a wrinkle of his flat and fixed expression, he suddenly croaked, "Kid, you die!"

Joe wasn't ready for those words. He also wasn't ready when Croaker lunged at him, knocking him down onto the deck. Croaker started to pin him down, and Joe could feel the shape of a revolver as Croaker's chest pressed against his.

Joe struggled against the bulk of the muscular body. Croaker was strong, but Joe knew the thug wasn't as agile as he was. Wiggling like an eel, Joe managed to free one arm. He brought his fist down on the back of the stocky man's neck. The blow stunned Croaker just long enough for Joe to shift his body and push, toppling Croaker onto his side.

Another powerful shove and the thug went sprawling on the deck. Joe sprang up then and pounced. But as he landed, Croaker wasn't there. The ship, hit by a heavy wave, had heeled over, sending a salty spray over the two. Croaker had rolled away, and Joe missed. A second later Croaker was trying to pin him again.

The two of them rolled from side to side with the pitching and tossing of the ship. It seemed as though the fight was alternating between slow motion and fast forward. Balance was the key. And each time one had the advantage, the movement of the ocean liner upset that balance, and the other wound up on top.

Joe was on the bottom now. Croaker had one hand on Joe's throat; the other hand was trying to extract his gun. Joe's left hand was clawed into Croaker's face as Joe tried to push the powerful little man off him. Croaker's neck was bent back as Joe kept pushing with all his strength. But Croaker didn't budge. Joe's right hand was busy trying to tear Croaker's fingers from his neck.

Joe saw Croaker's right hand come out from under his jacket with a gun grasped tightly in his fingers. Joe couldn't loosen his opponent's grip on his throat, nor could he push him away.

Releasing his hold, Joe suddenly locked his fingers together behind Croaker's neck and yanked. Croaker's head was pulled sharply downward until the thug's skull smacked into Joe's.

The pain was excruciating for Joe, but much worse for Croaker. At least Joe was expecting it—and it was certainly less painful than a bullet would have been. Joe recovered faster than his rival, and in two quick moves was on top of him, holding Croaker's gun.

Again the ship rocked. Joe kept his balance, but Croaker smashed out with his left forearm, sending the revolver flying from Joe's hand. The gun skittered across the deck, under the bottom railing, and into the violent waters.

Joe slugged the squat man in the jaw. Then he got to his feet, his fingers clasped tightly around Croaker. Croaker rose, offering little resistance. They stood less than five feet from the railing, and Joe's head was about six inches from the bottom of the lifeboat which hung overhead.

Then the boat pitched again. Joe's head slammed against the lifeboat, his grip loosened, and the stocky man slid to the ground. The ship rolled, and Joe was tossed against the railing, with Croaker leaping at him.

Frank was beginning to worry what was keeping his brother. Suddenly, between the sounds of the crashing waves, he heard a shrieking cry.

"Man overboard! Man overboard!"

He rushed out of the cabin, down the passageway, around the corner, and onto the deck.

Once again the cry carried through the sea air. "Man overboard!" It was coming from the deck above. Frank staggered aft against the rocking motion to an outside stairway leading up to B-deck, then made his way back toward the center of the ship.

"Joe!" he cried out.

Joe was holding on to the railing under one of the lifeboats. Two ship's officers were moving toward the youth from the opposite direction. Frank reached his brother shortly after one of the officers. He caught the end of Joe's excited story.

"Then the ship rolled, he lost his balance, and went right overboard."

"What was he doing out here in this weather?" the first officer asked.

"I have no idea. I just opened that door there to have a look outside and breathe some fresh air, and I saw him by the railing. He went over before I could even call out." Joe extended his hand, which was clutched around a small brown wallet. "This fell out of his pocket."

As the officer took the wallet and opened it, Frank caught a glimpse of the picture on a photo ID. He tried not to show any surprise at seeing Croaker's face. He put his hand on his brother's shoulder, and waited until the officers left before he said anything.

The officer closed the wallet and looked again at Joe. "Who are you?"

"Joe Hardy. I'm in cabin C-one-twelve."

"We have to get to the bridge," the second officer interjected, "and get the ship turned around. We might need to talk with you again, later."

Joe nodded, then turned to his brother as the officers left.

"Croaker!" Frank exclaimed in astonishment.

"I bumped into him on deck, and—"

"Tell me inside," Frank interrupted. "It's really rough out here."

"Wait a minute," Joe said. He braced himself on the underside of the lifeboat. "Croaker decided to fight. He went down and hit his head against the railing there."

"And went *overboard?*"

"He was knocked cold. But his gun went overboard during the fight, and that gave me an idea." Joe climbed to the top of the lifeboat and started undoing the canvas cover. Frank stared at his brother's struggle to keep his footing for a second, then climbed up to help with the knots. "I realized if we held Croaker captive, Kruger would be tipped off about us as soon as he knew Croaker was missing. But if everyone thought that Croaker had gone overboard—"

He pulled off the cover to reveal Croaker lying unconscious in the bottom of the lifeboat. "This seemed like a better idea. Now, help me get him out."

Removing the unconscious Croaker from the lifeboat was not easy. Joe climbed in and handed the lifeless body down to Frank, all the while afraid that someone might walk out on the deck at any moment. But the rough weather let them work unobserved. Then the two brothers propped the thug between them, went inside, and walked him back to their cabin like two men escorting a drunken friend.

"This is incredible," Frank said when they got Croaker back to the cabin. "You've managed to get an entire ocean liner to turn around! The crew will be searching for a body that doesn't exist."

"There was nothing else I could do without spooking Kruger. Let's hope he doesn't think Croaker's accident was suspicious."

"We should tell Montague." Frank furrowed his brow as he stopped to think out their next move. "We'd better stay in the cabin and have Montague tell the captain what happened. Then he can arrange to have Croaker locked in the brig."

Frank knocked on the door adjoining the two cabins. A second knock brought Alicia to the door.

"This rocking put me right to sleep," she said. "But it's put Dad right out of commission." The Hardys peered in the other cabin and saw Montague lying in bed, a white washcloth splashed across his green face.

"That's too bad." Joe shook his head. Then he looked at Alicia. "We need you to do something for us." Joe described his encounter with Croaker briefly as he pressed a wet towel against his forehead. Alicia's pretty face had made him forget his aching head for a few seconds.

"What happened to your head, Joe!"

"Nothing." He winced. "I just bumped it."

Alicia looked over at Croaker, whom she recognized as one of her captors. She grinned, pleased that he was now the captive. "Funny, your friend here has a forehead as red as yours. Must be something going around."

"He's coming to," Frank observed. "You should go now, Alicia, and tell the captain."

Alicia left. The Hardys used a sheet torn into strips to tie their prisoner's hands behind his back, and when Croaker regained consciousness, they began questioning him.

"How many more of you are there?" Frank asked the stocky man.

"There's just me. My mother didn't want no more children," he answered.

"I can see why," Joe told him. "But I want to know about your gang. Are there any more of you on the ship besides you and Kruger?"

"Will I get a shorter sentence if I tell you?"

"Yeah," Joe said sarcastically. "We promise we won't use sentences with more than six words."

Croaker looked confused. "There's nobody on this boat except me and Kruger."

"And what cabin are you in?" Joe asked.

"The one next to Kruger."

"What *number?*"

"Uh, B-twelve." Croaker's voice was like short bursts of machine-gun fire. Frank kept wanting him to clear his throat, but it *was* clear.

"Did you charge things on my dad's credit card so we wouldn't be able to use it?" Joe asked, remembering the three thousand dollars the card was over the limit.

"Yeah. It was Kruger's idea—to slow you down."

"And how did Kruger—?" A knock on the door interrupted Frank's question. It was Alicia with the purser and a rather large seaman dressed in khakis and a sailor's cap.

"The captain is in my office explaining to your friend the circumstances under which his traveling companion went overboard." The purser spoke as though he were on the stage. "It would be best for us to remove this gentleman at the moment, while the other gentleman is occupied. That way we can ensure getting him down to the brig unnoticed."

"Great," said Joe.

"Now we're up to the hard part," Frank reminded them after the two crewmen left with the thug. "We've got to stay out of sight until we land. Then we've got to be right on top of Kruger when he makes his move."

"Oh, dear," Alicia said, like a heroine from an old movie. "And to think I'm practically confined to my cabin like a prisoner for two whole days with no one to talk to but a seasick father and you two boys!"

The two days went quickly, and once the storm subsided, it was a relaxing voyage. Joe enjoyed the time he spent with Alicia—even if they did have a chaperon. Montague felt better the second day of the voyage, and he shared adventure stories with the two detectives. And they weren't cooped up for the entire trip. The captain, the purser, and the ship's doctor advised the group of Kruger's whereabouts. When Kruger was eating, they found it possible to spend some time out on deck. Kruger, meanwhile, spent most of his time in his cabin. He seemed to accept the captain's story about "poor" Croaker.

By the time the ship docked in New York City, Kruger was visibly nervous—he'd have been more nervous if he knew what was waiting for him: Fenton Hardy and a host of federal agents. But Kruger was smart—and cool. When he walked off the ship into customs, he looked like any other passenger.

Fenton Hardy and the others—three undercover feds—were stationed at different points in the large customs hall, past the customs checkpoint.

Joe stayed on board with Alicia, where he had a good view of the customs checkpoint set up on the dock below. Frank, meanwhile, followed Kruger, staying far back and out of sight.

Kruger, still in disguise and using a forged passport, passed through customs without any difficulty. He walked straight toward a tall, distinguished-looking gentleman in a gray suit, carrying an umbrella which he used as a cane. The New York ringleader lifted his head in a slow nod and proceeded into the large customs hall. Kruger followed him to the center of the large room. The head of the credit card scam in the United States and the chief of the counterfeiting operation in Bermuda shook hands, never suspecting that they were being observed.

Just then, a scratchy voice bellowed out above the din of the crowded customs hall: "Kruger, it's a trap! A trap!" It was Croaker, shouting from the side of the room. He was under the guard of two uniformed police officers who were leading him through the large building. Though his movements were restricted, his grating voice was not. "Run for it!'' he shouted again before the officers could quiet him.

The distinguished-looking man lifted his umbrella like a sword and ran swiftly in the direction from which he had just come. Kruger froze, staring in the direction of Croaker.

Joe heard Croaker inside the shed and immediately swung into action. Literally. He leaped over the railing, grabbing on to one of the ship's mooring lines. Then he rode the cable down onto the dock below, avoiding the crowd that was choking the gangway. Landing squarely on two feet, he rushed toward the checkpoint.

In the crowded hall, a commotion erupted as the dapper man carved a path for himself with his umbrella. The two federal men pursued him, but their progress was hampered by the curious onlookers. The crook passed through the door leading out of the large room—only to be tackled some three feet later by Fenton Hardy.

Meanwhile, Bernhard Kruger, still cool and still composed and looking completely innocuous, turned, walked slowly, and disappeared into the crowd that had stopped to watch the spectacle.

Chapter

15

KRUGER'S NEW YORK CONTACT was in the hands of the police, but the big man himself was walking to freedom. Frank tried to race after him but was held back by the crowds.

Joe was stopped at the checkpoint by the customs officer on duty. Before he had a chance to explain, a blue-suited gentleman ran up, flashed a badge at the official, and motioned for Joe to go through.

Montague and Alicia were still on the ship, trying to push their way through the crowd. They were too far back to participate in the chase, but they wanted to get into the main terminal in case Kruger tried to outsmart his pursuers and double back.

Frank was rushing through the crowd, with

Joe not far behind. Every once in a while he thought he caught a glimpse of Kruger, but he couldn't be sure. Still, there was only one direction the gang leader could have gone.

Frank ran through a large double door leading into the main terminal. The customs area seemed calm and orderly compared to the turmoil here. At least in customs everyone was moving in the same direction. Here people were coming and going, with patterns of cross-traffic merging and blocking the way.

Frank saw a couple of federal officers handcuffing the man with the umbrella. They were in a hallway. Kruger wouldn't have gone in their direction, Frank thought, turning toward the main exit.

Then he caught sight of Kruger. "Hold it!" His loud voice rose above the din of the crowded terminal. "The police have the exits covered."

Kruger peered over his shoulder at his pursuer. He knew he couldn't outrun the young detective, so he looked for the area with the most people. He turned right, away from the main exit, and darted down a corridor marked *Taxis/Buses*. Once again he disappeared into the crowd.

Frank ran as fast as he could without knocking anyone over. But there was no sign of the master criminal. Just when he thought he had lost Kruger for good, the counterfeiter came rushing out of the crowd—heading straight for him!

Frank was startled. He stood his ground, planting his feet firmly, wondering what the slick German was up to.

Then he saw it. Right behind Kruger was Fenton Hardy, running faster than Frank had ever seen him go. His father had a gun, and it seemed Kruger would rather face a youthful, unarmed athlete than a gun-toting private eye.

"I've got him, Dad!" Frank shouted, positioning himself in the middle of the corridor.

"Get out of the way, everyone!" Fenton ordered as he continued his pursuit.

The crowd thinned out, with people pinning themselves against the wall to avoid getting involved. Kruger knew he couldn't get past Frank, so he tried the next best thing—he ran smack *into* him!

Kruger was a heavy man, and he was in motion. There was no way Frank could brace himself. The impact knocked him off his feet. Kruger was down on one knee, but like a football player who doesn't believe the ball is dead, he scrambled up and continued his escape down the corridor.

Then he stopped short. Joe Hardy stood at the end of the corridor, blocking Kruger's avenue of escape, and he *was* braced and ready.

Kruger couldn't try the same trick again. But there was the crowd behind Joe. Fenton Hardy couldn't fire a gun where a bullet might hit an innocent passerby.

Kruger kept coming, passing a couple who had been on the boat and were now huddling against the wall. Sticking out of one of the bags they clutched were two bottles of duty-free rum. Kruger grabbed one of the bottles, smashing its bottom against the wall. He moved up the corridor toward Joe more slowly now, holding the broken bottle firmly by its neck. Then he whipped around as Frank came up behind him. The jagged edges of his bottle gleaming, Kruger pointed them at his challenger.

Frank backpedaled, whipping off the light windbreaker he had been wearing and wrapping it around his left arm. He was about four feet from Kruger now. The two began to circle around in the middle of the passageway, like two wrestlers preparing to get into a clinch.

"Give it up," Frank said, staring his opponent squarely in the eye.

"Never!" Kruger replied. "I have nothing to lose now—and *you're* responsible for everything I've lost already. You should be dead, and before they grab me, you will be."

Frank faked a charge to force Kruger into action. Kruger stepped back and to the side, then lunged at Frank with the broken bottle.

The sharp-edged glass ripped into Frank's jacket.

Kruger thrust again. This time Frank moved his arm quickly upward, and the bottle gouged out a piece of Frank's sleeve, coming close to his chest. Having drawn his opponent in toward him, Frank turned his left hand and grabbed Kruger's wrist. He pushed down on the man's hand, shoving the bottle away. Then, with his right hand, Frank delivered a mighty blow to Kruger's jaw, stunning him.

The bottle fell from Kruger's hand, crashing to the floor. Frank let go of his assailant's arm, wound up, and sent a smashing left hook into the side of Kruger's face, bringing the criminal to his knees. With both hands, Frank lifted him off the ground by his lapels. Kruger was beaten.

Frank was unhurt but winded. Joe and his father reached the fight from different directions at the same time, and Joe stepped in to put an armlock on Kruger while Frank unwound his windbreaker from his arm.

"Got you at last." Joe stopped as he saw Alicia and Montague running down the corridor, with two FBI men not far behind. He grinned when he saw Alicia's smile.

The Port Authority police and FBI took charge of the defeated criminal. They escorted him away in silence, leaving Fenton Hardy in charge of the rest of the group.

Frank and Joe turned to their dad. "Good to see you," they said.

"And you." The senior Hardy smiled. "So—how was Bermuda?"

Frank and Joe both laughed.

"Well, hello, Fenton." Montague beamed. And after a hearty handshake, he added, "This is Alicia."

"I've heard a lot about you," the elder Hardy said. Then he noticed the twinkle in Joe's eye as his young son gazed at this attractive girl. "And I guess I'll be hearing a lot more." Joe turned slightly red, and everyone laughed.

"I have a message for you from your pals," Frank told his sons. "Chet, Tony, and Biff are waiting at the pizza parlor. I think they ordered a pie with 'Welcome Home' written on it in anchovies."

"Sounds good to me," Frank said.

"Yeah. What do you say we get moving," Joe added.

"Wait a minute," Montague said. "There's the problem of Alicia."

"Alicia?"

"At first, immigration wouldn't let me off the ship," Alicia explained, "because I didn't bring a passport. In fact, I don't even have *any* identification—Kruger's men took everything I had. They let me through because of your father's reputation with the FBI. But we have to go back to immigration now in order for a U.S. citizen to take responsibility for me."

"Can you be put in *my* custody?" Joe asked, trying to keep a straight face.

"Never mind them," Fenton Hardy said through a smile. "I'll take care of everything."

"Oh, and there's one more thing," Montague interrupted with a more serious look on his face. "The FBI told me that Kruger and the New York head man are under indictment in the U.S. and will be arraigned here. But Croaker will have to be extradited back to Bermuda to stand trial along with Mickey, Gus, and Del."

"I hate to tell you this," Montague continued, trying to suppress a growing smile, "but it looks as if Joe and Frank are going to have to return to Bermuda in a few weeks to testify."

Frank gave a very loud—and phony—sigh.

Alicia broke into a big grin—and Joe blushed again.

"Well," Joe said as he took Alicia's arm, "these are the sacrifices a crack detective has to make."

The Borderline Case

Chapter

1

"WHAT IS THIS STUFF, ANYWAY?"

Joe Hardy held up a fork holding something he'd speared from his lunch plate.

His older brother, Frank, glanced up at the fork. "I believe it's squid, Joe."

Joe dropped the fork as if it were red-hot and stared down in mock horror.

"*Squid?* You serious, or just trying to gross me out?"

Frank leaned forward. "If you look closely, you'll see the little suckers on the tentacles—"

Joe continued to stare. "I *knew* I shouldn't have ordered anything I couldn't pronounce." Joe was talking about the food in Greece on his summer student exchange trip. He shoved the plate away.

"Lighten up," Frank replied. "Hamburgers and pizza will still be at home when we get there. You might give Greece and its food a chance before you put it down."

Sitting next to Joe was the Hardys' friend Chet Morton. He looked up from his plate long enough to observe, "You know, it really isn't bad. And this pink stuff is great on bread."

Frank laughed. "Chet never met a meal he didn't like."

The Hardys were part of a group of Bayport students sitting around a big table at an outdoor restaurant in Piraeus, the port of Athens. It was their first day in Greece. Later that afternoon they would board a ship to Salonika, Greece's second-largest city. Salonika was in the north, only forty miles from the border of Yugoslavia.

The exchange students included another good friend of Frank and Joe's, Phil Cohen, and a boy of Greek heritage, Peter Stamos, who spoke up then.

"That 'pink stuff' is called taramosalata, and it's made from fish eggs and oil—"

"Peter, please," Joe cut in. "There're some things it's better not to know."

The chaperon of the Bayport group was a fussy-looking man with glasses—a Professor

Morton Prynne. He had been frowning at Joe from his place at the head of the table. "One purpose of student exchange is to learn about the customs and habits of other lands. It wouldn't hurt you to try the food."

Joe muttered under his breath.

"Come on, Joe," Frank urged. "Don't you remember Dad telling us about eating camel hump in North Africa and rattlesnake in Arizona?"

Their father, Fenton Hardy, was an internationally known private eye. His work took him to all parts of the world.

Morton Prynne cleaned his glasses, then tapped the table with a spoon. "May I have your attention for a moment? As long as we have time before we board our ship, we might go over our schedule for the next few days."

"Bor-r-r-ing," Chet said through clenched teeth.

"After lunch we will go directly to the pier, where we will go aboard. The luggage is already loaded. We leave the harbor at three this afternoon, and reach Salonika at two P.M. tomorrow. You will be sleeping two to a cabin. You should already have your room assignments. If anyone has misplaced his or hers, please see me after lunch.

"We will be met in Salonika by Mr. Spiros Stamos, who will lead a Greek contingent of students to America. I remind you that Spiros Stamos is the uncle of our own Peter Stamos. They have never met, and in honor of that meeting, and to celebrate our arrival, there will be a party tomorrow night, hosted by Mr. Stamos and his son and daughter.

"For the next two days, Mr. Stamos will be our guide for the many interesting sights in Salonika and the area."

Joe Hardy stifled a groan. "Ruins," he stated darkly. "Ruins and more ruins—we'll be climbing over piles of old rocks."

Prynne interrupted Joe's gloomy prediction. "Please remember—especially you, Joe—that you represent American youth. Whatever Mr. Stamos may have planned for this visit, I expect that you will behave in a way that will reflect positively on our country. You will treat Mr. Stamos with more respect than you have given me."

Phil Cohen grinned. "In other words," he whispered, "shut up and eat your squid."

Opposite Prynne sat a Greek school teacher named Nicholas Kaliotis, serving as the professor's assistant and, when necessary, as an interpreter. He looked up, his broad grin taking some of the sting out of Prynne's stuffy speech.

"I'm told that we'll be visiting one of the many excellent beaches near the city." He smiled. "We Greeks want you to know that we have more than monuments and ruins. I might even be able to find some American-style hamburgers in Salonika."

As Kaliotis had hoped, the mood of the group brightened.

Chet tapped Joe on the shoulder. "If you don't plan to eat any of that," he pointed to Joe's untouched lunch, "do you mind if I take some of that . . . whatever the pink stuff is called?"

Joe slid the plate over. "Here you go, big guy. I'll stick to bread and water for now."

"Right," Frank said, "you go ahead and soak up some Greek culture, Chet."

Phil Cohen turned to Peter Stamos. "You've never met any of your relatives in Salonika? At all?"

Peter shook his head. "My father went to Greece for visits once or twice. But I've never been to Greece before."

"Do you speak any Greek?" asked Frank.

"I speak some, and I understand a little more. My folks didn't use it around the house—except when they didn't want us to understand what they were saying."

"Hey, Peter," said Joe. "Maybe you can help us out while we're on the boat with some basic vocabulary. I'm still having trouble with 'please' and 'thank you.' "

"Sure. I guarantee that by the time we reach Salonika, you'll be saying 'please' and 'thank you' just like a native. Maybe even—"

"Hey! Americans!"

The raspy shout cut off all conversation. On the sidewalk, behind a low white-metal fence, three scruffy men glared at the group. They wore old and dirty denim pants, and two had dark blue peacoats. The third wore a shabby sweater. All three looked as if they hadn't shaved or showered in the past few days. All three looked like sailors.

"What are you doing here, Americans?" the guy in the sweater snarled in heavily accented English. "Nobody want you in Greece! Why you don't go home?"

A second one joined in. "Go away, Yankee pigs. Greek people sick of you!"

Prynne leaned in toward the students. "Pay no attention. It seems they've been drinking. If you ignore them, they'll leave, but if you answer, it will only get worse."

"Hey, talk to me, Americans!" The first taunter leaned over the fence. "You think you too good to talk to me?" He spat on the ground near the table—right by Joe's foot.

Joe sat still, but his face flushed under his blond hair.

"Hey, pretty boy, what's the matter? You don't like Greeks now, pretty boy?"

6

The ringleader had an ugly grin on his skinny, pockmarked face.

"Joe—" Frank warned, his dark eyes flashing.

But Joe just held up his fork. "Greeks, yes," he said. "You, no."

Nicholas Kaliotis jumped up, shouting something in Greek, and the three toughs vaulted the low fence. A waiter rushed to intercept them but was knocked flat by one of the three with a disdainful backhanded swipe.

Suddenly there were large, ugly knives gleaming in the thugs' hands. They stalked toward the Americans, murder in their eyes.

Chapter

2

JOE LEAPED TO his feet as one of the men came for him. The thug stopped a few feet from Joe, sizing him up, staying in a half-crouch and occasionally feinting. His knife hand lazily moved from side to side, making short jabs toward his target. Then he stepped forward quickly, with his knife aimed at Joe's stomach.

Chet Morton, sitting unnoticed, had quietly picked up a Coke bottle. Now, moving with a speed and agility unexpected of someone his size and weight, he brought it down with a chopping blow on the wrist of the man's knife hand. The weapon clattered to the ground as the attacker grunted in pain, cradling his injured wrist in his other hand.

Wasting no time, Joe caught his enemy on the jaw with a right that had all his weight and strength behind it. The man hit the pavement like a sack of cement and lay motionless.

Meanwhile, a second assailant was going for Prynne. He circled the students, then zeroed in on the head of the table, his knife in front of him, edge up, as experienced blade-fighters keep theirs. Prynne scrambled out of his chair and backed up one step, staying just beyond range of the sharp point and looking terrified. His attacker grinned—this little fellow in the eyeglasses seemed like an easy mark.

But as the attacker started his lunge, Prynne snatched a cup of hot tea from the table and flung the steaming contents into the thug's face. Screaming, knife and attack forgotten, the man went down, clutching his scalded face.

The last of the attackers, the ringleader, had hung back. Now, seeing how things had gone, he spun away, cleared the fence in one bound, and took off running down the street. Frank sprang up, intending to chase him down.

Prynne called out as Frank started to move: "Frank! No!"

Frank wheeled and looked at Prynne in surprise. "Why not, Mr. Prynne? These guys should get arrested. I can have that one back here in—"

"Frank, that'll do! Just leave things alone,"

snapped Prynne. Then he softened slightly, explaining, "You haven't spent time in Greece, Frank. You can't imagine the amount of red tape we'd get tangled up in with the police. We might be stuck here for hours, even days. We'd miss our ship, wreck our schedule. The entire tour would be ruined, and all over a foolish business with a few men who had a few drinks too many. Best not to get involved."

Rubbing his bruised knuckles, Joe said, "What about the two guys lying here? Are we going to let them go, too? Maybe we owe them an apology for being so hostile—I mean, all they did was try to stick us with those Greek toothpicks!"

Prynne glowered at Joe. "Certainly we won't let them go. I'll just have a word with the manager here and see to it that they're turned over to the authorities. In the meantime we can be on our way to the pier. Justice will be served, and we won't have to be involved."

With that he signaled to the manager and drew him aside. As they talked, Joe tapped Chet on the shoulder.

"Hey, thanks for the help. I owe you one."

Chet blushed and smiled. "I already owe *you* a few, remember?"

Prynne paid for lunch, and for the damage done by the attackers. Then the manager shook hands and called out two waiters and a busboy to take charge of the thugs. Meanwhile, Prynne hurriedly got his students to their feet and shepherded them off the terrace and toward the pier.

Half an hour later the American students stood at the pier at the end of a long line of passengers. The procession moved very slowly—each would-be boarder went through a rigorous examination before being allowed to proceed.

Joe watched the lack of progress with growing impatience. "I don't see what all the rush was for back at the restaurant," he complained. "We could have spent the whole afternoon clearing that mess up with the police and still have been in plenty of time for this."

Frank sighed and ran his fingers through his brown hair. "Well, Prynne's right about one thing," he said. "We've never been to Greece, and he has. Maybe he's right about dealing with the local law. Let's just take it easy and assume he knows what he's doing."

"Okay." But Joe still wasn't very happy. "It just feels weird, ducking out like that after being attacked, almost as if we were the criminals. I bet Dad wouldn't be too crazy about it either."

Frank thought for a moment. "Maybe so," he said. "But we're here and he's not." Then he spotted Peter Stamos and waved him over.

"Hi, Frank, Joe! Too bad we can't fight our way through. That's some right you've got there, Joe. You put that ugly customer out with one punch!"

Joe smiled and said, "Thanks to Chet and his trusty Coke bottle."

"Peter," asked Frank, "you remember just before those guys came at us, Mr. Kaliotis jumped up and yelled something at them?"

Peter replied, "Yeah. What about it?"

Frank continued, "Did you understand what he said? Was your Greek good enough to follow it?"

Peter's forehead wrinkled in concentration as he thought back. Then he shook his head, saying, "I didn't really catch it, Frank. I mean, everything happened so fast. He was yelling something like 'These are important Americans, so don't mess with them . . .' Some kind of warning." He shrugged. "Why do you ask?"

"Oh, no special reason, I was just wondering," Frank said. "Hey, what do you know! This line actually seems to be moving. I was beginning to think we'd have to camp here for the night."

The American kids began to pull out their passports and tickets. They passed the check-in booth and started up the passenger ramp. At the top of the ramp, Frank turned back for a final look at Piraeus.

The pier was bordered by a busy waterfront street with a scattering of sailors' bars, shops, and a steady stream of traffic. At the corner nearest the pier, a man with a knit cap and jeans stood leaning against a wall. He had a thin ferret face and needed a shave badly. His eyes never left the group of Americans. The man walked over to a parked car and leaned in through a window to talk.

Then the car's passenger door opened, and two men got out. They were similarly dressed, in heavy wool coats, jeans, and knit caps.

As Frank turned away to step onto the boat, the three men joined the boarding line.

All through the afternoon and early evening, the ship sailed in relatively calm water between islands. But after dinner it reached the open sea and began to pitch and roll.

For the students from Bayport, the unfamiliar food and the constant swaying had a nasty effect on their stomachs. By nine in the evening, most of the group had retreated to their cabins, trying to find some comfort in bed.

Joe Hardy was one of the sickest of all. When Frank suggested a walk on the deck, Joe only groaned and turned his slightly green and sweaty face away. "Walking? Even talking is too much for me." So Frank went to search out other company.

But the only other young person who wasn't laid low for the night was Chet Morton, who happily agreed to take a little fresh air on deck. The two went out and leaned against the rail on their deck, looking out over the sea.

The moon laid down a white path for the ship to follow as it cut through the whitecaps. Frank thought that he could make out the shoreline in the distance, a thin smudge slightly darker than sea or sky.

Frank grinned at Chet. "We must be the only ones who have their sea legs."

"Yeah, I guess so," agreed Chet, who liked the notion that he was a better sailor than the others. He sucked in his belly and squinted out to sea, thinking of himself as an old salt. A few minutes passed in friendly silence.

"Say, Frank," Chet said at length, "this sea air is giving me an appetite. You think they have a snack bar anywhere on this boat? A hot fudge sundae would really be—"

"I don't think you'll find anything open this late," replied Frank with a grin. "Besides, even if they did have late-night service, it'd most likely be squid or octopus or fish eggs."

"I'd settle for that," Chet sighed.

Frank smiled. "Tough it out then. You'll have to wait until morning."

Suddenly a loud thump echoed from a nearby passageway. A harsh, whispering voice followed, too faint for the boys to make out the words.

Chet turned to Frank. "What was—?" Frank cut him off with a quick "Shhh."

He stood and listened intently and then looked around. The whispers changed to scraping sounds and seemed to be getting closer. Motioning for Chet to follow, Frank moved noiselessly to a point where they would be hidden in deep shadow. They pressed themselves against a bulkhead and waited.

Three figures shuffled onto the deck, visible only as darker shapes in the dim light. Frank saw two guys half dragging a third between them. As they neared the rail, the moonlight hit them.

With a jolt, Frank recognized the figure being pulled along as Morton Prynne!

Chapter
3

PRYNNE LOOKED HALF-CONSCIOUS. Frank and Chet exchanged a quick glance, and then charged forward from their shadowy hiding place.

The boys had the element of surprise on their side. Reaching the closer of the two, Frank grabbed him by the shoulder and yanked him around, breaking the guy's grip on Prynne. He stiff-armed the man in the midsection. His breath came out in one loud *whoosh* before he fell to his hands and knees.

Chet had taken the other one by the collar and belt and lifted him the way a pro wrestler might. He then bounced him off the bulkhead. The man hit with a metallic *clunk* and slid to the floor, where a weak side-to-side movement of his head showed that he was still breathing. He was probably trying to figure out what had hit him.

With both of the mystery men out of action, Frank turned to Prynne. From somewhere just beyond his line of sight a heavy body threw itself at him. Frank, caught completely off guard, was propelled toward the rail by the momentum of the surprise attack.

He slammed into the wooden railing and stopped, momentarily stunned. He felt himself being lifted then, and had a brief flash of churning water below him and of a distant, barely visible shoreline. There seemed to be no way of stopping whoever it was from sending him for a deadly moonlight swim.

And then, just as unexpectedly as the surprise attack had begun, Frank's still unknown enemy lost his grip, dropping Frank heavily onto the deck. Frank struck his head sharply against the rail on the way down. Stunned and breathless, he was only vaguely conscious that someone had come to his rescue. After a brief pause to recover his wits and his wind, he struggled to his knees.

He stayed that way until he was sure that no bones had been broken, and then, gritting his teeth, staggered painfully to his feet.

He saw Chet, leaning against the bulkhead

holding his head, and Prynne, who was now up on one elbow.

There was no one else around. The unknown men had vanished, leaving the three Americans, bruised but breathing, alone on the rolling deck.

Frank went to help Prynne get up as Chet slowly joined them.

"Thank you, boys," said Prynne faintly. "I feel all right now, I . . ." He swayed, and clutched at Frank's shoulder for support.

"Sir," said Frank, "I think you may need medical attention. You could have a concussion or internal injuries. Why don't I stay with you while Chet looks for the authorities."

Even though he was battered, Prynne hadn't lost his pride. "Don't be ridiculous!" he snapped, straightening his clothes and glaring at Frank. "I'm in no need of anything, except the opportunity to go back to my cabin to lie down."

Frank looked narrowly at the man's pale face. "Look, Mr. Prynne, someone has to let the ship's captain know what just happened. Even if you won't see a doctor, we can't just—"

"I have only one need right now," Prynne said, cutting him off. "And that is to get back to my bunk and rest. If you want to help me, you can help me there."

Frank and Chet looked helplessly at each

other as their teacher tottered into the passageway.

Chet stared after him. "What do you think we should do?" he asked.

Frank didn't speak at first. Then he shook his head. "I think if we follow him, we'll probably get our heads bitten off. Maybe we'd better do what he says. Let's turn in for the night and take care of business in the morning."

But Chet was still curious. "Do you figure those two guys really wanted to dump the professor over the side?"

"It looked that way from where *I* was standing." Frank gave Chet a puzzled look. "*Two* guys? Didn't you see the third guy?"

Chet stared. "What third guy? All I saw was the two we went after, the ones with Prynne. There was another?"

"There had to be," answered Frank. "After I took care of the one I grabbed, someone jumped me from behind and tried to dump me overboard. There didn't seem to be a thing I could do about it. Then someone took the new guy off me. I thought maybe it was you."

"Don't look at me," protested Chet. "I thought my man was down and out, but he tripped me up somehow, and I think he kicked me in the head before he took off. By the time

I came to again, there were just the three of us."

Frank was at a loss. Who could have saved him? He walked over to the rail and looked out at the sea, trying to put it all together.

Chet joined him. "There was something else kind of funny, Frank. I can't be sure of it, but—"

"What?" Frank turned to his friend.

Chet shrugged. "Everything was pretty mixed up and dark, but I thought the guy who attacked me was one of those guys from the restaurant this afternoon."

The Hardys got up at noon the next day to find the sun shining, the winds calm, and the sea smooth. Joe stretched and yawned, sitting up in his bunk while Frank did pushups, all the exercise their cramped cabin allowed.

Interrupting a pushup, Frank lifted his head to glance at his brother. "Looks like you're back among the living today," he observed.

Joe swung his legs out of the bunk and sat up, smiling. "It's amazing," he said. "Today I feel great and ready to eat about ten pounds of steak. Last night if someone had asked me to choose between food and being tossed over the side of the ship, I'd have had to flip a coin."

Frank got to his feet. "Funny you should

mention going over the side," he said. He told Joe about the events of the evening before.

Joe's smile faded as he listened. "Sounds like a pretty close call," he said.

Frank shrugged.

"I should have been there for you," Joe growled.

"Hey, go easy on yourself," said Frank. "When you're sick, you're sick. Anyway, Chet did a pretty good job standing in for you."

"I don't like this," Joe insisted with a frown. "Something's not right. Let's find the captain and let him know—"

"Whoa, take it easy." Frank raised his hands. "I think it'd be better if we talk to Prynne first. Whoever attacked him has no-where to go—they're still somewhere aboard."

Joe jumped to his feet. "Then let's get cleaned up, find Prynne, and talk to him—after we find something to eat."

Frank grinned as he pulled on a pair of jeans. "Trust you to get your priorities straight."

A few minutes later they entered a small snack bar on an upper deck. Phil Cohen and Chet Morton were sitting at a table, and Phil waved the Hardys over.

"Chet told me about the fun and games last night," said Phil as the Hardys sat. "You okay, Frank?"

"I've got some bruises where I hit the rail."

Frank rubbed his ribs. "No big deal—it could have been worse. How are *you* feeling?"

Phil smiled weakly. "Now that my stomach is back where it belongs, I'm fine. Last night it kept trying to crawl out through my throat."

Joe said, "I think some plain breakfast food will help keep mine in place. What's safe to eat here?"

Chet looked up from his plate. "Try some of these cakes, Joe. This one's my favorite. It's filled with chopped nuts and cinnamon, and the honey is the best I've ever tasted. And they have this soda, it's a kind of sour cherry flavor, I think it's called, uh, veeseenada, or something, and—"

"Easy, big fella," said Phil, laughing. "Don't strip your gears." Then he turned to Frank and Joe. "You'd probably like this spinach pie," he said. "And the cakes are good, if you have a serious sweet tooth, like our pal here."

They signaled to a waiter, who took the Hardys' order. Before he could leave, Chet stopped him. "Um, as long as you're here, bring a couple more of those spinach pies. Oh, and a couple of the ones filled with custard."

The waiter gaped at him, not certain he'd heard correctly. "You want two more of this *and* two more of this one here? Yes?"

22

"And another one of these veeseenadas to wash it down," finished Chet happily.

Chet noticed the others grinning at him, and shrugged. "It's the sea air," he said.

"Yeah, right," said Joe.

"Take it easy on Chet," Frank cut in. "He had a busy time last night.

"Speaking of last night," Frank continued in a more serious vein, "maybe it'd be better if we kept all of that to ourselves for a while. At least until we've talked to Prynne anyway."

Chet and Phil agreed to keep quiet.

"Have you seen Prynne yet today?" asked Frank.

"Nope," answered Phil. "We got up late and came right in here."

From outside came a babble of cheers and excited voices. Nicholas Kaliotis stopped in the entrance and saw the students.

"Better eat fast, friends, we've arrived! We are coming into the port of Salonika!"

An hour later the ship had docked, and the group was waiting on deck to disembark. There was still no sign of Morton Prynne.

"I don't think he wants to show himself until the last possible minute," Joe muttered. Then he nudged Frank. "There he is now, over there where the gangplank is being hooked up."

The Hardys made their way over to Prynne. He stood waiting, unsmiling.

"How are you feeling today?" asked Frank as they joined him.

"Thank you, I feel quite well," said Prynne. He turned back to look at the dock.

Frank kept on. "We didn't want to do anything until we had seen you and talked it over. But I think it's a good idea to report the attack before the guys responsible have a chance to get off the ship and disappear."

Prynne swung around to glare at Frank. "Attack?" he repeated. "I don't know what you're talking about!"

Chapter

4

FRANK AND JOE gave each other a startled glance. "You do remember last night, don't you, Professor?" he said. "The guys who were trying to dump you over the rail? The ones that Chet and I took care of for you? Does any of this ring a bell?"

"If I were you," Prynne answered coldly, "I would put such business completely behind me. The Greek authorities take a dim view of rowdy young people, even young people who carry American passports."

"Rowdy?" Frank exclaimed in disbelief. "Now, wait just a minute! I mean, I don't expect any medals or anything, but I don't call saving you from an attack being 'rowdy'!"

Prynne gave Frank an icy scowl. "Let us get this clear," he said. "For your information, Mr. Hardy, *there was no attack.*"

While Frank gawked, Prynne went on. "Last evening I was suddenly taken with a severe case of seasickness. I felt extremely weak, dizzy, and feverish, and feared that I might pass out. Two passengers very kindly offered to help me outside, where they thought the fresh air might help to revive me.

"No sooner had they assisted me to the deck than we were set upon by two maniacs. Quite understandably, my helpers beat a hasty retreat, frightened out of their wits.

"If I had not felt so wretched, I would have taken you to task then and there for your foolish behavior. Now let's have no further mention of this regrettable affair."

But Frank was not about to let it drop.

"Just a second, Mr. Prynne. What about the third man, who attacked me after we had dealt with the first two? And one of your 'helpers' looked just like one of the 'drunken sailors' who attacked us at the restaurant yesterday. What about that?"

Prynne's eyebrows rose in surprise. "You clearly saw his face?"

"I didn't. But Chet's pretty sure."

"I see," Prynne said with a smirk. "On a dark night, while the two of you were engaged in your disgraceful roughhousing, your friend was 'pretty sure' he recognized a face. Do you expect anyone to believe such a story?"

"But, what about the third man," Joe put in, coming to his brother's aid.

"Ah, yes, the third man," Prynne replied. "As to that, I'm afraid I have nothing to say. Perhaps you tripped over each other in the confusion of the moment. In any event, I strongly suggest that you put this embarrassing matter to rest. That, at least, is what *I* intend to do."

Prynne stalked away, to show that, for him, the subject was closed.

Joe was steaming. "Do you believe anything he said just then?" he demanded.

Frank shook his head. "There's something going on with Prynne, and it's not just seasickness. But if he won't open up, we're out. Let's just keep our eyes open."

After the ship moored, the crew ran down the gangplank and the passengers disembarked. At the foot of the ramp, Frank and Joe noticed a small knot of people waiting to greet them.

The American students circled around the little welcoming group and Morton Prynne performed introductions.

In the middle of the welcomers stood Spiros Stamos, a stocky man with jet black hair and a bushy mustache of the same color. With him was his sixteen-year-old son, Andreas, who was thin and intense, all bones and angles, like a greyhound.

Also on hand was Spiros's seventeen-year-old daughter, Clea. She had her father's glossy black hair, which she wore long and loose. It framed a beautiful face, with golden skin, highlighted by huge dark brown eyes. She was wearing a brightly colored skirt and a snow-white blouse.

When Joe Hardy's turn came to be introduced he shook hands with the father and son, saying he was pleased to meet them.

Then Joe was face-to-face with Clea. He took her hand and said, with his warmest smile, "I'm *really pleased* to meet you."

But Clea just gave him a "How do you do" and an impersonal handshake.

While Peter and his Greek relations embraced and exchanged bits of family news, the other Americans waited to board a bus to the hotel.

Phil moved next to Joe. "Clea is cute—you planning on getting to know her better?"

Joe looked shocked. "Hey, come on. This is a different country, a different culture. You can't just start talking to a girl the way you

28

would at the Bayport Mall. You have to take it slow. Just watch and learn."

Frank walked over then and tugged on Joe's arm, leading him away. "Don't be too obvious about it," he said quietly, "but take a look at the big car by the gangplank. See anyone familiar?"

Joe turned casually to check out the car. He recognized one drab figure moving through the crowd of brightly dressed tourists.

His code name was the Gray Man, and he worked for a supersecret government organization known only as the Network. He was a heavy hitter in the game of international intrigue.

"What's *he* doing here?" Joe wanted to know. "And what was he doing on our ship?"

"Maybe it's a coincidence," replied Frank. But he didn't believe it, and neither did his brother. The Hardys and the Gray Man had crossed paths before. Sometimes they'd helped one another, sometimes they'd found themselves fighting the Network.

Could the Gray Man have been the mysterious rescuer who'd come to Frank's aid last night? If so, why hadn't he made himself known?

Frank watched as the Gray Man got into the large American car and took off.

Frank turned to his brother. "One thing's for sure," he said. "If there's any connection between the Network's business and us, we're involved in something a lot more dangerous than a student tour."

Chapter

5

THE WELCOMING PARTY that evening was a serious party. The crowd of forty seemed to be carrying on about ninety conversations at the same time, and the air was full of shouts, laughter, and music. The tiny Old Quarter restaurant was bulging at the seams.

But from the moment he spotted Clea in the crowd, Joe had eyes and ears for no one else. If she'd looked good that afternoon, she was a knockout that night in a simple linen sleeveless dress.

Joe said to Frank, while never taking his eyes off her, "Is she or isn't she gorgeous?"

Frank had to agree. "Clea's something special, all right. But remember—the kind of stuff that goes over with the girls back home may flop over here. Take your time."

But Joe had a glow in his eye, and he wasn't about to be steered away from his target. "We're supposed to be getting acquainted, right?" he reasoned with his brother. "Well, I've got some acquainting to do."

He purposefully moved off through the crowded room.

Clea had been helping one of the Bayport students choose food from the buffet table, but by the time Joe got there, she had vanished into the mob. In her place stood Chet, who was busy getting acquainted with a dozen kinds of Greek noshes.

"You see Clea around?" Joe asked.

"She was here, but she went off that way," Chet replied, gesturing vaguely while maintaining his focus on the goodies. "Hey, Joe, you ought to try some of this stuff. It's good!"

"You must have a dolma," said a female voice on Chet's other side. He looked around to find a pretty girl whose big smile showed off the dimples in her cheeks. She fluttered long eyelashes at Chet, who blinked back uncomfortably.

"I am Alma," she said, taking Chet's plate and adding tidbits to what was already on it.

"Uh, hi. I'm Chet."

"Chet. I like that name. Chet. It's a strong

name, fit for a big man. Here." She handed his plate back. "This is a dolma, a grape leaf stuffed with lamb and rice."

Chet sampled, and his face lit up. "Hey, this is great! What's it called again?"

"Dolma. I made it myself. I am a very good cook. One day I will marry a man with a great love of food."

Chet squirmed, not sure how to reply to the girl. Joe grinned. "How do you like that? The way to this girl's heart is through *your* stomach."

Chet glared at Joe, and then turned back to Alma. Before he could think of anything to say to her, his eye met those of a hulking Greek teenager, who stood a few feet behind the girl. He had muscular arms folded across a barrel chest, short, bristly hair, and dark, flashing eyes.

When he saw Chet looking at him, his eyes flashed even more and his face gathered itself into a dark scowl. Chet turned back to Alma.

"Say, um, do you know who that big guy is?" Chet asked. "He keeps staring at me."

Alma looked over, then giggled. "Oh, that is only my older brother, Aleko. He is—I do not know the word in English—when he sees me with a boy, he is—"

"Jealous?" inquired Chet faintly.

Alma gave him a brilliant smile. "Yes, that

is the word. He is very jealous. One time he—
Where are you going?"

Chet dove into the thickest part of the
crowd, putting as much distance as possible
between himself and Alma. Alma frowned and
pouted, then followed him. A moment later,
the menacing Aleko followed her.

Frank had gotten into conversation with Andreas Stamos, whose initial shyness had given
way to enthusiasm when he spoke of the great
love of his life—long-distance running.

He announced proudly to Frank, "I'm going
to be a marathon runner. Pehaps by 1996 I can
compete in the Olympics for my country. I'm
the best junior distance runner in Salonika."

Spiros looked down at his son, clearly proud
of the boy's achievements. But he only said,
"Remember, past accomplishments mean
nothing, unless you go on working. All over
Greece, all over the world, there are strong,
fast boys. Winning will come to the one who
wants it the most and tries the hardest."

Andreas grinned. "Every week I run forty
to fifty miles."

"Wow—pretty heavy-duty," Peter Stamos
said, joining them.

"Next year I'll be running more. When the
time comes, I will be ready."

"I bet you will." Frank was deeply impressed by the young runner's determination.

Joe had been making polite chitchat for what seemed like hours, maneuvering to get close to Clea. Every time he got within feet of her, he found himself trapped in another round of introductions. But now, it looked as if his moment had finally arrived. Clea was standing by herself, rearranging the platters of food. Joe walked up to her.

"Can I give you a hand with anything?"

Clea turned toward him, looking at him from those amazing eyes. "No, thank you," she said with a smile. "I've just finished."

Joe toyed with some of the food, picking a few tidbits up and dropping them on a plate. "This is some party your family has put together. You went to a lot of trouble for us."

"To the Greeks, blood ties are important," she said. "This was a very special occasion, our first meeting with our American cousin. Also," she added after a pause, "we wished to give your group a proper welcome."

"Well, speaking for myself," Joe said, "I sure do appreciate it."

Clea continued to smile. "Do you?" she asked sweetly.

"Absolutely." Joe smiled broadly at her.

"Then what I suggest you do," Clea said, "is go to my father and tell him. He is, after all, the one who went to the greatest trouble."

"What I mean is," Joe persisted, "if you

ever feel like going to a movie, or the beach, or for something to eat . . ."

"Ah!" said Clea as the light dawned. *"Now I understand you. You do not want only to thank me. You want to have what you call a 'date.' "*

Joe wondered if he was being laughed at. "Well, yeah."

"You know, Joe, you're not the first American boy to ask me for a date. In your country a young man may approach a girl, even if he hardly knows her, and ask for a date. It is nothing—like picking up a newspaper."

"Well, I wouldn't say that it's nothing," said Joe, feeling his face start to flush.

"No respectable Greek boy would presume to ask such a thing so casually. It shows no respect for the young woman."

"Hey, wait a minute, I didn't mean—"

"While you're here, I hope you take advantage of the opportunity to learn about our customs, about which you clearly know nothing. But don't expect to pick up a girl with a nice smile and sweet words."

Clea walked away, leaving Joe red in the face, openmouthed, and wishing he could crawl under a table.

Now two musicians tuned up their bouzoukis—twangy Greek instruments that looked like a cross between a guitar and a mandolin—

and someone else shouted out, "Give us room to dance!"

Several Greek men began to move in a vigorous, stomping dance, urged on by the clapping of the spectators. They dipped and spun with grace and energy and were clearly having the time of their lives. Their joy in the dance spread to their audience, and even Joe felt his bruised spirits lift. The surging beat of the dancers had brought the party to its height.

And then, without warning, the lights went out.

In the pitch-blackness, a confused babble of voices, Greek and English, arose. Then a shrill scream burst out and was abruptly cut off. There were thumps, as of furniture colliding, then the nasty sound of flesh hitting flesh.

A dim rectangle of light appeared, as the restaurant's front door was opened. Acting on instinct, Frank and Joe both raced for the door. Frank bumped into someone—no telling who in the dark—and tripped over a chair leg. He fell headlong into the space that had been cleared for the dancers.

Joe was luckier than his brother and managed to stay close to the wall, avoiding the chaos of panicky people and fallen objects. He made it to the doorway and dashed into the street, just in time to hear the roar of an engine being revved to its limit. A battered old van screeched around a corner and disappeared into the night.

A moment later some order was restored. Lanterns were found and lit. Frank picked himself up as Joe returned.

"You see anything?"

"Just a beat-up old van taking a corner on two wheels. You okay?"

"Yeah," Frank answered, dusting off his clothes. "I just got blindsided by a chair."

"Peter! Peter!" Andreas was shouting wildly. *"Peter!* Where is he?"

Spiros Stamos took his son by the shoulders to calm him. "What about Peter?" he asked.

"He—he was just here, with me! I was talking to him when the lights went out, and now he's gone!"

The restaurant was small and a thorough search took little time. When it was over, there could be no doubt: Peter Stamos had disappeared.

Chapter

6

IT WAS QUITE late now, and the restaurant had been cleared up. The electric lights were back on—the intruders had simply unscrewed a fuse from the box outside. Local police had arrived on the scene, questioning Spiros' Stamos, Kaliotis, and Prynne, then departed.

The American students had all gone back to their hotel, a little scared and a lot shaken—all except for Frank and Joe Hardy. They'd stayed behind. Now they were approaching Morton Prynne, who stood off by himself, looking tired and drawn.

When he saw the Hardys moving toward him, he gave them his trademark cold stare.

"What are you doing here?" he demanded.

"I told you students to head back to the hotel and get some sleep."

"Well, we decided that this would be a perfect time for a heart-to-heart talk," replied Frank, crossing his arms over his chest.

"Now, look here, you two," snapped Prynne. "I am in no mood for nonsense."

"Nonsense!" Joe was indignant. "Maybe there's been nonsense going on around here, but we're not the ones responsible for it! The time's come for you to level with us."

"I don't know what you're babbling about," insisted Prynne.

"Number one," said Frank, "the 'incident' at lunch yesterday, when we were attacked by supposedly drunken sailors. Number two, the two guys who wanted to help you get rid of your seasickness—permanently. And now, Peter gets snatched by someone. I'm beginning to get a little suspicious. Two attempts on you, one on the nephew of our host. And you're trying to tell us there's no connection?"

"You may think we're rude and rowdy," added Joe, "but don't think we're stupid."

"Come on, Mr. Prynne," Frank urged. "Tell us what's going on. You never know. We might be able to help."

"Help! You think you can help? You're just a pair of fools!" Clea Stamos advanced on them, her eyes flashing in anger.

"What do you know of our country?" she demanded. "You Americans, you make me sick! Your interference in matters you cannot understand might cause my cousin's death. Don't give us your 'help,' please. Mind your own business and let us mind ours."

"Clea!" Spiros Stamos came forward and put an arm around his daughter, gently drawing her away from the Hardys and Prynne. "It is time you were at home. Come with me."

Clea sagged back against her father, closing her eyes and allowing herself to be led away. Spiros waved a good-night to the three Americans as he left the restaurant with his daughter.

Prynne took a deep breath before saying to Frank and Joe, "Come on, you two. I have a taxi waiting."

Sitting in the cab, the three remained silent during the short drive to the hotel. But as they reached the hotel lobby, Frank stepped in front of Prynne.

"You have nothing to say to us?" he asked.

"All I have to say has already been said," Prynne replied. "You're making something out of nothing."

Joe now spoke up. "Okay, in that case let's just add one last piece of nothing to the picture. This afternoon, Frank and I saw an old friend get off our ship and into a car at the pier—the Gray Man."

Prynne stared at them, his eyes narrowed. "The Gray Man?"

Frank continued, "That's his code name—what everyone calls him in the Network."

Prynne's suspicion had now given way to amazement. "You—you are familiar with the Network?" he asked at length.

Frank and Joe smiled at Prynne. "What's more," said Joe, "*they* are familiar with *us*."

"We *do* get around, you know," added Frank.

Morton Prynne stared at them, took off his glasses, and wiped them on his handkerchief. He said, "I can't tell you anything—not tonight at least. Be patient for tonight and let's plan to have breakfast together tomorrow. Perhaps then I can say more."

"Tomorrow morning then," Frank agreed. "But we'll be expecting some hard facts and not just a lot of smoke."

Prynne just nodded and headed for his room.

The following morning found Frank, Joe, and Prynne sitting at a table in the hotel café. Prynne had not said much, and the Hardys were getting annoyed.

It was Joe who broke the long silence. "Lis-

42

ten," he said, rattling a juice glass on the tile table, "if breakfast was all you had in mind here, I'd just as soon have slept a little later."

Prynne held up a hand. "No, no," he protested, "it's simply that . . . I think we'd better have our little talk someplace more private. I'm going to my room. You wait here for five minutes, looking around to see if anyone follows me out. If it's all clear, then come up and join me. Understood?"

Frank's eyebrows raised. "Is this really necessary?"

Prynne got up and surveyed the Hardys. "Once we've had our talk," he replied, "you can judge that for yourselves."

Joe and Frank knocked on Prynne's door and were quickly motioned inside. As they sat down, Frank said, "No one followed you, and as far as I can tell, no one followed us. Let's talk."

Prynne paced nervously for a moment, then stopped and faced the Hardys. "Everything I am about to tell you is highly confidential—not a word of this can be repeated. Is that clear?"

Joe nodded. "We know all about the Network's security."

"Very well," Prynne answered. "First of all, I *am* an operative of the Network.

"We have an agent who has been working under deep cover in various nations of the

Eastern Bloc, gathering sensitive military information. His code name is Atlas. Right now, he's making his way through Yugoslavia. Tomorrow he will reach the Greek-Yugoslavian border.''

"In other words," Frank cut in, "he may be within forty miles of here."

Prynne nodded. "Essentially correct, although the spot will be more like sixty by the mountain roads. My assignment was to lead a small force to get him back across the border, back to the West. Since being a professor is my usual cover, they put me in charge of a student tour to Greece."

Joe started to his feet, but Prynne waved him back down. "I'm not happy about using innocent students as part of an operation like this—but the decision was not mine.

"Upon our arrival here, American and Greek groups were to join together, under Spiros Stamos—our Network contact. He would take them on a tour, well away from the scene of the action, while I went north with my people to get Atlas."

"And then the wheels fell off your little wagon," Frank observed.

Prynne winced. "You put it crudely, but that's true. Our cover seems to have been completely blown. You were right, of course, seeing the connection between the attacks."

44

He shook his head. "Before we got to Greece, two key Greek operatives were taken out. The body of one was found two days ago, and the other has yet to be heard from. These men were supposed to go north with me. I'm planning to take Spiros now, but even so it will—"

A knock on the door stopped him. Prynne opened it to admit a very worried Spiros Stamos. He nodded a greeting to the Hardys and said to Prynne, "We must talk."

"Certainly, Spiros, sit down."

Stamos turned to Frank and Joe. "Boys, I must speak privately with Mr. Prynne, if you would not mind leaving for—"

"No, no, Spiros, it's all right," interrupted Prynne. "These young men seem to have known almost from the beginning that things weren't normal. What's more, when our friend got off the ship yesterday, they recognized him. They know about the Network and his connection with it."

Stamos stared at Frank and Joe. "How is it possible that these boys should know of such things?"

"Let's just say that we've gotten caught up in a couple of Network deals before," Joe replied. "It wouldn't do to go into the details, would it?"

"No, no, certainly not," Prynne agreed

45

quickly. "But, Spiros, you can speak in front of these two, and we must rely on their continued discretion. What have you come to tell me?"

Stamos walked to the window and stood looking out. "Very early this morning," he said with his back to the others in the room, "I had a telephone call from the ones who are holding Peter. They told me, if I wished to see the boy alive again, I must take no further part in what they called 'foolish criminal activities.' "

Stamos turned from the window and looked at Morton Prynne, the burden of a painful decision showing clearly in his face.

"Morton," he said, "at first I was supposed to do nothing more than lead a student tour—simple and hardly dangerous. Then, last night we talked about my joining you in place of one of the men we lost. This meant some risk, but I was willing to do it, because I believe in the cause.

"Now the danger is not mine alone. I do not fear to lay my life on the line if need be. You understand this. I am not a coward."

"Of course you're not, Spiros," said Prynne quietly. "No one could think such a thing."

"You must see, then," Stamos went on, staring fixedly at Prynne, "that I no longer have a choice in this matter. I cannot allow harm to come to the son of my brother, while he is in my care."

He hung his head. "That is why I cannot go to the border with you."

Chapter

7

"IT LOOKS LIKE you guys could use a little help," said Frank.

"And it just happens that our calendar is clear," continued Joe.

Prynne stared at the brothers in shock. "Are you two actually suggesting that you become actively involved in this business?"

"It did cross our minds," answered Frank.

"It'd sure beat touring ruins," replied Joe.

Spiros Stamos pulled a chair close to the Hardys and sat down. "Boys, we are dealing with very dangerous opponents. They won't hesitate to kill anyone who stands in their way."

He gave them a hard look. "Understand—as

long as they see you as students, you won't be harmed. They wouldn't dare create an international incident. But if it were known that you are members of our team, your youth would not protect you. You'd become targets."

Prynne jumped in. "Moreover, I don't have the authority to bring you in. I can't be responsible for exposing you to harm."

"Now, don't be too hasty," protested Frank. "I can see you think we're just kids who want to play cops and robbers and get in your way. I don't expect that we can convince you otherwise, not by ourselves."

"But if our old buddy, the Gray Man, is around, he can vouch for us," Joe said. "I know he can approve our coming aboard. So that'd take you off the hook, Mr. Prynne."

Prynne angrily blurted, "I don't care about being 'on the hook,' young man! I have a legitimate concern about your safety. However—wait here." He left the room.

"He probably has to get permission to change neckties," said Joe.

Stamos gave Joe an angry look. "I think that Morton Prynne might well surprise you," he said. "There's more to him than what you perceive."

Only a few minutes passed before Prynne returned with the Hardys' old acquaintance.

The Gray Man was not overjoyed to see Frank and Joe.

"If I had the slightest idea that you two might be included in this group," he said sourly, "I would have scrubbed the whole operation."

"Well, things go wrong." Frank looked at the agent. "By the way, do I owe you for a helping hand on the ship the other night? If it was you, then thanks."

The Gray Man waved it off. "Let's call that an even trade," he said. "After all, you were helping Mr. Prynne out of an awkward scrape."

"Look," Joe cut in, "I don't think you have any gripes about us being around to help. You need us now, and you've got us."

That got him a glare from the Gray Man. "We do *not* need you! Just because you've managed to keep from getting killed so far doesn't mean that you're trained agents. We'll get by without you."

"Is that a fact?" Joe asked. "Seems to me you've dug yourselves into a nice, deep hole so far. I don't see how we could possibly make things any worse."

"If this operation is as important as you say," Frank went on, "you have a problem getting a new team in here. We have a couple of friends here who are also very good in a crunch. Phil Cohen is a genius with anything electronic or technical, and Chet Morton may not look it, but he can be tough when it really counts. So—what do you say?"

The Gray Man simmered. They had him in a bind. The loss of Atlas would be a disaster, and almost as bad would be any public exposure of a Network fiasco. He thought hard for a second, and then spoke to Frank and Joe.

"Your analysis of our predicament may be a little overstated, but not too far off the mark. We don't have many options. But if we're going to try to pull this off, I have a few ground rules. First, you'll follow orders—exactly. Second, if it appears that you are in any immediate physical danger you'll stop whatever you are doing and bail out. At once. Agreed?"

Frank and Joe glanced at each other, then looked, with solemn faces, back at the Gray Man.

"Of course," said Frank.

"Makes sense to me," said Joe.

"Very well then," said the Gray Man.

Spiros Stamos came forward. "My children Clea and Andreas are concerned about their cousin and wish to help. Also, the girl Alma and her brother Aleko are closely tied to our family. I am Alma's godfather. And Nicholas Kaliotis will want to be of service as well."

The Gray Man frowned. "Kaliotis? What's his connection?"

"Nicholas was practically raised by my father," replied Stamos. "We are the only family he has. For a Greek, ties of family are sacred."

Taking Stamos's hand in both of his, Prynne said, "Thank you for your suggestions, Spiros. We will consider them. Now, go home. We will keep you informed."

After the Gray Man and Stamos departed, Chet and Phil were summoned to Prynne's room and briefed on what was happening and why.

"Here's the plan," said Prynne. "I'll lead a group north to the border rendezvous. We'll pass ourselves off as a teacher of classical history and his students—there are archaeological digs and a ruined fortress not far from the scheduled meet.

"We'll go with tools—picks, shovels, and the like—as well as some explosives. My party will include Joe, Phil, whose technical know-how may be of use, and Andreas, since we must have one Greek-speaker along.

"Frank, Chet, and the rest will begin a search for Peter Stamos. The other students will be taken on an innocent tour, to keep them out of danger, and fed a story to account for the absence of those of you who will be working with us. Any questions?"

No one had anything to add. The group broke up to make arrangements, get supplies, and pass on information to those who had not been present. At dinnertime they'd meet again at the hotel.

That evening found Frank, Joe, Prynne, Chet, Phil, and Kaliotis around the dinner table. Andreas, who was expected, had not yet arrived.

"We'll start without him," Prynne decided, pulling out a checklist. "Those of you going with me must be ready to leave by six A.M. I've gotten an all-terrain vehicle, just in case any problems force us to leave the main road.

"We'll take along a multiband radio receiver-transmitter, and we'll call in regularly. The Salonika party will have a similar radio. Listen for our calls every hour on the hour. When we have reached—"

Chet, who was facing the entrance to the restaurant, cut in on Prynne's instructions: "Here's Andreas."

Joe turned toward the door and frowned. "Here comes trouble," he said.

Andreas was not alone. At his side, with her jaw set and a challenge in her eyes, walked his sister. Andreas could hardly look at the people around the table, stammering, "She made me tell her what we are doing. She wants to . . . I couldn't . . ."

Clea spoke up. "I am going to the border too. If my brother can go, then I can as well."

"Now, wait a second," said Joe, holding up his hands. "There's plenty that you can do here in Salonika, Clea. From what Mr. Prynne says, we could find ourselves in rough country. We can't be held up by—by someone who isn't physically up to the job."

"Not up to it!" Clea's eyes shot fire at Joe. "Why do you assume that? I have spent much time in the places you are going, camping and climbing mountains."

She pointed to her brother. "Do you think *he* can keep up, because he is a boy? On flat ground, he can outrun me. But in the mountains, he is no match for me. And this way you will have another Greek along."

Joe glared, but Morton Prynne cut the debate off. "Very well, Clea, we have room in the truck, and you may join us. But understand, no allowances will be made for you if it becomes necessary to go on foot. You will be expected to keep up to our pace."

Clea smiled. "You do not have to worry about me," she said.

They were running through the final preparations when a waiter came through the room, calling Frank's name. Frank raised his hand. "Over here!"

"Mr. Frank Hardy? You are wanted on the telephone in the lobby."

Going to the booth, Frank picked up the phone.

"Hello?"

"Frank Hardy?" The voice was accented, unfamiliar. "Here is someone who wishes to speak to you."

After a momentary pause, another voice came on the line, shaky and very frightened.

"Frank?"

"Peter! Is that you?"

"Yeah, it's me. I have—"

"Listen, how are you doing? You okay?"

"I—I'm all right. A little shook up, but they haven't hurt me—yet. I'm supposed to give you a message from them."

"Go ahead, Peter."

"They say that you'd better not go ahead with your mission. You can't succeed. If you try, they'll—they'll kill me. They really mean it, Frank. I'm scared."

"Listen, Peter." Frank tried to make his voice a lot more confident and reassuring than he felt. "Take it easy. We'll get you out of this. We won't let anything happen to you. Understand?"

"Yeah, I guess."

Frank racked his brains, trying to think of

some way to keep Peter on the line and maybe pick up clues to his whereabouts.

"Listen, Peter, I want to ask you a few questions, if they'll let you stay on the line. Just answer yes or no. Got it?"

"Yes."

"Are you still in the city?"

But the only response was a sudden dry click.

Frank's knuckles whitened as he tightened his grip on the phone.

"Peter? Peter! You there?"

No answer.

Frank stared in helpless frustration at the dead receiver.

Chapter

8

BY SEVEN-THIRTY the following morning, the all-terrain vehicle, with Prynne at the wheel, had left Salonika far behind. Joe Hardy rode shotgun, with Phil Cohen, Andreas, and Clea Stamos in back, along with their gear—extra clothes, tools, and an emergency supply of gasoline.

The road had been straight and wide at first. But now they were going with some care along a twisting, two-lane ribbon of concrete that clung to a mountainside, full of hairpin turns. On one side they were hemmed in by a steep, rocky slope covered with boulders and scraggly bushes. On the other side was a dizzying drop into a deep gorge.

"Not much traffic on this road," Joe observed.

"It's too early in the day," answered Clea, leaning over the front seat. "Anyway, there is not much ahead on this road except the border, some ruins, and that old Turkish fortress."

"How come a Turkish fortress?" Phil wanted to know.

"The Turks ruled here for quite a long time," Prynne explained from behind the wheel. "So did the Venetians, the Franks, and various other groups over the years."

"Until we won our independence," Andreas added with pride.

Suddenly a large Mercedes sedan appeared behind them, moving much faster than they were. Prynne edged the ATV to the right, and the luxurious car glided past, quickly putting distance between them. The windows were so darkly tinted that it was impossible to see inside.

Phil whistled as they watched the Mercedes vanish around a curve ahead. "Pretty fast for a tricky stretch like this."

"Oh, I don't know," Joe answered. "A car like that has a low center of gravity and great suspension. Now, if you took *this* baby at that speed—"

"I don't even want to think about it," Phil said, with a shake of his head. "I have this strange fear of falling several hundred feet into a dry riverbed. Some hang-up, huh?''

Joe laughed as they whipped through a demanding set of mountain turns. Then, coming around on one especially sharp turn, they found the Mercedes that had passed them. It was parked diagonally across the road, blocking both lanes.

Prynne braked with a squeal of tires. Almost before they had stopped, a series of shots rang out from somewhere above them. A webbed hole appeared in the windshield, and a metallic clank indicated a bullet striking the body of the truck somewhere.

"Ambush!" shouted Joe.

"Turn around!" Andreas screamed.

"No room." Prynne threw the ATV into reverse and lurched away from the trap. More shots rang out as Prynne made the treacherous hairpin turn backward. About two hundred yards farther along he slowed the vehicle and backed it off the paved surface and into a cleft in the rock, protected on either side by almost vertical cliffs.

"Phil, get on that radio, and let the people back in Salonika know we've been attacked," Prynne ordered. "The rest of you, start looking for shelter. I imagine we'll have company soon, and we know they're well-armed."

"Andreas, Clea, let's move!" urged Joe, who was already out of the truck.

Behind the truck, the cleft ran deeper into the rocks but didn't seem to be more than a blind alley.

Phil had set the radio up and was listening with a frown to the static coming out of the speaker. "The mountains are blocking us here," he said. "I tried to send word, but I don't know if anything's getting out or *to* us." He turned up the receiver, which hissed with the static.

"Keep trying," Joe said, coming back and shaking his head. "It doesn't look like we've got much in the way of shelter here," he advised Prynne. "These cliffs are steep, and I don't see where—"

"Joe! Come here!" called Clea. "I think there is a place up there."

Joe ran over to her and followed her pointing finger, but all he saw was what appeared to be a slight break in a sheer cliff. He told her as much.

"You don't have a mountaineer's eye," she said impatiently. "I will show you."

She began to climb up quickly, finding little crevices for her hands and feet. About fifteen feet above them, she pulled herself up onto a ledge and looked down to the others.

"This is wide enough to hide us," she called down.

Prynne ordered Andreas to climb up, help his sister look for possible weapons, and stockpile them.

"What kind of weapons?" Andreas wanted to know. "We have no guns." Prynne had ordered them not to have guns in case they were caught. The guns would blow their cover.

"Rocks," replied Prynne. "Good throwing rocks."

"Rocks against guns?" Andreas muttered.

"They're all we have now," Prynne replied.

Andreas scrambled up to join Clea. Joe came back to Prynne. "I may have an idea," he said, explaining quickly.

Prynne nodded. "Set it up," he said. "I'm going to explore farther up into the cleft."

Joe ordered Phil to stow the radio, and gave him a length of rope, but Phil still looked at the steep rock face unhappily.

"Look, if Clea can do it, then *we* can do it," coaxed Joe. "It's not completely smooth, like glass. Look for little ridges, little cracks, use the plants for handholds. It's better than just sitting here and waiting for them."

With this encouragement, Phil carefully started up, the rope slung over his shoulder. With Clea shouting instructions and urging him on, Phil slowly got to the ledge, where he rolled himself onto the flat surface with a deep sigh of relief.

Then they hauled up a bundle of spare clothes and a can of gasoline. Morton Prynne came out from the inner reaches of the cleft, and Joe stopped to check with him.

"We're ready to go up there," he said. "Are you coming?"

"I've found a little hiding place back there," replied Prynne, gesturing with his thumb. "It's a kind of mini-cave that'll hold just me. It's better that someone stays on ground level, so we attack from two directions at once. Watch for my signal, and then let 'em have it."

Joe grinned at Prynne and said, "Well, here goes nothing." He started up the ledge, while the other man retreated into the crevice.

On the ledge, Joe found a good-size pile of rocks being gathered. He tied the spare clothes into bundles, soaking them in gasoline. Each makeshift torch also got a rock for throwing weight.

Phil studied them, then asked Joe, "Think these'll do any damage?"

"Well, they'll surprise whoever they're dropped on. Maybe that'll give us an edge."

Preparations finished, the four students lay in wait on their ledge, with Prynne below, tucked into his little niche. Minutes dragged by, and the silence was complete. It grew warm on the ledge, and Joe wiped the sweat from his eyes.

Then, a man's head peered cautiously around from the road. The scout saw the ATV, and called back over his shoulder. Seconds later, four men were standing near the truck, searching. The four above flattened themselves down and froze.

Joe whispered to Phil, "Those guns they have are AK-forty-sevens. Russian-made, automatic."

Phil whispered back, "How'll they stand up against manually operated Greek rocks?"

Joe nudged Clea. "What are those guys saying?"

"I don't know," she whispered back. "They aren't speaking Greek."

One of the gunmen now moved out of sight, down the road from where the Mercedes sat, off to see if the ATV passengers had fled in that direction.

"That cuts the odds down a little," Joe muttered. "Get ready."

Prynne leapt from his cover, landing on the back of the nearest opponent and clamping an arm around his throat. The other two wheeled around, but as they did, the four on the ledge hurled a hail of rocks, some of them trailing flaming torches. One of the men was smashed squarely in the side of the head and toppled.

The other had his aim spoiled when a torch nearly singed his face. He jerked away, only to have Joe drop from the ledge onto him.

The AK-47 fell to the ground. Joe lunged for the gun, but was grabbed from behind. Twisting, Joe saw that his man had him by the leg with one hand, while reaching for a knife with the other.

Joe kicked back with his free leg, catching the man hard in the chest and breaking his grip. A quick roll brought Joe to his feet. But his opponent, knife in hand, barred the way to the gun.

A wild slash sent Joe stepping back, looking for more room. But his foot landed in a shallow hole and he tumbled, landing hard. Sensing his chance for a quick kill, the thug started forward, but a sudden burst of automatic weapon fire from behind froze him in his tracks.

There stood Phil, glaring over the sights of the AK-47 in his hands. Joe's attacker dropped his knife and raised his hands. "Joe, you all right?" Phil asked.

"Can't complain," Joe said, getting up and dusting himself off. "Much obliged for the help."

"Any time."

Clea and Andreas by now had made their descent from the ledge, and Prynne stood alone, cradling an AK-47. At his feet lay another thug, lying flat out before him.

"Is he—dead?" Andreas asked in a shaky voice.

"No, just fast asleep. I didn't cut off his air supply long enough to do him any serious damage," Prynne said calmly. "Joe, pick up that gun, if you would, and then we'll wait for the fourth one, who should be here before long."

A few minutes later they heard a voice calling out a question in the same mysterious language their attackers had used. To the surprise of all the others, Prynne called out an equally unintelligible response.

A moment afterward the fourth attacker strolled into the recess, to find three AK-47s pointed right at him. Sensibly, he lowered his gun and joined his comrades.

The four disarmed gunmen were pulled back into the deeper part of the cleft in the rocks, where they were tied securely with rope and their own belts. While this went on, Joe asked Prynne, "What was that language you were speaking?"

"Serbo-Croatian," Prynne replied, his eyes still on the prisoners. "Phil, that rope needs tightening. That's more like it."

"You speak Serbo-Croatian?"

"I'm a bit rusty," Prynne said, smiling, "but good enough for the present purposes."

While the others finished with their captives, Phil and Joe headed for the ATV to try the radio again. As they neared the truck, Joe stopped short, noticing a pool of liquid spreading out from under the front end. He ran to the front of the vehicle and knelt down. Then he raised the hood and looked down at the engine. Phil joined him.

"What's up?" Phil wanted to know.

Scowling, Joe thumped the motor. "Look for yourself. We took a bullet in the radiator, and this engine is scrap metal. We're not going anywhere—at least not in this truck."

Chapter
9

WAITING, FRANK THOUGHT, is the hardest thing of all, especially while somebody else is out doing something. He and Chet, along with Alma and Aleko, sat in Frank's hotel room. He kept checking his watch, amazed at how slowly the time crawled along.

The multiband radio sat on the bureau. But the time to check for messages hadn't arrived yet, nor had Nicholas Kaliotis. Frank went back over the events of the past few days in his head.

Suddenly he sat up straight, and said, "Hey, I just remembered something from last night."

"Let's hear it," Chet exclaimed.

"Well," Frank went on, "while I was on the

phone with Peter, when he was giving me the word from the people holding him, I heard—I think it was a whistle. Yeah, like a boat whistle! Maybe that could help to narrow down the areas to search."

Aleko sighed and shook his head sadly. "In Salonika, you can hear whistles from ships almost anywhere. It is no help."

Frank slumped back in his chair. Finally he went over to turn on the radio.

"Phil should be in touch any minute now," he said. But the only sound to emerge was static. He turned the volume all the way up and paced the floor. Nothing. In frustration, he slammed the bureau top with the flat of his hand.

"You're sure that's the right frequency?" Chet asked.

Frank glared at him. "It's the right frequency, the right time, the right everything. Maybe—"

"Shhh!" hissed Alma, bending close to the radio's speaker. "Listen!"

Through the interference Phil's voice could just be made out, barely audible: "Ambushed . . . trapped on . . . road . . . automatic weapons . . . careful . . ." The static swelled, and the faint voice disappeared altogether. Frank attempted a transmission.

"Base to Northern Group . . . Base to Northern Group . . . Do you read me, Northern Group? . . . Phil, are you there? Over. Come in if you read me, Phil, over." But the only sound from the receiver was noise.

"Ambushed!" Frank snapped. "The other side was waiting for them up there. Someone's been one step ahead of us every move we've made."

There was a knock on the door, and Aleko opened it to admit Nicholas Kaliotis, who was immediately surrounded by Frank and the others in the room.

"We heard from Phil. They've been ambushed on the road by guys with machine guns!"

"We've got to do something fast!"

"Have you heard anything about Peter? Is he alive?"

"Listen, we have to get reinforcements up toward the border, they may be—"

"Quiet!" Nicholas's roar cut through the excited barrage. "Now, one at a time, if you please. Did you actually speak to them?"

"No, the interference was terrible," Frank replied. "We were able to make out bits and pieces and then we lost them completely. I tried responding, but I don't think I got through."

"Hmmm. Yes, in the mountains, radio reception might be difficult," said Kaliotis. "But you were able to establish that they were under attack of some kind?"

"The first word we heard was *ambushed*," Chet exclaimed.

"How quickly can you organize a relief party?" asked Frank. "They may not have much time."

Kaliotis cut off the discussion. "Right," he said. "Stay here for a few minutes. I will be back as soon as I can. I must see to getting a team prepared to go north. Wait." And he was gone.

Frank picked up where he had left off before the arrival of Kaliotis. "I can't see any other explanation for it," he said, flopping back onto the couch. "Somebody is passing information to the other side."

"But—but who?" Alma asked.

"Well, they took out two Greek agents before we arrived in the country," Frank answered. "That suggests the leak is someone from over here. I think we can eliminate Stamos and his family." And then noticing that Aleko looked ready to erupt, he added, "And we also can cross off those who are very close to the family." Aleko subsided.

"But what about Kaliotis? What's his story?"

Alma spoke up. "It could not be him. When he was a young boy his father and mother were killed in the civil war by Communist partisans. The partisans also kidnapped thousands of children over the border into the East. His only brother was taken away, never to be seen or heard from again. Spiros Stamos's father raised Nicholas as one of his own. They are the only family he has. It is not possible that he could betray them."

"Okay, if you say so," Frank said, as he stood and began to pace again. "But we have a weak link somewhere. So we'd all better be careful about who we talk to until we clear it up."

Alma's face was serious until she caught Chet's eye and gave him a beaming smile.

"It is a frightening thing that we are dealing with, but I feel lucky to have such strong, brave men to help us. Have you been involved in such matters before?"

Chet shifted his feet, looked at Frank and then away, and mumbled, "Not *real* often— not at all, hardly. Well, maybe a little."

Frank put a hand on Chet's shoulder. "Alma," Frank told her gravely, "you're looking at a real hero. Why, he saved my life once already this trip, and two days ago, I saw him take a knife away from a vicious criminal."

Alma's eyes gleamed. "I knew it," she whispered. "A tiger."

"Come on, Frank," Chet muttered, squirming in his chair. "Cut it out, will you?"

"Alma!" Aleko rumbled, giving her a dark scowl. "Enough of this foolishness! This is not the time or place."

There was a quiet tap on the door, and Kaliotis stepped inside. "We must leave at once. I have taken the necessary steps," he said. "Now we'll go to where the group is preparing to leave, but we must hurry. On the way, I will tell you what has been learned about Peter's present whereabouts. Hurry!"

The group followed him outside and piled into an elderly Volvo.

Kaliotis headed away from the newer, central district of Salonika and toward the waterfront. The areas they went through became shabbier and shabbier.

"Where are we headed?" asked Frank.

"It is what is called a 'safe house,'" said Kaliotis. "There we are gathering those who will go to help your brother, and there we will make our plans to rescue Peter Stamos. We will be there soon."

Shortly afterward they pulled up in front of a seedy, run-down building with metal shutters covering its windows. The stucco walls had faded until it was impossible to tell what color they had been.

"This is it?" Chet looked doubtful.

"This is it," answered Kaliotis. "You don't want a safe house to call attention to itself, do you? This place blends with its neighbors."

"That doesn't say much for the neighborhood," noted Chet as he and Frank left the car. With Kaliotis in the lead, they entered a dim hallway. Kaliotis opened a narrow door and stood back, gesturing them in.

"Be careful going down the stairs," he cautioned. "They are steep and the light is poor."

Frank led the way down the flight of creaky steps and into a cellar lit only by a couple of low-wattage bulbs in wall sockets. They found a number of men cleaning and loading pistols and automatic weapons.

"Looks like you've got a real task force here," Frank observed to Kaliotis.

Then his eyes fell on what seemed to be a bundle of clothes piled on the floor against a wall. As his eyes got used to the lack of light, Frank realized with a jolt that he was staring at the bound and gagged body of Peter Stamos.

Frank spun around to discover that most of the guns in the room were now aimed at him and his friends. Kaliotis had led them directly into the hands of the opposition!

Chapter

10

PRYNNE, JOE, PHIL, Clea, and Andreas stared unhappily at the ruined ATV. Joe slammed down the hood. "We need new wheels," he said.

Prynne took off his glasses and wiped them with a handkerchief. "There's a very nice Mercedes just around the corner," he said.

Phil shook his head. "There'll be guards—and I'll bet they won't be ready to lend it to us."

"Then I guess we'll have to persuade them. Got any ideas?" Joe turned to Prynne.

The agent shook his head. "The problem is getting close enough without getting shot."

Joe took Prynne's arm, leading him back to

where their four prisoners lay tied. Joe pointed to one of them. "He looks just about my size. With his clothes and that knit cap of his to cover my hair, I could pass for him."

"Maybe at a distance," Prynne said dubiously, looking at the prisoner's stubbly face.

"We could all walk around the curve with me holding you at gunpoint as captives," Joe went on. "We'd get as close as possible to the Mercedes, then all we'd need was some sort of distraction to let us rush the guards."

Joe smiled. "Phil could make a very loud distraction with the explosives in the ATV. Let me try this guy's outfit on for size."

When Prynne and Joe walked back to the others, Joe was wearing a pair of baggy khaki pants, a grimy black sweatshirt, and a black knit cap.

"Well, what do you think?" he asked.

"As a fashion statement," said Phil, "it's the pits. Is there a point to this?"

Joe swiftly outlined his strategy, then turned to Phil. "We need an explosion—something with a lot of noise and smoke but no damage. It should go off forty-five seconds from the time we start walking toward the Mercedes."

Phil examined the area, marking a spot with his toe. "About here, you'd get lots of echo, and it'd be harmless."

"Excellent," Prynne said. "You stay here,

with one of the AK-forty-sevens. When your explosion goes, fire a few short bursts, just to add to the noise and general confusion. After that, act at your own discretion. Understood?"

Phil nodded and went to work.

"You know," Joe said, "it would be a good idea if I knew a few words in their language."

"Serbo-Croatian." Prynne nodded. "Let's see, I'll teach you. 'It's all right, these are prisoners,' and 'Help! Come quickly!' That'll be enough for our purposes."

While Prynne was drilling the phrases into Joe, Clea came up with a handful of mud, which she smeared over Joe's cheeks, jaws, and chin.

"It will look like the face of an unshaven man, from perhaps thirty yards," she said.

Joe shrugged. "If we get that close and Phil's bomb hasn't gone off, we're in trouble anyway."

"It's ready." Phil picked up his AK-47.

"Right." Prynne started out of the cleft. "Phil, we'll be expecting your explosion forty-five seconds from when we go around the turn."

"You got it," Phil answered. "Good luck, guys."

A moment later, Prynne, Clea, and Andreas appeared around the curve, their hands clasped behind their heads. Joe came just behind, carrying an AK-47 and muttering his two Serbo-Croatian phrases under his breath. The Mercedes stood about one hundred and fifty yards away, with two men guarding it.

"Slow down," hissed Prynne. "We don't want to get too close too soon."

The guards had by now caught sight of them. One yelled something.

"Don't answer yet," whispered Prynne. "Make a show of not being able to hear him."

On they trudged, and the guard called out once more and brought his gun up to his shoulder.

Joe waved one arm over his head and shouted out what he hoped would pass for assurance that everything was all right. The guard lowered his gun and called out something else.

"What's he saying now?" whispered Joe.

"He wants to know where the others are. Try the first phrase again."

Joe repeated the first line as they moved steadily closer.

Fifty yards. The guard shouted out more sharply, and both men now trained their AK-47s on the approaching group.

Forty yards. Suddenly the roar of an explosion filled the air, followed by the rattle of an automatic weapon.

Joe spun around, yelling to the alarmed

guards. He kept his face turned away and fired a couple of short bursts in the general direction of the blast. The three "prisoners" moved aside.

The two guards came running up. Joe let the first go past, then tackled the second man. He caught him at knee level from behind, cutting him down and sending the man's AK-47 skittering away.

The other guard turned back, his gun wavering as he tried to find a shot that wouldn't hit his comrade. Before the guard had a clear shot, Prynne rushed in to knock the gun aside. The man pulled free but Prynne drove a shoulder into him, sending both of them sprawling into a gully.

Meanwhile Joe tried to pin his man, but the gunman kicked out, sending Joe flying. After a bone-jarring landing, Joe struggled to rise. He turned to see that the guard was scrambling for his fallen AK-47. With a desperate lunge, Joe caught the man's foot, and Clea darted in to snatch up the weapon.

The man now tried to kick loose and grab for Clea, but Andreas jumped in, kicking him hard as he could in the stomach. The guy sagged to the ground, while Joe took the AK-47 from Clea and covered him.

"Where is Mr. Prynne?" Clea asked, "and that other man?"

"I was hoping *someone* would ask," came Prynne's voice from alongside the road. They peered into the ditch. There lay the gunman. On top of him sat Prynne, holding a gun.

"Way to go, Mr. Prynne!" Joe exclaimed, as Phil came running up.

"How are you all doing up there?" Phil wanted to know.

"Everything's under control," Joe replied. Prynne looked up at the students, and they suddenly noticed that he was pale and sweaty. "My leg," Prynne said. "I think I've torn a ligament in my ankle. That means I won't be doing any long-distance walking for some time. Could someone give me a hand?"

Joe helped Prynne over to the Mercedes, while the others took the guards to join their fellow captives. Then, taking the radio and the captured guns, they piled into the liberated car and resumed their northward journey with Joe at the wheel.

Prynne watched the barren countryside roll by for a while and then spoke up. "What worries me now is that whoever set up that ambush is likely to take another shot at us. I wish we could get off this main route."

From the back seat, Clea spoke up. "There is an old road leading directly to the ruined fort."

"Our rendezvous is an abandoned shepherd's hut, right on the border," Prynne said. "Do you know it?"

"I don't know the cabin," admitted Clea. "But it should not be hard to find."

Prynne sighed. "I had hoped to make that hike myself, but under the circumstances Joe will have to undertake it, if he's willing."

"It'll be a pleasure," Joe said with a grin. "Clean mountain air, beautiful scenery—and I've never seen Yugoslavia. I wouldn't miss it."

"And *I* will go with you," announced Clea.

Before Joe could protest, Prynne nodded. "You'll need a guide," he said. "But there is the possibility of a great risk."

"Don't worry, Mr. P.," Joe answered, "I'll look after her."

Clea smiled. "We will look after each other."

The road began to climb until at the crest of a hill they saw the fort. Some of its walls were crumbling, but one tower stood intact, rising about twenty-five feet. The only way to the top of the tower was a narrow set of steps. It was an easily defended stronghold.

With Andreas and Clea helping Prynne, they brought their gear up the stairs. Joe and Clea began preparing backpacks for their hike.

Phil, who was standing lookout, seemed troubled. "How will anyone coming to reinforce us know where we are? That turnoff we took—there's no way we would have found it without Clea's help."

"Ah!" Andreas exclaimed. "I can go back to the place where the road meets and show them."

"What do you mean, 'go back'? You might drive right into the enemy," said Joe.

"Not drive—run!" Andreas said. "I can do that distance in less than one hour."

"And when we raise Salonika on the radio, we can advise any relief force to look for him," Phil added.

"It sounds like our best choice," Prynne mused. "Phil and I will hold down the fort here, while Joe and Clea are—" He stopped abruptly and held up a hand for silence. "We have company."

Phil darted to the wall nearest the road. He called back over his shoulder, "Two cars—ten or more guys with guns getting out of them."

Joe joined Phil. They watched as the group of men fanned out and began to search the area. Prynne positioned himself near the top of the stairs. Shortly afterward a couple of heads peered up at him. Prynne fired two rounds, and the heads vanished.

"Joe!" called Prynne. "How are they armed? Can you tell?"

"I saw more AK-forty-sevens," Joe replied.

"Nothing heavier? No mortars or any kind of artillery?"

"No, just small arms."

Prynne let out a sigh of relief. "Then they can't get up here, and we can't get out. Except we *have* to get you out of here, somehow."

Clea had been exploring the walls. Now she called out, "Joe! Andreas! Over here. I think I've found a way out, if we can keep those men occupied on the other side."

She pointed down the wall, saying, "Do you see the vines here—the way the stones in the wall are uneven? I am sure we have enough footholds and handholds to get down."

Joe surveyed the immediate area, which was almost halfway around the fort from the road. At the foot of the wall, the ground sloped down, but not too steeply. There were scattered boulders, and stunted trees and bushes.

"Once we're down," he said, "it looks as if there's enough cover to let us work our way clear. I think it's our best shot."

Leaving Phil to patrol the wall, Joe outlined the plan. Prynne listened, and when Joe finished, he thought it through for a second.

"It'll have to do," he muttered. "Are you set to move out?"

"Whenever you say," answered Joe, and Clea and Andreas nodded.

Prynne looked at his watch. "In one minute

Phil and I will open up with a heavy covering fire. Give us fifteen seconds to catch the enemy's attention, then make your move. Good luck." Gravely, he shook hands with each of them.

A minute later Prynne and Phil opened up on their side of the fort, firing in frequent, short bursts. The force beneath the walls began firing back. After counting off fifteen seconds, Clea, the most experienced climber, swung herself over the top of the wall.

She made her way carefully, using the tiny crevices between the stones of the wall and the climbing vines. Joe noted the route she took, impressed by her strength and agility, as well as her nerve. He looked over at Andreas.

"Here goes nothing," he said. "See you on the ground floor." Joe swung himself over and began the difficult descent.

Below him Clea had reached a point only three feet from the ground.

But as she dropped, some bushes a few feet from her rustled. Out stepped a man with an old Tokarev pistol—a scout for the attacking party.

And he had Clea dead in his sights!

Chapter
11

THE CELLAR WAS dim, musty, and bare. The men who had kidnapped Frank and the others obviously had faith that they couldn't escape because they removed Peter Stamos's gag and ropes and left his friends unbound. The prisoners were alone now.

As soon as the door had closed, Frank began a quick but thorough search of their dark cell. There was a single, small window, set high into a wall, and protected by a thick steel grill. As a source of light, it was too dirty to be of much use; as a possible escape route it was entirely hopeless.

Moreover, there was nothing—no carelessly dropped tool or removable length of pipe—

nothing that could conceivably serve as a weapon.

Alma huddled, weeping, in a corner, with Aleko hovering over, trying to comfort her.

"What—what will they do to us?" she asked in a shaky, whispery voice.

Aleko knelt before her and put his hands on her shoulders."

"I will not let them hurt you," he said. "They will have to kill me first."

At this, Alma's tears built into sobs that shook her whole body. Chet approached the terrified girl. He bent down and spoke in a calm, casual voice.

"They're not going to do anything to us, Alma. All they want is to keep us out of the way for a while."

She looked up at Chet, wanting to believe him. "Do you think that we are safe?" she asked.

Somehow Chet managed a comforting smile. "Sure, they'll probably hold us until tomorrow and then let us go. Why don't you try to get a little rest?"

She smiled quickly and leaned her head back against the wall, closing her eyes.

For the first time Aleko looked at Chet without hostility. He muttered in gratitude, then began pacing, smacking one massive fist into his other hand with a loud crack.

Moving away from Alma so as not to disturb her, Aleko whispered fiercely, "Frank, I do not know how he could do this."

"Who? Kaliotis?" questioned Frank.

"When we were little, we called him Uncle Nicholas. How could he turn on those who gave him love, gave him *life?* When his parents were killed and his brother taken, he was a small child who would have died if the Stamos family had not taken him in."

He stared at Frank, his burst of anger spent. "I cannot understand it. It is—it is the worst of crimes."

Just then the door at the head of the stairs was flung open, and some men clomped down the steps. Two carried automatic pistols, the third had an Uzi. Fanning out, they trained their guns on the five students.

Then a fourth figure clomped noisily down the wooden steps as everyone watched silently. He surveyed the group with an ugly smirk. And Frank realized that his thin, ferret face was a familiar one—he'd been the ringleader in the attack at the restaurant. Chet gasped and whispered, "Frank! That's the guy from the ship, the one who—"

"You will be silent!" snapped the man in a cold, cutting voice. He looked over to one of the armed men and in the same chilling tone commanded, "Get a brighter light."

"At once, Theo," responded the other, who hastily trotted back up the steps, reappearing a moment later with a long, multicelled flashlight that he handed to Theo.

Theo played the light slowly over the five young faces. Stepping forward, he grasped Frank's collar and jerked him forward a couple of paces.

"Well, well, my meddling young Yankee friend! You have a nasty habit of sticking your nose in where it doesn't belong. I think the time has come for you to pay for your interference."

Frank stared straight into Theo's eyes, refusing to show any fear, concentrating on breathing deeply and evenly.

"Pay?" he said. "Sorry, I didn't think to bring much cash. You take credit cards?"

Switching the flashlight to his left hand, Theo lashed out with his right, catching Frank on the jaw with his open palm and sending him reeling into the wall. Alma gasped, and Chet took a step forward, but stopped when the Uzi was swung around and pointed straight at his chest.

"Enough of this foolishness!" Theo said, slapping the long, heavy flashlight into his palm like a policeman's nightstick. "We have some questions for you." He pointed the flashlight at Frank. "You will answer them immediately and save yourself and your friends unpleasantness."

Frank's jaw hurt, but he would not give Theo the satisfaction of rubbing it and admitting to the pain. "I don't know what kind of information you think you can get out of me. I'm just a student on an exchange program."

"Either you are a fool, which I doubt, or you take me for one." Theo leaned in until his face was inches from Frank's. "I want to know exactly where your criminal accomplices are to meet with the American spy. He will not escape the forces of justice in any case, but if you tell us the exact location of the meeting, it will be easier for him—and for you."

Frank took a deep breath, but let none of the relief and happiness he felt show in his face. Maybe Joe and the rest of the northern party had somehow managed to get free of the ambush.

"Spy? Criminal accomplices? Listen, Theo, I'm telling you, you're making a mistake. We came here to study history and culture.

"I tell you what, check with my brother Joe. He'll be happy to explain how we've always wanted to visit Greece and soak up all this ancient history."

"I look forward to the chance of having a long, long meeting with your brother, when such a thing is possible. But for now," Theo said, "I am talking to *you*. So, stop this pointless lying. Where is this meeting to be?"

Frank shrugged and shook his head. "Sorry, but I'm afraid I can't help you."

Theo's eyes narrowed, and his lips pressed together into a thin, bloodless line. He handed the flashlight to one of his henchmen and reached into his jacket, pulling out a large, nickel-plated 9mm automatic pistol. Holding it casually at the bridge of Frank's nose, he asked, "Perhaps this will help your memory a little?"

To Frank, the barrel of the gun looked about the size of a manhole cover. But he gave Theo his most innocent, puzzled look and replied, "There's nothing I can tell you. And if you shoot me, then there definitely will be nothing I'll be able to tell you."

"Shoot *you?* Oh, no, my young student friend, I would never dream of shooting *you*." Theo's mouth curved up into a smile, and that smile was the ugliest expression he had shown yet—the look of a shark that had just sniffed out a tasty meal.

"No, *you* are to remain alive for the time being," Theo went on. "But I am going to introduce your friends here to a very old custom of our country—one which your brother and you, with your great interest in Greek history, will no doubt find fascinating."

Theo put his gun away and climbed the steps out of the cellar, returning a moment later with a small clay pot in his hand. "It is a kind of lottery," he explained.

Pulling a knife from a sheath on his belt, Theo crossed the basement. The wall there had once been decorated with black and white tiles. Many were now missing or broken. Theo pried several of the tiles loose, then slipped the knife back in its sheath.

"You see," Theo said, holding the tiles out in his hand, "I have three white tiles and one black one. When the ancients had to choose one person from a group to suffer an unpleasant fate, they put tiles or rocks in a pot, like so."

He dropped the tiles into the pot and shook it up. "Then each member of the group would pick a tile. The person with the bad luck to draw the black tile—that one would suffer. Now we relive this old Greek custom. Fun, eh?"

Frank reached for the pot, but Theo shook his head.

"Oh, no, my friend, you may only observe our little lottery," Theo said. "But the rest of you"—he swung his gaze over Chet, Peter, Alma, and Aleko—"will reach into the pot and choose a tile. Whoever chooses the black tile, that unhappy soul will suffer if Frank refuses to answer my questions."

He smiled again. "Whether you live or die will be entirely Frank's responsibility."

Chapter

12

JOE HARDY CLUNG to the rocky surface of the old fortress tower like a fly to sticky paper. He was only halfway down when the gunman had appeared to subdue Clea.

Apparently the enemy scout had seen only her and decided on a quiet capture. He had clamped a hand over her mouth and begun dragging her backward.

But Clea refused to cooperate. She sank her teeth into the guy's hand. He grunted in pain and lost his grip on the girl, who darted away. He recovered quickly and lunged after her.

Twelve feet above, Joe pushed out from the wall. Falling like dead weight, he hit his unsuspecting target squarely on the back. They both fell heavily, with the man taking most of the impact.

Joe kicked free and got to his feet, while his dazed opponent wobbled to his hands and knees. Before he got up any farther, Joe delivered a roundhouse right to the side of the guy's head with enough power to send him flat on his face, down and out.

Clea rushed up as Joe removed the unconscious gunman's pistol and checked the clip. There was a full load of eight shots. He made sure the safety was on and stuck the gun in his belt.

"Are you all right?" Clea asked.

"Never felt better," he answered, pulling a coil of rope from his pack. "Let's drag him over behind the bushes there and tie him up."

They left the scout behind a dense growth of plants, a gag stuffed in his mouth and his hands and feet bound behind his back. By this time, Andreas had joined them. They still heard occasional firing from the other side of the tower.

"Okay," Joe said. "Clea and I will circle in front of the tower and create a diversion with this." He patted the pistol.

"I figure if they think they're under fire from two sides, that ought to let Andreas move down the hillside without being seen. Andreas, you have a watch?"

"A stopwatch for my running," he replied, pulling one from a pocket.

"Great!" exclaimed Joe. "Give us, say, ten minutes from the time we move out before you take off. And one last thing—when you get to that junction, stay out of sight until you're sure that the people you see are *friendly*. Got that?"

Andreas's eyes gleamed with excitement. "I understand," he assured Joe. Then he smiled at his sister. "Take care, and good luck."

Clea gave Andreas a quick hug. "Run well, my brother."

Leaving Andreas looking at his watch, Joe and Clea worked their way down the slope. They carefully started around the fortress, using all available cover once they were within sight of the attack force.

Dodging from scraggly bush to little hillock of earth, to one of the many boulders scattered around the area, they moved in behind the enemy. They climbed a hill, at their opponents' backs. The gunmen never noticed a thing.

"Over here," Joe whispered. He'd seen just what he wanted—a thick tangle of bushes on the hill's crest. From there they could see a section of road where Andreas should soon appear. The nearest of the opposition was about sixty yards away. Joe checked his watch and found that eight minutes had passed. They had two minutes to establish their diversion.

Joe motioned Clea to lie flat and pulled out the automatic pistol, flipping off the safety. He drew a bead on the rock the nearest enemy was using for cover. Then, gripping the heavy pistol in two hands, as his father had taught him, he squeezed off a shot.

Sixty yards away, the bullet smashed into a rock only a foot from the gunman, who jumped in fear and stared wildly around. Joe fired again, and a bullet ricocheted off a rock on the man's *other* side, sending up a shower of stone chips.

Joe and Clea could hear the man cry out in shrill, panicky tones. Joe kept shooting until the clip was empty. The result was a frantic scramble as the bewildered attackers looked for better hiding places against gunfire from both the tower and this new threat. A burst of wild automatic fire tore through the top of a tree, but the gunner had no idea where to aim.

Clea reached out to tap Joe on the arm. "Look! On the road!" she whispered urgently.

Joe swung around and saw Andreas, arms churning, thin legs pumping, as he sprinted away, completely unseen by the enemy. The diversion had worked!

Seconds later heavy fire erupted from the tower, and the attackers, now totally rattled, turned back to face their original target.

Joe nudged Clea. "I think Phil and Prynne

are giving us some cover. Let's take advantage of it and get out of here. Stay low and move slowly—at first.''

They put some distance between the fortress and themselves before they felt it was safe to take off across the jagged terrain at a rapid clip. The noise of shooting soon faded behind them.

They moved through a landscape of barren earth and stone. Drab, colorless, low trees and bushes were the only silhouettes breaking up the monotony. There were no buildings, no signs of paved roads, in fact, no evidence that people had ever set foot there. Clea had some knowledge of the country and led the way. At one point, Joe called a brief halt and discarded their pistol, hiding it under a pile of small rocks.

Clea asked, "Why don't we keep the gun?"

"If we're stopped by anyone," answered Joe, "it's better if we look like a couple of innocent backpackers. And an empty pistol isn't going to be of much use anyway."

They plodded on for a while in silence, each wrapped up in his or her own thoughts and worries about friends and relations.

Joe began to be aware of the straps of his pack cutting into his shoulders. And his legs were sending painful messages that all this up- and downhill was getting very old very fast.

He stopped and drew in a deep breath. "Listen, Clea." She turned to face him. "Uh, how are you doing? You want to take a breather?"

"A breather?" she asked with a mocking smile. "Can it be that the all-American athlete is tired already?"

Joe felt his face reddening. "Hey, give me a break!" he protested. "I'm fine, I just figured maybe you might be a little—"

"You needn't worry about *me*," replied Clea coldly. "Any Greek could outlast you in cross-country hiking. I see how the American tourists won't go anywhere if they can't take a bus or car. You're soft and weak, all of you."

Joe's aching legs and back were forgotten in a rising tide of anger and resentment. He marched alongside her, demanding, "Why do you hate America anyway? What's your problem?"

Clea stared at him in puzzlement. "Hate America? I don't. We Greeks owe a great deal to your country. America saved us from terrible things when my parents were young."

Joe frowned. "I don't get it."

"After World War Two ended, there were those who wanted Greece to become a Communist state. Many died in the fighting, and thousands of children, babies even, were carried off to be raised in Communist countries.

When we became a tyranny, they would return as our new leaders.

"If it had not been for American assistance, the Communists might have won. But when I see rich, spoiled American tourists who only want their comforts, I wonder if they could fight for their liberty if they had to."

Joe had forgotten his anger as he listened to Clea's story. He walked a way before answering.

"I never heard any of what happened in Greece back then," he said finally. "I'm glad you told me. But I do know a bit about America. Sure, there are some folks like the ones you're talking about, who come over for a good time only.

"But I look at Bayport, where Frank and I live, and people don't look so lazy or spoiled to me. They work hard. My father, for instance, makes a good, comfortable living as a detective, but I can tell you, he's worked hard to help a lot of people."

He looked down. "I guess that's one of the reasons my brother and I want to be like him."

Clea shook her head. "What you say may be true, but that's just one town and only a small number of people."

"Frank and I have met a lot of Americans. I'm not saying they're all perfect, but I don't think we're all that bad. In fact, I bet we're a lot like you. We look at some things differently, we do some stuff differently. But I guess we're the same in more important ways than we're different.''

Joe broke off, seeing Clea smile at him. He looked away, embarrassed at having gone on as he had.

"Well, anyway, that's what I think," he mumbled. "Maybe it sounds pretty dumb, but—"

"No, not at all," Clea protested. "I don't think it's dumb at all, Joe. I think that it is probably so. Perhaps I do not know Americans as well as I thought I did. Maybe we're both learning important things from each other."

They went on in silence again—a friendlier silence than before.

Near the crest of what seemed to Joe like the two hundredth hill they'd climbed, he raised his hands in mock surrender and said, "Okay, I give up. *I* want to take a breather, because *I* could use a break, all right?"

Clea began to pull off her backpack. "If you hadn't said anything, I would have in a minute or so," she admitted. "I think we could both use a little rest and something to eat."

Joe noticed a flat ledge of rock nearby. He walked over to it, shedding his own pack as he did. "This looks like a pretty good spot to sit down for a couple of—"

Whap! Something smacked into the pack, ripping it out of his hands. Startled, Joe yelled to Clea, "Get down!"

She stared in surprise but dove for the ground.

Crouching, Joe scanned the barren hillsides around them. Somewhere out there, someone had targeted them. But there'd been no sound of a gunshot.

"We've got to get behind those rocks," he said to Clea, glancing at the only cover nearby.

Joe and the Greek girl managed to crawl only a foot toward shelter.

Then something went *spang* off the rocks right between them.

Chapter
13

THEO SHOVED THE small pot with the four tiles inside at Chet Morton, saying, "We'll begin with you, fat boy. Put your hand inside and pick out a tile. Quickly!"

Glaring at the man, jaws clenched tight, Chet reached in and pulled out a tile. It sat in his large fist as he swallowed, then opened his hand. The tile was white!

Theo was clearly enjoying the game and the fear it caused his prisoners. He moved over to Aleko, who scowled sullenly. "Now you, make your choice. Don't be afraid, boy, the odds are still in your favor."

"I am not afraid," muttered Aleko as he pulled out a tile. It, too, was white.

"It is the turn of the young lady," Theo said, offering her the pot. Alma stared at him, eyes wide, frozen, like a bird hypnotized by a snake. She couldn't move.

"Come, now," Theo went on, shaking the pot so that the two remaining tiles rattled. "Get it done with, girl. You are making me angry, and that is a very bad idea. *Take the tile*, or I will make your brother my first victim!"

"No! Please!" cried Alma, groping inside the pot with a trembling hand. Looking at what she had chosen, she let out a soft moaning sound. Her hand fell to her side, and the black tile dropped to the cellar floor.

Theo grabbed Alma by the wrist. He pulled her forward, away from the others, drawing the big automatic with his other hand.

"Let her go," roared Aleko, springing for Theo's throat. The henchman with the long flashlight clubbed the brawny young Greek on the back of the head, dropping him in a crumpled heap on the ground. Alma screamed, but Theo silenced her abruptly, pointing the ugly gun at her nostrils. The room grew quiet.

"Now then! There will be no more heroics, I hope," Theo said, looking over at Frank.

"If you wish this girl to live, you will tell me all you know about where the meeting has been set with the criminal spy—now!"

Frank gauged the distance that separated

him from Theo—but with three other armed
men facing him, the odds were too long. Theo
held Alma by the wrist, and now, deliberately,
he cocked his gun with a dry click that echoed
through the room. Then the door at the head
of the steps opened.

"Theo!" called out a voice, and Nicholas
Kaliotis stormed the cellar. Theo sullenly lowered his weapon. The two men shouted angrily
at each other in Greek. Kaliotis turned to
Frank, giving him a grim look.

"We do not wish to hurt anyone. You will
all be released unharmed, if you are coopera-
tive."

"Traitor!" Alma shrieked. "How can anything you say be believed?"

Kaliotis bit his lower lip but did not look at
her.

"I tell you, we are not here to shed blood.
You must tell us what you know, and you and
your friends will be safe. I swear it."

Frank studied Kaliotis for a few seconds.
"Maybe you actually believe what you're saying," he answered. "I wish that *I* could. We've
seen too much, we know too much, and your
buddy Theo seems like a guy who would shoot
because he doesn't like the way we cut our
hair. I don't think it matters if I say anything
or not."

"No! You are wrong, I tell you!" Kaliotis

grabbed Frank's shoulders with both hands. "I would not have done this—do you think I would have brought you here to be *shot?*"

Theo stepped forward between Kaliotis and Frank and shoved the Greek back and out of the way. He gave Kaliotis a look of contempt.

"We have tried your method, and you see where it has gotten us. Now we are short of time, and we will use *my* way. I will shoot a prisoner now, and one for each additional minute that this stubborn American refuses to talk."

Kaliotis started to protest, but Theo grabbed Alma once again, saying, "You are weak, my brother."

He aimed the pistol at Alma, and once more looked over at Frank. "Well? What will it be? Nothing? Very well, then. Her death is on your head, Yankee."

"Theo! No!" Just before Theo pulled the trigger, Kaliotis hurled himself at Theo. The pistol roared, and Kaliotis was flung back against the wall.

Seeing his chance, Frank drove a shoulder hard into Theo's chest, knocking him down and sending the gun clattering into a corner. Chet wrenched the flashlight away from the distracted guard and brought it down on the man's arm as he raised *his* pistol. Then he rammed an elbow into the face of the disarmed gunman, who fell to his knees, all the fight knocked out of him.

Screaming, Alma rushed the man with the Uzi, clawing at his eyes. Peter jumped on the guy's back, pinning the man's arms to his sides, hanging in with grim determination. The man, bleeding from the scratches that Alma had left on his face, tried to shake Peter loose, but the boy wouldn't let go.

The remaining guard leveled his pistol, hoping for a clear shot at one of the young demons. But in the dim light the action boiled so rapidly around him that he dared not shoot.

While he hesitated, Chet threw the long multicell flashlight at him. It struck him a glancing blow that didn't do much damage. But it was followed immediately by Chet himself, who slammed the guard against the wall of the cellar and knocked the wind out of him.

Theo was tough and agile, quickly getting up and going for the gun lying in the corner. When Frank tried to hook an arm around his leg, he kicked back, landing a heel on Frank's forehead hard enough to leave him briefly stunned.

Now Theo had eyes only for his gun—*he* wouldn't hesitate to shoot the wrong person. But as he strode toward the gleaming automatic, a hand reached out to trip him up. Aleko, only partially conscious, was still in the fight. Theo landed hard, the gun a few feet beyond his outstretched hand.

Snarling in frustration, Theo jerked his foot loose from Aleko's grip and kicked back with his heavy boot on Aleko's arm. Then he started to crawl forward but stopped short and sagged in defeat. Frank Hardy, bleeding slightly from a cut on his forehead, stood with the silvery pistol in his hand. He fired a single shot, which split the air with an ear-shattering roar. A moment later all the guns had been collected by Peter and Chet. Alma knelt beside her brother as he started to come around.

Nicholas Kaliotis lay motionless, the sleeve and body of his shirt marked by a spreading stain of red. Frank started over to him. "Mr. Kaliotis? Nicholas?"

When Peter and Chet also turned to Nicholas, Theo saw his opportunity. With a single lithe movement, he was on his feet, and before anyone could react, he had an iron grip around Alma's neck, and a knife at her throat. Furious at his own carelessness, Frank trained his gun on Theo, who sneered, pulling Alma back toward the foot of the stairs.

"No, no, young American, don't be hasty. I am going to take my leave of you now—but I am certain that we'll be seeing each other again, quite soon."

Keeping his eyes fixed on the guns held by

Frank, Chet and Peter, Theo climbed the steep flight of stairs, pulling Alma up step by step, using her as a shield. When he reached the top landing, he held the knife against Alma, and reached back with his other hand to push open the door. With one last malevolent stare at Frank, Theo vanished through the doorway, leaving Alma standing alone and trembling.

"C'mon, Frank, let's get him," urged Chet.

But Frank let his gun hand drop to his side. "No, we'd never catch him—he knows this city, and we don't. Besides, we have some people who need looking after. He'll keep, for the moment. Alma, are you okay?"

Alma had her arms crossed, hugging herself tightly. She took a ragged breath and said, "Yes, I think so. I am not hurt, only . . . I was very frightened. But I am well." She started back down the steps.

Peter was kneeling by Kaliotis. "Frank! He's alive. His eyes are open, and I think he's conscious."

Frank got down next to Kaliotis, who looked up with a mixture of pain and remorse. The man panted with effort. In spite of his shoulder wound, he reached out with his other hand to grip Frank's arm. "You must believe that I never thought he would shoot. I was wrong, and you were right."

Frank gently removed Kaliotis's hand and

spoke quietly. "Just try to relax, and we'll get some help for you."

Kaliotis nodded weakly. "I am not seriously wounded, I think. No immediate danger."

"Mr. Kaliotis—Nicholas," Frank went on. "Theo called you 'brother' a while back. Why did he do that?"

Kaliotis's eyes closed, and he sighed. "He *is* my brother by birth—he was taken across the border many years before. Some months ago, he revealed his identity to me, telling me things about our family that only my brother could possibly know."

A bitter look came over the man's face. "He said that things had changed since the civil war, that he was fighting for a just cause, and that he would permit no killing. I wanted to believe. But now . . ." His face hardened. "We may have had the same mother, but we are brothers no longer."

"Don't talk any more," Frank said as Chet came up with an old blanket he had found to cover the wounded man. "Just take it easy, and help will be here in a little while." Frank stood up, and looked over to where Alma was tending Aleko. The muscular young Greek was sitting with his back against a wall, fully awake and alert.

Frank surveyed him a moment. "How are you making out?"

Aleko managed a faint grin. "My head—it hurts very bad. But I will be all right. I—*we* owe you much."

Frank waved a hand. "Hey, we all did our bit. You, too, for that matter. But we still have a lot to do. Peter and Alma, you had better stay here with Nicholas and Aleko. Chet, let's get moving."

"First thing," Frank continued, "we find a phone and let Spiros Stamos know what's happened—that we've found Peter, and that Kaliotis needs a doctor. Then we try to make radio contact with Joe and the others up north."

He looked grim. "With Theo on the loose, we're likely to find a hot time on the border—all too soon."

Chapter
14

JOE LAY FROZEN in the open, thinking that if there was anything worse than being shot at, it was not knowing where the shots were coming from. He waited to see what would happen next. If people were sniping at them, he and Clea couldn't try anything until they showed themselves.

From the cover of a gnarled and stunted tree trunk thirty feet away, a boy stepped forward. The kid couldn't have been more than thirteen or fourteen. He wore a ragged T-shirt, old jeans belted with a piece of rope, and sandals on his feet. He was carrying a long piece of rawhide. He glared at the two strangers.

Clea spoke to Joe in a whisper, never taking

her eyes off the boy. "He is a shepherd, and he shot at you with that sling he is holding."

As she spoke, the boy pulled a smooth stone a bit larger than a marble from a pouch hanging from his rope belt and fitted it into the sling. He addressed them in Greek, sounding angry to Joe. Clea replied, and there was a short conversation between the two. Joe heard a familiar word—*Amerikanos*—Greek for American.

The boys eyes widened. *"Amerikanos?"* he echoed softly, dropping the stone back into the pouch and letting the sling fall. He was transformed, now carrying on with a stream of friendly chatter.

"He is called Giannis," Clea translated. "He says that border guards have been coming from Yugoslavia and raiding his flock, taking his sheep for food. He has been making patrols lately and moves his flock frequently."

There was another interval of talk between Clea and Giannis in Greek, and Clea turned to Joe in some excitement. "He knows the cabin we are looking for! It is no more than a fifteen minute walk from this spot."

Clea resumed her talk with the shepherd, who spoke for a longer time, with Clea listening and nodding her head in agreement. She explained to Joe: "It will not be hard to find— it is just over that hill, there." She pointed to a gentle slope about half a mile away. "But he warns us that we must be very careful and watch for the border patrols. He says the guards are the kind who shoot first and ask questions later, if at all."

Joe smiled at the boy, saying to Clea, "Be sure to thank him for me."

Clea spoke to Giannis, and the boy looked down shyly, then stepped closer to Joe, saying something directly to him for the first time. Joe looked questioningly at Clea, who tried to hide a grin.

"Giannis said that, since you are from America, perhaps you know his uncle George, who lives in America in a town called Chicago."

Joe looked at the shepherd, who stared at him hopefully, and shook his head.

"Uncle George drives a taxicab," Clea added.

"Tell him I'm sorry, but I've never met Uncle George," Joe said, keeping his face serious as he did so. "But if I ever do run into him, I will tell him that his nephew Giannis was very helpful to me."

When Clea relayed this speech, Giannis glowed with pride. Opening their packs, they took out food and offered some to Giannis. The young shepherd hesitated, and then took what was offered, wolfing it down as if he hadn't eaten in days. Joe and Clea finished their meal, thanked the boy once more, and headed off toward the last hill and the cabin beyond.

As they hiked, Joe looked back once more at Giannis, who stood watching them. "He seems kind of young to be out here by himself."

"He is not so young that he cannot help his family make their living," Clea answered. "People in the mountains are very poor. They can't afford to be children for very long."

They climbed the hill that Giannis had pointed out to them and began to descend the far side. Partway down, they caught sight of a small tumbledown hut standing by itself near the foot of the hill. Joe stared at it. "Calling that a cabin gives it the benefit of the doubt. If you ask me, I'd call it a shack."

The place seemed to be deserted. They waited for a few minutes; there was no sign of activity.

Joe slipped out of his pack and handed it to Clea. "I'm going down to check it out. You stay here." He scrambled down the slope till he reached the cabin. He peered in through a hole in the wall, then came to a crude door. It swung open with a loud creak.

Inside the dim light was alive with dust motes. A very old mattress lay along one wall and a three-legged table was on its side nearby. Otherwise the room was empty.

Joe climbed back up to Clea and squatted down near her. "All clear. We're the first to arrive, and I think we should stay up here, where we have a view of anyone coming. Let's get comfortable—we might be a while."

They found good cover and settled in to wait. Joe was half-asleep in the late-afternoon sun when Clea poked him with her foot. "I think someone is coming."

Joe stared where Clea was pointing. A man was indeed heading toward the cabin from the north. He was plainly straining, pushing on despite the fatigue that made his stride a little wobbly. From time to time he paused to look behind him.

As the man neared the cabin, Joe and Clea began to pick their way toward him. They walked through a patch of gravel, and the man spun to face them.

Clearly, they weren't what he was expecting. He tried speaking to them, first in a language that neither Joe nor Clea knew, then in Greek.

Joe now took a few steps toward the man, who was obviously on his last legs. The agent hadn't shaved in days. His eyes were red rimmed and glazed; only willpower was keeping him on his feet. He took another quick glance back in the direction from which he'd come.

Finally Joe decided that he had to be their contact. "It's all right. You must be Atlas. We're, uh, friends of Mr. Prynne—I think you know him as Ajax—anyway, he couldn't be here himself because of an accident, and—well, it's a long story. So here we are instead, okay?"

The man stared and shook his head slowly. "I can't believe it. You're just a couple of kids."

Joe straightened up and said, "Well, I'm seventeen, and so's Clea here, if that's what you mean. Sorry, I tried to get older, but this is the best I could do."

The man squatted down, staring up at Joe and Clea, raking his hair back with his fingers. "You two have any weapons?"

"Afraid not," Joe answered. "Sorry."

"You wouldn't, by any chance, have something to eat and drink? It's been quite a while since I had any food."

Joe stripped off his pack and found him some bread and cheese. The man tore at the bread and stuffed hunks of cheese into his mouth. Clea wordlessly gave him her canteen, and he took several long swallows.

"Can't tell you how much I needed that," he said once the little meal was done. "Wish I had time for an after-dinner nap, but we'd better get moving. We're going to have company any minute now. We are on the Greek side of the border, aren't we?"

"Yes, you are in Greece," Clea said. "The line is just north of that cabin."

The man slowly got to his feet and stretched. "We'd better head out of here anyway. With what I'm carrying, the people on my tail aren't about to let a little thing like a national border get in their way. You two kids actually work for . . . I mean, I knew they'd been having some recruiting problems, but . . ."

Joe shrugged back into his pack. "We're not exactly Network operatives, if that's what you're getting at. We sort of fell into this job. Things haven't been going according to plan, but it doesn't sound like we have time for a long story just now. Shall we get going?"

"Lead on. By the way, what do I call you two?"

"She's Clea and I'm Joe. Joe Hardy."

"Pleased to meet you. I wish it had been under different circumstances." Clea took the lead as they began to retrace their steps back toward the south. As they climbed the hill, agent Atlas kept looking behind them, as he strained to keep up the pace. Joe observed Atlas's concern. "Who are you expecting to follow us?"

"There was a Yugoslav patrol about ten miles back. I managed to give them the slip and must have built up a little lead. But I know they're back there somewhere.

Joe peered into the distance, but saw no signs of movement. They returned to their hurried climb. As they neared the top, Atlas no longer kept glancing back. He seemed to be rapidly running out of energy: his breathing had become more labored, and he was limping slightly as if there were a rock in one of his shoes.

"You okay?" Joe asked him.

"Don't bother worrying about me. How far do we have to go, and do you have any friends waiting when we get there?"

"It's between an hour and a half and two hours, and there's at least a few friends there—with guns. Maybe more of them by now."

"Very good," said Atlas. "Okay, Joe, you and Clea don't have to worry about me. I'll do what I have to, to get back home. I'd just feel better if we had a weapon, but—"

Crack! The unmistakable sound of a high-powered rifle rang out, and a puff of dust and dirt spouted a few feet to Joe's right side.

"There they are," said Atlas, pointing north. Joe quickly counted about a dozen men in tan uniforms, all armed, jogging down the slope of the next hill over, perhaps three hundred yards behind them. More shots were fired, and a ricochet whined off a nearby rock.

The sight of the pursuers seemed to destroy Atlas's energy. His shoulders slumped, and he reeled as if someone had hit him.

"Let's go!" snapped Joe. "Let's stay about ten yards apart and take advantage of all the cover you can find—at least till we're over the crest of the hill. Move!"

As they clambered up their hill, Joe risked another look back. The border guards had formed a ragged line, picking up speed as they came. They had their target in sight, and they'd guessed right that the target couldn't shoot back. A few of them had even broken into a full run.

The hunters were closing in rapidly—and there wasn't a thing that Joe, Clea, or Atlas could do to stop them.

Chapter
15

A CAR SPED north along the same road that
Joe, Prynne, Clea, and the others had taken
earlier. At the wheel was Spiros Stamos, with
Frank Hardy next to him, the multiband radio
in his lap. In the backseat were the Gray Man
and Chet Morton.

After Frank and Chet had left the cellar
where they'd been held captive, things had
come together in a hurry. Medical attention
had been provided for Nicholas Kaliotis and
for Aleko, both of whom would recover.

In the case of Kaliotis, there were legal
matters to be dealt with once he left the hospital, and he was in police custody. But he was

willing, even eager, to help bring Theo and his thugs to justice.

Earlier, when Frank had gotten in the car, he exclaimed, "This is the big rescue force you talked about? The four of us? What's the deal here, is the Network running on a supertight budget or something?"

The Gray Man had replied, "Take it easy, Frank. The Greek military can't get involved in this, and neither can any other official arm of the Greek government, unless we want serious diplomatic problems. It can't seem that they took any official interest in this matter at all. And there *is* a larger party, which will come after us. We're just the vanguard, so to speak."

Now they were twisting and turning along the mountain roads, carefully taking the switchbacks and hairpins. Frank fiddled with the radio, but he didn't hear anything except static. He was feeling edgy and tried not to let it show. There hadn't been any information about Joe and the others for hours.

Abruptly, Stamos braked the car to a stop and backed it up. Half-hidden in a cleft between some rocks stood an all-terrain vehicle.

"That must be the ATV Prynne was driving this morning," he said.

They pulled in next to the truck and behind it found a group of men, tied up. The bound men wouldn't speak, but the Gray Man noticed a piece of paper pinned on one guy's shirt. He reached down and pulled it loose.

"Somebody's left a note. 'To whom it may concern,' " the Gray Man read. " 'We had to borrow a car from these guys after they shot up our truck. We're on our way north. See you soon—we hope. Joe.' "

After Spiro Stamos radioed in to arrange for the prisoners to be picked up, they headed back out on the road. Frank took control of the radio, switching it to the proper frequency. Before he had a chance to try a transmission, the voice of Phil Cohen crackled out of the speaker. Eagerly, Frank grabbed the microphone.

"Phil! This is Frank, Phil! Do you read me? Do you read me? Over?"

Phil's response was audible through a slight filter of static and interference. "Affirmative, Frank, you're coming through pretty well. Good to hear a friendly voice over this thing!"

"What's happening with you up there? We're on our way to join you. Over."

"It's kind of involved, so I'll try to keep it simple. Wc drove the Mercedes we took from that bunch of heavies, but we decided to turn off from the main route and take a side road that goes right by this old Turkish fort. Prynne got hurt when we took the car, by the way— messed up his leg, so he can't walk."

The radio hissed and popped with static for a second, then Phil's voice came through again. "He and I are holed up on top of the fort's tower, and there're maybe five guys with small arms down below. We can hold 'em off as long as our ammo holds out, because they haven't got anything heavy enough to knock the tower down."

Frank cut in on Phil. "How's Joe? Is he with you? Over."

"Joe and Clea have gone out to make the meeting at the border and bring Atlas back. So it's just me and Prynne here right now, but that'll be enough—till our ammunition runs down. Over."

Spiros Stamos took the mike from Frank. "Listen, Phil—you say you took another road, off the main route. How will we know where that road is? Is there any kind of sign or landmark? Over."

"We sent Andreas down from here on foot, to point out where you turn. He should be there now. Keep an eye out for him. Over."

Frank took the mike back. "I copy that," he said. "We just passed your ATV and the bunch you left tied up there."

"Then you'll get to the road junction in less than half an hour." Suddenly the volume of static rose, and Phil's voice faded. Frank turned his volume control as high as it would go and strained his ears, but all he could make out was "See you . . . hurry . . . luck . . ." Then the noise took over completely.

Frank stared in frustration at the radio and flicked the set off. The Gray Man leaned forward over the front seat. "Radio contact is tough when you're going through the mountains. But it sounds like they're doing well."

Frank wasn't about to get his hopes up too easily. "Yeah, they're doing all right—unless they run out of ammo, or heavier guns show up for the bad guys. And we don't know what's happening with Joe and Clea. Can't we get any more speed out of this thing?"

"The idea is to arrive there in one piece." Spiros Stamos didn't take his eyes off the road as the car lurched along a roller coaster-like dip, followed by a tight turn. "We cannot help anyone if we wind up in the bottom of that ravine beside us."

Stamos's knuckles were white as he took the car through another hairpin, bringing the right front wheel within less than a foot of the drop. "Be patient, Frank. To go faster in this area is crazy—suicide."

Frank forced himself to be cool and let Stamos do the driving. He stared silently out at the drab countryside flying by. But he could restrain himself for only so long, as grim thoughts about Joe kept popping up in his mind. He turned back to look at Stamos.

"Maybe I ought to drive for a while. You could probably use a break."

Stamos continued to stare straight ahead. "I know you are worried about your brother, Frank. But do not forget—my son and daughter are there as well, facing the same dangers. We will do all that can be done, but we must not let our worries make us try foolish things."

Frank settled back in his seat, feeling a little ashamed. He *had* forgotten that he wasn't the only one in the car with a strong personal interest in getting safely and quickly where they were going.

Frank suddenly sat bolt upright, focusing his eyes farther down the road. Had he actually seen something flashing by the roadside, or was he imagining— No! There it was again, a glint of metal from the bushes—a signal, maybe?

"Mr. Stamos," Frank began, "do you see a bright—" and he broke off. From the clump of brush where the flashes had come, he could just make out something moving. It was an arm! Someone was hiding there, pointing upward. Why?

Frank looked up, trying to figure out what the unseen figure was pointing to.

The hillside rose steeply, though it wasn't

sheer cliff at this spot. Frank's gaze moved up, then he shouted, "Stop! Look out! Up there, on our left!"

Bouncing down the hill like a giant, misshapen bowling ball, a huge boulder was crashing its way toward the road.

And it was headed right for their car!

Chapter
16

CLEA, JOE, AND ATLAS cleared the top of the hill and plunged down the slope on the other side. They were able to put some more distance between themselves and their hunters, but only for a while. The border guards knew their quarry would run and not fight. The gap had to close again and quickly.

Atlas hadn't complained, but he was clearly in no shape for a long running chase. He had reached the outer limits of his endurance. But they had no choice other than to keep moving, heading south.

Behind them, the faster, more ambitious guards raced ahead of their comrades. Joe could hear them calling to one another.

One guard in particular had a sizable lead over the others. He cleared the top of the rise and broke into a near-sprint, ignoring the shouts of the others who couldn't match his pace. This target would be his, and his alone!

Running grimly ahead, he closed the distance. A hundred yards between them— eighty—sixty . . . Now the man they had been chasing for so long had begun to lag behind. The spy was running awkwardly, only twenty yards ahead. He looked back over his shoulder, saw the patrol guard coming, and turned to face him.

The guard knelt down, propping his AK-47 on a flat rock to steady it. Then he drew a careful bead on his prey.

Up ahead, Joe looked back to see the guard aiming at Atlas. There was no cover for the American, and the guard was too close to miss.

Then the guard flung a hand up over his face and slumped sideways, his gun rattling on the rock. He lay motionless. Joe saw Atlas dart forward toward the mysteriously fallen gunman, when he realized that a voice was whispering to him from some nearby undergrowth.

"*Amerikanos!* Hey *Amerikanos!*" Branches parted, and a thin, young face appeared between them. It was Giannis! The young shepherd waved his sling and made frantic beckoning gestures. Joe waved back in agreement, turning to locate Clea, who was staring in surprise at the downed guard.

"Clea! This way! Come on, move it!" She scrambled toward him. Atlas, Joe noted, had now grabbed the guard's gun and ammunition, and was starting back downhill. Soon all three were lying behind the concealing undergrowth along with Giannis.

Clea introduced Atlas to the shepherd, and Atlas admired Giannis's sling. "You tell him he's quite a marksman with that thing. He saved my bacon just now."

Clea passed on the compliment to Giannis, who grinned broadly.

Atlas was checking out the captured automatic weapon. "I think we may be able to slow our friends down some, if this young fellow with the sling will help us out some more."

Clea translated the request, and Giannis replied eagerly.

"He says that he's happy to help. Maybe they will think twice before stealing a lamb for their dinner."

Atlas knelt down facing the others.

"Okay. These clowns out there think we're unarmed and helpless. Now, one gun and a little ammo isn't much good in a real fight, but it'll be fine for *show*." He looked like a new man with a weapon in his hands.

"Suppose you two head on down to the foot

of the hill and find cover. Clea, you tell Giannis that I'm going to fire a few bursts at those guards when they get closer. When I do that, I want him to plink another one of those sheep-rustlers for me. Just put one of them out of action.

"Once they realize that we *do* have guns, that'll slow them down. They won't know that it's just the one weapon. Also, they can't afford to leave their wounded here, on the wrong side of the border where the Greek police might find them. So they'll have to detail men to stay with the injured guys, to make sure they get back home.

"Then I'll join you two at the bottom of the hill. Tell Giannis to stay buttoned up here until the guards have gone by, then hightail it out of here. He'd better move his flock away for a while, too."

After shaking hands with Giannis, Joe and Clea started down the hillside again, keeping the bushes between themselves and the border guards as much as possible. A few scattered shots were fired, but the patrol members were out of effective range.

Joe turned back when he heard the burst from Atlas's AK-47. He saw a man sprawl forward on the ground, while his comrades scattered, looking for cover from the unexpected gunfire.

"Giannis strikes again," remarked Joe to Clea. "Let's find a place to wait for Atlas."

Presently Atlas came limping down to the bottom of the slope, glancing back toward the pursuers. "They seem to have gotten our message. There are only seven or eight following us—and they're likely to keep a respectful distance. We ought to be able to mount a pretty good rear-guard action and get back to your buddies in the tower."

They set off, at a less frantic pace than before. The border patrol seemed content just to shadow them.

After a while Joe tapped Clea on the arm. "I figure we should be getting close to the fortress by now. See any familiar landmarks?"

Clea studied the area. "We ought to be very—listen!" The breeze brought the sound of shooting, coming from not too far ahead of them.

"We're back," said Joe, "and they're still holding on at the tower."

Atlas was making his way in their direction, looking back over his shoulder periodically. Joe ran out to meet him.

"The fortress is just a little bit ahead and to our right," Joe reported. "We heard some firing from that direction."

"Great. Let's get someplace where we can see how it lays. If we can surprise the guys attacking the tower, maybe we can break through before they know what's going on.''

In front of them the ground sloped gently, but to their right it became steeper. From the echoing gunfire, the fight was going on just on the other side of that hill.

"Let's get ourselves to the top, and see what we can," Atlas said. They began to climb, slowly and cautiously, not knowing how close they were to the action beyond. At the summit, they looked down into a little valley, beyond which was a somewhat higher hill. "I guess that's your fortress, up on that peak over there."

"That's it." Joe squinted. "But we're too far away to see what's up."

Atlas stood, cradling the AK-47. "Let's get moving. We don't want to find ourselves pinned between the border patrol and these guys."

Fifteen minutes later, they were about a hundred yards from the tower, lying behind a dense thicket of thorny scrub. Joe poked his head up to look around.

"You can see a little bit of the road, off to the right and beyond the tower. The doorway leading to the top of the tower is over on the left."

Atlas raised his head and scanned the area. "Looks like there's a bunch grouped around that doorway. I think they're going to try storming the stairs."

Joe said, "We'd better hurry up. I don't think Prynne and Phil can hold off much longer."

The remaining members of the attack team were scattered in front of the tower, taking potshots at the top from their places of concealment.

Atlas frowned. "You see the two over on the left of their line? The ones closest to the entrance? We might just be able to take them without the others realizing it."

The men in question shared the same cover, a large outcropping of stone. They were separated from the rest of the group.

Joe nodded. "If we can get their guns, we could charge the ones trying to storm the entrance."

They dropped on their bellies and crawled around the dense bushes, Atlas cradling the gun against his chest. To Joe, the crawl seemed endless—if any of the enemy just happened to look back for a second, matters could get very unpleasant very fast. But the men behind the rock kept their eyes on the tower.

When they came close enough to the two heavies, Atlas looked back at Joe, who nodded, scarcely breathing. Then he sprang forward, with Joe and Clea close behind.

Before the gunmen had time to move, Atlas was on them. He clubbed the first man on the back of the head with the automatic weapon. The other guy spun around, trying to get his gun into position, but Joe launched himself from a crouch to knock him down.

Joe grabbed his opponent, pulling him forward. Then he brought his right knee up into the man's jaw. The gunman's eyes went glassy, and he rolled onto his side. It was over in a few seconds.

None of the attackers had seen or heard a thing. Atlas removed the unconscious men's guns and ammunition. Joe took one AK-47 and passed the other to Clea, who took it reluctantly.

"It's set for automatic fire," instructed Joe. "Just squeeze the trigger to shoot. Remember: fire up in the air. This is just for effect, to scare those guys away from the stairway. Ready?"

Clea looked pale, but she nodded. "Even if I can't shoot, I can scream."

They grinned at each other.

Atlas slapped another magazine into his gun. "Right, here we go. Make a lot of noise. Joe, you sing out and make sure your friends don't mistake us for bad guys."

At a signal from Atlas, they sprang out from behind their shelter, guns pointed high, racing for the tower.

Five men knelt near the archway when the chaos exploded. They looked up to see three screaming maniacs practically on top of them, firing automatic weapons. Forgetting that they, too, had guns, they took to their heels in a total panic.

Joe Hardy fired his AK-47 and screamed as loud as he could: "Phil! Mr. P.! Hold your fire! We're coming in! Don't shoot!"

They dove into the archway as bullets from the attackers kicked up dust clouds and stone chips. But Phil and Prynne held their fire as Joe, Clea, and Atlas hurtled up the stairs and onto the tower roof, panting but unhurt.

Phil watched the three tumble in. "All right!" he said. "I'm glad you could drop by. Sorry I don't have time right now for socializing." He swung back and fired out at the gunmen below.

Atlas walked over to Morton Prynne, who sat with his back against a wall, covering the stairs. "Mr. Prynne, I presume? How's the leg?"

Prynne gave Atlas a thin smile. "Well, it isn't any better. But it isn't any worse either. Good to see you."

Atlas squatted down beside Prynne. "These kids of yours—I don't know where you picked them up—but they sure did a job."

Prynne's smile broadened. "Clea! Joe! Well

done! Now man a battle station. We still have to hold on until help arrives, but it's on the way."

"More company coming!" yelled Phil. "Looks like eight new arrivals down there!"

Joe, who had propped his gun on the wall near Phil, said, "Oh, yeah, we forgot to tell you—these guys have been on our tail all the way from the border."

Atlas joined the two at the wall and looked down, where the border patrol was now joining forces with the other group. "I make it to be about fifteen altogether." He frowned and looked at Joe. "Can't say that I like the odds."

Joe thought about their situation. "I don't know. There're more of them, but there're more of us, too, now."

"No," the agent said. "Having so many men down there gives them more firepower and mobility."

Atlas shook his head. "If they want me bad enough, they may just decide to take the casualties and try an all-out attack."

Chapter

17

THANKS TO FRANK'S WARNING, Spiros Stamos had two seconds to deal with the boulder. He stood on the brakes, bringing the car to a screeching stop. In the backseat Chet and the Gray Man were flung forward.

The boulder, with a thunderous roar, hit the road just ahead of the car, then tumbled down into the ravine. It had missed the front bumper by about a foot.

All the people in the car sat silent for a moment as they thought about the narrowness of their escape. Even the engine had stalled out.

Chet sat back in his seat with a soft "Wow!"

The Gray Man asked, "Is everyone okay?" Everyone seemed to be.

"You've got sharp reflexes, Mr. Stamos," Frank observed.

Andreas Stamos popped out from the bushes in which he had been hiding and dashed to the car. In his hand he held a small pocket mirror. "You saw my flashes?"

"They probably saved us from being squashed just then," said Frank. "Hop in, Andreas." Chet opened the back door and Andreas scrambled inside. His eyes were large with excitement, his words spilling out.

"I ran here and saw a car coming and hid because the car was full of strange men. Two of them climbed up—they were doing something to a big rock on the hill. When your car came they started pushing the rock, so I tried to signal you and—"

"And you succeeded and saved our lives," Stamos cut in. "Excellent work, son."

The Gray Man leaned across the back seat toward Andreas. "Did you see what happened to the men after they started the boulder downhill?"

Andreas nodded. "They ran that way," pointing toward where the secondary road branched off from the main one, "and then started down the hill."

"Then this is the turnoff we want to take to the fortress?" asked the Gray Man.

"It's about eight miles," Andreas said.

The Gray Man tapped Stamos on the shoulder. "They probably rejoined the others in their car, on their way to the fortress, or—"

"*Or*," cut in Frank, "they're planning a surprise for us ahead on the road."

"Well, whichever it is, we'd better get moving," the Gray Man responded.

Stamos brought the car's engine back to life, and they headed up the side road. It was narrower than the main route. Two cars meeting head-on would have had to pass each other very carefully.

They drove on, not too fast. Any curve could hide a trap set to spring on them. The minutes crawled by and each twist of the road became an adventure. The Gray Man reached down to the floor and began distributing guns. "Just in case. We don't want to be taken unprepared."

Frank examined his weapon, an American AR-14, which he had some experience with. He went back to watching the road. Was Joe back at the tower by now? Had he and Clea managed to bring the American agent back with them? Or—but there was no point in this kind of guesswork. He forced himself to concentrate on the matter in hand. Joe could take care of himself. Or, at any rate, he would have to, for the time being.

"Must be getting pretty close by now," Chet said. "Maybe those other guys just drove on up to the fortress."

"We are very near," Andreas agreed. "It will be up on a hill, to our left. You will go around a long curve, just ahead, and—"

Suddenly the rocky hills that bordered the road on the left broke off, forming a crevice, and out of that crevice a van appeared just behind them, greeting them with a hail of gunfire. Men leaned out of windows on both sides with automatic weapons blazing.

Stamos pressed down heavily on the gas pedal, trying to get a little distance between the two vehicles. Frank rolled down his window and aimed his gun back at the van. But in the bouncing, swaying car, it wasn't easy.

Chet peered back at the van from the back window. "Hey, Frank! You recognize the one riding shotgun?"

Frank knew that sharp face with the cold eyes, even when the eyes were squinting over the blazing barrel of an Uzi. "It's our old buddy, Theo. I figured we'd see him again before this was over." He fired a short burst, then corrected his aim.

"Go for the engine or the radiator!" the Gray Man shouted.

Frank grabbed at the door as the car took a sharp turn on two wheels. "I'll be lucky to hit anything, rocking and rolling like this!"

A series of metallic *thunks* and a shudder in the car showed that a gunman had stitched the trunk with bullets. Frank fired again, aiming lower.

The right front tire of the van blew out with a pop that could be heard in Salonika. The van lurched and swung wildly to the right, and then back the other way as the driver fought the wheel to keep the vehicle on the road. It fishtailed again with its tires squealing in protest, the van driver slamming on the brakes. Finally the van flipped over on its side and skidded.

Stamos brought the car to a halt, and Frank started to get out, but as he did, Theo pushed open the van door, firing at the car and forcing Frank back inside.

With Theo covering, another rider from the van managed to work his way out, carrying something in his arms. Both men sprinted away from the overturned van and away from the road. Frank realized that they were headed for the fortress.

Stamos grabbed Frank by the arm and pulled him into the car. "Shut the door! We must get up there fast."

Frank did as he was told, but as Stamos

gunned the car forward, he asked, "Why the big hurry?"

Stamos kept both eyes on the road. "Did you see what that fellow was carrying when he ran off toward the fort?"

"I couldn't tell what it was."

"Well, I've seen those things in action before. It was a mortar. They'll be able to lob shells right into the tower."

Stamos coaxed the car along the road while Theo and his friend ran cross-country.

"There it is!"

Andreas pointed to the fortress rising above the road.

Stamos stopped the car and the five passengers got out to look the situation over. They could hear firing, but from the road, there was no view of the action.

Suddenly the volume of fire increased sharply. "I'm going to take a look." Frank darted out from behind the car and worked his way uphill, toward the fort.

Moments later he raced back. Ducking down with the others, he drew a rough map in the dirt. "This is the fortress. And here is where they're setting up that mortar. They've got most of their firepower concentrated over *here,* well away from the mortar position, and they've opened up with heavy firing from that line.

"My guess is that the heavy firing is a diversion, to keep the defenders from noticing the mortar. Then they'll start lobbing shells into the tower. We'd better get that mortar out of commission fast."

The five moved hurriedly to the crest of the hill. Two men knelt by the mortar, stacking shells beside it.

"Where's Theo?" whispered Chet.

Frank whispered, "Maybe he's over where the shooting is coming from."

"We'll have to drive those men away from that field piece, that's the first priority," the Gray Man said.

They poured a hail of bullets over the heads of the two men, who immediately abandoned their position, dashing for cover.

The Gray Man called out, "Hold your fire!" The chattering of the guns stopped. "Frank, you and Chet stay here and keep anyone from reaching the mortar. If you can knock it out of action without exposing yourselves to any undue risk, do it. Spiros, you and Andreas come with me—we'll give those people doing all the shooting something else to worry about—a flank attack. Let's go."

While the Gray Man and the two Stamoses set off, Chet and Frank found cover. The mortar stood fifty feet away, with a pile of shells to one side and a few shells lying on the ground nearby.

"Maybe we could just rush out and grab that stovepipe," Chet suggested.

Frank shook his head. "Try it, and the crew will start sniping at you."

"Yeah, I guess. Boy, I feel like I haven't eaten in a week. You have any snacks, Frank?"

Shots rang out, *behind* Frank, and he actually heard the whine of a bullet zipping by him. He whipped around, and heard Chet cry out.

"Frank! It's Theo!"

The thin-faced thug had crept to within twenty feet of Frank and Chet, but his burst of fire had missed. Frank sent a short blast at the gunman, who ducked for the shelter of the thick, heavy branches of a dead tree.

Frank fired again, moving out to his left to get a better angle. Theo popped out from behind his tree trunk, aiming another volley at Frank, who dove headlong, hugging the ground as the shots passed harmlessly over his head. He heard a mocking laugh from behind the tree.

"You see, my young Yankee friend, I told you that we would meet once again."

Flat on his stomach, Frank raised his gun high, firing a long burst. Theo flinched back, but the bullets went over his head. He stepped round the tree, his face an ugly mask of triumph as he leveled his Uzi at Frank. "I want you dead, Yankee."

Then the massive tree branch that Frank's shooting had torn loose from the trunk dropped on Theo's head. Frank smiled as Theo folded into an unconscious heap. "You're lucky I wanted *you* alive," he said.

He dragged Theo over to the tree and tied him so that his arms circled the trunk. Then he hurried back to Chet, who said, "I thought he had you there for a second."

"Good thing that tree was dead, or I don't know if that trick would've worked. Now, about that mortar . . . I wonder if we could set off one of those loose shells over there by shooting it."

"Want to try?"

"If it goes up, it'll probably take those other shells with it, so let's back off."

They moved away to some rocks that stood forty yards from the mortar. Frank tapped Chet on the shoulder. "If this works, don't stand there admiring the explosion. Hit the dirt."

They began firing short bursts at the shells. The first few did nothing but raise dust clouds. Then there was a loud *crack!* and a fiery flash, followed almost immediately by a really thunderous roar.

Frank and Chet dove behind their shelter

with the first explosion. But they felt the shockwave and the heat from the big blast as the entire stack of shells went up. A scattering of debris fell around them. They waited a bit, and then slowly raised themselves up for a look.

The mortar lay some distance from where it had been, a twisted and bent metal tube. There was a shallow crater where the shells had been.

"Awesome!" Chet's eyes were wide.

Frank's ears were ringing. "Come on," he said to Chet. "Let's give the others a hand. We're not out of the woods yet."

They found Spiros and Andreas Stamos with the Gray Man exchanging fire with a group of enemy gunmen. The Gray Man twisted around to give Frank a startled glance.

"Five or six men have us pinned in place here, and I think most of the rest are trying a last-ditch attack on the tower."

The intensity of gunfire abruptly rose, coming from the vicinity of the entryway leading to the tower, and from the top of the tower itself.

"This could be it," the Gray Man muttered.

Spiros Stamos called out from his position, "What can we do?"

Frank thought of his brother, up there facing an all-out assault. "We've got to do something!"

The Gray Man reached out and gripped Frank by the shoulder. "Listen to me. Trying to get over to them now would be suicidal. They have us pinned down here. We wouldn't—"

"Hey!" Chet piped up. "Listen a second!"

Frank listened, frowning. "I can't hear—Wait a minute! It sounds like—a car."

A khaki-colored troop carrier with the Greek flag painted on its door pulled up. Troops hopped out, forming up in ranks.

Chet jumped up. "Look! The attackers are splitting!"

The men who'd been massing to attack the tower were now retreating in haste, into the hills and back to the Yugoslav border. The wounded were being hauled along by their comrades.

"Why don't you go and round them up?" Chet demanded.

"We have what we want—it's much better to pretend all this never happened." The Gray Man shot a look of warning at Frank and Chet.

"I hope we can count on you never to talk about this, to anyone, under any circumstances whatever. You went to Greece, looked at ruins and the countryside, made a little side trip, and you went home. Period."

"What about Peter being kidnapped?" asked

Frank. "The students all were there when that went down."

"They've been told that it was all a misunderstanding. Peter went home with some relatives and didn't tell us in advance. And the attack at the restaurant had nothing whatever to do with us. Clear?"

"Clear," said Chet with regret in his voice.

"Frank! Hey, Frank!" Joe Hardy walked toward them, supporting Morton Prynne on one side while Atlas supported the other. "I never thought I'd be so happy to see you again!"

Andreas Stamos dashed ahead and hugged Clea. Peter and Spiros ran over, too, and the four Stamoses met in a big embrace. Atlas and the Gray Man started to move away with them, but Frank stopped the Network agent.

"Just about a hundred yards back that way, you'll find a guy tied to a tree," he said. "His name is Theo, and he's the head bad guy."

"Nicholas Kaliotis will tell us all we need to put Theo away," said Spiros Stamos. He shook hands with Frank and Joe in turn and said, "Thank you, both. I cannot say how grateful I am."

Stamos turned to the Gray Man. "These young men are valuable assets. Perhaps one day you might formalize their position."

The Gray Man coughed. "Ah, yes, I must admit that they did quite well, considering—"

"That we're only amateurs," said Frank and Joe in chorus.

"Frank. Joe." It was Morton Prynne, now supported by two Greek soldiers in fatigues. "You're a couple of very remarkable young men. And you have some remarkable friends."

Joe stepped forward. "And you're a tough dude, Mr. P. Take care of that leg, now."

"Joe," said Clea softly, coming toward him. Joe smiled and stuck out his hand.

Clea ignored the hand, reached up, and kissed him softly on the cheek.

"I'll try not to think so badly of Americans," she said, smiling. "Or, at least, I will always think *very* well of one young American man."

Joe looked into those deep, dark eyes. "Clea, you're something else. There's no one I'd trust more in a tight spot, male *or* female."

Frank pulled Joe to one side. "Can I believe my ears? Or am I hallucinating?"

Joe glared at Frank. "Hey, give me a break! There's an exception to every rule, and she happens to be it."

Frank nodded, pretending to consider Joe's statement very carefully. "Well, then, can I tell our friends back in Bayport that you now realize that there are women who can stand up

148

to men in physical endurance and clutch situations?"

Joe said, "That can only be revealed on a need-to-know basis." He grinned. "And I hope *that* is something no one will *ever* need to know!"

Simon & Schuster publish a wide range of titles from pre-school books to books for adults.

For up-to-date catalogues, please contact:

International Book Distributors
Campus 400
Maylands Avenue
Hemel Hempstead
Herts
HP2 7EZ

Tel. 0442 882255